Su

Legends Awaken

J.B. Corgard

Subzero Quest
Legends Awaken

Table of Contents

Prologue

In the late 21st century, rapid climate change led to a catastrophic failure of the planet's environmental systems. Massive storms, droughts, and heatwaves became commonplace, leading to crop failures and mass migrations. The UN had several meetings with top scientists to combat the massive warming of the earth.

To combat the crisis, world governments began a massive geoengineering project to cool the planet's temperature. This project involved releasing millions of tons of reflective particles into the atmosphere which caused a global cooling effect.

However, the project had unforeseen consequences. As the planet continued to cool, ice sheets began to expand and cover vast swaths of the globe. Soon, the world was plunged into a new ice age with temperatures dropping to -50 degrees Celsius in many areas. Most of the world's population died off in the ensuing chaos, war over what little recourse existed. With only a few hardy survivors managing to seek out a living in the frozen wasteland.

The people left in the barren empty land, they made small colonies in the abandoned cities when most migrated south, to the new and poorly built new USA. A megacity that not only expanded from the coast of Georgia to Dallas Texas, but into the sky. It quickly became a hub for drugs and crime lords. Became a rundown slum place to live and not much better out in the cold waste of the rest of the USA.

As the ice age took hold, the equator became the only area on the planet where temperatures were warm enough to sustain human life. However, the equatorial region was also the most desirable and lucrative area on the planet, home to vast wealth and power. The world's elite had long recognized the strategic importance of the equator, and they had invested heavily in securing its resources and defending its borders. They built massive walls blocking the poor from getting in.

As the rest of the world plunged into chaos, despair, war, famine, death, cold, and unrest, the equatorial region became an island of stability and prosperity. Its cities were sprawling metropolises, filled with towering skyscrapers, gleaming shopping malls, and luxurious estates. The people who lived there enjoyed all the trappings of wealth and privilege, including fine dining, high-end fashion, and the latest technologies. The poor wished for this lifestyle before the new ice age.

However, life in the equatorial region was not without its challenges. Global cooling had disrupted weather patterns and caused extreme weather events, such as hurricanes and monsoons, to become more frequent and severe. The elite had to use their wealth and power to build massive infrastructure projects, such as seawalls and weather control systems, to protect themselves from these dangers.

Chapter 1

In the year 2124, the world changed drastically. The once-thriving city of Chicago had become a shadow of its former self. The streets were empty and silent, with only several survivors seeking out a living amongst the ruins. The city was abandoned, it got ruined. Hannah, an 18-year-old girl, was one of those survivors.

Despite the harsh realities of life in the new ice age, Hannah remained hopeful. She lived with her parents and younger sister, Grace, in a small run-down apartment building on the outskirt of downtown. The building was one of the few still in livable condition and the family was appreciative that they had a roof over their heads. They shared the space with several other families, all of whom were struggling to survive. The lack of high-paying jobs made it hard for families to make a living.

Hannah spent her days scavenging for anything that might be useful, picking her way through the rubble in search of food, water, and other supplies. It was a dangerous task, as the freezing temperatures and treacherous terrain made every outing a risk. But she was determined to keep her family alive, no matter the cost. The icy and high snow-covered streets made it hard for trucks to get much-needed supplies to the city.

The city of Chicago was a grim reminder of the world that once was, so alive and vibrant. Only about 1/30th of the population still lived there, and most of them were barely hanging on. The people who still live in this area are either physically or financially unable to move south. The skyscrapers that had once towered over the city were now little more than crumbling ruins, and the streets were littered with debris and garbage. The once-vibrant neighborhoods were now ghost towns, with only a few stubborn survivors remaining.

Hannah's family was among the lucky ones. Her parents worked long hours doing odd jobs to bring in a little bit of money, but it was never enough. They struggled to put food on the table and keep the lights on, let alone pay for Hannah's father medicine.

That treatment her father needed was only available in the Equatorial Zone (EZ), a place reserved for the rich and famous. It was a world away from the cold and snow that Chicago had become. In the Equatorial Zone, the sun shined bright and the temperatures were warmest year-round.

Hannah dreamt of one day being able to afford a ticket to the Equatorial Zone. It seemed like an impossible dream, but she clung to it nonetheless. She knew that the odds were stacked against her, but she refused to give up. She would do whatever it takes to give her family a better life, even if it meant risking everything she had.

Hannah stood at a height of 5'7 with an average body build. Her dirty blonde hair hung in loose waves around her face, framing her sharp features. Her striking blue eyes were her most noticeable feature, and they seemed to sparkle with a determined glint.

Despite the harshness of her surroundings, Hannah refused to let it get to her. She was a fighter, and she had to be to survive in a world that was constantly trying to beat her down. She had a sharp wit and a fierce determination that had seen her through some of the toughest times.

Despite her toughness, Hannah had a kind heart. She was fiercely loyal to her family and would do anything to protect them. She was also quick to lend a helping hand to others in need even if it meant risking her own safety.

Hannah had never been to the Equatorial Zone, but she had heard stories about it from others. She knew that it was a place of unimaginable luxury and wealth, where the rich and famous lived like kings and queens. Hannah longed to experience that kind of life, even if it was just for a little while.

Hannah's love for video games was something that had been with her since she was a child. She had grown up in a world where entertainment was scarce, and so she had learned to find solace in virtual worlds. Most of her free time was spent playing games, immersing herself in the stories and adventures that they offered.

Although she couldn't afford any of the latest games or equipment, Hannah didn't mind. She was content with the games from the past that she had scavenged, finding joy in the simplicity of their graphics and mechanics. Something was charming about the old games, something that she couldn't quite put her finger on. Perhaps it was the nostalgia that came with them, a reminder of a time when the world was a much different place.

Hannah's love for old things didn't stop with video games. She had a fondness for anything that had a sense of history to it. She loved to collect old books, trinkets, and artifacts that she found on her scavenging trips. Her room was filled with all sorts of oddities, each with its own story to tell.

Despite her love for gaming and collection, Hannah always made time for her family. They were the most important thing in her life. Whether it was playing board games with her sister or cooking a meal for her parents, Hannah treasured every moment that she spent with them.

Despite her best efforts, Hannah knew that her family was still struggling to make ends meet. To help contribute to the household income, she had taken up a part-time job at the local grocery store. The store was only open thrice a week, for limited hours, due to the limited supply of groceries. It was a constant struggle for the store to keep its shelves stocked, given the challenges of transportation in a world covered in ice and snow.

Hannah's job at the store was a necessary evil. She didn't particularly enjoy it, but she knew that it was important to do her part for her family. Three times a week, she would make her way through the snow-covered streets to the store, pulling on her thick winter coat and wrapping a scarf around her neck. The walk was always a cold and lonely one, the only sounds coming from the crunch of her boots on the snow-covered ground.

Once she arrived at the store, Hannah would spend a few hours restocking shelves, organizing inventory, and helping customers find what they needed. Sometimes she cashiered if needed. The store was small, and the selection was limited, but Hannah did her best to make sure that everyone who came in was taken care of. She would smile and chat with customers, offering a small ray of light in an otherwise bleak world around them.

The limited supply of groceries was a constant source of frustration for everyone in the community. The snow and lack of infrastructures made it hard for trucks to make deliveries and the few suppliers that still existed were often overworked and under-resourced. Hannah had seen the desperation in the eyes of the customers who came into the store, their faces lined with worry and anxiety. It was a stark reminder of just how fragile their world had become.

Hannah walked to work every day, passing by the remains of what once was a bustling metropolis. Broken buildings, abandoned cars and piles of snow were all that remained of what used to be Chicago. It was a harsh reality, but one that Hannah had grown and accustomed to. She trudged through the snow, her boots sinking into the slushy mixture with each step.

As she walked, she couldn't help but glance at the electronic store that she passed by. It was one of the only places in the city that still sold electronics, but the prices were outrageous and the models were mostly outdated. She knew that her family could never afford to buy anything from there.

Despite the high prices, the store still managed to display the world news station on the TVs in the window. It was one of the four stations that reached the area, and Hannah often stopped to listen to what was happening in the world. She couldn't help but feel a sense of longing as she watched the images on the screen, wishing that she could experience the world beyond her city.

The news was often bleak, reporting on the worsening conditions of the world due to climate change. Coastal cities had been flooded while others were being ravaged by extreme weather conditions. Food and water shortages were becoming extremely common and diseases were spreading rapidly in some areas.

Hannah felt a mix of emotions as she watched the news. She was scared for what the future held, but she also felt a sense of determination to make a better life for herself and her family. She knew that she couldn't change the state of the world, but she could try to improve her situation.

With these thoughts in mind, she continued on her way to work, ready to face another day of stocking shelves and helping customers.

Hannah couldn't help but stop and stare at the news broadcasts that played on the screens in the store windows. The news anchors reported on the latest political scandals and international conflicts, but what caught her attention the most were the reports on the state of the planet. The ice age caused massive devastation with many cities around the world being completely uninhabitable. The equatorial region was now the only place where people could live in any sort of comfort.

Hannah felt a pang of envy every time she saw footage of the luxurious estates and high-end shopping centers in the equatorial region. It was a world away from the crumbling buildings and scarce resources of her city. But she quickly pushed those feelings aside and reminded herself why she worked so hard every day.

She had to support her family and help her father get the treatment he needed to survive. The job at the grocery store was far from glamorous, but it paid enough to help keep some food on the table. Sometimes she even managed to save a little extra money to put towards her dreams.

As she walked towards the grocery store, Hannah couldn't help but wonder what it would be like to live in a world where things weren't so difficult. A world where she didn't have to work three days a week just to afford necessities. But for now, she focused on the present and did what she could to make life a little bit easier for her family and help her parents out.

Chapter 2

On this particular day, Hannah woke up to a sight that was all too familiar to her. The view outside her window was bleak and desolate. The world was shrouded in a thick layer of snow and the sky was a deep shade of gray. The snow drifts had accumulated to a point where walking was almost impossible. Hannah had to make her way through the high snow and the biting cold to get to work.

Hannah's thoughts were consumed with worry for her father. His terminal illness was taking a toll on him and the family, and there seemed to be no hope for a cure. As she walked, she clenched her fists in frustration. "What can I do?" she thought, "I can't just sit around and watch him suffer."

As Hannah walked into the grocery store, she was greeted by her co-worker Jane, who was a little older than her and had become a good friend. Jane was already stocking the shelves, and the two of them chatted as they worked. Hannah picked up a copy of the World of Electronics (WOE) magazine, which they sold at the store. It was the only way she could keep up with the latest tech trends.

Hannah flipped through the magazine, looking at all the new gadgets and electronics. Her eyes lit up when she saw the virtual reality deck she had been following for years. She showed it to Jane and said, "I would love to have one of these."

Jane responded with a sigh, "We can barely afford food, so keep dreaming."

Hannah put down the magazine with a resigned look on her face. "At least I have dreams of getting out of this frozen land," she said, feeling a sense of helplessness washed over her.

As they finished stocking the shelves, Hannah's mind wandered back to the virtual reality deck. She had always been fascinated with video games and the idea of immersing herself in a virtual world. She had saved up a little money from her job, but it was nowhere near enough to afford the deck.

Hannah sighed, knowing that her family's financial situation made it impossible to even dream about luxuries like that. Her thoughts drifted back to her father's illness and the treatments he desperately needed. She felt helpless and frustrated, wishing there was something more she could do.

After work, Jane could see the sadness in Hannah's eyes as she walked through the snowy streets. She knew that Hannah was going through a difficult time with her father's illness, and she wanted to do something to help.

"Hey, why don't we hang out?" suggested Jane. "We can play your favorite game and take your mind off things for a while."

Hannah looked up at Jane, grateful for the kind offer. "Yea, that'd be great," she said, her voice still tinged with sadness.

They walked to Hannah's house, which was a small apartment building with 8 units on the edge of town. They made their way to her room, where Hannah's gaming setup was located. The room was dimly lit, with colorful LED lights adorning the walls and the ceiling.

Jane was impressed by the setup. Hannah had managed to build her gaming PC from scratch, and she had a collection of retro consoles dating back to the early 2000s. Jane saw an old Nintendo GameCube console sitting on a shelf and just smiled.

"Is that the one we're playing?" she asked, pointing to the console.

Hannah laughed, "Yeah, that's my favorite. We can play some Super Smash Bros and some Mario Party."

They settled down in front of the TV, each grabbing a controller. They played for hours, laughing and shouting at each other as they battled it out in the virtual world. For a brief moment, Hannah forgot about her troubles and felt free just like a kid again.

As they were packing up to leave, Jane turned to Hannah. "You know, you have a gaming talent, have you ever considered pursuing it as a career?"

Hannah shrugged, "I don't know. It's always been more of a hobby for me, plus that's not feasible out here"

"Well, you should think about it," Jane replied. "You're really good at it, and with the right training, you could become a professional gamer."

Hannah's eyes widened at the thought. She had never considered that gaming could be more than just a fun pastime. "Do you think so?" she asked.

"As your best friend, why would I lie to you," Jane noted. "And I'll be here to support you every step of the way."

Hannah smiled, feeling a newfound sense of purpose. Maybe pursuing gaming as a career was exactly what she needed to do.
"If only the internet was better out here," thought Hannah with a sye as she lay in bed.

Hannah made her way to her parent's room, which was always a refuge for her. She had spent countless hours in this room, either listening to her parents' stories or telling them about her own. As she pushed the door open, she could hear the sound of her father's labored breathing. His condition was worse today than most days.

"How are you, Dad?" she asked as she walked in with a glass of water.

"Oh, I'm just fine, kiddo," her dad replied, catching his breath.

"I'm not your kiddo anymore," Hannah said, smirking at him. She was 18 now, and while she still loved being with her parents, she was aware of the fact that she was an adult.

"Could have fooled me, Hannah," her father said, chuckling softly.

Hannah walked over to her father's bed and sat down beside him. She placed the glass of water on the bedside table and took her father's hand in hers. "Don't worry, things will get better soon," she said, squeezing his hand.

Her father smiled weakly, grateful for his daughter's words of encouragement. "I know they will, Hannah. I just have to keep pushing through".

Hannah nodded in agreement, but she couldn't shake the feeling of helplessness that consumed her every time she saw her father like this. She wished she could do more for him, wished that she could take away his pain and make everything better.

As she sat there with her father, she couldn't help but think of the future. She had dreams and ambitions, just like any young person, but she knew that her family's struggles were not over yet. She would do whatever it takes to help them, to make sure that they could have a better life. Just as much as they helped me.

A week later, the sun rose early on the day of the monthly basketball game, casting a warm glow across the town. People began to stir from their homes, preparing for the day ahead. They could feel the excitement in the air, a buzz that always surrounded the game. It was a day when the town came together, north side versus south side, to compete on the basketball court.

The basketball court was located in the center of town, in an old high school gym, and it had been put together years ago by volunteers. It was a symbol of pride for the community, a place where people gathered to socialize and cheer on their friends and family. The court was well-maintained, with freshly painted lines and new nets that were replaced every year. The stands were also updated and now boasted comfortable seating, thanks to a local business that had donated money for the upgrades.

Everyone in town looked forward to this day. Children woke up early, put on their basketball jerseys, and headed to the court to watch the teams warm up. Adults made plans to tailgate, bringing food and drinks to share with friends and family. The local radio station began broadcasting live from the court, providing play-by-play commentary on the game.

The teams were made up of local players, most of whom had grown up playing on this very court. There were no big-name players or fancy uniforms, but that didn't matter. The game was about community and coming together, not about who had the most skill or the best gear. The players were respected by their peers, and they knew that this game was more than just a competition. It was a chance to show their pride for their town, their families and themselves.

The basketball game was one of only two events in the area that was locally broadcasted. The other was the annual town parade, which was a celebration of the town's history and traditions. But the basketball game was special. It brought people together in a way that nothing else could. It was a time to forget about the challenges of daily life and simply enjoy the moment.

As the day went on, the excitement grew. The town became a sea of color as people donned their team's colors, either red for the north side or blue for the south side. The sound of basketballs bouncing and sneakers squeaking filled the air as the players warmed up. The stands were packed with people of all ages, eagerly awaiting the start of the game.

Hannah and Jane were eagerly anticipating the monthly basketball game between the north and south sides of town. This event was a highlight for the community, as it was one of the few forms of entertainment in the area. The rivalry between the two sides was intense, with both sides determined to come out on top.

Hannah lived on the north side of town, and she had always been a proud supporter of their team. She would paint her face with blue and white stripes, the colors of the team, and wear a matching shirt and hat to show her support. Jane, on the other hand, lived just over the line on the south side, but she was still passionate about her team. She would make a sign every month, with clever slogans and team colors, to show her spirit.

As the day of the game approached, both girls were filled with excitement. They made plans to meet up early and get a good spot in the stadium. Hannah packed a cooler with snacks and drinks, while Jane brought a bag of noisemakers and other gear to cheer on her team.

When they arrived at the game, the atmosphere was electric. The stands were packed with fans wearing team colors, waving flags, and chanting. Vendors selling hot dogs, popcorn, and other snacks, and a live band playing music to pump up the crowd.

Hannah and Jane settled into their seats, with Hannah on the north side and Jane on the south. They both held up their signs and cheered loudly for their respective teams.

Finally, the moment arrived. The players took to the court, and the crowd erupted into cheers. The game was on, and everyone watched with rapt attention, cheering on their team with every basket and steal. The game was intense, but in the end, the north side emerged victorious. The celebration that followed was nothing short of epic, with people dancing, hugging, and high-fiving each other. It was a day that would be remembered for months to come, a day when the town came together and showed its true spirit.

The game was intense, with both sides scoring back and forth and the tension mounting with every shot

As the clock ticked down to the final seconds, the score was tied. The crowd was on its feet, screaming and shouting for their teams. Then, with just seconds left on the clock, the north side made a last-minute shot and won the game.

Hannah jumped up and down with joy, hugging her friends and high-fiving strangers in the stands. Jane was disappointed but still proud of her team for putting up a good fight. They both left the game feeling exhilarated and proud to be a part of such a passionate community.

In the end, everyone was a winner. They got to enjoy a fun and exciting game. Got their minds off the daily grind of life and everything happening outside the stadium.

Chapter 3

The morning sun slowly filtered in through the curtains, illuminating the room and casting warm rays of light across Hannah's face. She squinted as she stretched her arms above her head, taking in a deep breath of fresh morning air. Today was the day she had been looking forward to for weeks - a day of scavenging in search of hidden treasures.

As she got out of bed and began to prepare for her journey, her mind raced with excitement at the possibility of discovering some rare finds. She had heard whispers of an old GameStopped store on the far side of town, and she was determined to find it. Hannah knew that this could be her chance to add some gems to her growing collection of retro games and consoles.

She packed her backpack with some water, snacks, and a map of the area. She also brought along her trusty walking stick, a flashlight and a custom sled she and her dad built for hauling her treasures. Hannah knew that the journey would not be easy, as the GameStopped store was located in a remote and less-traveled part of town. She estimated that it would take her at least four to five hours of walking to reach the area where it was rumored to be.

With everything ready, Hannah set out on her journey, eager to find the treasure trove of retro games that awaited her. She walked through the quiet snowy streets of her town, passing by empty shops and stores, each one holding the potential of hidden treasures. However, her heart was set on the GameStopped store and nothing could distract her from that goal.

As Hannah continued on her journey to the GameStopped store, her mind was filled with anticipation and excitement. She thought about all the possible treasures that could be waiting her, and each step brought her closer to fulfilling her dreams of adding rare and unique games to her collection.

The walk was long and tiring, but Hannah was determined to find what she was looking for. She passed by many different stores and buildings, each one catching her attention with its unique architecture and charm. A glimpse of what the past was like. She stopped to admire some of them, taking pictures and making mental notes to come back and explore some of them later.

As Hannah continued on her journey, she couldn't help but feel the weight of the world on her shoulders. The cold was getting worse and the wind was picking up, making her feel as if she was being pushed back. She walked past the empty buildings, staring up at their once-impressive architecture now eroded by time and the elements.

As she approached the high-rise buildings, she could see the LastBuy Electronics store on one side and a restaurant on the other. Both had seen better days with broken windows and boarded-up entrances. Hannah's heart sank at the sight, but she knew she had to check them out.

She began with LastBuy Electronics, cautiously making her way through the snow-filled entrance. The store was dark, and the only light came from the small flashlight she held tightly in her hand. Hannah moved to the back of the store, hoping to find something that had been overlooked by others.

As she searched, she could see that the store had been thoroughly ransacked and there wasn't much left. But then, she stumbled upon an old motherboard tucked away in a corner, covered in dust and forgotten. “No way, a motherboard,” said Hannah, eyes widened with excitement as she realized what a gem she had found. She carefully wrapped it in a cloth and put it onto her sled, grinning from ear to ear.

Leaving the electronics store behind, Hannah made her way across the street to the restaurant. She knew that finding food was unlikely, but she had to try. As she pushed the door open, a wave of musty air hit her in the face, and she wrinkled her nose in disgust. The restaurant was in ruins, with broken furniture and shattered glass scattered everywhere. The kitchen was in the back, and Hannah made her way there, her flashlight illuminating her path.

She searched through cabinets and drawers, hoping to find some canned food or anything she could take home to her family. But as she suspected, there was nothing. "Not surprised I didn't find anything," said Hannah, closing cabinet doors. The pantry was bare, and all the appliances were broken or rusted beyond repair. Disappointed, Hannah turned to leave, feeling the weight of her failure. This wasn't the first time she had been unable to find food in an abandoned building and she knew it wouldn't be the last.

Taking a deep breath, Hannah walked back out into the cold night, determined to continue on her journey. She pulled her coat tighter around her, the weight of her backpack slowing her down. But she wouldn't give up. Hannah was determined to find something else of value, no matter how small, to make the trip worth it.

Finally, after what seemed like an eternity, Hannah arrived at the location where the store was supposed to be. Her heart sank as she saw the old, abandoned building that looked like it had been forgotten by time. "This better not be a waste of time," thought Hannah walking up to the building, pulling the sled.

Hannah's eyes scanned the outside of the abandoned building, looking for any signs of life. She noticed that the windows were boarded up, and the door was locked with a rusty padlock. Despite this, she knew that this was the right place. She could feel it in her bones.

As she approached the door, she pulled out a set of lock-picking tools from her backpack. She had learned how to pick locks from her grandfather, who used to be a locksmith. Carefully and quietly, she began to work on the padlock, feeling a rush of adrenaline as she did so.

After a few tense minutes, the padlock clicked open, and the door creaked as she pushed it open. The inside of the store was dark and musty,

But Hannah didn't let her doubts get the best of her. She knew that sometimes the best treasures are found in the most unexpected places. She took a deep breath and walked towards the old building, ready to explore and discover what treasures might be hidden inside.

Hannah pushed open the rusty doors of the abandoned building and stepped inside. The building was massive, towering above her with three stories of darkened windows and empty storefronts. Hannah's footsteps echoed loudly against the tiled floor, making the silence of the place even more eerie. The once bustling mall was now a ghost town, long forgotten and left to decay.

As she walked deeper into the mall, Hannah marveled at the remnants of its former glory. There were rows of empty storefronts, their display windows shattered and their interiors long since looted. The faded signs of long-closed stores hung crookedly above their entrances, hinting at the mall's former grandeur.

Despite the decay and destruction, Hannah couldn't help but feel a sense of awe at the scale of the place. It was like a time capsule, frozen in a bygone era. She imagined the shoppers and the hustle and bustle of the mall's heyday, a stark contrast to the desolate emptiness that now surrounded her.

As she continued her search, she couldn't help but feel a sense of excitement at the thought of what treasures the GameStopped store might hold. And finally, after wandering through the desolate mall for what seemed like hours, she caught a glimpse of the GameStopped sign in the distance.

Hannah hurried towards the store, her heart pounding with anticipation. The GameStopped store was smaller than she had expected, but the brightly lit interior was a stark contrast to the dimly lit mall. The walls were lined with shelves filled with old games, consoles, and accessories. The air was thick with the smell of musty cardboard boxes and plastic.

As she began to search through the stacks of games, Hannah found a few items that caught her eye. There was an old Atari console that she had always been curious about and a few classic Nintendo games that she remembered reading in a magazine. Although she didn't strike gold with any rare finds, Hannah was still pleased with her haul.

Finally, after hours of searching, Hannah emerged from the store with her arms full of retro gaming treasures. She looked around the abandoned mall once more, feeling a sense of melancholy mixed with triumph. Hannah had found her treasure trove, but it was bittersweet knowing that the mall and the era it represented were long gone.

With her arms full of gaming treasures, Hannah made her way back through the deserted mall. She couldn't help but feel a sense of nostalgia as she looked around at the empty storefronts and abandoned escalators. As she left the mall, Hannah felt both satisfied and wistful, knowing that the era of retro gaming was fading into the past.

As Hannah began her journey back home, she couldn't help but feel a sense of satisfaction at the treasures she had found at GameStopped. But then the sun had already started to set, casting an orange glow across the snow-covered streets. The snow crunched beneath her feet with each step, and she shivered as a gust of wind whipped past her.

She knew that it was getting late and the temperature was dropping rapidly. It was going to be a difficult walk back home, but she had no choice. The sun was quickly disappearing below the horizon, and Hannah knew that it was not safe to be out at night.

The weight of her newly acquired retro gaming treasures began to take its toll on her, slowing her down. The custom sled helped but it was still a lot for the long journey back. The cold was biting, making her ears and nose numb, and she could feel her breath turn into frost in the frigid air.

As the sun disappeared completely and darkness enveloped her, Hannah quickened her pace. The temperature continued to drop, and it felt like the world around her was freezing over. She could feel the chill seeping through her clothes and into her bones. She knew she had to keep moving, or risk being trapped in the cold.

The thermometer on her old phone showed a terrifying number: the temperature had dropped below -70 degrees Fahrenheit. Hannah knew that it was beyond dangerous to be outside in such conditions, but she couldn't stop now. She gritted her teeth and pushed through the biting cold, determined to make it back home with her precious gaming haul.

Hannah trudged through the deep snow, the freezing wind biting at her cheeks and numbing her fingers. She knew she couldn't stay out in the cold for long without risking frostbite or hypothermia. She had to find shelter, and fast. “I need to find shelter for the night and fast,” thought Hannah looking around for a good place to spend the night.

Looking around, she saw the towering high-rise buildings that lined the street. Most of them were abandoned, with no electricity or heating to speak of. But they offered cover, at least, and that was something she desperately needed.

She made her way towards the closest building, her boots crunching through the snow with each step. As she approached the entrance, she noticed that the door was locked. She tried the handle anyway, hoping for a stroke of luck, but it wouldn't budge.

Undeterred, she searched the surrounding area and found a way to climb up to the first floor. She made her way to the nearest apartment and tried the door, but it was locked as well. She tried a few more doors, growing more anxious with each failure. "Why is everything locked," thought Hannah walking from door to door to find the lock.

Finally, after what felt like an eternity, she found a door that was slightly ajar. She pushed it open and stepped inside. The apartment was dark, with broken windows and peeling wallpaper. But it was better than being out in the cold.

Hannah quickly set to work, searching the kitchen for any food or supplies. She found a can of corn, which wasn't much, but it was better than nothing. She then moved to the living room, where she spotted a few books and an old chair. She grabbed them and started to build a fire. Using her flint and steel she had brought.

It took her a while, but she eventually got the fire started. The flames crackled and danced, casting a warm glow across the room. Hannah huddled close to the fire, wrapping herself in the blanket she found in the bedroom.

She spent a restless night, dozing off here and there, but always keeping an eye on the fire. By morning, the temperature had risen slightly, making the room more tolerable. "Finally morning and much warmer," said Hannah, tired from the long night before. Hannah felt a sense of relief as she gathered her things and made her way back out into the cold.

As she walked back home, she couldn't help but feel grateful for the small amount of warmth and shelter she had found in the abandoned apartment. It wasn't much, but it was enough to keep her alive for one more night in the unforgiving winter wilderness.

Hannah was relieved as she opened the door to her building, her frozen fingers aching from the cold. She stepped inside, and as she made her way to the kitchen, the warmth of the heater enveloped her, melting away the chill of the harsh winter. Her mom was sitting at the table, a warm cup of tea in hand, and a book open beside her. Her mother was a petite woman with kind eyes and a warm smile that always managed to make Hannah feel safe and loved.

"So what did you bring back this time?" her mom asked, putting down her book and giving Hannah a knowing smile.

"First, I have this can of corn," said Hannah, digging into her backpack and pulling out the can. "Not much, but it's something."

Her mom took the can and examined it, nodding her head in appreciation. "It's a start," she said, smiling at her daughter.

Hannah then pulled out an old computer motherboard, an ancient Atari console, and two Nintendo NES games. "And I found all of these!" she exclaimed, her eyes sparkling with excitement.

Her mom looked at the treasures and smiled. "I'm glad you found something," she said, a note of caution in her voice. "But remember, you need to be extra careful in that part of town. It's not safe."

"I know, Mom," replied Hannah, grateful for her mother's concern. "I'm always careful. And besides, I can't let a little danger stop me from exploring."

"I care about you, Hannah," said her mom, giving her a warm hug. "I don't want you to go missing like that Billy kid did."

Hannah hugged her back tightly, feeling her mother's love and protection surround her like a shield. "Thanks, Mom," she said, feeling grateful for her mother's unwavering love and support.

Chapter 4

A few days had passed since Hannah's adventure through the snowy city. She had spent most of her time resting, reading books, and tinkering with the old electronics she had found during her scavenging trip. However, it was time for her to return to her job. As she walked to work, she noticed Barb, a woman she often saw on her daily walks. Barb was a friendly woman in her mid-fifties who loved to walk and explore the city. She would often stop by the electronic stores like the one Hannah had visited during her scavenging trip.

As Hannah walked past the electronic store, "What was that," said Hannah, walking backward as she noticed something on the news caught her attention. The news anchor was talking about a new virtual reality game console that was about to be released. Hannah had always been fascinated by technology, and the idea of a game console that could transport a person's consciousness into a virtual world intrigued her.

On the TV screen, the news anchor spoke with a sense of excitement in his voice, "In other news, we have a story for the avid gamers out there. One that could change your life and your family's forever." Hannah's eyes lit up with excitement as she leaned closer to the screen, eager to hear more.

"We are here with Dr. Johnson, the creator of the Virtual Deck, and he has a big announcement to give us," said the news anchor, turning to the guest next to him. "But first, tell us about this new virtual reality game console.
How does it work?"
"Thank you for having me," Dr. Johnson replied, adjusting his glasses.

"We have spent many years trying to build a system that reads the electricity in your brain and takes your consciousness and projects that into a mind and body in a virtual world."
The news anchor looked concerned and asked, "Is this safe to use?"
"We have finally gotten it to a state where there is only a 1.7% chance of any harm happening. That comes from the brain interpreting the virtual world as reality," Dr. Johnson reassured him.
The news anchor held up a full head-covering helmet and asked, "So, this is what you would wear?"
"Yes, this helmet reads the electricity from your brain and comes out these cables in the back that are connected to the deck. The deck that you lay on reads and interprets it into the game. The deck also reads the vitals of your body and displays it on this screen, while the game is on the other screen," Dr. Johnson explained.
"Wow, this is all so fascinating. Now, tell us about your big announcement," the news anchor said with excitement.
"To test out the product, we are holding a competition at our headquarters. This will involve 10,000 players playing in a massive medieval world. We are inviting some of the best gamers from around the world to compete. We are also asking gamers to send in their video of their skill," Dr. Johnson said, his voice rising with excitement.
"Now, what would one win in this contest?" the news anchor asked.
"This will change the life of one family. They will get a full ride to live in the EZ. Everything will be paid for throughout the rest of their lives. Not only that, but they will come to work for us as well," Dr. Johnson said, his eyes lighting up with enthusiasm.
"Anything else to add?" the news anchor asked.

"Lastly, we will be streaming everything over the internet. Every player will have a stream of their own, so you can watch the players or family members you follow. Not only that, but we will have three streams going at all times, giving you highlights of all the epic moments going on," Dr. Johnson said, beaming with pride.
"Thanks for coming on and sharing this exciting news. Now, if you want to know more, head to the website below," the news anchor concluded.

"This is just what I needed" deemed Hannah, so thrilled that she quickly wrote down the website and ran to work to tell Jane all about it.

Hannah rushed into work, her heart still racing with excitement from the announcement she had just heard on the television. The manager was waiting for her, arms crossed and a stern look on his face.
"You're late Hannah," he said, glancing over her shoulder to see if any customers were waiting to be served.
"I know, it won't happen again,' she replied, brushing past him and making her way through the store.

As she hurried down the aisles, Hannah's mind was buzzing with thoughts of the virtual reality tournament. She knew that this was her chance to make a name for herself in the gaming world, to prove that she had what it takes to compete at the highest level. She finally found Jane, who was busy stacking shelves with the latest products.

"Hey, Hey Jane," said Hannah, rushing towards her.
"Slow down Hannah, slow down," replied Jane, trying to calm her down.

"You will never guess what I just heard," said Hannah, jumping for joy.
"What's so important, Hannah?" asked Jane, intrigued by her friend's excitement.
"They just announced a virtual reality tournament with the virtual deck," said Hannah, barely able to contain herself.
"No way, really?" replied Jane, her eyes widening with excitement.
"They are asking for people to apply and I want your help," continued Hannah, all giddy.
"Tomorrow, we will work all day to make it perfect," said Jane, getting back to work.

"This is going to be the longest day of my life," she thought to herself as she clocked in and made her way to the register.

Jane led a solitary life, existing in a state of detachment from her family. The bond that typically binds relatives together was notably absent in her case. While she harbored no ill will or animosity towards them, the emotional connection that usually thrives within a close-knit family was simply not present in her life.

Living alone, Jane found solace in the tranquility of her solitude. Her home, a sanctuary of quiet contemplation, offered respite from the complexities and demands of familial relationships. Without the responsibility of caring for others, she was free to pursue her passions and navigate life on her terms.

Though some may perceive her lack of familial connections as a void to be filled, Jane embraced her independence. She reveled in the freedom to make decisions without the influence or expectations of family members. She relished the ability to shape her path, unburdened by the ties that often come with close familial bonds.

Jane's self-reliance and autonomy allowed her to explore her individuality fully. She sought fulfillment through personal endeavors, immersing herself in creative pursuits, intellectual growth, and meaningful relationships outside of her family circle. The absence of familial obligations gave her the space to cultivate deep connections with friends and develop a network of support that was uniquely hers.

In the absence of familial ties, Jane's chosen family became her closest confidants and companions. These were the individuals she turned to in times of celebration and times of hardship. They formed an intimate circle that provided the emotional support, understanding, and sense of belonging that she craved.

While some might question her decision to lead a life seemingly detached from her family, Jane was content with her choices. She had crafted a life that allowed her to define her sense of happiness, free from the expectations and pressures that often accompany familial relationships. The absence of a traditional family structure did not define her but rather empowered her to forge her path and embrace the unique journey that awaited her.

For the next five hours, Hannah worked the register, checking out customers and making small talk as she went. The store was quiet for the first two hours, giving her a chance to read up on the virtual deck and the tournament that was coming up. She scoured the internet, jotting down notes and ideas for her application. Finally, the rush hour hit, and the store was filled with customers, leaving Hannah with little time to think about anything else. "Where did all these customers come from," thought Hannah, scamming items one after another, with a click of each scan.

As Hannah rushed back home from work, she couldn't contain her excitement any longer. She was practically skipping through the snow-covered street with every step, her mind buzzing with the endless possibilities of what could happen if she won the virtual reality tournament. As she entered her house, the aroma of her mom's hearty beef stew filled her senses, making her stomach grumble with anticipation.

"Mom, Dad, you'll never guess what I heard on the way to work!" she exclaimed, her words tumbling out in a rush, door slamming behind her. Her parents looked up from their respective activities, intrigued by her excitement. Her mom was stirring the bubbling pot on the stove while her dad was reading the newspaper at the kitchen table.
"Whoa, slow down there, Hannah. You're going to give your dad a heart attack!" her mom joked, placing a gentle hand on her shoulder to calm her down.

Hannah took a deep breath, trying to compose herself.
"There's a virtual reality tournament happening and I want to participate in it," she said with a big smile on her face.
"And the grand prize is an all-expenses-paid life in the EZ!"
"That's amazing, Hannah," her dad said, putting down his newspaper and looking at her with a glimmer of hope in his eyes.
"But let's not get too ahead of ourselves. We'll worry about that if and when you get picked. For now, it's just a dream."
"Grace, dinner" shouted Mom towards her room.

Hannah's heart sank a little at the thought of her dad's condition. He had been struggling with a chronic illness for a while now, and the treatment was expensive.

As the 4 sat down to enjoy the delicious stew that her mom had made, they took turns discussing their day, the conversation ranging from work to school to their plans for the future. For a moment, all of their worries and fears faded away, and they were just a happy family, enjoying each other's company and the comfort of a warm home-cooked meal.

As the sun rose, the next day.
"Today's the day," said Hannah, who was already up, eagerly awaiting the day ahead. The grocery store was closed today, which meant she had the entire day to focus on creating her video application for the virtual reality tournament. She began by tidying up her room, ensuring everything was in its proper place. She dusted off her shelves and arranged her retro video game collection neatly, wanting to showcase her love for classic games in her application.

"Everything is in the right place," said Hannah looking around her room at her collection.
With her room looking perfect, Hannah moved on to the next step: picking out an outfit. She had two options in mind, and she couldn't decide which one to wear. The first was a playful ensemble featuring a pink plaid skirt with black lace, knee-high striped socks, and a pink Super Mario shirt. The second was a custom-made dress that she had designed with her mom, inspired by the beloved franchise, Pokemon. The dress had a white skater-style base with various Pokemon characters

printed all over it, and it was adorned with a jean jacket and black boots.

Hannah admired both outfits for a while, pondering which one would be the better choice for her video application. As she contemplated, she called out to her sister, Grace, who came running into her room. "Hey, what's up?" Grace asked, eyeing the outfits on the bed. Hannah explained her dilemma and asked for her sister's opinion.

Grace took a few moments to think before holding up the custom-made Pokemon dress. "I think you should go with this one. It's more personal and unique. Plus, you can share a story about it in your application," Grace suggested holding up the dress.

"You're right, that would be the perfect outfit," said Hannah, smiling, realizing that her sister was right. The Pokemon dress would set her apart from the other applicants and showcase her creativity.

"Thank you, Grace. You always have the best ideas," Hannah said, giving her sister a tight hug. With the outfit decision made, she went to take a shower and do her makeup before Jane came over.

An hour later, Jane arrived at the door.

"Hey, you made it," said Hannah as she opened the creaky door.

"Yea, we're gonna have so much fun today," said Jane walking through the door, closing it behind her.

Hannah led her to her room where they both sat down on the bed. Hannah was beaming with excitement while Jane had a look of admiration on her face.

"You look amazing, Hannah," Jane exclaimed as she took in Hannah's appearance. "Thanks, I wanted to make sure I looked good for the video," Hannah replied with a smile.

After a brief exchange of pleasartries, Hannah quickly got to work. She turned on her camera and started to introduce herself. "Hi, my name is Hannah and I'm a huge fan of virtual reality gaming. I've been playing video games ever since I was a little girl and I've always been fascinated with the possibilities of virtual reality." She paused for a moment before continuing. "I'm so excited to apply for this virtual reality tournament and showcase my skills."

Jane nodded in agreement and chimed in, "Hannah is an amazing gamer and I know she's going to do great in this tournament." Hannah blushed at the compliment and continued with the video. She talked about her experience with different types of games and how she's honed her skills over the years. She then went on to explain her strategy for winning the tournament and how she planned to use her unique skills to come out on top.

As they continued working on the video, Jane suggested they add some visuals to make it more engaging.
"How about we add some footage of you playing some of your favorite games?" Jane suggested. Hannah thought it was a great idea and quickly pulled up some footage on her computer.

As they worked on the video, Hannah and Jane joked around and reminisced about their favorite gaming moments. They took breaks to snack on some chips and soda, laughing and chatting the entire time. Finally, after several hours of hard work,

"We finally finished the video," said Hannah, giving Jane a big hug, jumping with excitement.

Hannah was thrilled with how the video turned out and couldn't wait to submit it. She thanked Jane for all her help and they hugged before Jane left. As Hannah watched her go, she felt a rush of gratitude and happiness. She knew that she couldn't have done it without her friend's support and encouragement.

Hannah then went online to the website she had saved from the day before. There, she filled out the 10-page application. It took about an hour to fill out and she was elated as she finished the application for the virtual reality tournament. She had worked hard on her video, making sure it was perfect and showing off her skills and personality. As she hit the submit button, a wave of nervousness washed over her.
"What if I didn't get accepted? What if someone else had a better video?" said Hannah, pushing those thoughts aside, reminding herself that she had done her best and that was all that mattered.

After submitting her application, she clicked on the confirmation email that had arrived in her inbox. It gave her all the details about the tournament, including the dates, location, and rules. She read through it carefully, taking notes on anything that might be important. She also checked the website daily, hoping to see any updates or news about the tournament.

Despite her best efforts to keep herself occupied, the wait was starting to weigh on Hannah. She would check her mailbox every day, hoping to find a response from the tournament. But day after day, there was nothing but bills and advertisements.

Hannah began to worry that perhaps she had not been selected for the tournament. She wondered if her video was not good enough, or if there were simply too many other applicants. But she refused to give up hope, and instead poured herself into practicing her gaming skills.

As the weeks passed, Hannah tried to stay positive. She would often remind herself of the excitement she felt when first learning about the tournament, and how much she wanted to be a part of it. She would also talk to her friends and family about her passion for gaming and how much it meant to her to have the opportunity to compete on a national level.

Then, one day, Hannah finally received the long-awaited package in the mail. It was a large box with the tournament logo on the front. She could hardly contain her excitement and couldn't wait to tear into it and see what was inside.

The tournament logo embodies the spirit of awe-inspiring competition, captivating viewers with its dynamic design and symbolic representation. At its core, the logo features a fierce mythical creature, rendered with intricate detail and bold strokes, exuding power and determination. Its majestic wings spread wide, symbolizing the soaring ambition and limitless possibilities that await participants. The creature's eyes, ablaze with intensity, reflect the passion and unwavering commitment of the competitors. Surrounding the central figure, a swirling vortex of vibrant colors and dynamic shapes signifies the exhilarating energy and ever-evolving nature of the tournament. With its striking visuals and captivating symbolism, the logo stands as a testament to the grandeur and excitement that await those who dare to partake in this extraordinary contest.

As soon as Hannah saw the package waiting for her at the doorstep, she knew it was something big. Her heart raced with anticipation as she rushed inside to open it. She couldn't wait to share the news with Jane, her best friend since childhood. She picked up her phone and dialed Jane's number, barely able to contain her excitement.

"Hey, what's up?" Jane answered.
"You have to come over now!" Hannah interrupted, her voice filled with joy and excitement.
"Slow down, I can't understand you," said Jane, trying to calm her down.
"I got a package from the company running the tournament," said Hannah, her voice trembling with excitement.
"No way! I'll be over as soon as I can," said Jane with equal enthusiasm.

Hannah sat by the box, waiting anxiously for everyone to get home. She couldn't bear the thought of opening it without her family and friends around her. When her parents arrived home, they were just as surprised as she was to see the package. The next two hours seemed like an eternity as they waited for Jane to arrive.
"Finally, everyone is here. Now we can open the package" said Hannah to her family and friends.

The group gathered around the box, eager to see what was inside. Grace, Hannah's little sister, was practically bouncing with excitement.

"Come on, open it," she said, unable to contain her curiosity.

Hannah took a knife to the top of the box, carefully slicing it open. She could feel her heart pounding in her chest as she reached inside and pulled out a tan envelope. Her hands shook as she opened it and began to read the letter.

"Thank you for applying to be a part of our launch tournament. We'd like to inform you that you have been selected for this once-in-a-lifetime opportunity at a better life," Hannah read aloud, her voice filled with excitement.

"The tournament will take place just outside Miami, Florida, at our US testing facility. The tournament will take place in two months, on June 30th. All contestants will need to arrive 1 week before the start date and are allowed to bring one person with them. Everything will be paid for as long as you are still competing in the tournament. Once you lose, you'll be asked to head back home the next day. In the box is a portable virtual deck that you will use to create your character before the tournament. This must be done before your arrival, and we will upload your info onto your full-size virtual deck. Thank you for applying; we'll see you in Florida. Good luck in the tournament."

Hannah finished reading the letter with a smile on her face, feeling like she had won the lottery. She couldn't believe it - she had been chosen for the tournament! She looked up at her family and friends, their faces beaming with pride and excitement.

"Well, come on now, look in the box," said her mom, unable to contain her curiosity.

Hannah rummaged through the packing peanuts until she found the helmet and virtual deck console. The helmet was sleek and futuristic, with a visor that covered her eyes and a series of buttons and switches along the side. The virtual deck console was a small, handheld device that looked like something out of a sci-fi movie.

Hannah couldn't wait to get started. She knew she had a lot of work to do before the tournament, but she was ready for the challenge. She was going to train harder than ever before, and she was going to win.

As Hannah pondered over the decision of who to take with her to the tournament, she felt a sense of pressure building up inside her. The choice was not an easy one, and it seemed as though both options held equal weight in her heart. She knew that whoever she chose to bring along would play a crucial role in her overall experience at the tournament.

On one hand, there was Jane, her best friend since childhood. They had grown up together and shared many adventures. Hannah could imagine spending the entire trip laughing, having fun, and making unforgettable memories with Jane by her side. But on the other hand, there was her father, who had always been her biggest supporter. He had sacrificed so much for her and had always been there to encourage her every step of the way.
"This might be the last time I could spend quality time with him before his illness gets the best of him," said Hannah, wanting to have one last good time with him.

As Hannah weighed her options, she thought about all the fun times she had shared with Jane, and how much she valued their friendship. But at the same time, she couldn't help but think about how much her father had done for her over the years. He had always been there for her, even when things were tough, and had always been her biggest fan. She knew how much it would mean to him to be able to share this experience with her.

Hannah tried to imagine what it would be like if she chose to bring Jane along instead. She pictured herself laughing and joking with her friend but also felt a twinge of guilt at the thought of leaving her father behind. She knew that he would be disappointed and that the two of them might never have another chance to bond like this again.

In the end, Hannah knew what she had to do. She took a deep breath and made the difficult decision to bring her father with her to the tournament. She knew that it would mean the world to him and that the two of them would have an unforgettable experience together. This might be the last time that the two would have a chance to spend time together.

She also knew that her friendship with Jane would endure and that they would have plenty of opportunities to have fun and make memories in the future. Jane would understand that Hannah's dad didn't have much time left. Hannah loved her parents dearly and spent a lot of time with them. Jane knows that her father's illness weighed heavily on her too.

Hannah couldn't believe it - she had been selected to compete in the tournament of a lifetime, and she was going to need all the help she could get. That's why she turned to her best friend, Jane, for support. "Come back first thing in the morning. I want you here with me when I put the helmet on," Hannah said, her nerves getting the better of her.

"I'd love to be here to help you out," Jane replied, giving her friend a reassuring hug before heading out the door. As soon as Jane was gone, Hannah sat down at the table and began to study the letter from the tournament organizers. She read it over and over again, taking in every detail about the competition, the location, and the rules.

As she sat there, looking at the letter and the helmet, Hannah felt a mix of excitement and trepidation. She knew that this was a once-in-a-lifetime opportunity, but she also knew that the competition was going to be fierce. She needed to prepare herself mentally and physically for the challenge ahead.

For the next couple of hours, Hannah studied the rules of the tournament, took notes, and practiced her skills. She also spent some time researching the other competitors, trying to get a sense of who she would be facing in the competition.

Despite her nerves, Hannah was still mesmerized by the fact that she had been chosen to compete in the tournament. She felt grateful for the opportunity and excited about the adventure that lay ahead. And with Jane by her side, she knew that she had the support and encouragement she needed to succeed.

Chapter 5

As the sun slowly rose in the sky, Hannah lay in bed, her mind racing with thoughts of the upcoming tournament and the incredible headset that would soon change the lives of thousands. Despite her excitement, she had barely slept, her nerves getting the best of her. This was a completely new experience for her, and she couldn t help but feel a little overwhelmed.

Finally, after what seemed like an eternity, the day had arrived. Hannah had spent hours preparing her room, setting up the headset, and connecting it to her TV so that her friend Jane could watch everything that was happening. She was eager to lose herself in a new world, to experience something that she had never experienced before.

As she sat on her bed, Hannah was interrupted by her little sister Grace, who appeared in the doorway of her room.

"Can I watch, Hannah?" Grace asked, her eyes wide with excitement.
"Yes, you can watch," Hannah replied, though she made it clear that Grace was not to interfere or distract her in any way.

Grace sat down in a chair to the left of the bed, trying her best to stay quiet and out of the way.

A little while later, Jane arrived, buzzing with excitement and ready to see how the headset worked. She was an avid gamer herself, but Hannah was on a whole other level.

"Are you ready for this?" Jane asked as the two of them made their way to Hannah's room.
"I'm excited and nervous, Jane," Hannah admitted, her palms sweating with anticipation.
"You'll be fine, Hannah. This is something you've wanted ever since they announced it," Jane reassured her.
"Yeah, you're right," Hannah nodded, taking a deep breath to calm herself down.

As they settled in, Grace broke the silence, giving Hannah a thumbs up and telling her she'd do great.

"Alright, let's do this," Hannah said, lying back on her bed. Jane turned on the TV, the virtual deck, and the mask visor, which flickered to life in a dim glow.
"Here we go," Hannah said, taking a deep breath before putting on the helmet.

At first, nothing happened. Minutes ticked by, and the TV remained stuck on a blank white screen, while Hannah lay there, still conscious and feeling frustrated.

"What's going on? Why isn't anything happening?" she demanded, her frustration mounting.

Jane quickly went to work, rifling through the instruction manual to try and figure out what the problem was. Finally, she had an idea.

"Close your eyes, Hannah," Jane instructed, placing the manual down.

"I'll hit the sync button on the helmet." Hannah followed her friend's directions, closing her eyes tightly as Jane pushed the button.

For a few moments, nothing seemed to happen, and Hannah felt a wave of disappointment wash over her. But then, suddenly, a red light lit up on the left side of the helmet, and text began to appear on the TV screen. Hannah's heart leaped with excitement as the world around her began to come to life, and she was finally able to fully immerse herself in the virtual reality experience.

Hannah's heart raced as she found herself in a strange, virtual world, with nothing but a blank, white expanse in all directions. She gazed around, taking in the eerily silent surroundings, and tried to steady her nerves. "Hello, anyone there?" she called out tentatively. Suddenly, a soft, calming voice filled her ears, seemingly coming from all directions at once.
"Hello and welcome, Hannah," it said.

Hannah spun around, looking for the source of the voice, but found nothing.
"Who are you? Show yourself!" she demanded, her voice rising in panic.
"I'd like to congratulate you on being picked for a once-in-a-lifetime opportunity," the voice said smoothly, ignoring her outburst.

Hannah gritted her teeth.
"Who are you?" she repeated, her voice tight with frustration.
"I am your AI," the voice replied patiently.

"I will guide you through the process of creating your character."

"Please show yourself," Hannah begged, desperation creeping into her voice. Suddenly, a blue, vaguely humanoid figure appeared in front of her, its contours shimmering and rippling like a mirage. Jane and Grace leaned in closer to the old CRT TV, their eyes glued to the screen.

"I'm going to go make popcorn. Do you want anything?" Grace asked, already heading towards the kitchen.
"Bring me a Mountain Dew," Jane replied absently, still entranced by the unfolding scene.

Grace returned to the room with a bag of popcorn just in time to see the blue figure appear on the screen. Hannah couldn't help but feel a bit intimidated by the figure's appearance.
"What is this place?" the figure asked, looking around the empty space.
"This is the plane between the real world and the virtual world. This is where all new players start before entering their respective virtual world," explained the blue figure.
"So where do we start?" Hannah asked, eager to get started.
"Here," said the voice, gesturing to a pop-up box. Hannah reached out and touched the box, and a keyboard popped up with
"Enter character name" displayed in the box. "Here you will enter the name of your character you will be playing. You will be in a medieval setting, so pick accordingly," instructed the figure.

Jane was glued to the screen, watching every move Hannah made.

"Pick something awesome," she said encouragingly. Hannah took a moment to think of a name that would truly stand out in the tournament. She wanted something epic and unique. "Aurora Stormblade" she shouted excitedly as she typed in her character's name. It was the name of a comic book character she liked reading.

"Great name!" exclaimed Grace, her eyes glued to the TV screen. The pop-up box vanished as soon as Hannah hit "submit". "Well done! You've picked a unique name. Be proud of it as you play. Now, let's move on to your character's appearance," said the blue figure. Suddenly, a mirror materialized in front of Hannah, and she could see herself in the real world.
"For now, you will look mostly like yourself, but in some virtual reality worlds, you'll look completely different. Here, you'll have some changes based on the settings you pick," explained the blue figure as she moved to the left side of the mirror.
"Swipe up with your hand, and a menu will appear."

Hannah did as she was instructed, and a menu of races appeared on the screen. Elf, Dwarf, Human, Small-foot, and Orc were the options available to her. Each race had its own unique ability that could benefit her in the game. Hannah scrolled through the races, and as she did so, her appearance changed accordingly in the mirror. "Pick Elven, pick Elven!" chanted Grace. However, Hannah decided to keep it simple and picked humans as her race.

The human race had the ability "Quick Learner" Human characters can learn new skills and abilities faster than other races, giving them an advantage in the long term.

"I'll pick humans as my race," said Hannah, tapping it on the menu.
"You have chosen the human race. They are the most common and reliable among all the races," said the blue figure, snapping her fingers to change the appearance of Hannah's character.

The only things that changed were the clothing she was wearing and how her hair was styled. She wore a long, dark blue tunic with light brown pants and black boots. Her hair was woven into a long French braid, adding a touch of elegance to her appearance.
"Ooo, I look nice," said Hannah, turning from side to side, and looking at herself in the mirror.

Hannah was both excited and nervous as she swiped up to reveal the class list. Each class had its own unique abilities and traits that would determine how she would play the game. She knew this was a big decision, one that would greatly impact her virtual gaming experience. The blue figure beside her watched with great interest as she scrolled through the list.

"Picking your class says a lot about you," the blue figure said, emphasizing the importance of her decision.
"Take your time and choose wisely."

Hannah studied the list carefully, weighing the pros and cons of each class. Paladin, Warrior, Rogue, Ranger, Sorcerer, Bard, Cleric, and Druid. Each class had its own unique set of skills, and she was having a hard time deciding which one to choose.

After much contemplation, Hannah ultimately chose the Ranger class. She was drawn to their light feet and excellent tracking abilities, and she loved the fact that their main attack style was from afar. She could see herself becoming a skilled archer, taking out enemies from a distance.

"I thought she would have picked Warrior or Sorcerer. She always picks thoughts classes" Jane said, surprised by her friend's selection.
"I don't know what any of them mean," Grace chimed in, looking confused and just wanting to be a part of the action.

The blue figure explained to Hannah that each class had its own set of strengths and weaknesses and that the Ranger class was a great choice for someone who valued agility and precision. Hannah looked at herself in the mirror and admired her new appearance. She was proud of her decision and couldn't wait to start playing.

But there was one more decision to make. The blue figure instructed her to swipe again to reveal a list of abilities. She had to choose two from the list of ten, and she had to choose wisely as selecting one would mean that five others would be unavailable to her in-game.

Hannah studied the list carefully, reading and re-reading each ability. It was a tough decision, but after some time, she picked Basic Bowman and Minor Healing. The former would give her the upper hand with a bow, while the latter would allow her to heal herself or others with a low number of health points.

"Congratulations, Aurora. You have taken the first step to competing in the virtual reality tournament. May you do well my new wonderer" said the blue figure cheerfully.

The blue figure congratulated her on creating her character, Aurora Stormblade, and saved it to her portable virtual deck. Hannah felt a sense of satisfaction and accomplishment as she realized that she was now ready for the tournament. She couldn't wait to see what adventures lay ahead in the virtual world.
"What do I do now?" asked Aurora, wondering what happens next.

Suddenly, in a blink of an eye, the blue figure disappeared, leaving Hannah standing alone in the empty room. She looked around, feeling a bit disoriented. Everything had happened so fast. She had created her character and now she was supposed to be ready for the tournament.

After Hannah confirmed her character creation, the screen faded into a plain white color, and the visors went dark. She felt a momentary jolt as if she was waking up from a dream. As the visors lifted, she saw Jane and Grace standing by the side of her bed, eagerly awaiting her feedback.

"How was it?" Jane asked excitedly, her eyes wide with anticipation. Hannah felt a broad smile spread across her face.
"It was amazing!" she exclaimed.
"It felt so real like I was there. The blue figure was so detailed."

Grace nodded approvingly, clearly satisfied with Hannah's response. "And how do you feel now?" she asked, checking on her friend. Hannah paused for a moment, running a mental check on her body. "I feel perfectly fine like nothing has happened. It's incredible how immersive the experience was."

"I just wish there was more to it," Hannah added wistfully. "I want to try it out more, explore the virtual world, and see what other adventures await me." Jane nodded reassuringly. "Don't worry, you'll get plenty of opportunities once the tournament starts. It's going to be an amazing experience, and we'll be there with you every step of the way" said Jane, encouraging Hannah with confidence.

Hannah's eyes widened with excitement. "The tournament! I can't wait. It's so far away, though.
"She let out a sigh, longing for the chance to dive back into the virtual world. "But I know it will be worth the wait."

Jane smiled at Hannah's excitement.
"Well, in the meantime, we can research more about the game and how to improve your skills," she suggested.

Grace nodded in agreement.
"Yeah, and maybe we can find some tips and tricks online from other players who have already played it," she added.

Hannah grinned. "That's a great idea. But the game isn't out yet" she said, feeling grateful to have such a supportive sister.

As the days passed, Hannah became more and more obsessed with the idea of the tournament. She would spend hours each day reading and researching the game, trying to find any clues about what the challenges might be.

In her research, she discovered that the game was called "Realm of Adventure." It was supposedly known for its incredibly detailed and immersive world, as well as its challenging quests and battles.

Hannah found herself becoming more and more excited about the tournament, imagining herself exploring the vast virtual world, battling fierce monsters, and completing challenging quests. She was determined to be the best, to come out on top and win the grand prize.

Despite her excitement, however, there were still several weeks to go before the tournament. In the meantime, Hannah decided to continue practicing and preparing for the competition.

She knew that the tournament would be a challenge, but she was determined to overcome it and emerge victorious. The thought of the grand prize – a life in the EZ kept her motivated and focused.

Chapter 6

As Hannah arrived at her workplace, she couldn't help but feel a bit nervous about the upcoming tournament. Her mind was filled with thoughts of strategies and tactics, all aimed at winning the competition. But as she walked towards the entrance, something caught her eye. There was a sign in the window that read "Go Hannah, you'll do great!"

Her heart swelled with pride as she realized that her coworkers had put up the sign to show their support. Hannah had always been close with her colleagues, but she never expected them to go this far to cheer her on.

Her manager greeted her with a wide smile, saying "Congratulations, Hannah! We're all so proud of you."

"What's with the sign?" Hannah asked, genuinely curious.
"Oh, that. Jane put it up," her manager replied. "She said something about rallying the town behind you or something."

Hannah couldn't help but smile at the thought of Jane going out of her way to support her. "Thank you," she said, feeling a sense of warmth and gratitude towards her coworkers.

As she went about her day, she couldn't help but notice the extra attention she was getting from her coworkers. They seemed to be going out of their way to congratulate her and wish her luck for the tournament.

Later on, Hannah found Jane stocking the shelves and decided to thank her personally for the sign in the window.
"You told everyone, huh?" she asked, approaching her friend.

Jane grinned.
"Of course I did! You need people cheering you on. This is a big deal, Hannah. You should be proud of yourself."

Hannah couldn't help but feel touched by Jane's words.
"Thanks, Jane. I appreciate it," she said, grateful to have such a supportive friend.
"Just wait till the next basketball game," Jane teased. "You'll be the star of the show!"

Hannah rolled her eyes, but couldn't help but laugh.
"Please don't. You know I don't want to be put on the spot," she said, but deep down, she was grateful for the support and encouragement of her coworkers.

After work, Hannah decided to go for a walk to clear her mind. As she strolled through the town, she noticed more and more signs congratulating her and wishing her luck in the tournament. It was both overwhelming and humbling at the same time. She couldn't believe that so many people cared about her success.

As she walked, she thought about how far she had come since she first put on the virtual reality helmet. It was amazing to think that her passion for gaming had led her to this point, where she was about to compete in a major tournament. It was a dream come true.

As she turned a corner, she heard a group of kids playing in the park. She stopped to watch them for a moment, feeling a sense of nostalgia for her own childhood. She had always loved playing in the park, but as she got older, she found herself more drawn to gaming. It was a different kind of competition, but it was still thrilling in its way.

As she continued her walk, she came across a small store that sold vintage gaming merchandise. She couldn't resist going inside and browsing the shelves. She was amazed at how many old games and consoles were still available, and she spent a long time reminiscing about the games people used to play.

As she walked away from the store, Hannah realized that the tournament was about more than just winning. It was about the connections she would make with other gamers, the support she was receiving from her community, and the sense of accomplishment she would feel just by competing. She was more excited than ever to see what the tournament would bring.

As she walked, Hannah couldn't help but think about the virtual world she had experienced. The thought of competing in it made her heart race with excitement. She imagined herself exploring new landscapes, defeating monsters, and solving puzzles. But more than that, she was eager to meet other gamers from around the world and build relationships with them.

Hannah had always been shy and reserved, but something about the virtual world made her feel more confident and outgoing. She realized that the tournament was not just about winning, but about the experiences and connections she would make along the way.

As she continued walking, Hannah thought about the upcoming tournament and her virtual deck at home. She had created her character. She was disappointed that she couldn't interact with other players or play around in the virtual world. Nevertheless, she was excited about the possibility of teaming up with someone for the tournament and the prospect of building relationships with other gamers.

With newfound confidence, Hannah walked towards home, determined to practice for the tournament and make the most of the community aspect of the competition. She couldn't wait to see what the virtual world had in store for her.

Hannah arrived home and immediately went to her room to turn on her virtual deck. As she waited for it to load, she couldn't help but feel a little disappointed that she couldn't connect with other players or receive messages as she had hoped.

Finally, the virtual deck finished loading and Hannah logged into her account. However, to her dismay, she discovered that there were no games available for her to play. All she saw was a message that read "Character already created."

"That's disappointing," said Hannah, wanting to do more with the virtual deck.
Hannah sighed and slumped back onto her bed. She had been so excited to participate in the tournament and connect with other gamers, but it seemed like she was stuck with a virtual deck that couldn't do anything. However, she refused to give up so easily. She was determined to find a way to make the most of her situation and still participate in the tournament.

Despite the setbacks, Hannah was determined to make the most of her situation and still participate in the tournament. She was confident that her hard work and dedication would pay off in the end.

The day had arrived for Hannah to head off to work again, but she couldn't resist making a quick pit-stop at the electronic store on the way. She sauntered in, eyes glimmering with excitement, and her attention was immediately caught by a commercial playing on one of the screens. It was advertising the upcoming tournament she had been accepted to, and she watched it with rapt attention, hoping to glean any new information or strategies she could use to improve her chances of success. Alas, there was nothing she hadn't already learned from her extensive research and hours of practice, but the mere sight of the advertisement was enough to give her a renewed sense of determination and vigor as she continued to work.

Upon arriving at her job, she was greeted with a surprise that nearly took her breath away. She counted four old TVs in the store's front window and two more hanging from the ceiling, all tuned to the same channel. Curiosity piqued, Hannah approached one of her coworkers standing at the end of a register and asked what was going on.

"The owner must be overly excited about you being in that tournament of yours," the coworker explained with a chuckle. "Good luck, Hannah," a regular chimed in as he walked by, flashing her a supportive thumbs-up.

Hannah made her way to the back of the store to see if the owner, John was around.

"John, you here?" she called out as she peered around the shelves. A few moments later, he emerged from behind a stack of boxes, clipboard in hand.
"Oh, Hannah! Congratulations on your acceptance to the tournament. We're all rooting for you," John exclaimed, beaming with pride. "Now, what can I do for you?"

Hannah wasted no time getting to the point. "What's with all the TVs up front?" she inquired, though she had a pretty good idea of what the answer was.
"Yeah, I'm getting ready for the tournament. I'm going to stream you on all the TVs. I want to show our utmost support for you. I just ask that you mention the store a few times during your adventure," John explained as he jotted some notes down on his clipboard. Hannah couldn't help but feel touched by his enthusiasm and support.
"Thank you so much, John," she said, feeling grateful for his unwavering encouragement.
"One last thing. If you don't win, your job is always available," John added with a chuckle as he turned to walk away.

Hannah couldn't help but smile at his words, feeling a sense of comfort and belonging at the grocery store that had been her workplace for so long. She left the store that day with a newfound sense of confidence, ready to take on whatever challenges the tournament may bring, and knowing that she had a team of supporters behind her every step of the way.

As the days passed by at a snail's pace, Hannah's excitement for the virtual reality tournament continued to grow. She couldn't wait to compete against the best gamers from all over the world. However, she had to wait for two weeks before the tournament began, and it seemed like an eternity.

Finally, the day of the monthly basketball game arrived, and the town was buzzing with excitement. Everyone in town had turned up for the game, and the atmosphere was electric. Hannah put on her team's northern blue colors, and she met up with her friend Jane to hang out before the game. They caught up with some colleagues from the grocery store and decided to tailgate before the game.

They grilled hotdogs and hamburgers, and they drank beer while huddled together to keep warm in the cold. It was -21 below zero, and the 10mph wind made it feel even colder. But the group didn't mind; they were all having a great time.

After a couple of hours of hanging out, it was finally time for the game to begin. Jane wore her red colors while Hannah wore her blue colors, and they headed into the gym together. To Hannah's surprise, Jane took her to a special spot up front. Hannah wondered what Jane had planned for her.

As the players warmed up, a man came out to center court and asked for everyone's attention.

"Hello, everyone in attendance today. I wanted to make an announcement brought up by a nice young lady," said the man as he gestured toward Hannah. She was taken aback and felt embarrassed by the attention. She slowly and nervously walked to the center of the basketball court.

"Hannah here has been picked for something big, something that could change her life. She has been selected to compete in the virtual reality tournament down in Florida," continued the man.

"I want everyone to congratulate her and give her a round of applause," he said as the crowd erupted in applause, cheers, and shouts of encouragement. Hannah's face turned red with embarrassment.

Jane gave Hannah a big smile and hugged her tightly, "Congratulations, Hannah! You deserve it."

However, Hannah was feeling irritated and embarrassed, "Please don't do that again," she said to Jane.

The rest of the game went by in a blur for Hannah. She couldn't wait to get back home and start practicing for the tournament. She was determined to do her best and make her town proud.

As the days dwindled down before the tournament, Hannah kept a low profile. She was still reeling from the embarrassment she endured at the basketball game. Everywhere she went, people would stop her and congratulate her on being picked for the tournament. She appreciated their well wishes, but she couldn't help feeling a bit uncomfortable with all the attention.

As she was packing her bags for the long train ride down to Florida, Hannah couldn't help but feel a sense of excitement and nervousness. She had never been to a tournament of this magnitude before, and the thought of competing against some of the best gamers in the world was both thrilling and intimidating.

Two weeks before the tournament, a package arrived in the mail for Hannah. Inside were two passes to get into the EZ.

These passes were highly coveted and incredibly hard to come by. They gave special access to the EZ.

Chapter 7

The day had finally arrived for Hannah and her father to embark on their journey to Florida for the virtual reality tournament. With no other means of transportation due to the heavy snow, they were set to take a horse taxi to the train station, which would take about 3 hours. Hannah had meticulously packed her belongings, making sure to include everything she needed for the tournament. In her backpack, she had her phone, a Game Boy Advance with a working copy of Pokemon Yellow, the highly coveted EZ passes, and the letter. Meanwhile, her pink sparkly suitcase was packed with her clothing, helmet, virtual deck, and bathroom essentials. She even packed the Pokemon dress she and her mother made.

As they were getting ready to leave, Hannah couldn't help but feel worried about her father's health, given his history of heart problems.
"So Dad, you're up for this, right?" she asked, her voice laced with concern.
"I'll be fine. You don't need to worry about me. You just focus on winning that tournament," her father reassured her, albeit slowly and with a hint of shortness of breath.

Before they left, Hannah's mother, Grace, gave her a big hug and told her she would be watching the tournament closely. Jane also gave her words of encouragement and hugged her tightly. Finally, Hannah and her father picked up their bags and headed outside to the horse taxi, where a large group of people had gathered to see them off. They cheered them on, offering their support and well wishes as they loaded their bags onto the wagon. There were quite a few people from work, ready to send her off.

As they made their way through the snow-covered streets, Hannah couldn't help but feel a sense of excitement and nervousness about what lay ahead. She knew that the tournament was the biggest thing in the world since the EZ was set up, and the thought of being a part of it made her heart race.

After three long hours, they finally arrived at the train station that was under downtown Chicago. They stepped off the horse taxi and made their way inside, where they would wait for the train to arrive. In the meantime, they picked up their tickets, which cost a hefty $376 for the both of them, 2 weeks' worth of work, a price that Hannah knew was a lot of money for her family.

As they sat and waited, Hannah couldn't help but feel grateful for the outpouring of support she had received from her family and friends. She knew that they were all rooting for her and it gave her the strength and determination she needed to succeed in the tournament.

The station was small and silent, with only one other traveler sitting on a bench against the wall. Hannah looked around in amazement, taking in every detail of the station. She had never seen anything like this before and the quietness of the place made her feel a bit uneasy. She glanced at her dad, who seemed to be taking everything in stride.

The two of them settled down on a bench. The anticipation and excitement of the journey ahead made the time pass slowly. Finally, after what felt like an eternity, the train slowly rolled into the station from the south, its sleek and imposing presence sending shivers down Hannah's spine. She felt a sudden sense

of awe and wonder, realizing that she was about to embark on a journey that would take her to a place she had only dreamt of. "You ready for this, Hannah?" asked her father, as he got up and looked at Hannah still sitting on the bench.
Hannah hesitated while sitting on the bench, "let's do this" she said, getting up off the bench and heading to the train.

The two of them boarded the train, carefully picking seats close to the front of the train. Hannah could feel the train's vibrations beneath her feet as they settled in their seats. She couldn't help but wonder what kind of experiences awaited her on this journey. As the train slowly picked up speed heading out of the station, she gazed out the window, marveling at the snow-covered scenery that passed by in a blur.

Fifteen minutes later, the train was off. Hannah felt a rush of excitement and fear mixed, as this was the first time she had ever left her town, and had never been on a train before or even a car for that matter. She held on tight to her backpack as they headed down the tracks.

As the train journey continued, Hannah felt a sense of liberation and excitement at the new experiences that awaited her. She couldn't wait to see what the future held and what amazing adventures were in store for her.

As Hannah and her father traveled through the countryside, they left behind the quiet and familiarity of their small town to venture into the unknown. The cities they encountered along the way were mere remnants of their former selves, Indianapolis, Louisville, and Atlanta with their once-bustling streets now empty and desolate. Despite the eerie quiet of these former metropolises, Hannah and her father were filled with a sense of excitement and anticipation as they journeyed toward their destination.

As the train rolled along, Hannah's thoughts turned to the upcoming tournament. She had spent countless hours studying and preparing for this event and she was determined to win. However, she was also worried about her father, who was suffering from a serious illness. She kept a watchful eye on him, making sure he was comfortable and taking his medicine on time.

During the journey, they enjoyed some simple and convenient frozen meals that they had brought with them, and Hannah occasionally played her favorite game, Pokemon Yellow, on her Game Boy Advance.
"I still remember the day I found this small yellow cartridge" thought Hannah to herself as she played. However, most of the time, she was gazing out of the window, taking in the breathtaking views of the countryside and the changing scenery.

As the train chugged closer to the border of the New USA, Hannah peered out the window in awe. The once tranquil and serene countryside had gradually morphed into an ominous concrete jungle, with towering skyscrapers that seemed to touch the clouds. The cityscape was a tangled mess of metal and glass that spanned for miles with no end in sight. It was as if the city had been built to stretch towards the heavens and take over the sky. From the coast of Georgia to the former city of Dalles, Texas.

As the train pulled into the station, Hannah was immediately struck by the thick smog that clouded the air, making it difficult to see anything beyond a few feet. She could barely make out the tops of the skyscrapers towering above, as they disappeared into the murky haze. The stench of rotting garbage filled her nostrils, making her gag. The streets were lined with mounds of trash that seemed to stretch on for blocks, with rats scurrying in and out of the piles. It was a stark contrast from the pristine countryside she had left behind.

As they stepped out of the train, the city of New USA welcomed them with a not-so-warm embrace. The streets were crowded with shady individuals who looked like they had been up all night, and buildings were crumbling and covered in graffiti. It was like the sketchiest part of a city that Hannah had ever seen. She couldn't help but feel uneasy as they made their way through the city, trying to avoid the sketchy people and the piles of garbage that littered the sidewalks.

But despite the grimy appearance of the city, something was mesmerizing about it. The buildings that towered above them seemed to go on forever, creating a skyline that was both intimidating and awe-inspiring. The mix of architectural styles was bewildering, with ancient brick buildings standing shoulder-to-shoulder with sleek and modern glass structures.

Everyone had to get off, and a conductor came down the platform to check their IDs and passes.
"Do you have our passes and paperwork out?" said her father, making sure they had everything they needed.
"Yes Dad, I have them all right here, the paperwork, our IDs," she said a little snippy, showing her dad.

There was only one other person left on the platform, and the conductor approached Hannah and her father. He politely asked to see our IDs and passes, and they handed them over. Hannah presented her letter of invitation to the tournament, and the conductor checked everything thoroughly before congratulating them and handing back their documents.

After passing the checkpoint, they hopped back onto the train and continued their journey toward the EZ. They were excited to finally reach their destination and start the tournament. Despite the challenges they had faced along the way, Hannah felt more determined than ever to succeed and make her family proud.

As Hannah and her father passed through the border and entered the EZ, they couldn't believe their eyes. It was as if they had entered a whole new world. The snow was way less here and the landscape started transforming into lush green grass and trees. As they traveled further south, the temperature rose, and they could feel the warmth of the sun on their faces. The sky was clear, and the air was filled with the sweet scent of flowers. It was a stark contrast to the cold and snowy environment they had left behind.

After traveling for 50 miles into the EZ, they came across the clean and well-maintained building, the first sign of civilization. The building was surrounded by beautifully landscaped gardens, and the roads were smooth and free of potholes. They were in awe of the advanced infrastructure and the level of cleanliness maintained throughout the area.

As they traveled further south, they arrived at Orlando, where the snow had disappeared entirely. The weather was a pleasant low 60s at its average high, and everything seemed more alive down here. The trees were in full bloom, and the grass was lush and green. It was a sight that they had never seen before.

Finally, after a few more hours, they arrived in West Palm Beach, the furthest south that the train would take them. The weather was so pleasant that they didn't need to wear their winter gear. The locals were dressed in light clothing, making them realize they had to do some shopping.
"Wow, it's nice here," exclaimed Hannah as she took off her jacket, scarf, gloves, and hat.
"Never once have I been able to walk outside and not need a jacket," said Hannah enjoying the nice weather, well nice to her.
"Don't get too attached to the nice weather. It may not last for us" cautioned her father.

Upon reaching the front of the station, they were greeted by a taxi driver who was designated to take them to Miami, where they would be staying during the tournament. The taxi ride was smooth and comfortable, and they had an opportunity to see the beautiful surroundings. They passed through small towns with colorful houses and people riding bikes and walking their dogs. It was a whole new world for them, and they couldn't wait to explore it more.

After a long and exhausting journey, Hannah and her dad finally arrived at one of the hotels where the contestants were staying. The building was an impressive feat of architecture, standing tall and grande with a sleek and modern design. The hotel was one of 7 that had been set up for contestants from all over the world. This one was for North and South America players. As they walked into the lobby, Hannah couldn't help but be impressed by the luxurious and spacious interior. The

lobby was adorned with beautiful artwork and chandeliers hung from the ceiling, casting a warm glow over everything.
"This place is super fancy. Never seen anything like this" said Hannah, mesmerized by the beauty of the hotel.

As they approached the front desk, a friendly receptionist greeted them with a warm smile. She was dressed in a professional uniform and her hair was pulled back into a neat bun.
"Checking in for Hannah Anderson," said Hannah's dad to the lady. The receptionist nodded and began to type on the computer, her fingers moving quickly over the keys.

After a moment, the receptionist set a tablet on the counter and turned to Hannah's dad.
"Just going to need your fingerprint here and here," she said, pointing to two spots on the screen. Hannah's dad obliged, signing his name with his thumbprint.

"Great, thank you," said the receptionist, handing them a map and a set of keys.
"You'll be in room 278 on the third floor. Just take the elevator over there and head to your left. Follow the signs, and you'll find your room."

Hannah and her dad thanked the receptionist, then followed the directions and made their way to their room. The room was spacious and well-lit, with two comfortable beds, a large flat-screen TV, and a cozy armchair in the corner. The walls were painted in a soothing shade of blue, and the carpet was plush and soft underfoot.

After they had settled in, they made their way back down to the lobby to check in for the tournament. They joined the long line of people waiting to check in, which stretched all the way around the lobby. It took them a good 45 minutes to reach the front of the line, but finally, it was their turn.

"Congratulations and welcome to the tournament!" said the friendly man behind the counter.
"May I see your letter and EZ passes, please?" Hannah handed him the necessary documents, and he quickly scanned them into the computer.

"Great, thank you," he said, printing out a schedule and a set of badges. "Here is your itinerary. It lists all the dates and times of everything going on this week, and when you need to be at the arena for the tournament. Everything this week, except linking your helmet and virtual deck, is optional. But I'd recommend at least going to one practice. You'll get a feel for how everything works."

He handed them each a badge, which they were instructed to wear at all times while at the tournament. "Any questions?" he asked.

Hannah's dad spoke up. "Is food included, or do we have to pay for that?"

The man smiled. "Each hotel has a restaurant, and they are all included in the tournament. Just show your badges, and you can eat for free. Here's a map of the city with all the included hotels marked."

Hannah and her dad thanked the man and headed off to explore the hotel and get some much-needed rest before the practice week began.

Chapter 8

It was the first full day of the practice week, and Hannah was filled with excitement as she looked out the hotel window at the bustling city below. She had been dreaming of this moment for months, and she couldn't wait to see what the day had in store for her.

As they ate a hearty breakfast in the hotel's restaurant.
“What do you think it's going to be like, Dad,” asked Hannah, taking a bit of her toast with blackberry jelly on it.
“It’s going to be a whole new world and a new body. But you’ll do great in the tournament” said her Dad, wishing he could adventure with her.
“Well, when I created my character, it felt so natural. Like it was my body in the game. Plus, I can't wait to get into the game and see how it works said Hannah just wanting to play now and not wait till Wednesday.
“According to this itinerary, you have a lot you can do to learn about the game and everything it has to offer. Seminars, workshops, and even plenty of time to practice” said Dad, taking a bite of his eggs while looking at the itinerary.
“On another note, how are you feeling today,” asked Hannah, concerned for her father's illness, taking a bit of a waffle she ordered.
“Well, this fresh warm air makes it easier to breathe, the air is not so cold and harsh here and I love it,” Dad said, sounding not so winded today.
“Even so, you should still take it easy as to not overdo it because I care a lot about you Dad and I want you to be around for a long time,” said Hannah leaning forward to hold his hand.
“You need not worry about me. You need to focus on the tournament and winning” said her Dad comforting Hannah, as he finished his breakfast. “Shall we get going, Dad” said

Hannah, who was eager to go get to the arena and check out the tournament floor. Also not finishing her breakfast.
Hannah and her Dad made their way to the tournament area. The sun was shining bright, and the cool breeze was a welcome change from the chilly weather back home. As they drove through the scenic countryside, Hannah couldn't help but marvel at the lush greenery and the towering trees that seemed to go on forever.

Finally, after a 30-minute drive, they arrived at the tournament area. The building was massive, stretching across 20 city blocks, and it was easy to see why it had been chosen as the venue for the tournament.

As they stepped out of the car, Hannah could feel her heart racing with excitement.
"Wow this place is massive " said marveling at the size of the building.
She clutched her helmet and virtual deck tightly in her bag, eager to link them up to the table and start practicing for the tournament.

Hannah and her dad made their way into the massive building that would serve as the battleground for the upcoming tournament.
"There are an offal lot of players here already," said Hannah to her Dad as she looked around.
"That there is," responded Dad, looking for where to go.
The lobby was bustling with activity as players and their families milled about, getting ready for the day ahead. The pair joined the queue for the bag check and metal detectors, a necessary precaution against any potential threats from the outside world. They watched as security personnel

meticulously inspected each bag and scanned every person who walked through the detectors.

As they approached the check-in desk at the end of the hall, Hannah felt a flutter of excitement in her chest. She couldn't wait to see what the day had in store for her. The line here was mercifully short, and they were quickly ushered through to the front. The man behind the desk greeted them with a smile.

"Badge please," he said, holding out his hand.

Hannah fished her badge out of her pocket and handed it over. The man thanked her as he scanned it with a handheld device. After a brief pause, he handed it back to her.
“Here,” she said, hanging her badge on the man.
"Thank you,” he said, scanning the badge into the computer system.
“Now, if you head through those doors to the area floor, join the line, and wait for your turn, they will help you link your steam deck to your table" he instructed, pointing to his left at a set of doors.

Hannah and her dad followed his directions, pushing open the heavy doors and stepping onto the tournament floor. It was like nothing she had ever seen before. The sheer size of the space took her breath away. Bleacher seats rose all around the room, holding thousands of fans who had come to watch the competition. The tables were arranged in neat rows, each one looking like a giant concrete slab with a black top and green lines forming squares.
“There has to be a thousand tables here” thought Hannah looking around the room in sheer awe.

As Hannah walked towards the tables, she felt a shiver of anticipation run down her spine. This was it. This was where she was going to compete against some of the best players in the world. She looked at the monitors that were set up at each table, one for the player's perspective and the other for the audience to see the player's vitals.

As Hannah and her father made their way to the end of the line, her excitement for the tournament was suddenly interrupted by a commotion nearby. A group of people was gathered, arguing with the security guards, waving signs, and shouting slogans. Hannah tried to make out what they were saying, but it was difficult to decipher through the cacophony of voices. It became apparent that they were protesting for something related to equality and fairness.

As she stood there, bewildered by the situation, Hannah remembered her father's warning about a rogue group that was advocating for a different approach to the tournament. The group, known as the Equalizers, believed that everyone in the EZ should have an equal chance to win, regardless of their skill or ability. They had been causing disruptions throughout the EZ, protesting against what they believed was a flawed system that favored the privileged few over the disadvantaged many.

Hannah couldn't help but feel a twinge of worry as she watched the group getting more agitated by the minute. She hoped that they wouldn't cause any trouble and that the tournament would go on as planned. She knew that the EZ was not perfect, but it was still a better place to live than most of the world.

After waiting for what felt like an eternity, Hannah and her father finally made it to the front of the line. The hustle and bustle of the registration area was a dizzying spectacle of people and technology, with countless tables and machines scattered about. Hannah could feel the excitement building within her as they approached their assigned table.

"Finally," she thought to herself, tapping her foot impatiently.

A man in white and black striped overalls greeted them with a smile. "Number, please?" he asked, gesturing towards Hannah's badge.
She quickly checked the number on her badge and replied, "6783."
Perfect, "the man said.
A moment later and after looking at a clipboard, "If you would follow me, please. That number assigned you to a table you will compete on" mentioned the man as they made their way to the upper left of the room.

As they approached table 6783, the man instructed Hannah on what to do next.

"Please place your virtual deck on the table," he said, motioning towards the sleek device in her hand. Hannah did as she was told, placing the device gently on the table. The man then took the virtual deck, deftly attaching three cords to it before slotting it into a port on the right-hand side of the table.

"Your deck is not connected to the table. Now, I need you to lay on the table and put on this helmet," he continued, holding out a large helmet. "The table will scan your body, and I'll be attaching these wrist monitors to keep an eye on your vitals during the tournament." he mentioned as Hannah lay on the table.

Hannah climbed onto the table, feeling a bit apprehensive. She took the helmet from the man and placed it on her head, closing her eyes as the visor dimly lit up. As she lay there, a green line traced back and forth across her body, scanning her in intricate detail.

"The scanner helps register your exact size onto the virtual world," the man explained, gesturing towards the screens on the table. "And it'll continue to scan every hour during the tournament to monitor your vitals. Your health is very important to us"

Hannah's father looked on nervously, asking, "This is safe, right? I don't want anything to happen to my daughter" he nervously watched his daughter.

The man smiled reassuringly. "We've got it down to a 1.7% chance of anything major happening. Some do come out with trauma from the same, also rare, but found mostly in people who already have mental problems. But that's why we have all these measures in place. We'll have 75 trained nurses on the floor at all times, watching over the players. The company takes safety very seriously."
"Only 75 for this amount of players," her Dad said concerned, talking to the man.
"Well, 75 might be a little low for this. There is also a system that monitors to help out and let us know right away if anything happens to our players. I assure you sir, that this is completely safe and your daughter has nothing to worry about " reassuring him that everything will be fine.
"If anything happens to her, you'll be hearing from no " said her dad with a stern voice fading into a cough.

After a few minutes, the scan was complete, and Hannah was fully linked to the table. The man pressed a button on the helmet, prompting the system to save her data and exit the virtual world. Hannah removed the helmet and sat up, feeling a bit disoriented.
“You are now all set for the tournament. You may return Wednesday to start your practice” said the man to Hannah, sitting on the edge of the table.
"So, how was that?" her father asked, looking very concerned.

"I feel a little tingly and disorienting, but other than that, I'm fine," Hannah replied, swinging her legs off the table. The man nodded, adding, "The first couple of times, you might experience some minor symptoms as your brain gets used to the machine."

Hannah looked up at the man, feeling overwhelmed. "Now what do we do?" she asked, feeling a bit lost.

"Well," he said, "now that you're linked, we'll go ahead and load the training program and the game world. Starting on Wednesday, you can come here and play in a very small world to get used to the virtual environment. I recommend that everyone spends a few hours getting familiar with the basics before diving into the tournament. You don't want to go in blind."
“I can’t wait to try this out,” Hannah exclaimed in anticipation.
“I've needed it many times and I can say that it is something otherworldly. You’re going to have a great time in the tournament” said the man walking them back to the entrance.

Hannah nodded, feeling grateful for the man's advice. She couldn't wait to start exploring the virtual world and learning the ropes before the tournament began.

After completing the necessary preparations for the upcoming tournament, Hannah and her father decided to head to a place they had only ever seen on television and in pictures. They drove for 45 minutes to reach the beachfront, which was lined with private homes and large hotel properties. As they stepped out of the taxi, the fresh sea air filled their lungs and the sound of the waves crashing against the shore filled their ears.

Hannah's excitement was palpable as she took her first steps onto the sandy beach. She couldn't believe how soft and warm the sand felt between her toes.
"Wow, would you look at that," she exclaimed, gesturing towards the vast expanse of blue water stretching out before them. Her father couldn't help but smile at her enthusiasm.
"Yes, it's truly something magical," he replied, taking in the stunning scenery around them, the sounds of the rushing water and kids at play.

The beach was alive with activity. People of all ages were out and about, playing games, building sandcastles, and soaking up the sun. Hannah and her father found a quiet spot away from the crowds, where they could relax and enjoy the peacefulness of the ocean.
“I, with mom and Grace, could be here to see this,” said Hannah, sitting next to Dad with her head resting on his shoulder.
“They would have loved to see this too” mentioned her Dad as they watched the ocean fully alive and not frozen.

Hannan took out her phone and took a picture of them two on the beach and sent it to Mom and Jane.
"Maybe one day we can enjoy this as a family" said her Dad thinking of what life would be like.
They spent the next few hours walking along the shore, collecting seashells, and enjoying the warm weather.

As they walked, Hannah couldn't help but marvel at the beauty of the ocean. The water was a deep shade of blue, and she could see fish swimming just beneath the surface. She felt a sense of wonder and awe at the vastness of the sea, and she couldn't wait to explore it further.

As the sun began to set, Hannah and her father decided to head back to their hotel. They left the beach feeling refreshed and rejuvenated, ready to tackle whatever challenges lay ahead. They knew that the next few weeks would be intense, but they were grateful for this brief moment of peace and tranquility before the tournament began.

The following day marked the start of the highly anticipated gaming event, commencing with a series of informative seminars that delved into the intricacies of the game, providing participants with a comprehensive understanding of the gameplay mechanics. Hannah and her dad eagerly headed down to the lobby in the morning for breakfast, eager to start their day. They indulged in a scrumptious breakfast spread consisting of fluffy pancakes, scrambled eggs, crispy bacon, and freshly squeezed orange juice to energize themselves for the long day ahead.

After breakfast, they joined the queue for the first seminar, standing in line for an excruciating three hours. To pass the time, Hannah whipped out her treasured Gameboy Advance, a classic device that always held a special place in her heart, and immersed herself in the captivating world of Pokemon Yellow. As she played, a curious player standing in front of her took notice of her vintage console and inquired about it.

"What's that there?" he asked with a hint of curiosity in his voice.
"Oh, it's just a Gameboy Advance. Super old and rare," Hannah replied with a smile, looking up to meet his gaze.
"I'm James from the UK," said the man, introducing himself.
"I'm Hannah from Chicago," replied Hannah, extending her hand for a shake.
Well, nice to meet you, Hannah, maybe we can get to know each other. We could maybe work together in the tournament" exclaimed James checking Hannah's hand.
Ya, maybe we could help each other get far. We'd have a lot of talking to do, getting to know each other" said Hannah, putting down the Gameboy.
Over the course of the next two hours, the two of them exchanged stories about their past gaming experiences, discussing their favorite titles and consoles. Hannah found James to be an amicable and knowledgeable person, and they quickly became friends.

As the clock struck ten, the queue began to move, and they headed towards the seminar hall, eager to learn everything there was to know about the game. Hannah and her dad secured seats at the front of the hall, keen not to miss a single detail.
I've got my notebook and I'm already taking notes" said Hannah, flipping to the first open page.
"Aren't you going to take notes?" said Hannah to James who sat next to her.

“I have a really good memory and don’t need to write it down, " exclaimed James, looking in Hannah's direction.
“I think he likes you” whispered her dad into her ear.
“Dad, would you stop that,” said Hannah, blushing and lightly pushing him.
As they waited for the seminar to begin, a man walked out on stage, and the lights dimmed, signaling the start of the session.

The lights dimmed down as the audience watched with rapt attention, eagerly waiting to hear more about the game that they would soon be immersing themselves in. The lead developer, an impressive figure with an air of authority and confidence, stepped forward to greet the audience. He introduced himself with a name that sounded exotic and foreign, instantly grabbing the audience's attention and piquing their curiosity.

"I am pleased to welcome you all to the world of 'Arcadia'," he announced, his voice carrying an air of pride and accomplishment.
"As the lead developer on this project, I can assure you that you are in for an unforgettable experience." With a flick of his hand, he began to switch through slides, showcasing the stunning graphics and intricate details of the game world that lay ahead.

But it wasn't just the visuals that were impressive.
"In 'Arcadia', you have the freedom to choose your race and class," he continued, "and the decisions you make in character creation will have a direct impact on your performance in the game. But that's not all - we've taken it a step further. Your physical appearance in the real world will also affect your performance in the game. As you level up and gain better

abilities, your body will start to change in subtle ways. We wanted to make this game as immersive and realistic as possible, and I believe we've achieved that."

The audience erupted into a buzz of excitement, their minds racing with the endless possibilities that 'Arcadia' offered. The lead developer paused, allowing them to calm down before delivering the next bombshell. "But be warned," he said, pacing back and forth on stage. "In this game, we've implemented the need to eat, drink, and sleep. These stats will affect your performance, and if you neglect them, it could be fatal. You can die in the game from lack of any of these basic needs. So, keep a close eye on them and manage them well."

The lead developer cleared his throat and continued his speech, "In this game, we have incorporated advanced AI to give you the most realistic experience possible. Your character will have its personality, emotions, and behavior, which will be influenced by the choices you make in-game. Your decisions will affect your character's relationships with other NPCs and players, and it will determine how the game will unfold.

"The world of Arcadia is vast and full of mysteries waiting to be discovered. You will be able to explore different environments, from lush forests to treacherous mountains, to vast deserts. Each location has its unique challenges, quests, and secrets. Speaking of quests, we have added a dynamic quest system that will change based on your choices and actions in-game.

"The combat system is also realistic and immersive. It is not just about attacking and dodging, but also about strategy and tactics. You will have to use different types of weapons, spells, and abilities to defeat your enemies. The better you are at planning and executing your attacks, the more successful you will be.

"And last but not least, we have created a multiplayer system that will allow you to play with other players around the world. You can form alliances, join guilds, or engage in PvP battles. The choice is yours. We believe that this game will revolutionize the gaming industry and change the way people perceive RPGs. We cannot wait to see you all in-game!"

The audience listened in awe, the magnitude of the game's realism and complexity dawning on them. The lead developer smiled, satisfied with their reaction.
"I hope you're all ready for the adventure of a lifetime," he said, his eyes gleaming with excitement.
"Welcome to 'Arcadia'."

The audience erupted in applause as the lead developer stepped off stage, leaving the attendees excited and eager to try out the game.

As the three of them left the seminar hall, the excitement and anticipation for the upcoming tournament was palpable in the air.
"That seminar was awesome! I'm so pumped for the game now," he exclaimed with a large smile of joy on his face.
“Ya, it looked awesome, but it will be even better when we are in it, " said Hannah, just as excited.
“How about me and you hang out and talk about the game and strategy,” said James inviting Hannah to hang out.
Hannah, however, was more hesitant.

"I don't know, James. I came here to spend time with my dad, not just play the game," she said, her eyes flickering to her father.
Her dad, who had been leaning against the wall, catching his breath, interrupted them.
"Don't worry about me, kiddo. You two go ahead and have some fun. I'll just relax by the pool," he said, a reassuring smile on his face as he winked at Hannah.

Hannah was still hesitant, though.
"Are you sure, Dad? What if something happens?"
"I'll be fine, honey. You go have some fun with your friend," he said, his voice firm but gentle.
"Okay, Dad. But we're going to that Japanese restaurant for dinner, right?" she asked, a hint of excitement in her voice.
"Of course, we are. Just don't be late," he said, his tone teasing.

As they walked towards the lobby, James couldn't help but notice the sadness on Hannah's face. "Not to be rude or anything, but is your dad okay?" he asked, his tone gentle.

Hannah took a deep breath before responding.
"Unfortunately, my dad has this illness that can only be treated in the EZ. It's why we're here. I'm fighting for him in this tournament," she explained, her voice tinged with sadness.

James's expression softened.
"I'm so sorry to hear that, Hannah. But you're not alone. I want to help you and your dad too. As much as I want to win myself, I want to support you and your goals," he said, a determined look on his face.

Hannah's eyes filled with tears, touched by James's words. "Thank you, James. That means a lot to me," she said, her voice breaking slightly.

As they walked towards the arcade room, James couldn't help but feel a sense of purpose. Helping them would be a nice thing to do, but he wanted to win.
"Telling her what she wants to hear will get her on my side. Another person to a line with" thought James scheming his way to the end.

After spending hours at the arcade, Hannah and James were both feeling invigorated and carefree. They had played on some of the newest machines and some of the rarest ones that Hannah had never even seen before. The two of them had a blast and were so engrossed in the games that they forgot about all the worries of the world. As they took a break to eat lunch and talked about the game. James suggested that they hang out again tomorrow to talk more about games, and Hannah's face lit up with excitement.
"I would love that," said Hannah as they talked more about the game.
"We can hang out for half the day and then you can hang with your dad the rest of the day. How does that sound" said James, coming up with a way for her to hang out with him and her dad?
"Ya, I don't know. I don't know, I'll be practicing all day. Here's my number so I can message you to let you know" said Hannah, writing her number down.
"Alright thank you," said James, putting it in his phone.
After launch, they headed to the pool to hang out for the rest of the afternoon.

After some time, they walked back to the lobby and saw Hannah's dad waiting for them.
"Are you ready to go?" he asked.
"Yes, I'm starving!" exclaimed Hannah, rubbing her belly with a grin. As they walked towards the front of the hotel, James said goodbye and parted ways with them. Hannah and her dad hailed a taxi and made their way to another hotel, one that was heavily inspired by Asian culture.
What's Japanese food like" asked Hannah, never having had it before.
"Well, I have never had it but as far as I know, they eat a lot of rice and raw fish of all kinds' ' said her dad as they rode in the taxi.
"That sounds gross," said Hannah, getting a sickly feeling in her stomach.
"You never know if you like it until you try it and we both are going to try as many new things as we are here" exclaimed her father as they pulled up to the other hotel.
"Yes father," said Hannah as they got out.

This was an Asian-themed hotel, mostly Chinese and Japanese, those were the 2 restaurants they had in the hotel.
As they stepped into the lobby of the hotel, they were surrounded by stunning Asian-inspired decor. The walls were painted with colorful murals, and traditional Japanese paper lanterns hung from the ceiling. Hannah was mesmerized by the intricate details of the artwork and the vibrant colors that adorned the walls.

The restaurant that they were heading to was also heavily inspired by Japanese culture, and as they sat in their booth, Hannah and her dad were eager to try Japanese food for the first time. Back home, there weren't very many restaurants, especially foreign cuisine restaurants. With what little money they had, they never ate out, so this was a special treat for them. The menu was filled with items that were foreign to them, but they were excited to try them all.

The restaurant was filled with the aroma of exotic spices and the sound of sizzling woks. The decor was stunning, with wooden accents and traditional Japanese paintings adorning the walls.

The sun was setting and the air was cool as Hannah and her dad walked into the restaurant. They were greeted by the warm smile of the waitress who offered them a table for two. As they sat down, the waitress handed them their menus and asked if they wanted something to drink.

"Hello, can I get you anything to drink?" said the waitress, holding out the menus.

"We never really had Asian food and would love to try Japanese food," said Hannah's dad, excitedly explaining to the waiter.

"Perfect, you came to the right place. I'll bring you some traditional hot and cold tea for you to try. I'll be right back," replied the waitress, eager to provide them with an unforgettable experience.

As they waited, they looked through the extensive list of dishes. The menu was a work of art, with pages upon pages of dishes arranged by country, from Chinese to Thai, Korean to Japanese. The options were overwhelming, and Hannah and her dad took their time perusing each page, trying to decide what to order.

A few minutes later, the waitress returned with a traditional tea set with two teapots. She poured the hot tea into delicate ceramic cups and handed them to Hannah and her dad. They took a sip of the hot tea, and it warmed their throats as they felt the tea's bitter taste. They also tried the cold tea, which was refreshing and had a subtle sweetness to it.

"Now, are we ready to order or do we need a minute?" asked the waitress, ready to write it down.

"Can we get two bowls of two different Ramen, the mixed tempura vegetables, and three of your best sushi, please?" said Hannah, hoping they got all the big dishes from Japan.

"You guys picked a good feast from Japan. You will not be disappointed. I'll be back soon with your food," said the waitress, heading into the kitchen.

As they waited for their food, they continued to sip on their tea. Hannah wasn't a big tea person, but she appreciated the effort and tradition behind it. Her dad, on the other hand, savored each sip, taking in the intricate flavors and aromas of the tea.

About six minutes later, the sushi arrived. The waitress placed the dish in front of them with a smile. Hannah and her dad marveled at the colorful array of sushi rolls, each looking more delectable than the next.

The waitress explained the sushi to them. The first roll was a classic California roll, filled with crab meat, avocado, and cucumber. The second roll was a spicy tuna roll, featuring a spicy blend of tuna and mayonnaise, topped with avocado and scallions. And the third roll was a dragon roll, with a crispy exterior and a creamy interior, featuring eel, cucumber, and avocado.

They gave each roll a try, savoring each bite as they explored the subtle flavors and textures. Hannah enjoyed the sushi immensely, but her dad couldn't get over the raw fish.

Moments later, the waitress returned with the tempura vegetables. The dish was a work of art, featuring perfectly crispy vegetables coated in a light, fluffy batter. The dish was accompanied by a special dipping sauce, made from a blend of soy sauce, ginger, and garlic.

"Here is the vegetable with a special dipping sauce. How was the sushi?" she said, putting the plate down.
"Oh, so good," said Hannah, taking another bite.
That's what I like to hear, I'll be right back with your Ramen" said the waitress as she walked away from the table.

They gave the tempura vegetables a try, and the crunchiness on the outside and softness on the inside was delightful. They enjoyed it so much that they vowed to try and make it back home. Even the sauce was a hit, with its savory and spicy flavors.

Finally, the waitress brought the 2 bowls of Ramen to the table. a savory-sweet flavor. The aroma of the noodles wafted through the air, and they could see the steam rising from the bowls. The broth looked rich and flavorful, with slices of tender pork, soft-boiled egg, and a medley of vegetables floating in the bowl.

Hannah and her dad eagerly picked up their chopsticks and dug in, slurping up the noodles and savoring the rich broth. The spicy ramen had just the right amount of heat, enough to make their taste buds tingle, but not too overpowering. The savory-sweet ramen, on the other hand, had a delicate balance of flavors that complemented each other perfectly. They enjoyed the variety of textures in the dish, from the tender pork to the crunchy bamboo shoots and soft noodles.

As they ate, they couldn't help but marvel at the complexity of the dishes. The broth alone had so many layers of flavors, with a hint of umami from the dashi, sweetness from the mirin, and depth from the soy sauce. The noodles were perfectly cooked, not too soft or too firm, and the toppings added an extra layer of flavor and texture to the dish.

After they finished their meal, Hannah and her dad were both completely satisfied. They couldn't believe they had never tried Japanese food before, and they were already planning their next visit to the restaurant. They thanked the waitress for the wonderful experience and left feeling happy and content.

"That was so good, we should go back before we leave" explained Hannah with excitement in her voice.
"We will try as there is so much I still want to give a try," said her Dad with a full belly of great-tasting food.

Chapter 9

It was finally the big day - the day Hannah had been waiting for. It was the first day of the virtual world's debut and she couldn't wait to get into the game and test it out. Despite having a hard time sleeping the night before, Hannah was up exceptionally early, eagerly waiting to dive into the virtual world.
"Today is the day," Hannah said with enthusiasm and excitement, unable to contain her eagerness any longer.

Before heading out to the arena, Hannah's dad insisted that they grab breakfast.
"First, breakfast," he said, being the responsible parent that he was. Hannah let out a sigh, not wanting anything to get in the way of her being able to enter the game. Despite her reluctance, she followed her dad to the lobby and made her way to the breakfast area.

As they walked towards the breakfast area, Hannah spotted James sitting with another boy. Her heart fluttered with excitement at the thought of meeting with him and talking about the game.
"Hey James, who's this?" Hannah asked as she set her plate on the table. James introduced her to his best friend, Donny, who had accompanied him to the tournament.

"We are headed to the arena after this to start practicing if you guys want to join us," Hannah's dad chimed in. James' face lit up with excitement.
"That'd be great," he said, taking a bite of his food. "I can't wait to see what this virtual world has in store."
“This is some much-needed practice and we’ll be doing a lot of it,” said Hannah ready to face any challenge that came her way.

The four of them sat at the table, chatting and eating for the next half hour, enjoying each other's company. Even Hannah's dad was having a good time not knowing half of the conversation. Hannah couldn't wait to see what the virtual world had in store for her and she was excited to spend the day with James and Donny.

After finishing their breakfast, the group of four excitedly headed toward the front of the hotel and hailed a taxi to take them to the arena. As they sat in the taxi, Hannah could feel the adrenaline pumping through her veins, ready to immerse herself into the virtual world and begin practicing for the game. The taxi ride took around 45 minutes to an hour due to the heavy traffic, with a plethora of people eagerly making their way to the arena for the same reason.
“Ugh, I hate this. Can we move any faster? "Hannah said out loud, wanting to be at the arena already.

Upon arriving, the sheer amount of people gathered outside of the arena was overwhelming. The lobby was full of players and fans alike, all buzzing with anticipation for the day's practice sessions. Hannah's excitement was palpable as she surveyed the scene, eagerly counting down the minutes until they could enter the virtual world.

"How long until we can get in?" Hannah asked, unable to contain her curiosity.
"About another 20 minutes," replied a guy standing in front of them, a friendly smile on his face.
Hannah's dad gave her a reassuring pat on the back. "See, wasn't it a good thing we had breakfast?"

"Yeah, I guess," grumbled Hannah. "But now we have to wait in this line."

As the minutes ticked by, Hannah and James continued discussing their game strategy, planning out how they would tackle each challenge that came their way. Finally, after what seemed like an eternity, the doors to the arena opened, and the group surged forward like a herd of wild animals. Hannah estimated there were at least 300 players all eager to get in as much practice as possible.

The guests made their way to the stands to watch, while the players headed to their assigned tables. Hannah couldn't wait to put her skills to the test in the virtual world, feeling the excitement bubble up inside of her as she walked to her table. The arena was buzzing with energy and anticipation, and Hannah knew that this was just the beginning of an incredible journey, not only for her but for every player throughout the tournament.

Finally, Hannah had arrived at her table, feeling a rush of excitement coursing through her veins. She eagerly lay down on the bed, donned her virtual reality helmet, and closed her eyes, eagerly anticipating the next few hours of gaming that lay ahead. After a moment or so, she found herself back in the familiar white room, with the holographic blue figure appearing before her.

"Welcome back, Hannah," the figure greeted her warmly. "Swipe to assess the main menu, there you'll be able to select the virtual world you'd like to play in."

Hannah swiped her finger across the air in front of her, her eyes scanning the menu of virtual worlds that appeared before her. She felt a sudden sense of anticipation when she saw that the only option listed was the tournament practice world. With a thrill of excitement, she selected the world, and everything went dark as the system loaded the game.

The first thing Hannah noticed as she started to come back to consciousness was the soft rustling of the grass beneath her feet. As her eyes adjusted to the bright sunlight, she realized that she was standing just outside of a small, rustic village that seemed to have been lifted straight out of a medieval fairy tale. A health bar appeared at the upper right-hand corner 20/20.

The village was situated in a verdant, rolling meadow that stretched out as far as the eye could see. The houses were constructed out of wood and stone, with thatched roofs and small windows that let in the warm sunshine. The streets were narrow and winding, and there was a bustling market square at the center of the village, filled with people going about their daily business.

The air was filled with the sweet scent of freshly baked bread, and the distant sound of church bells ringing in the distance. Hannah couldn't help but feel as though she had been transported to a different world entirely, one that was teeming with life and vibrancy.

She walked around the village, taking in every detail, feeling the rough texture of the wooden buildings, the smooth stones underfoot, and the cool breeze on her skin. She even caught the eye of a few of the villagers, who smiled at her warmly and went about their business, seemingly unfazed by her presence.

As she explored the village, Hannah couldn't help but feel a sense of wonder at the intricate and elaborate design of the game. Everything looked and felt so real, and she marveled at the incredible attention to detail that had been put into creating this virtual world.

"This place looks so real," she murmured to herself in amazement, as she continued to wander around the village, her mind racing with excitement and anticipation at what lay ahead.

As Hannah admired the breathtaking beauty of the village, a villager approached her with a sense of urgency.
"Greetings, Aurora. I've been expecting you," the villager said with a respectful bow.
"Please accept this gift," he instructed, holding out a short sword and a small wooden shield.
“What's this for?” asked Hannah, unsure of what was going on.
“Everything will be explained to you shortly,” said the villager holding out the sword and shield.

Hannah accepted the sword and shield with a curious look, feeling the weight of the equipment in her virtual hands.

"This feels so real, It's like I'm holding them" she thought, examining the details of the items she was given. Suddenly, a pop-up appeared on her screen, informing her that she had acquired a "short sword and wooden shield."

The villager gestured for her to follow him as they walked towards a larger stone building. As they approached, Hannah noticed the intricate details of the building's architecture, marveling at the skill and craftsmanship of the virtual world's designers.

Once inside the building, the villager led her to a large room where a man sat in an ornate chair at a table. "Sir, she has arrived," the villager announced with a respectful bow.

"Ah, yes. Come on over," the man said, gesturing for Hannah to join him at the table. She walked over and sat down, noticing that the man was in the middle of eating when she arrived.

"Thank you for coming on such short notice," he said, taking a bite of some chicken.
"We are having trouble with a group of goblins and need you to take care of them," he explained.

Aurora listened intently, nodding along as he spoke.
"Anything else I should know?" she asked, eager for more information.

The man handed her a parchment paper, saying, "Here is everything we know so far." As she grabbed the parchment, a notification popped up on her screen, indicating that a quest had been started - "Defeat the Goblins."

Feeling the thrill of the adventure, Aurora looked over the parchment paper as she walked out of the building, ready to embark on her quest to defeat the goblins and protect the village from harm. The parchment paper was added to her inventory.

As Aurora walked through the village, she couldn't help but admire the intricate details of the houses and shops. She noticed the way the colorful flowers bloomed outside the houses and how the sunlight made everything glow. Suddenly, a compass tracker popped up at the bottom of her screen, reminding her of her current objective. She swiped the screen to open the main menu, revealing different options such as Quests, Stats, Abilities and Skills, and Equipment.

Aurora opened the quest list and selected the task at hand, causing her current objective to appear on the right side of the screen. "Ok, so I need to talk to someone named Galen," she murmured to herself, scanning the village for the person she needed to talk to.

Following the direction on the compass, she walked north through the village to a hut on the edge of the village. Aurora knocked at the door, and moments later, the door opened. She walked into the small one-room hut and talked to the man there.

"Hi, I'm here to talk about the goblins," mentioned Aurora, standing in the doorway.
"I had a run-in with them while hunting not too long ago. I could have held my own, but there was way more for me to handle," said the man as he stared at a pot of stew.
"Do you remember where that was?" asked Aurora, curious about the goblin's whereabouts.
"Yes, it was in the greenwood forest, not too far from here. But it might be hard to find them," mentioned the man, looking at Aurora with a worried expression.
"How many did you see?" asked Aurora, trying to gather as much information as possible.
"I saw 6 or 7 headed my way before I headed out," he said, his expression serious.

“Anything else I should know” asked Aurora, making sure she got all the info needed from the man.
“I'm afraid that's all I have to give. You'll have to find them on your own" said the man with a worried look on his face.

Aurora left the hut, and the status of the quest changed to finding the goblins in Greenwood.
"I don't know what level the goblins are at, but I know I need to level up first," she said to herself, making her way back to the starting area outside the village.

As she looked around, she saw some rats scurrying around and realized that she could use them to level up. She ran up to one and swung her sword, hitting the rat with ease. A -3 popped up above the rat, indicating the damage she had inflicted. The rat tried to retaliate, but Aurora swiftly dodged the attack. She swung again, this time missing her target.

The rat took advantage of her mistake and bit her, causing her health bar to drop by 1. Aurora quickly regained her focus and swung with all her might, hitting the rat head-on. A -4 popped up, and the rat let out a shriek as it died.

A +5 popped up, and a blue bar appeared below the red health bar, indicating her experience points. She had gained 5 out of 50 experience points needed to level up. She searched the inventory of the rat and found rat meat and 2 copper coins, which she took.
“It’s not much but I'll take it,” Aurora said to herself as she picked up the items.

Aurora continued to work on the rats until she reached level 2, stopping once to rest and gain her health back. Finally, she killed the last rat, and a cheerful ring sounded out as a box popped up “Level Up - level 2. Her health bar rose by 2 points, and she felt a sense of accomplishment wash over her. She ended up with 5 rat meat, 12 copper coins, and a broken sword. She knew she was ready to face the goblins in Greenwood.

After a ten-minute walk from the village, Aurora finally arrived at the entrance of the Greenwood forest.
“Here's the start to big adventures," said Aurora as she stepped inside, the canopy of trees overhead creating a serene, yet slightly eerie atmosphere. The compass on her screen started glowing, indicating that she was in the right area.

Aurora walked cautiously, trying to locate the goblin encampment. She kept an eye out for any signs of movement or sound, as she was wary of being ambushed. As she progressed deeper into the forest, she spotted a few boars foraging in the undergrowth, and a locked chest tucked away under some foliage. However, her focus was on finding the goblins, so she moved on.

Finally, after a while, Aurora caught sight of the encampment. It was a small clearing with makeshift tents made from animal hide and wooden poles, scattered around the perimeter. A few goblins were milling about, some sharpening their weapons, while others were lounging on the ground.

Aurora knew she had to be strategic in how she approached them. She couldn't risk rushing in and getting overwhelmed by all of them at once. She picked up a rock lying nearby and threw it in the opposite direction, hoping to lure one of the goblins away from the camp. Moments go by and the plan works, and one of them starts wandering towards the sound.

As the goblin moved away, Aurora made her move. She crept towards the camp, keeping low to the ground to avoid detection. She unsheathed her sword and swung at the goblin closest to her. A -6 popped up, indicating a successful hit. The goblin turned around, agitated, and brandished his spear. He lunged towards Aurora, and the spear grazed her side, -4 to her health.

Aurora quickly regained her composure and retaliated with a swift slash, which broke the goblin's spear. A -2 popped up. The goblin recoiled in pain, giving Aurora the upper hand. She continued to engage in battle with the remaining goblins, dodging their attacks and striking when the opportunity presented itself.

Aurora was no stranger to challenges, but the task of defeating the goblins was a new one for her. She had never encountered anything like this before, and the experience was daunting. Nevertheless, she refused to give up without a fight. Her training and quick thinking came into play, and she engaged in a fierce battle with the goblins. Despite the chaos and the numerous obstacles she faced, she managed to emerge victorious, with the goblin encampment now in ruins.

As she took a moment to catch her breath and survey the damage she had inflicted, Aurora checked her health bar, which was now less than half. The adrenaline rush of the battle was beginning to wear off, and the fatigue was starting to set in. However, with a deep breath, she knew that this was only the beginning of a long and arduous journey. She steeled herself for the challenges that lay ahead, determined to face them head-on and emerge victorious.

Aurora, feeling accomplished from her recent victory over the goblin encampment, continued her journey by exploring the surrounding areas. She had used her minor healing ability to bring herself back to full health, and with newfound confidence, decided to search the dead goblin's inventory. After a quick search, she discovered a set of goblin armor, 23 copper coins, and some herbs that could be useful for future battles.

With a sense of accomplishment, Aurora felt a surge of adrenaline as she realized that she had gained 180XP from the encounter, bringing her just 20XP shy of reaching level three. Despite her excitement, she knew that she had to make her way back to the village to rest and wait for the morning.

As Aurora walked through the village, she couldn't help but feel a sense of gratitude towards the villagers for the hospitality they had shown her. She noticed an inn nearby and, feeling weary from her recent battles, decided to check in for the night.
“Greeting young traveler, what may I do for you tonight?” asked the innkeeper from behind the counter.
“I’d like a room and a warm meal please” stated Aurora looking around the room.
“Very well then, that'd be 10 copper for the night and 4 copper for the meal.
“Yes yes,” said Aurora as she put the coins on the counter.
“Perfect, I'll have the food ready shortly.
Aurora walked over to a table by the fire to wait for the hearty meal she had ordered. When the meal arrived, Aurora was pleasantly surprised by the hearty portion and the delicious smell of the food. The meal consisted of a thick, savory stew

with chunks of meat, vegetables, and herbs, along with a side of warm bread and a mug of ale.
“This looks like my mom made it,” thought Aurora, ready to savor the meal.

As Aurora savored her meal that night, her mind was filled with reflections.
"I definitely need more training," she thought, taking a moment to chew on a particularly juicy morsel.
"I require a solid foundation in the basics if I'm going to survive in this world, I need some guidance." thought aurora looking around the room for an answer.

Aurora's determination burned bright as she contemplated her next steps. She realized that she couldn't rely solely on her instincts and natural abilities alone. She needed to further hone her skills and knowledge, to be better equipped to face the challenges that lay ahead. Her current encounter with the goblin encampment had shown her that there were still gaps in her understanding, and she needed to fill them if she was going to continue her quest successfully.

Lost in her thoughts, Aurora finished her meal, her mind already racing with plans for her next moves. She knew that finding proper training would not be easy, but she was willing to put in the effort and dedication required. With renewed determination, she resolved to seek out the best training available, learn the basics thoroughly and become a formidable force in this new world.

Aurora turned in for the night, her thoughts drifting to her recent battle and the treasures she had obtained. Time in the practice world passed twice as fast as in the real world, and before she knew it, morning had arrived.

Before leaving the cozy inn, Aurora sat at the table by the fireplace, sipping on a warm mug of tea. As she looked around the room, she noticed a group of adventurers chatting in hushed tones at a nearby table, and a bard strumming a lute in the corner. She couldn't help but feel a bit envious of their skill and experience.

Feeling determined to improve her abilities, Aurora approached the innkeeper, a kind-looking man with a friendly smile.
"Excuse me, sir," she said, "but do you happen to know of anyone who could train me in sword and shield combat?"

The innkeeper stroked his beard thoughtfully, his eyes scanning the room as if searching for an answer.
"Well," he said slowly, "there are a few skilled fighters in the area, but I can't say for sure if any of them would be willing to train you. However, I do know a squire who works at the stables to the left of the stone building. He might be able to help you out. His name is John, and he's a bit of a rough character, but he knows his way around a sword."
“Thanks for the help,” said Aurora turning to head out, with her sword and shield clanging softly at her side.

Aurora made her way to the stone building to turn in her quest. The man was seated at a table, poring over parchment as she approached. "I have vanquished the goblins for you," she said confidently, bowing in appreciation.

The man looked up from his work and nodded.

"Thank you for saving our village from the goblins. Here is your reward," he said, sliding a bag of 50 copper coins towards her.

As Aurora accepted the bag, earning 200XP, a box popped up on her screen “Level Up - Level 3.” She heard the sound of the game chime indicating that she had finally reached level three. “Yes, I completed my first quest,” said Aurora with excitement in her voice, ready for another quest.
With newfound strength and abilities, she couldn't wait to see what other adventures awaited her in this virtual world.

With determined strides, Aurora made her way towards the stables where she hoped to catch Brad, the squire. The stables were located about 500 feet away from the inn, and Aurora took in the scenery around her as she walked. The sun was shining brightly, casting a golden glow over the fields and the horses grazing nearby.

As she approached the stables, Aurora noticed a man standing in the field with a horse. She made her way around the stables, stepping carefully over the hay-covered ground until she was face-to-face with the man. "Are you Brad?" she called out, walking towards him.

Brad, a burly man with a no-nonsense expression, looked at Aurora with a hint of curiosity.
"Can I help you?" he asked, not sure what was going on.
"I was told you could potentially teach me a thing or two about using a sword and shield," mentioned Aurora, her voice steady with determination.

Brad's eyebrows raised in surprise.

"Yeah, I could do that," he said, scratching his head. "Just follow me." He led the way toward the stables, and Aurora followed closely behind.
"So, how long have you been a squire?" asked Aurora, making small talk.
"I'm not much of a squire here. I'd call myself more of a horse breeder. I raise horses for the duke mostly" mentioned Brad

Once inside the stables, Brad retrieved his short sword and wooden shield, and they headed out into the field a little bit. Aurora pulled out her sword and shield, holding the shield in her left hand and the sword in her right, ready for the lesson to begin.

Brad started by instructing Aurora on her stance.
"You need to keep your shield out in front of you, covering your body," he said, demonstrating the proper posture.
"And make sure to have one foot in front of the other, so there's less area to hit."

Aurora nodded, absorbing Brad's instructions and mimicking his stance. She could feel the weight of the shield in her hand, and the grip of the sword as she held it firmly.

Brad then guided her through basic swings and blocks, explaining the importance of defense in combat.
"The best offense is a good defense," he mentioned, emphasizing the need to protect oneself while also being able to counterattack.

They practiced for the next couple of hours, with Brad patiently correcting Aurora's form and providing guidance. Aurora felt her muscles strain and sweat forming on her brow, but she was determined to learn. She focused intently on Brad's instructions, gradually improving her technique and gaining confidence with each swing and block.

As the sun began to set, Brad finally nodded in approval. "You've got the hang of it," he said with a smile. "Keep practicing and you'll be a formidable fighter in no time."

Aurora thanked Brad gratefully, feeling a sense of accomplishment and satisfaction. She knew that mastering the sword and shield would not be easy, but she was willing to put in the effort to become a skilled warrior. A box popped up saying “Basic Sword Skill”. With a newfound sense of purpose, Aurora left the stables, her heart filled with determination and her mind set on her next adventure.

Aurora carefully navigated her way through the virtual world, taking in the stunning scenery around her. After several hours of gameplay, she realized that she needed to take a break and leave the game. She slowly swiped up to the main menu, then swiped again to exit. A pop-up box appeared, asking if she was sure she wanted to exit. She confirmed her choice and within minutes, Aurora was back in the real world.

As she removed her helmet and sat up, she felt a wave of exhaustion wash over her. It was as if she had truly been transported to another world, with all its sights, sounds, and sensations. Aurora was so engrossed in the game that she had lost track of time. When she looked up, she saw her father walking towards her, his face etched with concern.

"How was that, Hannah?" he asked intriguingly as he walked up to Hannah.

"It was amazing," Hannah replied, her voice filled with wonder. "It felt so real. The smells, the feeling of the wood, the softness of the grass...it was like I was there. Physically touching everything with my own hands," said Hannah wondering what was real.

Her father nodded, smiling knowingly. "You were in there for six or seven hours," he said, "and you were completely immersed in the game. It's no wonder you're exhausted."

Hannah yawned and stretched, feeling the weight of her body settling back into reality.
"How about some food?" her dad suggested, "and then a nap too."

"That sounds perfect," Hannah agreed, eager to refuel and recharge. They made their way towards the exit, passing by James's table. He was still plugged in.

Hannah couldn't help but wonder what he was up to, but she was too tired to linger. As they walked away, she thought to herself that the virtual world was truly amazing, but nothing could ever compare to the real world and the people in it.

As they walked towards the exit of the arena, Hannah couldn't help but feel a sense of disorientation. The transition from the immersive virtual world to the real world was always jarring for her. She shivered as the cold wind hit her face, a stark contrast to the warm and sunny digital world she had just left behind.

A wave of homesickness hit Hannah, and she realized that this was the longest time she had been away from seeing her friends and family. But she knew that it would all be worth it once she won the tournament.

As they reached the exit, Hannah's dad held the door open for her, and she walked out, taking a deep breath of fresh air. The sound of traffic and people talking filled her ears, and she marveled at how loud everything was compared to the virtual world.

They walked towards the taxi, parked outside the area. Hannah's dad helped her get in, and they drove towards their hotel. The silence in the taxi was only broken by the sound of the engine.

Hannah looked out of the window, lost in thought. She was still amazed by the virtual world and how real it felt. She wondered how people would react if they knew how immersive the game was.

As they reached the hotel, Hannah's dad suggested they do something fun like watch a movie or go out for dinner. But Hannah was exhausted, and all she wanted was to lie down and sleep.

"I think I'll just go to bed, Dad," she said as she headed to her room.

Hannah closed the door behind her and lay down on her bed. She was still thinking about the game and how much it had affected her. She wondered what else she could do in the game and how far she could go.

Chapter 10

Hannah's schedule revolved around the virtual world for the next few days. With the upcoming tournament looming over her, she knew she had to dedicate herself to rigorous training and preparation. Day in and day out, she delved into the immersive digital realm, honing her skills and mastering the intricacies of the game.

The hours seemed to blur together as Hannah immersed herself in various virtual scenarios, challenging herself to overcome formidable opponents and conquer difficult quests. She pushed herself to the limits, determined to emerge victorious in the upcoming tournament. From perfecting her combat techniques to refining her strategic thinking, every moment spent in the virtual world was a step closer to her ultimate goal.

However, amidst her intense training, Hannah found solace in occasional conversations with James. They formed an unlikely bond, sharing their experiences, strategies, and knowledge. Late nights were spent engrossed in discussions about the game, exchanging valuable insights and uncovering hidden secrets.

Together, they explored uncharted territories, discovering hidden treasures and unlocking new abilities. They pushed each other to their limits, engaging in a friendly competition to test their newly acquired skills. As they exchanged ideas and strategies, their virtual avatars became formidable allies, their strengths, and weaknesses seamlessly complementing each other.

Their camaraderie extended beyond the game, as they shared personal stories and aspirations. In these moments of respite, they forged a genuine friendship, finding comfort in the shared pursuit of excellence. While the virtual world served as the backdrop for their encounters, it was their mutual passion and determination that bond them together.

Outside of their training sessions, Hannah made sure to maintain a balance between her virtual endeavors and her real-world responsibilities. She set aside time to connect with her family and friends, recognizing the importance of nurturing relationships beyond the confines of the digital realm. In their presence, she found a sense of grounding and support, reminding herself that life existed beyond the confines of the virtual world.

As the tournament drew nearer, Hannah's dedication to her training intensified. The long hours spent in the virtual world were fueled by a relentless desire to succeed. She analyzed her opponents' strategies, sought out the most challenging quests, and fine-tuned her combat techniques. Every decision she made, every action she took was with the singular goal of emerging victorious in the tournament.

The next few days were a whirlwind of excitement, anticipation, and hard work. Hannah knew that she had done everything in her power to prepare herself for the challenges that lay ahead. The virtual world had become her training ground, a place where dreams turned into realities. With James by her side and the support of her loved ones in the real world, Hannah was ready to embrace the tournament with unwavering determination and a burning passion for victory.

As the much-anticipated day of the tournament dawned, Hannah's anticipation mingled with nervous excitement that made it difficult for her to find restful sleep the night before. Thoughts of the impending challenges and the weight of expectations swirled in her mind, causing her heart to race and her palms to grow clammy. Nonetheless, determination burned within her, fueling her desire to prove herself on the grand stage of the virtual reality arena.

Hannah and her dad, both early risers that day, embarked on their journey to the tournament venue with time to spare. They arrived at the bustling arena while the sun was still low in the sky, casting a warm glow over the sprawling city of Miami, Florida. The energy in the air was palpable as participants, spectators, and tournament staff converged upon the site, each person bringing their unique blend of excitement and nervous energy.

Following the instructions they had received, Hannah and her dad made their way through the bustling crowds toward the designated area. The early hour provided them with an opportunity to observe the unfolding scene and witness the arrival of fellow competitors. The atmosphere crackled with tension and camaraderie as players from diverse backgrounds and skill sets converged in a united pursuit of victory.

“Hannah, you're going to do great in this tournament and if you lose, we will still be proud of what you accomplished,” said Dad, giving words of encouragement.
“Thanks, Dad,” said Hannah, thanking him with a big hug.
“Now remember that we all will be watching and right there with you all the way,” said Dad with words of wisdom.
“Dad, it's time to go in now,” said Hannah as the clock struck 8 a.m and the doors opened to the arena.

As the clock approached 8 a.m., the designated starting time for the tournament, Hannah walked to her table, passing James's table and giving him one last good luck before the tournament started.
“Good luck, you’ll need it,” said James with a creepy smile on his face.
“What was that all about,” thought Hannah with a weird confused look on her face as she walked to her table.
Once there, she settled into her designated spot. She arrived ahead of schedule, allowing her ample time to soak in the vibrant ambiance and observe the competitors as they filtered in. The room was abuzz with conversations, the clatter of equipment being set up, and the occasional burst of laughter as friendships were forged and rivalries kindled.

With a keen eye, Hannah studied her opponents discreetly. She marveled at the array of players representing a diverse spectrum of all walks of life. Some participants exuded an air of confidence, their body language and equipment signaling years of experience. Others appeared more reserved, their focus evident in the way they meticulously adjusted their gear and mentally prepared themselves for the challenges that lay ahead.

As the final minutes ticked away, an electrifying energy filled the air, spreading like wildfire through the ranks of the participants. The anticipation was palpable, each competitor eagerly awaiting the moment when the virtual world would come alive, and their skills would be put to the ultimate test.
“This is it, it’s all or nothing, you can do this' ' said Hannah, her heart beating out of her chest.

Hannah felt her heart pound in her chest, a mixture of nervousness and determination intertwining within her. She double-checked her equipment, ensuring every strap was secure and every setting was calibrated to perfection. A surge of adrenaline coursed through her veins, heightening her senses and sharpening her focus. This was the moment she had been preparing for, the culmination of months of dedicated training and sacrifice.

As the tournament director's voice boomed through the loudspeakers, instructing everyone to assume their positions, a hushed silence descended upon the room. All eyes turned towards the central stage, where the virtual reality world awaited its valiant champions.

With a deep breath and a glance towards her dad, who offered her a reassuring smile, Hannah adjusted her headset, allowing herself to be engulfed in the immersive experience that awaited her. The moment the virtual world materialized before her eyes, all distractions faded away, replaced by the adrenaline-fueled rush of competition and the burning desire to prove her worth.

As the clock struck 9 a.m., signaling the official start of the tournament, Hannah's gaze swept across the expansive venue, taking in the sight of the other players who had gathered from far and wide. A wave of nervousness washed over her as she observed the array of skilled and determined competitors surrounding her. Doubt began to creep into her mind, questioning her abilities and whether she truly belonged among such formidable adversaries. She wondered, "Am I good enough for this? Will I fare well in this competition?"

Her eyes flickered from one competitor to another, each clad in their unique attire, showcasing their play styles and personalities. Some exuded an air of quiet confidence, their steely gazes, and composed postures hinting at years of experience and countless battles fought. Others wore expressions of focused intensity, their hands, their gear.

As Hannah battled her inner doubts, the lights in the arena dimmed, casting a hushed atmosphere over the expectant crowd. A single spotlight illuminated the center stage, drawing all eyes to its focal point. In the midst of the spotlight, an announcer emerged, stepping onto the stage with an air of authority and charisma.

The announcer, a charismatic figure with a commanding presence, stood tall with an athletic build and a warm, reassuring smile. His voice boomed through the speakers, resonating with an infectious enthusiasm that permeated the entire venue. He possessed an uncanny ability to captivate the attention of the audience, effortlessly instilling a sense of excitement and anticipation.

Dressed in a tailored suit that exudes sophistication, the announcer's attire juxtaposed the virtual realm with a touch of elegance. His passion for the tournament was palpable, evident in the way he gestured with grand gestures and infused his words with unwavering enthusiasm.

The announcer stood at the center of the stage, basking in the electrifying energy emanating from the crowd. With a deliberate pause, he took a deep breath, his voice resonating with a mix of anticipation and authority.
"Ladies and gentlemen, boys and girls, welcome to the pinnacle of virtual reality gaming, the Virtual Reality Tournament of the World. Are... you... ready?" His words hung

in the air, teasing the crowd's excitement, and the arena erupted in a thunderous roar of applause and cheers. From every corner of the globe, spectators tuned in, their eyes fixed on screens, cheering for their national heroes, ready to witness the extraordinary feats that were about to unfold.

"In this monumental event," the announcer continued, his voice amplified to reach every corner of the world, "we have gathered representatives from a staggering 103 different countries, each brimming with talent and skill. A whopping 10,000 players have converged here today, prepared to leave an indelible mark on the virtual landscape. This tournament is a testament to the passion, dedication, and sheer love for the game that unites players from across the globe."

As the crowd's cheers subsided, the announcer shifted his attention to the rules of engagement. His voice carried the weight of authority, ensuring every participant was well aware of the challenges that lay ahead.
"Now, let us delve into the intricacies of this tournament. Here, in this vast and meticulously crafted virtual world, everyone starts as equals—level zero, thrust into a randomized starting location. From the very beginning, you will live and breathe this virtual realm, where survival hinges not only on your gaming prowess but also on your ability to sustain yourself. Remember, food and water are vital commodities, essential for your virtual existence. The only escape from this realm is either through defeat at the hands of an enemy or emerging as the last player standing—the true victor of this grand competition."

The weight of the moment settled upon the competitors as they absorbed the gravity of the announcer's words. The challenges they would face were not to be taken lightly. The battle for survival loomed large, and the journey ahead would test their mettle like never before.

The announcer's voice reverberated through the arena, seamlessly transitioning from the rules to the exhilarating opportunities awaiting the players.
"Amidst this epic clash, each player has a dedicated stream, allowing viewers worldwide to follow and support their favorite contenders. Additionally, we have three spotlight streams that capture the most extraordinary moments and showcase the exceptional talents of featured participants, elevating them to the status of virtual legends."

The crowd erupted once again, their excitement mounting with each passing word. The prospect of witnessing breathtaking feats and unforgettable showdowns fueled their enthusiasm. The announcer's voice carried an air of reassurance as he continued,
"To ensure an immersive and seamless experience, we have an army of 800 dedicated staff members within the game, ready to assist you at every step. They are here to answer your questions, join your party, and provide guidance whenever needed. You are never alone in this virtual realm."

A charged silence descended upon the arena, anticipation palpable as the players prepared themselves for the epic journey ahead. The announcer's voice boomed, filling the space with an air of finality.
"Now, my fellow warriors, it is time. Don your helmets, ready your spirits, and get set to embark on this unparalleled adventure. Once every participant has entered the virtual realm,

the game will commence, and the battle for supremacy shall commence."

As the announcer's voice echoed through the stadium, the competitors felt a surge of adrenaline coursing through their veins, their hearts pounding in anticipation.

Hannah adjusted her helmet, her hands trembling slightly with a mixture of nerves and excitement. The magnitude of the event sank in, and she realized that she stood among the best virtual warriors from around the globe. Doubts and insecurities tried to creep into her mind, but she silenced them with a resolute determination. She had trained tirelessly for this moment, honing her skills and strategizing every move.

Around her, the other players were preparing as well. Their faces were a tapestry of emotions—focused determination, unwavering confidence, and quiet contemplation. Each competitor represented a unique story, a journey that had led them to this very point. Their diverse backgrounds, cultures, and experiences converged within the virtual realm, transcending boundaries and fostering a sense of unity among the players.

The crowd, a sea of eager faces, chanted and waved flags, rallying behind their respective nations. The air crackled with anticipation, the energy contagious. It was a global celebration of talent, resilience, and the power of virtual worlds to bring people together.

As Hannah glanced at the vast crowd, she felt a renewed surge of determination. The knowledge that millions of eyes were fixated on this tournament both thrilled and humbled her. She was not just playing for herself but for all those who had supported her throughout her journey—the countless hours spent practicing, the sacrifices made, and the unwavering belief in her abilities.

The announcer's voice rang out once more, commanding attention.
"Remember, dear competitors, within this virtual realm, you possess the power to create legends, forge alliances, and to make your mark upon history. Embrace the challenges, savor the victories, and learn from the defeats. This is your chance to showcase the limitless potential of virtual reality and redefine what it means to be a champion."

As the final words reverberated through the stadium, the players felt an electric energy surge through their bodies. The time had come to enter the virtual realm and embark on an adventure of a lifetime. Hannah took a deep breath, steadying her nerves, and closed her eyes. With a sense of purpose, she activated her helmet and allowed the virtual world to envelop her senses.

In an instant, she found herself transported to an immersive landscape, a breathtaking fusion of vibrant colors, awe-inspiring landscapes, and fantastical creatures. The weight of the real world faded away, replaced by the exhilaration of the virtual realm. She was no longer Hannah; she was Aurora, a warrior ready to conquer the challenges that awaited her.

The countdown began, and as the clock struck zero, the game commenced. A wave of exhilaration washed over Hannah as she embraced her new virtual identity. She would navigate treacherous terrains, engage in fierce battles, and forge friendships amidst the chaos. The possibilities were endless, and she was determined to seize every opportunity that came her way.

With her eyes fixed on the horizon, Hannah took her first steps into the virtual world, her heart filled with a mixture of determination, excitement, and a burning desire to leave her mark on the Virtual Reality Tournament of the World.

As Aurora stood in the open field, her senses heightened, taking in the beauty and vastness of the virtual world surrounding her. The emerald hues of the forest behind her beckoned with mystery and adventure, while the village perched atop the distant hill exuded an aura of bustling activity. She felt a surge of determination as she realized that her journey had truly begun.

Taking a deep breath, Aurora glanced at the counter in the upper left corner of her vision, which displayed the dwindling number of players. The intensity of the tournament was palpable, with a few players already succumbing to the challenges that lay ahead. She knew she had to act swiftly and equip herself with the necessary weapons to ensure her survival.
"This is it, time to make everything count. Time to become a legend. Make my name feared by other players" thought Aurora taking her first few steps in the tournament.

Aurora's gaze focused on the village, her footsteps guided by a mixture of caution and excitement. She hoped to arrive before other players, eager to secure an advantage. The village came into view, its humble buildings forming a tight-knit community. The market, nestled in the heart of the town, offered a glimpse of hope for Aurora's quest to obtain weapons and provisions.

As she entered the market square, Aurora was greeted by a vendor who seemed well-versed in the ways of trade. The man behind the table wore a friendly smile, his eyes gleaming with a hint of curiosity. A prompt appeared in front of her, asking if she would like to engage in a shopping experience. With a tap, Aurora confirmed her intent, and a comprehensive list of available wares materialized before her.

Bow - 30 silver
Crossbow - 60 silver
Short Sword - 40
Long Sword -70 silver
2-handed sword - 125 silver
Arrows - 15 - 15 silver

Aurora, being a skilled Ranger, knew the importance of a reliable bow in her arsenal. She scanned the options before her, weighing the costs and benefits of each item. The short bow caught her attention, its price of 30 silver seeming reasonable. She also considered acquiring a short sword and a bundle of arrows to ensure she had options for close-quarters combat.

Aware of the limited funds at her disposal, Aurora realized that she would need to prioritize her purchases. However, she couldn't overlook the importance of food and water to sustain her during her arduous journey. Carefully considering her choices, she mentally calculated her available silver, understanding the need for a balanced approach.

Moments passed as Aurora made her selection, her mind assessing her immediate needs and potential future requirements.
“I’ll take the short sword, bow, and 15 arrows,” said Aurora to the vendor.
“That will be 75 silver and you will not find a better price for that anywhere” mentioned the vendor waiting to collect the silver.

A confirmation box appeared, offering her the options to confirm, barter, or cancel. Curiosity tugged at her, compelling her to explore her budding bartering skills. With a tap, she selected the barter option, prepared to test her negotiation abilities.
“I'd like 10 silver off in exchange for buying arrows from you only,” said Aurora trying out her barter skills.
The vendor paused for a moment, contemplating her proposition.
"If you pledge your loyalty to my wares and purchase your arrows exclusively from me, I agree to deduct 10 silver from the total price," he responded, meeting her halfway.
“Deal,” said Aurora, handing over 65 silver to the vendor, feeling a sense of accomplishment as the weapons appeared in her inventory. A box materialized before her, emitting a cheerful chime that echoed through her virtual ears.
"Congratulations! You have gained a level in bartering. You are now level 2," the message proclaimed, filling her with a newfound sense of proficiency and potential.

Surveying her surroundings, Aurora's gaze swept across the bustling market in search of a suitable quest or job. Determined to bolster her skills and gain valuable experience points, she craved an opportunity that would provide a boost without overwhelming her at this early stage. With a thoughtful expression on her face, she meandered through the market, examining the various notice boards and listening for whispers of potential quests.

However, it seemed that luck was not on her side as no immediate prospects presented themselves. Undeterred, Aurora decided to seek guidance from the innkeeper, a seasoned observer of the village's happenings. Making her way to the inn, she pushed open the creaky door and was greeted by a warm and welcoming atmosphere.

The innkeeper, a jovial figure with a kindly face, acknowledged Aurora's presence with a friendly smile. "Welcome, weary traveler. What can I do for you on this fine day?" he chimed in a chipper voice, displaying genuine interest in Aurora's purpose.

Taking a moment to compose herself, Aurora leaned against the counter and met the innkeeper's gaze.
"Ah, yes. Hi. I'm looking for some work," she replied, her voice filled with a sense of purpose.
"Do you have any quests available, or perhaps know someone who does?" Said Aurora with a curious tone to her voice.

The innkeeper stroked his chin thoughtfully before responding. "It so happens that I am running low on meat for our patrons' meals. I'd like you to embark on a hunting expedition and bring me the meat of five boars," he said, pointing towards the field from which Aurora had recently arrived.

A quest notification promptly appeared before Aurora, displaying the details of her new endeavor. "Quest started -

Hunter: Kill 5 Wild Boars," it proclaimed, igniting a sense of excitement within her. She nodded appreciatively at the innkeeper and accepted the challenge with a determined expression.

Stepping outside into the refreshing air, Aurora instinctively swiped up to access the main menu, where she tapped on the inventory option. The interface materialized before her, showcasing a range of equipment she had acquired. With a confident smile, she selected her trusty bow and equipped it, feeling its weight settle comfortably on her back. Next, she reached for the short sword and fastened it securely to her side, ensuring she was armed for any eventuality.

With a satisfied nod, Aurora closed her inventory and gazed out at the sprawling field before her.
"There, now I'm all ready," she affirmed, her voice brimming with determination. Walking through the village and taking her first step into the field, she embraced the upcoming challenge, eager to put her skills to the test and emerge triumphant.

With her bow slung across her shoulder and her short sword at her side, Aurora ventured further into the field, her senses heightened and her determination unwavering. The vibrant foliage rustled in the gentle breeze as she scanned the surroundings, searching for any signs of the elusive wild boars.

Aurora's footsteps tread lightly as she navigated the terrain, mindful of her presence in this virtual world. The soft grass beneath her boots offered a comforting sensation, grounding her as she focused on her task at hand. Her eyes darted from one patch of dense vegetation to another, hoping to catch a glimpse of the boars she was tasked with hunting.

As she traversed deeper into the field, Aurora's acute hearing picked up faint rustling sounds. She froze, her senses honed to pinpoint the direction from which the noise emanated. Carefully, she crouched low, concealing her from behind a cluster of shrubs, her heart pounding with anticipation.

Silence enveloped the field for a brief moment, and then, like shadows emerging from the depths, a group of boars materialized. Their sleek, muscular bodies snuffled the earth, unaware of Aurora's presence. Her eyes widened, a mix of excitement and focus reflecting in her gaze. "This is my moment. You can do this. You've trained for this" said Aurora softly to herself, calming her nerves.

Drawing her bow with practiced ease, Aurora notched an arrow, aligning her sights on the largest boar in the group. Her fingers trembled slightly, a testament to the adrenaline coursing through her veins. She took a deep breath, steadying her aim, and released the arrow with precision.

The projectile sliced through the air, swift and true, before finding its mark. The boar let out a startled squeal as the arrow embedded itself in its flank. Sensing danger, the other board scattered in a flurry of movement, but Aurora remained steadfast, her gaze locked onto her wounded prey.

Moving swiftly, Aurora unsheathed her short sword and closed the distance between herself and the injured boar. Her movements were fluid, a testament to the hours she had spent honing her combat skills. With calculated strikes, she engaged in a brief but intense melee, expertly maneuvering to avoid the boar's tusks while delivering precise blows.

The clash of steel against flesh echoed through the field as Aurora's skills as a hunter came to the fore. In a final display of prowess, she delivered a decisive blow, dispatching the boar with a swift, well-aimed strike. The victorious moment hung in the air as Aurora caught her breath, admiring the fruits of her labor.

Four more boars remained to fulfill the innkeeper's quest, and Aurora continued her pursuit with renewed determination. She traversed the field, tracking each boar with the precision of a seasoned hunter. Each encounter tested her agility, her ability to read her adversaries' movements, and her resourcefulness in adapting to the ever-changing battlefield.

As she triumphed over the final boar, Aurora felt a sense of accomplishment swell within her. With each boar she killed, she was rewarded with 5xp. The quest that had started as a mere task to gather meat for the innkeeper had transformed into a personal journey of growth and self-discovery. She had honed her archery and combat skills, gained valuable experience points, and cemented her place as a formidable contender in the Virtual Reality Tournament.

Returning to the inn, Aurora presented the innkeeper with the spoils of her successful hunt. A smile of satisfaction graced his face as he inspected the quality of the meat.
"Well done, my young hunter. Your prowess is commendable," he commended, rewarding her with a generous sum of silver coins, a token of gratitude, and 200xp.

Aurora, basking in the warm glow of the innkeeper's praise, found herself yearning for more adventures and opportunities to hone her skills within the virtual realm. Just as she was about to bid farewell to the innkeeper and venture out into the world, the wise old NPC extended another quest, a chance for Aurora to gain valuable experience points and further strengthen her abilities.

"I have another task for you, young adventurer," the innkeeper said, his voice filled with a mixture of wisdom and anticipation. "Tonight, we are in need of a good supply of wood to keep the inn's hearth ablaze. Venture into the enchanted forest and gather ten bundles of wood. To aid you in this endeavor, take this enchanted ax. It will make the task easier and allow you to harvest the wood more efficiently."

Grateful for the opportunity to embark on another quest, Aurora accepted the innkeeper's offer with a nod of determination. A notification appeared before her, indicating the initiation of a new quest - "Wood Gathering." With the weight of the ax in her hand and a sense of purpose in her heart, she set off on her journey once again.

Leaving the comforting confines of the inn, Aurora passed through the small village that had become her temporary home. The villagers greeted her with warm smiles and nods of recognition, acknowledging her growing reputation as a skilled adventurer. Their encouragement fueled her resolve as she made her way into the vast expanse of the surrounding fields.

As she ventured through the fields, her gaze fixed on the enchanted forest that loomed in the distance. The forest's ancient trees stood tall, their branches interlaced like a protective canopy, their leaves whispering secrets carried by the gentle breeze. The air grew dense with anticipation as

Aurora stepped onto the well-trodden path leading into the heart of the forest.

With every step she took, the ambiance of the enchanted forest enveloped her senses. The sunlight filtered through the dense foliage above, casting a kaleidoscope of dancing shadows on the forest floor. The melodious chirping of birds and the occasional rustle of unseen creatures created a symphony of nature that seemed to accompany her every move.

Aurora's eyes remained sharp and vigilant as she ventured deeper into the forest, her enchanted ax gripped firmly in her hand. Along the way, she spotted several boars grazing peacefully in a small clearing, their presence offering an opportunity for both experience and resources.

Drawing upon her honed combat skills, Aurora approached the boars with caution. Her movements were precise, each swing of her weapon calculated to dispatch her foes swiftly and efficiently. The clash of steel against hide reverberated through the forest, punctuated by the victorious cries of experience points gained - 5XP for each defeated boar.

With every successful encounter, Aurora's confidence soared, her battle prowess increasing with each swing of her enchanted ax. The boars fell one after another, their defeat forming a testament to her growing strength. She only sustained minor injuries, losing a mere 3 HP, while gaining a substantial 25 XP.

Satisfied with her triumphant display, Aurora resumed her original quest, delving further into the enchanted forest's depths. Her senses attuned to the subtle signs of timber, she sought out the sturdiest and most abundant trees. With each swing of the enchanted ax, she felt a connection to the forest, the rhythmic thud of wood against wood a harmonious symphony.

As the sun began its slow descent, casting a warm golden hue over the forest, Aurora became acutely aware of the dwindling daylight. She knew that venturing too deep into the enchanted forest at night carried a heightened risk. The darkness could become a breeding ground for formidable creatures, and being caught off guard could spell danger for even the most skilled of adventurers.

With a cautious glance at the sky, Aurora decided it was prudent to start making her way back before the veil of night enveloped the land. The bustling virtual world seemed to mirror the fading light as the number of players dwindled to below 9500. She understood that the forest held its own secrets and perils, particularly after sundown.

Carefully cradling the ten bundles of wood she had diligently gathered, Aurora retraced her steps, following the path that had led her into the heart of the enchanted forest. Each cautious footstep carried her closer to the safety of the village, where she could secure her reward and rest for the night.

However, just as Aurora rounded a bend in the path, a sharp twinge of intuition prickled at her senses. A rustling sound, faint but distinct, reached her ears. Her heart quickened as she instinctively sought cover behind a cluster of ancient trees, their gnarled branches providing a shield from prying eyes. "What was that?" whispered Aurora, peering through the foliage. Aurora glimpsed two shadowy figures approaching, their footsteps crunching against the forest floor. The dimming light revealed their short and stout forms, unmistakably goblins, armed with menacing spears. Her grip tightened around her bow, her fingers expertly notching an arrow in anticipation of a potential confrontation.

Aurora's mind raced as she assessed the situation. Though goblins were considered low-level adversaries, their numbers and cunning tactics could still pose a threat, especially in an ambush scenario. She knew she couldn't afford to underestimate them, not with her goal of reaching safety before nightfall.

Drawing upon her experience and training, Aurora steadied her breathing and focused her gaze on the goblins, waiting for the opportune moment to strike. The goblins seemed oblivious to her presence, engrossed in their banter, their crude voices carrying through the stillness of the forest.

As the goblins drew nearer, Aurora's moment of action arrived. With a deft motion, she pulled back the bowstring, her muscles coiled with precision and intent. The arrow, fletched with feathers of vibrant hues, glinted in the waning sunlight as she aimed for her target, the goblin in the lead.

Time seemed to stand still as Aurora released the arrow, its flight swift and true. It soared through the air, closing the distance between her and her unsuspecting foes. The twang of the bowstring echoed through the forest, a sound as piercing as the goblins' startled cries when the arrow found its mark.

The goblin in the lead stumbled, its momentum disrupted as the arrow struck its shoulder. A mixture of pain and rage contorted its grotesque features as its companion turned to face the unexpected assailant. Aurora seized the opportunity, knocking another arrow and taking aim at the second goblin.

The forest erupted into chaos as Aurora unleashed a flurry of arrows, each finding its target with uncanny accuracy. The goblins, now fully aware of the danger they faced, lunged at her with primal ferocity. Aurora's instincts kicked into high gear as she deftly evaded their spear thrusts, her nimble movements a testament to her honed agility.

As the battle waged on, Aurora's skill and determination began to take their toll on the goblins. Her arrows found their marks with unerring precision, striking vulnerable spots and chipping away at their strength. The goblins' movements grew sluggish, their roars of rage turning into pained grunts.

But even as fatigue threatened to seep into her limbs, Aurora's resolve remained unyielding. Her heart pounded with adrenaline, fueling her every action, while her mind remained focused on the task at hand. She relied on her extensive combat training and experience, using her agility and quick reflexes to dodge the goblins' frenzied attacks.

With each well-placed shot, Aurora whittled down the goblins' numbers, never wasting an arrow or underestimating her opponents. Her eyes remained locked on their every move, analyzing their patterns and exploiting their weaknesses. She unleashed a flurry of arrows, each shot a testament to her unwavering aim and her unwavering resolve.

As the forest echoed with the clash of steel and the cries of the goblins, Aurora's determination only grew stronger. She could sense victory within reach, but she knew that complacency could be her downfall. With every breath, she reaffirmed her focus and sharpened her senses, keenly aware of the ever-changing dynamics of the battle.

The goblins, sensing their impending defeat, resorted to desperate tactics. They lunged and thrashed, their movements wild and unpredictable. But Aurora's unwavering composure kept her one step ahead. She evaded their attacks with graceful agility, her body moving as an extension of her sharpened instincts.

Time seemed to slow down as the battle reached its climax. Aurora's heart pounded in her chest, her veins coursing with adrenaline. Her vision narrowed, and her attention honed solely on the remaining goblin. With one final, well-aimed shot, her arrow found its mark, piercing the goblin's heart with a resounding thud. 50xp popped up after each goblin was killed.

In the aftermath of the hard-fought battle, a box materialized before Aurora, resonating with a resounding chime of heroism. Its message glowed in radiant letters: "Level Up - Level 2." The realization of her progress washed over her, infusing her with a newfound sense of strength, agility, and unwavering confidence.

As the notification faded, Aurora's senses heightened, attuned to the subtle shifts within her own body. She felt a surge of vitality coursing through her veins, her muscles tingling with newfound power. The challenges she had overcome, and the battles she had fought had molded her into a more formidable warrior.

The forest fell silent, save for the sound of Aurora's heavy breaths. The goblins lay defeated at her feet, their threat vanquished by her unwavering skill and determination. She stood tall amidst the triumphant scene, her chest heaving with a mixture of exhaustion and exhilaration.
"And that's how it's done," said Aurora, taking a moment to collect herself. Aurora retrieved her arrows and wiped the sweat from her brow. She felt a surge of pride and satisfaction welling up within her. This battle had tested her limits, both physically and mentally, but she had emerged victorious.

With the threat eliminated, Aurora continued her journey out of the enchanted forest, clutching the bundles of wood she had risked her safety to gather. Each step forward was a testament to her bravery and resilience. She had not only fulfilled the innkeeper's quest but also proved her mettle as a skilled adventurer.

With the last vestiges of daylight slipping away, Aurora hastened her steps, determined to reach the safety of the village before darkness engulfed the land. The encroaching shadows seemed to dance around her, a haunting reminder of the perils that lurked in the unknown. As she approached the village, the fading light revealed a scene shrouded in an eerie ambiance.

The inn, usually bustling with warmth and cheer, now lay cast in a dim glow. The absence of a crackling fire in the hearth left the room enveloped in a somber stillness, broken only by the flickering candles that cast eerie shadows on the walls. Aurora's footsteps echoed softly as she entered, the silence amplifying her awareness of the encroaching night.

"Welcome back, Aurora," greeted the innkeeper, his voice hushed, filled with concern.
"It's not safe to be out at night. You should stay here. It's a lot safer within these walls."
"Yes, I'd love a room for the foreseeable future," Aurora nodded, appreciating the innkeeper's advice. The air of caution hung heavy, reminding her of the unpredictable dangers that awaited in the darkness. She wasted no time and approached the counter, her gaze meeting the innkeeper's weary eyes.

"Oh and some food. But first, here is the wood," she added, reaching into her inventory to retrieve the bundles of wood she had diligently collected.

The innkeeper's expression softened as he accepted the offering, grateful for Aurora's contribution. With the wood in hand, he skillfully arranged it in the fireplace, coaxing a small flame to life. The room slowly bathed in a warm glow, as if welcoming the respite from the encroaching darkness.

A notification box materialized before Aurora, signaling the completion of her quest. "Quest completed - Wood Gathering," it declared, accompanied by a melodic chime. A surge of satisfaction washed over her, affirming the significance of her efforts.

Grateful for her accomplishment, Aurora collected her well-deserved reward from the innkeeper. Ten gleaming silver coins were placed into her waiting palm, their weight signified a tangible reminder of her growing wealth. Alongside the coins came a generous dose of 200 experience points, a testament to her growing expertise in the virtual realm. The knowledge that her skills were steadily advancing brought a sense of fulfillment, fueling her desire to embark on even greater adventures.

Satisfied with her successful endeavors, Aurora allowed herself a moment of respite. She settled into a cozy corner of the inn, relishing the warmth of the crackling fire and savoring the aroma of a hearty meal wafting through the air. As she nourished her body, she contemplated the possibilities that awaited her in this vast virtual world, her mind abuzz with anticipation.

With the warmth of the inn's crackling fireplace caressing her face, Aurora sat comfortably in a plush armchair, the flickering flames casting a mesmerizing dance of light and shadow across the room. The hearty meal had fortified her body, nourishing her with its comforting flavors and filling her with a renewed sense of vigor. As she savored the remnants of the delicious repast, a tranquil ambiance enveloped her, providing a momentary respite from the rigors of the virtual world.

The day's trials and triumphs had taken their toll on Aurora. The initial foray into the virtual realm had proven to be an exhilarating and demanding experience, stretching her physical and mental limits to their utmost capacity. But even as fatigue settled into her bones, a flicker of anticipation burned brightly within her heart. For tomorrow held a myriad of possibilities—a cascade of quests, encounters, and challenges that awaited her valiant spirit.

Resting in the inn, Aurora knew all too well that she couldn't afford to simply sit idly by, waiting for the dwindling player count to reach a solitary figure. No, she understood the importance of proactive action of being ever ready for the unexpected encounters that might arise. Her strategy was finely honed—a delicate balance between leveling up her skills and maintaining a shroud of secrecy that would shield her from the prying gazes of other players.

Determination coursed through her veins, fueling her every thought and action. She possessed an unwavering resolve to emerge victorious in this grand tournament, to surpass all obstacles that lay in her path. The taste of triumph lingered on her tongue, driving her onward, instilling in her an unyielding spirit that refused to accept anything less than triumph.

Yet, amidst her solo expedition, there was a vital element that Aurora recognized as necessary for her success—an ally, a companion with whom she could forge an unbreakable bond. James's character, a trusted confidant and fellow warrior, held the key to a formidable alliance. Their meeting would be a pivotal moment—a convergence of strength and strategy that would amplify their chances of overcoming the formidable challenges that awaited them.

In her mind's eye, Aurora envisioned the moment of their union—the quaint town square bustling with life, vibrant and teaming with players from all walks of life. As she gazed upon the bustling crowd, anticipation surged within her, knowing that among the throng, she would find James's character. Their eyes would meet, and an unspoken understanding would pass between them—a pact that bound them in friendship and cooperation.

As the warmth of the inn embraced her, Aurora contemplated the trials yet to come. Tomorrow held untold adventures and untamed realms, waiting to be conquered. She knew that rest was essential, that the respite within the inn's comforting walls would fortify her for the battles ahead. With each passing moment, her determination grew stronger, and her resolve hardened. The virtual world beckoned, and Aurora would answer its call with unwavering courage and an unbreakable spirit.

Chapter 11

In the bustling town of Chicago, the preparations for the monumental viewing party reached new heights of dedication and resourcefulness. Jane, driven by her unwavering loyalty and determination to make Hannah's journey an unforgettable experience, embarked on a series of endeavors that would leave an indelible mark on the community.

With a clear vision in mind, Jane recognized the pivotal role that a high-quality projector would play in creating a truly immersive and captivating viewing experience. Determined to procure the best equipment, she ventured into the heart of the city, seeking out the local electronics store. With passion and conviction, she presented her case to the store owner, sharing the tale of Hannah's extraordinary quest and the profound impact it had on their community.

"What can I do for you, mam?" asked the man behind the counter as Jane walked to the counter.
"I'm Looking to see if you would be so kind as to donate or let us use a projector for a viewing party for Hannah, who's in the big virtual reality tournament" explained Jane hoping he'd be sympathetic.
"I did hear about that tournament. Didn't know we had a local in the tournament though" mentioned the man as he is surprised.
"Yes, Hannah's my best friend and I'm railing the community around cheering her on," said Jane with a cheerful tone.
"Let me see what I have in the back and get back to you," said the man heading to the back to look through his extra stock. Moments go by and she hears parts being shuffled, boxes moving around, and a loud crash at one point. Finally, the man comes back to the front from the back room with a smaller box.

"Here, I have this one you can use. It should get you about a 100-inch screen. Will that work for you" said the man, setting down the box on the counter. Jane looked at the older projector, thinking about the project.
"Yes, this is perfect. We will need a screen and can we get some speakers too" asked Jane thinking of everything she needs.
"Sure, that's not a problem, I'm happy to help out," mentioned the store owner with a happy smile.
"One last thing, can you deliver all this to the Evergreen High School gym? That'd be great" said Jane, crossing off the projector on her list.
"That's no problem and good luck with the event," said the owner as Jane walked out of the store.

But Jane's tireless efforts did not stop there. She approached a talented local artist, renowned for her craftsmanship and creativity, to commission the creation of vibrant banners that would adorn the gymnasium. Jane knocked on the front door of the house the artist lived in. She waited a couple of minutes with no reply, she knocked again and waited. Finally, the door opened to an older lady.
"Can I help you?" asked the older lady, opening the door with a soft creaking noise.
"Are you Eleanor Winslow, by any chance?" asked Jane, hoping it was her.
"Why do you ask?" said the lady, irritated, wondering what she wanted.
"I'm looking to get some artwork done for an event we are having soon" mentioned Jane with a tone of voice.
"Come on in, I'll let my sister know you're here," said the old lady.

Jane ventured into a narrow passageway of the front of the house, where time had left its gentle touch upon the weathered wooden stairs that gracefully curved along the right-hand side. The corridor seemed to whisper with intrigue as the walls, adorned with a series of doors, silently beckoned her to embark on a journey of exploration. To her left and right, rooms stood in quiet anticipation, their closed doors tantalizingly hinting at the untold tales and hidden wonders concealed within. At the far end of the hallway, a solitary chamber nestled in the depths, veiled in an aura of anticipation and enigma. The very air itself seemed to vibrate with the potential for adventure and discovery, urging Jane to embrace her curiosity and unlock the secrets that lay dormant within each room, ready to transport her into a world of mystery and enchantment.
"May I help you?" said Eleanor Winslow walking down the creaky stairs.
"I'm looking to get a banner painted for an event we are doing soon," said Jane with excitement in her eyes.
"I can do it, but it won't be cheap" Eleanor mentioned with concern in her voice.
"I was hoping you would donate your services to a good cause. My friend Hannah got into a big virtual reality tournament and I'm putting together a viewing party for her" said Jane, hoping to win her over.
"Sure, why no, I'll help you out. You get 1 banner that's 6ft by 15ft. Will that work for you" said Eleanor, giving in and helping out.
"Thank you so much for helping out, here is everything you need," said Jane cheerfully, ripping a piece of paper out of the notebook.

With that, Eleanor got right to work, with intricate brushstrokes and meticulous attention to detail, the artist would bring

Hannah's virtual avatar to life on the fabric, capturing the essence of her heroic journey. Each brushstroke was infused with the hopes and dreams of the town, transforming the banners into symbols of unwavering support and admiration.

To ensure that the viewing party was not only a visual spectacle but also a delight for the senses, Jane turned to the local grocery store where she worked. Recognizing the magnitude of the event and the importance of nourishment, Jane approached her manager, outlining the significance of the occasion and the community's desire to celebrate together.
"Hey John," said Jane walking into his office before her shift started.
"Hey, Jane, what can I do for you today," said John looking up from the papers he was looking at.
"I'm working on setting up a viewing party for Hannah's live stream and I was wondering if you could provide concessions. We'll pay you back for everything sold out of the money make" said Jane with a strong proposal.
"I'd love to help cheer her on even more, let's do it," said John with a warm smile and an understanding of the town's spirit, the manager gladly agreed to donate an abundance of snacks, warm beverages, and treats that would fill the air with comforting aromas and satisfy the palates of the attendees.

With each step, Jane's passion ignited the generosity and support of those around her. The town of Chicago was awash with a renewed sense of unity and purpose. As news spread of the collaborative efforts and contributions pouring in from various corners of the community, a palpable excitement enveloped the frozen town. The upcoming viewing party was no longer just an event; it became a testament to the resilience and indomitable spirit of the townsfolk.

Jane, fueled by the collective enthusiasm, poured her heart and soul into ensuring that every detail was meticulously attended to. From coordinating the logistics of transportation and setup to personally handpicking the snacks and organizing them into enticing displays, she left no stone unturned. Her dedication shone through in every corner of the transformed gymnasium, radiating an atmosphere of warmth, celebration, and unwavering support for Hannah's journey.

As the day of the grand event approached, the gymnasium stood as a testament to the power of community and the triumph of human connection. Jane's unwavering commitment and resourcefulness had rallied the town of Chicago, transforming it into a beacon of hope amidst the frozen wasteland. The collective efforts and contributions from the electronic store, the talented artist, and the local grocery store elevated the viewing party into a truly immersive and unforgettable experience.

After weeks of tireless dedication and meticulous preparation, the momentous day arrived, casting a spell of excitement and anticipation over the once-desolate gymnasium. Jane, with a heart full of pride and a sense of accomplishment, gazed at the transformed space that had become a vibrant hub of collective energy. It was not just a local event anymore; it had transcended boundaries and captured the attention of the world.

The sun's feeble rays struggled to penetrate the thick layer of frost that coated the windows, casting an ethereal glow upon the crowd that had gathered in the gymnasium. The seating arrangement, carefully set out to accommodate every eager spectator, buzzed with a sense of camaraderie and shared purpose. The chairs were filled, and the aisles overflowed with a sea of faces, united in their unwavering support for Hannah's extraordinary journey.

The town of Chicago had come alive with anticipation, for such grand events had become rare in these frozen times. It was not just the locals who flocked to witness this once-in-a-lifetime spectacle, but curious onlookers from far and wide had also made the journey to be a part of history. The gymnasium, long devoid of such enthusiasm, reverberated with electric energy that transcended its four walls.

As Jane settled into her seat upfront, her eyes scanned the room, taking in the sea of expectant faces. Sitting next to Hannah's family. The attendance surpassed any previous gathering in recent memory, a testament to the indomitable spirit of the town. There were easily three to four hundred people in attendance, an extraordinary turnout for a community often overshadowed by the cold that surrounded it. Even the monthly basketball games paled in comparison to the attention and excitement that filled the air that day.

With bated breath, Jane awaited the start of the tournament, her determination unwavering. The lights dimmed, casting a veil of anticipation over the hushed crowd. A surge of adrenaline pulsed through the room as an introductory video splashed across the large screens, transporting everyone into the virtual realm that had captivated their imagination. It showcased the awe-inspiring arenas, the players engaged in thrilling battles, and the boundless adventures that awaited within the virtual world.

The video's energetic rhythm and fast-paced cuts mirrored the heartbeats of those present, fueling the growing excitement within the gymnasium. And then, as the last frame faded, a figure stepped onto the stage, commanding attention and igniting a chorus of cheers that reverberated through the rafters.

"Ladies and gentlemen, boys and girls!" the voice boomed, resonating with an authoritative yet welcoming tone. The crowd erupted in thunderous applause, their unified voices filling the room with a symphony of anticipation. The man, a symbol of the event's significance, stood tall and proud, embodying the spirit of competition, camaraderie, and the boundless possibilities that the virtual world held.

Jane's heart swelled with a mix of emotions – pride, excitement, and unwavering support for her best friend. She knew that this moment marked the beginning of a remarkable journey, one that would test Hannah's mettle, redefine her limits, and present her with an opportunity to reshape her family's future.

As the opening ceremony continued, enveloping the gymnasium in an aura of grandeur and anticipation, Jane settled deeper into her seat. She knew that her role was not just that of a spectator but a pillar of unwavering support for Hannah. Night and day, she would remain by her side, celebrating each victory and providing solace in moments of defeat.

In that dimly lit gymnasium, amidst the frozen wasteland that surrounded them, a small town united to witness the extraordinary. Their eyes gleamed with anticipation, their collective breath held in suspended excitement. The air crackled with electrifying energy as if the hopes and dreams of the entire community had converged within those hallowed walls.

As the resounding echoes of applause faded into the air, signaling the end of the mesmerizing opening ceremony, the attention of the crowd shifted to the colossal screens that now showcased the vastness of the tournament arena. The camera panned gracefully across the expansive floor, capturing the scene below in all its splendor.

Jane, her eyes shimmering with excitement, couldn't contain her enthusiasm as the camera lingered on the players. "Quick, switch to Hannah's live stream!" she exclaimed, her voice filled with a mix of anticipation and pride. The technician manning the control panel swiftly responded to Jane's plea, deftly manipulating the switches and buttons with practiced precision. The screens flickered, momentarily displaying a flurry of shifting colors before settling on a single stream.

And there she was—Hannah, the protagonist of their collective aspirations and the beacon of hope for her family's future. In the virtual realm, she stood tall and resolute, her avatar a reflection of her unwavering determination. The open field surrounding her exuded a serene beauty, a testament to the remarkable attention to detail within the game.

To the spectators in the gymnasium, the virtual world appeared eerily realistic, blurring the lines between the physical and digital realms. The graphics were stunningly immersive, capturing every intricate detail with uncanny precision. The textures of the grass swayed gently in the virtual breeze, and sunlight cascaded through the virtual sky, casting a warm glow upon the scene. It was as if the boundaries of reality had dissolved, transporting the viewers into a realm of limitless possibilities.

As the live stream showcased Hannah's virtual form, the crowd leaned forward in their seats, their eyes fixated on the screens. They marveled at her avatar's agility and grace, mirroring Hannah's unwavering determination and perseverance. Every step she took resonated with their hopes, her every movement a testament to the strength of their collective spirit.

Jane's heart swelled with pride as she watched her best friend navigate the virtual landscape. She knew the magnitude of Hannah's undertaking—the immense pressure she carried on her virtual shoulders and the weight of her family's aspirations resting upon her. But Hannah, like the true warrior she was, faced the challenges with unwavering resolve, pushing boundaries and defying limitations.

In the gymnasium, a hushed silence settled, broken only by the occasional gasp or murmured word of admiration. The spectators, captivated by the enthralling virtual world unfolding before them, felt a renewed sense of purpose and possibility. It wasn't just about a game anymore; it was about the collective dreams and aspirations of an entire community, bound together by a shared desire for a brighter future.

As the live stream continued, the camera panned across the virtual landscape, showcasing the intricacies of the game's design. Majestic mountains rose in the distance, their snow-capped peaks glistening under a virtual sun. A bustling town came into view, its streets teeming with virtual inhabitants, each with their own unique stories and quests to pursue. The virtual world was a tapestry of richly crafted environments, a testament to the tireless efforts of the game's developers.

Amidst the awe-inspiring scenery, Hannah's avatar stood as a beacon of determination and resilience. Her armor gleamed in the virtual light, each piece a testament to her courage and the trials she had overcome. The spectators in the gymnasium couldn't help but feel a surge of admiration, their hearts swelling with a mixture of hope and pride.

Hannah's family had come prepared for the day-long spectacle, recognizing the significance of their daughter's debut in this monumental tournament. Their arms laden with a humble feast, they had brought forth a spread of simple yet hearty dishes that were the embodiment of comfort and sustenance.

In a basket lined with a checkered cloth, the scent of freshly baked bread wafted through the air, teasing the senses and igniting appetites. The crusty loaves, lovingly baked by Hannah's mother, held a promise of warmth and nourishment. Their golden exteriors concealed a soft, pillowy interior, a testament to the care and attention poured into their creation.

Alongside the bread, a medley of simple fare lay on platters. A rustic potato and vegetable stew, simmered to perfection, emanated a tantalizing aroma that enveloped the gymnasium. Chunks of tender potatoes, vibrant carrots, and assorted vegetables nestled in a rich broth, seasoned with herbs and spices to elevate the flavors. The stew provided comfort, warmth, and sustenance, a reminder of the simple pleasures that nourished both body and soul.

Accompanying the stew was a plate of freshly baked pastries, their golden crusts adorned with a dusting of powdered sugar. Hannah's grandmother, renowned for her baking prowess, had contributed her signature recipe—flaky and buttery turnovers filled with a sweet mixture of seasonal fruits. With each bite, the delicate layers melted in the mouth, offering a delightful contrast to the savory stew.

As Hannah's family settled in their seats, they extended an invitation to Jane, who had become an integral part of their lives. It was an unspoken acknowledgment that Jane's unwavering support and tireless efforts in organizing this momentous event had elevated her from a mere acquaintance to an honorary member of their family. With heartfelt gratitude, they offered her a taste of their culinary offerings, a small token of appreciation for her indispensable role in making this day possible.

Jane accepted their gesture of kindness with a smile, feeling a swell of warmth within her. She understood the significance of this shared meal—the breaking of bread together signifying not only nourishment of the body but the forging of deeper bonds and the celebration of unity. At that moment, the gymnasium transformed into a makeshift dining hall, where the aroma of simmering stew mingled with laughter and the clinking of utensils.

With every bite, the flavors of the simple yet lovingly prepared food transported the spectators to a place where the worries of daily life momentarily faded. It was a reminder that even in the face of adversity, there was solace and joy to be found in the simplest of pleasures. The communal act of sharing this humble feast not only nourished their bodies but also strengthened the ties that bound them together as a tight-knit community.

As the evening sun bathed the gymnasium in a warm glow, the sense of togetherness permeated the air. The shared meal had nourished more than just empty stomachs—it had fed the collective spirit and reinforced the profound gratitude that each member of Hannah's family felt towards Jane. It was a poignant reminder that the power of community lay not only in the grand gestures but in the small, heartfelt acts of kindness that formed the backbone of their bond.

With their bellies content and their spirits uplifted, the spectators settled back into their seats, ready to resume their unwavering support for Hannah. The cheers and applause that accompanied her virtual triumphs carried an extra note of appreciation, echoing not only the thrill of the game but also the deep gratitude for the connections forged through this shared experience.

Chapter 12

As Aurora embarked on her second day in the vast expanse of the virtual world, she marveled at the seamless integration of reality and imagination. Every detail was meticulously crafted, from the gentle rustling of leaves in the wind to the authentic textures that adorned the walls of her virtual abode. The familiarity of her surroundings, reminiscent of her room in the real world, provided a comforting sense of stability amidst the ever-changing landscape.

With a keen sense of purpose, Aurora set out from her virtual sanctuary, her destination set on the small market nestled in the heart of the bustling virtual town. It was here that the posting board stood, adorned with an array of tasks and quests that promised both adventure and valuable experience points. As she meandered through the streets, the vibrant tapestry of the virtual world unfurled before her eyes, captivating her senses with its lively ambiance.

However, as Aurora approached the market, her trained eyes detected an anomaly, a disturbance in the carefully orchestrated reality. Instinctively, she retreated into the shadows, her heart pounding in her chest. Peering through the veil of secrecy, she observed a peculiar scene unfolding before her—another player, a telltale sign of a fellow player's presence. This encounter held significant weight, marking Aurora's first encounter with another denizen of this digital realm.

Uncertainty gripped her mind as she grappled with the implications of this unexpected rendezvous.
"Should I engage in combat, striving for dominance over the virtual domain? Or should she bide my time, observing the

player's movements and waiting for an opportune moment to strike?" Thought aurora, watching the other player intently. The stakes were high, the player count dwindled to a mere fraction of its original number—approximately 9000 souls remaining. The harrowing reality of this world pressed upon her, knowing that every encounter and every decision carried the weight of life and death.

Silently, Aurora shadowed the mysterious player, their footsteps echoing through the market square. Her eyes darted from vendor to vendor, analyzing the merchandise with a shrewd gaze. A plan formulated in her mind—a strategy forged in the crucible of survival. She could not afford to let her guard down, for the presence of another player signaled danger, an ever-looming threat that demanded her utmost vigilance.

Positioning herself behind a dense thicket of bushes, Aurora found solace in the concealment it offered. The distance between her and the unsuspecting player measured roughly fifty feet—an optimal range for her skills as a skilled Ranger. With bated breath, she drew her bowstring taut, the arrow nestling neatly in place. Time seemed to hang in suspension as she aimed at her target, gauging the perfect moment to release her arrow.

In a swift motion, the arrow soared through the air, propelled by Aurora's unwavering determination. Its trajectory was true, finding its mark in the lower back of the player. A surge of adrenaline coursed through her veins as she swiftly readied another arrow, her aim unwavering. However, this shot proved less accurate, errantly striking a nearby vendor's stall, eliciting a surprised gasp from the onlookers.

The sudden chaos disrupted the tranquility of the market, causing the player to bolt towards the left side of the square, his figure rapidly disappearing into the distance.
Aurora, caught in a maelstrom of emotions, pondered her next move. Should she give chase, driven by a thirst for victory and self-preservation? Or should she regroup, recalibrate her strategies, and await the next opportunity to assert her dominance?

With the taste of battle lingering on her tongue, Aurora knew that the path ahead would be riddled with peril and uncertainty. Every encounter and every decision would shape her destiny within this digital realm.

Determined to forge her destiny within the virtual realm, Aurora took a deep breath, her mind racing with possibilities. The fleeting glimpse of the player's retreating form served as a tantalizing reminder of the ever-present challenges that lay ahead. She knew she couldn't let this opportunity slip away. With resolute determination, she decided to give chase, her agile form blending seamlessly into the virtual landscape. "You're not getting away from me," said Aurora, chasing after the other player.

Bounding through the market square, Aurora weaved through the maze of stalls and carts, her footsteps a symphony of determination and anticipation. The sights and sounds of the bustling marketplace blurred into a cacophony of colors and voices, her focus laser-sharp on her elusive target. She deftly navigated the winding paths, her instincts guiding her towards the path less traveled.

As she reached the outskirts of the town, the open field leading to the cliffside and into a deep ravine stretched out before her, an unforgiving reminder of the perilous world beyond the safety of the settlement. The biting wind pierced through her virtual armor, mirroring the intensity of her desire to claim victory. With each step, she grew closer to the player who had unwittingly become her rival in this digital theater.

Aurora's mind raced with questions and possibilities. "What motivated this player? Were they seasoned warriors, strategic masterminds, or simply adventurers seeking their path?" Thought Aurora as she ran after him. The enigma of their presence fueled her determination, driving her to unravel the mysteries that lurked within this virtual realm.

With calculated precision, Aurora narrowed the distance between herself and the fleeing player. She observed their movements, deciphering their patterns, and identifying vulnerabilities she could exploit. Her experience as a Ranger granted her heightened senses and formidable archery skills, empowering her to strike from a distance, maintaining the element of surprise.

Cloaked in the shadows of a towering cliffside, Aurora prepared for her next move. She drew her bowstring once more, her fingers caressing the worn texture of the wood. The anticipation swelled within her as she steadied her aim, her breath steady and measured. With a fluid motion, she released the arrow, watching it slice through the frigid air, its trajectory honed towards its intended mark.

The arrow found its mark, piercing the player's armor with precision. A moment of stunned silence followed, shattered by the player's anguished cry. The sound echoed through the desolate wasteland, a testament to the unforgiving nature of this virtual realm. Aurora, fueled by the rush of adrenaline, felt a mixture of triumph and empathy, understanding the weight of defeat and the resolute drive for redemption.

As the player hunched over, kneeling on the unforgiving ground, Aurora's gaze intensified. Her fingers tightened around the hilt of her sword, a silent testament to the gravity of the situation. Though a flicker of compassion danced within her, she understood the cruel reality of this virtual realm—the fine line between mercy and self-preservation.

Approaching the fallen player, Aurora's steps were deliberate and measured. She yearned for camaraderie, a chance to forge an alliance in this perilous journey. However, the treacherous landscape of the virtual world demanded caution. She couldn't risk her own life for the sake of an uncertain alliance.

As she drew nearer, the player's trembling hands clutched their sword, a stark reflection of their fear and desperation. Their voice, laced with vulnerability, pleaded for mercy, a plea that tugged at Aurora's heartstrings. Yet, the fire within her eyes burned unwavering, fueled by the relentless pursuit of victory.

"I'm sorry, but I have no choice," Aurora responded, her voice carrying an air of cold determination.
"I, too, seek triumph, just like any other player in this realm." Her words hung in the air, heavy with the weight of impending fate.

Moments stretched into eternity as the player continued their pleas, their desperation echoing in the desolate landscape. Aurora remained steadfast, her resolve unyielding.
"Rise and face your fate with honor, or I can sever your head from your shoulders right here," she declared, her words a chilling ultimatum.

As the player wrestled with their decision, Aurora's own thoughts raced. The gravity of her own words struck her—a stark realization of the lengths she was willing to go in pursuit of victory. It was a sobering moment, a glimpse into the depths of her transformation within this digital realm.

Finally, the player rose, their trembling form a testament to their fear of imminent demise. Their grip tightened around their weapon as they launched a desperate swing toward Aurora. Instinctively, she raised her sword, parrying the blow with practiced precision. The clash of steel reverberated through the stillness of the landscape as the battle between the two unfolded.

Blow after blow, they traded strikes, each maneuver a testament to their skill and determination. In a moment of vulnerability, the player managed to land a hit on Aurora's right arm, causing her to wince in pain as she lost five precious points. The battle raged on, a fierce dance of swords and survival.

Then, in a surge of strength, Aurora's defensive maneuver gained unprecedented force, knocking the player's sword from their grasp. It clattered against the unforgiving cliffside, a poignant echo of their faltering defense. Sensing the opportunity, Aurora pressed her advantage, her blade poised at

the player's neck, holding them captive in the grip of uncertainty.
"I'm sorry but it must be done," said Aurora looking into the sad eyes of the other player.
"Please! Let me go. I have a family I'm fighting for" said the player as he wept and begged for mercy.
"Sorry, but I have a family I'm fighting for too," said Aurora, unleashing her final strike—a swift, precise movement that severed the player's head from their body. A spray of crimson burst forth from the severed neck, staining the ground beneath them. In the wake of the battle, a notification box materialized before Aurora, displaying a victorious "+1000xp," accompanied by a cheery chime that reverberated through the virtual expanse.

As the player's lifeless body slumped to its knees, then collapsed onto the ground, Aurora's mind reeled with a mix of emotions—relief, disbelief, and the weight of what she had just done. She had taken a life, extinguishing it within the confines of this virtual world. The consequences of her actions, though intangible, bore a weight that lingered within her consciousness.

The bittersweet symphony of victory and regret played on as Aurora stood amidst the aftermath of the battle. Her heart ached with conflicting emotions, torn between the euphoria of triumph and the haunting presence of remorse. The once vibrant and bustling virtual landscape now felt tinged with a somber undertone—a reminder of the delicate balance between ambition and the consequences of her actions.

Blood pooled beneath the lifeless body, a stark visual reminder of the finality of death within this virtual realm. The cheerful chime that accompanied her level-up notification seemed hollow and out of place, its joyous melody clashing with the gravity of the situation. Aurora couldn't help but question the price she had paid for her ascent, the toll it took on her soul.

She knelt beside the fallen player, her hand reaching out tentatively, almost instinctively, to close their vacant eyes. A profound sadness washed over her, as she contemplated the loss of another life in this ethereal existence. Despite the necessity of her actions, she couldn't shake the gnawing sense of guilt that settled within her core.

Aurora allowed herself a moment of silence, a respite from the relentless pursuit of victory. She contemplated the fragility of life within this digital realm, the poignant reminder that behind every avatar, there existed a human soul, fraught with dreams, hopes, and fears. The weight of responsibility pressed upon her, urging her to question her motivations, to seek a higher purpose within this virtual labyrinth.

The wind whispered through the desolate landscape, carrying with it echoes of battles fought and lives lost. It served as a haunting symphony, a reminder of the transience of existence within this ever-evolving realm. Aurora's gaze lingered on the horizon, her eyes tracing the jagged contours of the virtual world, a tapestry of endless possibilities and unforeseen consequences.

In that moment of introspection, Aurora made a silent vow—to wield her newfound power with compassion, to honor the lives she encountered, and to strive for a balance between her ambitions and the preservation of her humanity. She acknowledged the weight of her choices, knowing that every victory gained would be tempered by the knowledge that it came at the cost of another's defeat.

With a heavy heart, Aurora rose from her kneeling position, her resolve solidified. She moved the body up against the cliffside and put his head in his lap. Then she laid the sword next to him. She would carry the burden of her actions, seeking redemption and growth within this virtual crucible. The path ahead was treacherous, filled with untold challenges and unpredictable encounters, but she would navigate it with integrity, her moral compass guiding her through the labyrinthine corridors of this digital existence.

Just as the adrenaline from her recent victory was starting to subside, a notification box popped up before Aurora's eyes, bearing the words, "Moment captured - airing on highlight live stream." The shock of the message jolted through her virtual being. She had never anticipated that her intense encounter with the other player would be broadcasted to the masses, especially considering the vast number of participants still engrossed in the tournament. It was an unexpected intrusion into her privacy, a window into her virtual life exposed to the prying eyes of the world.

As Aurora tried to make sense of the situation, a mix of emotions surged within her. She felt a flicker of excitement at the thought of her moment of triumph being witnessed by others, but it was quickly overshadowed by a sense of vulnerability and unease. She hadn't anticipated the potential consequences of her actions being scrutinized by the vast audience. Nevertheless, she resolved to use this new experience as a stepping stone for her next adventure in the virtual world.

With a determined spirit, Aurora strode back into the bustling marketplace, the echo of her footsteps drowned by the cacophony of merchants hawking their wares. Her eyes scanned the posting board, filled with a myriad of quests and opportunities for her to undertake. She sought something more lighthearted and straightforward to balance out the intensity of her recent battle. Perhaps a simple gathering quest to replenish her supplies or a delivery quest to assist a local merchant.

Aurora weighed her options, deliberating over the choices before her. She knew she needed to pace herself and conserve her energy for the challenges that lay ahead. After all, there were still many players in the tournament, and she couldn't afford to let her guard down. With a deep breath, she reached a decision and plucked a parchment from the board, her choice made. Deliver medicine to a cottage out in the enchanted forest.

In the bustling marketplace, amidst the vibrant tapestry of colorful stalls and animated conversations, Aurora made her way towards the Merchant Guild. The guild's booth stood as a small oasis of order amidst the lively chaos, its modest exterior adorned with a sign bearing the emblem of interconnected gears. It was here that the merchants congregated, ensuring the smooth flow of goods and services within the village.

As Aurora approached the booth, she noticed a middle-aged man with a weathered face and a meticulous beard attending to the assortment of parcels and documents that adorned his work surface. His attire, a blend of earthy tones and practicality, hinted at a life spent traversing the virtual landscapes in service of commerce.

With a polite yet determined voice, Aurora announced her presence. "Excuse me, sir. I'm here to collect a package for delivery." She held up the parchment detailing the specifics of the task, its inked words speaking of an urgent mission that awaited her.

The man's eyes, the color of warm honey, flickered with a mixture of relief and urgency. He glanced briefly at the document before nodding, a slight crease forming between his brows.
"Ah, yes," he replied, his voice carrying the weight of responsibility. "We need this medicine sent to a house deep within the Enchanted Forest. Someone's life depends on it" said the merchant with haste.

Aurora's heart quickened at the gravity of the situation. She understood the importance of her role in this mission, entrusted with delivering a lifeline to someone in need. She accepted the small wooden box that the man presented to her, its contents representing hope and healing.

As her fingers wrapped around the smooth surface of the box, she could sense the subtle vibrations emanating from within. The weight of the task settled upon her, and she met the man's gaze with a firm nod.
"I will make haste," she assured him, her voice laced with determination. "Time is of the essence."

With a renewed sense of purpose, Aurora left the Merchant Guild booth and embarked on her journey towards the Enchanted Forest. The forest, shrouded in an ethereal mist, beckoned her with its mystic allure and hidden perils. She knew that this delivery was not merely about navigating physical terrain; it would also require her to navigate the unseen forces that danced within the enchanted realm.

As Aurora ventured deeper into the forest, the ambient sounds of the marketplace faded, replaced by the rustling of leaves and the distant calls of creatures unknown. Shafts of sunlight pierced through the dense foliage, casting a dappled pattern on the forest floor, as if nature itself had crafted a pathway for her.

The path ahead was not without its challenges. She encountered treacherous terrain, ancient trees with gnarled roots that threatened to trip her, and the occasional elusive woodland creature that observed her with curious eyes. Aurora's senses remained heightened, her every step a calculated blend of caution and purpose.

As Aurora ventured deeper into the enchanted forest, the dense foliage whispered secrets and mysterious melodies. The scent of moss and wildflowers hung in the air, intertwining with the musty aroma of ancient wood. It was in this ethereal realm that she encountered a majestic being, a towering tree-ent that stood proudly at a height of fifteen feet. Its imposing figure was adorned with branches and leaves, resembling the graceful elegance of a willow tree.

The tree-ent's movements were deliberate, almost languid, as if time itself moved at a different pace for this ancient creature. Its voice emerged as a deep rumble, resonating with the wisdom accumulated over centuries.
"Hello, weary traveler," it greeted Aurora in a voice that carried the weight of ages.

Aurora's heart skipped a beat, her eyes widening in astonishment at the sight before her. She cautiously held her sword at the ready, unsure whether this towering being was a friend or a potential adversary.
"Friend or foe?" she called out, her voice filled with both caution and curiosity.

The tree-ent, its gaze kind and steady, replied in its deliberate manner. "I am a friend of the forest and anyone who holds its harmony dear. Fear not, for I mean no harm."

Relief washed over Aurora as she slowly lowered her sword, realizing that this living guardian of the woods posed no threat. Gathering her composure, she spoke with a mix of respect and urgency.
"I seek a cottage hidden within these woods. Do you know its whereabouts?"

The tree-ent introduced itself with a name that resonated with nature's tranquility, "I am known as Verdant, guardian of these ancient wood. And yes, I am aware of the cottage you seek."

Time seemed to stretch as their conversation unfolded, for the tree-ent spoke with a measured pace, carefully choosing each word. Minutes passed with each sentence, as if the ancient being savored every syllable, drawing upon the very essence of the forest itself. Aurora listened intently, captivated by the tree-ent's gentle wisdom and ancient knowledge.

Impatience began to creep into Aurora's voice as she interjected, "I appreciate your wisdom, Verdant. However, I am in urgent need of reaching the cottage as swiftly as possible."

Verdant, unmoved by Aurora's haste, nodded sagely. "Ah, urgency can be a restless companion, but fret not, for the cottage lies just beyond yonder path," the tree-ent gestured slowly, indicating the way.

Grateful for the guidance, Aurora's tone softened as she expressed her gratitude, albeit tinged with impatience. "Thank you, Verdant," she murmured in a voice laced with irritation. She yearned to quicken her pace, fulfill her task, and delve deeper into the secrets the forest held.

With a gentle rustle of leaves and a resonating sigh, the tree-ent bid Aurora farewell. As she hurried along the designated path, her footsteps echoing in the tranquility of the enchanted forest, she couldn't help but marvel at the intricate web of encounters and experiences that awaited her, knowing that every interaction held the potential to shape her journey and the world she inhabited.

Finally, after what felt like an eternity of traversing the forest's labyrinthine trails, she reached the destination marked on her quest parchment. A humble cottage, nestled amidst a clearing adorned with vibrant wildflowers, greeted her weary eyes. This was the place where the package must be delivered, where a life hung in the balance.

As Aurora approached the door, a surge of anticipation and responsibility coursed through her veins. She knocked gently, her heart beating in synchrony with the rhythm of her actions. Moments passed before the door creaked open, revealing a figure cloaked in shadows.

Aurora presented the small wooden box, her voice steady yet tinged with empathy. “I bring the medicine that could offer hope and healing," she announced. The figure, whose features were obscured by darkness, nodded in acknowledgment and motioned for Aurora to enter. Stepping into the cottage, she was greeted by a warm and comforting ambiance. Soft candlelight flickered, casting dancing shadows on the walls adorned with tapestries depicting mythical creatures and enchanting landscapes.

As Aurora's eyes adjusted to the dim light, she caught a glimpse of the figure who stood before her. A hooded cloak draped their form, concealing their face from view. The air in the room seemed to hold an air of anticipation as if the weight of the moment permeated the very atmosphere.

With cautious steps, Aurora approached the figure, her senses attuned to the subtle energy that enveloped them. She extended the small wooden box, offering it as a lifeline.
"This medicine was entrusted to me. Its potency holds the promise of healing," she said, her voice carrying a gentle urgency.

The figure took the box from Aurora's outstretched hands, their movements deliberate yet shrouded in an aura of mystery. As the hooded figure carefully opened the box, a soft glow radiated from within, illuminating their face. Aurora found herself staring into eyes that mirrored the depths of the Enchanted Forest itself, swirling with ancient knowledge and profound gratitude.

"Thank you," the figure spoke, their voice laced with a mixture of relief and reverence. "You have brought hope to a weary soul, and your journey is not in vain."

Aurora felt a surge of fulfillment wash over her, knowing that her efforts had touched someone's life in a profound way. She couldn't help but wonder about the individual who would benefit from the healing properties contained within the small wooden box. Their story, their struggles, and their triumphs remained a mystery, a tale waiting to unfold.

With a sense of accomplishment, Aurora bid farewell to the hooded figure, their unspoken connection lingering in the air. She exited the cottage, stepping back into the embrace of the enchanted forest, now imbued with a renewed sense of purpose and wonder.

As she made her way back towards the bustling marketplace, Aurora couldn't help but reflect on the significance of her journey. The encounter with the hooded figure, the delivery of the life-saving medicine—it was a reminder that every quest, no matter how small, had the potential to shape destinies and weave the tapestry of the virtual world.

Arriving back at the marketplace, Aurora's eyes were drawn once again to the familiar posting board, adorned with a fresh array of quests. Gathering her resolve, she scanned the options, searching for her next adventure. Today's battle had been fought with weapons of healing and compassion, and she longed to continue her exploration of this vast virtual realm, ready to embrace whatever challenges and triumphs awaited her next.

Meanwhile, inside the grand gymnasium, a hushed anticipation filled the air as the small crowd gathered to witness Hannah's second day in the virtual world. Among them were Jane and Grace, their eyes fixated on the large screens displaying the enthralling events unfolding before them. The atmosphere was charged with excitement and curiosity as Hannah's journey unfolded, captivating the spectators with each calculated move and display of her formidable ranger skills.

The live stream transmitted the vivid imagery of Hannah's battles, her every action bringing forth gasps and whispers of awe from the onlookers. The tension grew palpable as she clashed against another player, their weapons colliding in a symphony of steel. The nimble dexterity with which she maneuvered, combined with her unwavering determination, left the audience spellbound. Each swing of her sword, each arrow she unleashed with unerring accuracy, showcased the searing strength that dwelled within her.

The entire encounter unfolded like a heart-pounding saga, with the crowd on the edge of their seats, their eyes widening in anticipation of the next breathtaking moment. Silence enveloped the gym as the climactic clash approached, and everyone held their collective breaths, entranced by the mesmerizing spectacle that was unfolding before their eyes.

The final clash, sword against sword, was a culmination of skill, strategy, and sheer willpower. The intensity of the battle radiated from the screens, infecting the spectators with an exhilarating energy. The crowd erupted in exultant cheers, their fervor reverberating through the space, as Hannah emerged triumphant, delivering the decisive blow that secured her first player kill. The room pulsated with a shared sense of victory and admiration for her indomitable spirit.

But the jubilation didn't end there. As the virtual world acknowledged Hannah's achievement, a radiant box materialized on her screen, displaying the words, "Level Up - Level 2." The crowd erupted once again, jubilant cheers resonating through the gymnasium. Hannah's prowess and determination had not only brought her a player kill but had also propelled her further on her path of growth and success. The spectators, witnessing this remarkable feat, now comprehended why she had been chosen to partake in the prestigious tournament.

However, Hannah's journey extended beyond the realm of player-versus-player encounters. The live stream continued to captivate the audience as they witnessed her fateful encounter with the enigmatic tree-ent named Verdant. This mesmerizing creature stood as a testament to the intricate and thoughtful design of the virtual world. Its towering form, reaching a height of fifteen feet, was a magnificent fusion of humanoid and arboreal elements. Verdant exuded an air of ancient wisdom, with the lines of age etched into its bark-like skin, and its voice resonated with a deep and melodic timbre that seemed to echo the whispers of the forest itself.

The onlookers marveled at the attention to detail and realism exhibited by the tree-ent creatures and non-player characters within the virtual world. Verdant, in particular, embodied the essence of a living, breathing entity, with its intricate movements, deliberate gestures, and the way its leaves rustled with every word spoken. It was as if the tree-ent had truly sprung to life from the depths of the virtual realm, enchanting all who bore witness to its presence.

As the live stream continued to chronicle the awe-inspiring adventures of Hannah and other players, the audience found themselves immersed in the vibrant tapestry of this expansive virtual world. Though physically outside of its boundaries, they lived vicariously through the players, their lives interwoven with the virtual realm through the lens of the live stream. It was a testament to the power of technology and the boundless imagination that breathed life into this captivating virtual world. The spectators, unable to physically traverse its landscapes, found solace in the immersive experience the live stream provided. They marveled at the intricate details, the lush environments, and the seamless integration of reality and fantasy that unfolded before their very eyes.

With each passing moment, the audience grew more enamored with the vastness and intricacy of the virtual world. They revealed in the stunning visuals that unfolded, from sweeping vistas of sprawling landscapes to the subtle play of light filtering through the dense foliage of the enchanted forest. The colors danced with vibrancy, captivating the senses and transporting the spectators to a realm where imagination knew no bounds.

As Hannah ventured deeper into the virtual realm, encountering mythical creatures, navigating treacherous terrains, and unraveling captivating quests, the crowd couldn't help but feel a shared sense of exhilaration. They became invested in her journey, her victories fueling their sense of triumph, while her setbacks evoked a collective determination to see her succeed.

The live stream had become a lifeline, a portal into a world that transcended the limitations of their everyday lives. It provided an escape, a chance to be part of something extraordinary, where dreams and fantasies melded into a cohesive reality. Through the medium of technology, the spectators found themselves swept up in the magic and wonder that permeated every aspect of the virtual world.

As Hannah made her way through the bustling marketplace, seeking her next quest, the spectators eagerly awaited the choices she would make. They yearned to see her navigate the intricate web of possibilities and witness the ripple effects of her actions. Would she embark on a daring rescue mission, delve into the depths of a treacherous dungeon, or perhaps uncover the secrets of a hidden artifact? The anticipation was palpable, and the crowd hung on every decision Hannah would make.

The virtual world had become more than just a game; it had transformed into a shared experience, a collective journey that transcended the confines of the gymnasium walls. The spectators found themselves united by their fascination, their imaginations ignited by the wondrous tales unfolding before them. They revealed in the camaraderie that sprouted among the players, the alliances forged, and the friendships kindled in this extraordinary realm.

As Hannah's adventure continued to unfold, the crowd remained captivated, their spirits intertwined with the virtual world through the live stream. It was a testament to the power of technology, as it bridged the gap between reality and fantasy, offering a glimpse into a world where anything was possible. And at that moment, as they immersed themselves in the grand tapestry of this digital universe, they realized that their own lives had been forever enriched by the wonders and magic of the virtual realm.

Chapter 13

Day 3 dawned upon Aurora, enveloping her in the familiarity of her newfound virtual life. The novelty had started to wear off, leaving her yearning for more meaningful connections. Though the non-player characters (NPCs) provided a semblance of companionship, their scripted dialogues and predictable responses began to feel repetitive and lacking in depth. As Aurora sat on the edge of her bed, contemplating her solitude, a pang of homesickness tugged at her heartstrings. The warmth of her family's presence felt like a distant memory, and she yearned for their comforting embrace.

With a sigh, Aurora reminded herself of the greater purpose behind her journey. This virtual world held the key to a brighter future for her entire family, and she knew that winning the grand prize would bring them prosperity and security. It was a sacrifice she willingly made, even as the days stretched on longer than she had ever been apart from her loved ones.

Day 3 began with a slower pace, Aurora allowing herself a moment of respite. She relished the chance to explore at a leisurely rhythm, taking in the intricate details of the virtual world that had become her temporary reality. Clad in her chosen attire, she descended the inn's staircase and entered the bustling tavern below. There was an unexplained shift in the atmosphere, a subtle energy that caught Aurora's attention. As she scanned the room, her eyes met the gaze of a dwarf standing amidst the crowd, a formidable ax resting upon her sturdy frame.

Intrigued yet cautious, Aurora found herself on guard, uncertain of the intentions of this new arrival. The dwarf

approached with a genial smile, breaking the silence that hung in the air.
"Hey there! How are you faring in this brave new world?" she greeted Aurora warmly, her voice filled with genuine curiosity. Aurora's apprehension slowly dissipated, replaced by a glimmer of hope that she had found a kindred spirit.
"Don't worry, I can't harm you because I'm here to help out players" said the dwarf with a warm smile.

Relieved to hear that the dwarf was incapable of harming other players, Aurora allowed herself to relax. The dwarf, introducing herself as Brynn Ironheart, had been observing Aurora's journey from a distance, moved by the determination and strength she displayed. It was an unexpected offer of assistance, a genuine gesture of camaraderie in this vast virtual realm.
"I could help you further yourself in the tournament if you'd like, " mentioned Brynn with an open invitation.

Aurora's smile widened, and she nodded gratefully.
"Yes, I could use some company. Having someone to talk to would be a great comfort," she confessed, her voice tinged with genuine longing. The dwarf's presence seemed like a beacon of light in the midst of solitude, offering a respite from the solitary nature of her quest.

"Join me for breakfast, and we can continue our conversation," Brynn invited, gesturing toward a table adorned with a spread of hearty dishes. As they settled into their seats, Aurora and her newfound companion savored the aroma of freshly cooked food, their conversation meandering through a myriad of topics. They shared tales of their respective journeys, exchanging strategies, and laughing at the occasional mishap.

Time seemed to melt away as they forged a bond that transcended the virtual confines. The breakfast turned into an extended rendezvous of heartfelt confessions, dreams, and shared aspirations. Aurora found solace in Brynn's presence, their shared experiences weaving a tapestry of camaraderie and support.

In that cozy tavern, surrounded by the vibrant virtual world and the comforting aroma of a nourishing meal, Aurora and Brynn Ironheart discovered that companionship, even in a virtual realm, had the power to soothe the ache of loneliness and invigorate their spirits. They embraced the newfound alliance, eager to face the challenges ahead together, their hearts buoyed by the knowledge that they were not alone in their virtual journey.

Brynn, with her sturdy frame and mighty ax, emanated a sense of resilience and wisdom. Her weathered face bore the marks of battles fought and victories earned, and her eyes sparkled with determination. As Aurora observed Brynn's battle-worn hands, she couldn't help but feel a sense of admiration and gratitude for this newfound ally. She had also reached level 4 already.

As they shared their plans for the day, Aurora expressed her desire to delve deeper into the enchanted forest, seeking further adventures and valuable treasures. Brynn, in turn, offered her expertise in navigating treacherous terrains and battling formidable foes, her knowledge of the virtual world proving invaluable.

With their bellies filled and spirits lifted, Aurora and Brynn donned their gear and embarked on their journey, their camaraderie bolstering their resolve. The virtual landscape unfolded before them, teeming with breathtaking vistas, hidden dangers, and the promise of untold treasures.

As they ventured deeper into the enchanted forest, their steps synchronized and their senses attuned to the slightest rustle of leaves or distant echoes of mythical creatures. Brynn shared tales of legendary artifacts rumored to be hidden within these mystical woods, while Aurora marveled at the intricate details of the ancient trees that whispered secrets from centuries past.

Together, they navigated through the dense foliage, their trust in one another growing with each passing obstacle overcome. Aurora found comfort in Brynn's steadfast presence, her unwavering loyalty and unwavering determination inspiring Aurora to push beyond her limits, to become a warrior worthy of her virtual realm.

In the company of their shared laughter, whispered strategies, and the symphony of their combined strength, Aurora and Brynn forged a bond that transcended the boundaries of the virtual world. They were no longer mere players; they were a formidable duo, their combined skills and indomitable spirit ready to leave an indelible mark on this virtual realm.

As their footsteps echoed through the enchanted forest, the virtual world bore witness to the birth of an epic partnership, their names whispered with reverence among both friends and foes alike. For Aurora and Brynn Ironheart, the journey had just begun, and together, they would carve their names into the annals of virtual legend.

As Aurora and Brynn Ironheart ventured further, their path led them to a familiar encounter with the tree-ent named Verdant. The towering figure of Verdant stood before them, his branches swaying gently in the breeze as if greeting old friends. His deep voice resonated slowly, each word carrying the weight of centuries.
"Hello again, Aurora. What brings you here today?" he inquired, his voice imbued with a sense of ancient wisdom.

Aurora looked up at Verdant, her eyes filled with curiosity and hope. "We came by looking for a quest, and I thought you might have one to offer," she stated, her voice echoing with determination. Verdant pondered for a moment, his eyes seemingly lost in the depths of the forest.
"I don't have anything to give you right now, but let me commune with my fellow trees. They hold the secrets of this forest," he responded, his voice trailing off into a soft murmur.

Aurora and Brynn settled down on the moss-covered ground, patiently awaiting Verdant's connection with the forest's intricate network of roots. Time seemed to stretch as the minutes turned into hours. Verdant, rooted firmly in the earth, stood motionless, his form blending seamlessly with the surrounding foliage. The forest itself seemed to hush as if holding its breath in anticipation of the impending communication.

Restlessness began to creep into Brynn's demeanor, as she fidgeted and shifted her weight from side to side.
"How much longer is this going to take?" she finally voiced, unable to contain her impatience. Aurora, too, found herself growing restless, pacing back and forth, her eyes fixated on

Verdant.
"Verdant, how much longer until you're done?" she called out, her voice filled with a mixture of anticipation and frustration.

Verdant's response came slow and deliberate as if carrying the weight of the ages. "You cannot rush our language. It predates this world itself. It takes time for the signals to travel from one tree to another," he explained, his voice echoing through the forest.
"However, I have received word that a group of spiders has nested deeper into the forest, causing unrest among the trees. I suggest heading down this path and taking a left at the fork," he continued his words unfolding at a leisurely pace. With a gentle wave of his branch, Verdant added the location to Aurora's map, a mark upon the vast expanse of the enchanted forest.

Aurora's fingers danced across the interface of her virtual menu, swiping to the main map. As the image unfolded before her, she realized the true scale of the enchanted forest. The map revealed a dense tapestry of unexplored paths, hidden clearings, and mysterious landmarks.
"Looking at this, the enchanted forest is much larger than I ever imagined," Aurora murmured, awe evident in her voice.

The duo exchanged glances, their eyes filled with a mixture of excitement and trepidation. With the newfound knowledge of the spider infestation, their quest took on a renewed sense of purpose. They knew that venturing into the depths of the enchanted forest would test their skills and mettle. Yet, the prospect of exploring uncharted territories, uncovering hidden secrets, and facing formidable challenges fueled their determination.

With the guidance of Verdant's wisdom and the map as their compass, Aurora and Brynn embarked on their next adventure. The enchantment of the virtual world pulsed around them as they traversed the winding path, their footsteps blending with the symphony of nature. The enchanted forest beckoned, its mysteries waiting to be unraveled by their courage and resourcefulness. And so, hand in hand, they delved deeper into the heart of the forest, their spirits buoyed by their newfound camaraderie and shared purpose.

As they made their way through the dense foliage, sunlight filtered through the towering canopy, casting dappled patterns on the forest floor. The air was infused with the sweet scent of blooming flowers, intermingled with the earthy aroma of moss and ancient wood. Birdsong filled the air, their melodic chirping providing a melodic backdrop to the adventurers' journey.

Occasionally, the duo would come across peculiar sights and sounds. A mischievous sprite darting through the branches, leaving a trail of sparkling dust in its wake. Ethereal wisps of magic weaving through the air, captivating their senses with their ethereal beauty. Aurora and Brynn marveled at the wonders of this virtual world, their eyes wide with childlike wonder.

As they pressed on, the forest grew denser, and a sense of anticipation tingled in the air. Suddenly, a low growl reverberated through the trees, causing Aurora and Brynn to halt in their tracks. The sound came from nearby, accompanied by the rustling of leaves and the snapping of twigs under heavy footsteps.

Aurora unsheathed her sword, her grip firm and resolute, while Brynn tightened her grasp on her trusty ax. They shared a knowing glance, their eyes reflecting both determination and trepidation. Ready to face whatever awaited them, they cautiously moved toward the source of the disturbance.

Emerging from the undergrowth, their eyes widened at the sight before them. A majestic, yet fearsome, creature stood tall and proud—a mystical guardian of the forest. Its magnificent form was a fusion of human and beast, adorned with intricate patterns and adorned with nature's blessings. It regarded them with wise eyes, emanating an aura of ancient knowledge.

"Greetings, travelers," the creature spoke, its voice a harmonious blend of human and animal. "I am Elowen, the Guardian of the Enchanted Forest. What brings you to my realm?" Aurora and Brynn exchanged glances, their awe mingled with respect for this majestic being. Aurora stepped forward, her voice filled with reverence. "We seek to rid the forest of the spider infestation and restore balance to this sacred place," she proclaimed.

Elowen nodded in understanding, a sense of gratitude emanating from its presence. "Your noble quest aligns with the forest's harmony. The spiders have become a blight upon its delicate ecosystem, and their presence threatens the very essence of this realm," the guardian explained. "I shall bestow upon you my blessings and guidance. May you find strength and resilience in the face of adversity."

With a graceful motion, Elowen extended a hand towards Aurora and Brynn, and a gentle surge of energy passed through them. They felt invigorated, their senses heightened, and a deep connection to the natural world around them. It was a gift of empowerment, a symbol of trust and partnership between mortals and guardians.

Emboldened by Elowen's blessing, Aurora and Brynn continued their journey with renewed purpose. Their path led them through winding trails, ancient ruins, and moss-covered bridges that spanned babbling brooks. Along the way, they encountered other forest denizens—playful fairies, wise old owls, and mischievous woodland creatures—each offering their own insights and aid.

As they progressed, the presence of the spider nest loomed closer, it's dark influence palpable in the air. The forest grew still, as if holding its breath, anticipating the imminent clash between light and darkness. Aurora and Brynn shared a resolute nod, their resolve unshaken.

With their weapons at the ready and Elowen's blessings guiding their steps, they braced themselves for the coming battle. Their hearts beat in unison, synchronized with the pulse of the enchanted forest. They were not alone in this quest—the forest itself stood beside them, its ancient guardians and creatures lending their strength and support.

In this vast virtual world, Aurora and Brynn had discovered a sense of purpose, friendship, and an unyielding spirit to protect the beauty and harmony of the enchanted forest. Hand in hand, they forged ahead, ready to face the challenges that awaited them, for they were not merely players in a game but heroes in a grand adventure.

After a grueling journey through the winding paths of the enchanted forest, Aurora and Brynn reached their destination—the heart of the infected region. It was a sight that struck them with a mix of awe and dread. The once serene and lush surroundings had succumbed to the spiders' relentless siege. The towering trees were now shrouded in gossamer veils, their branches weighed down by intricate webs that shimmered like ethereal tapestries.

Sticky strands crisscrossed the forest floor, impeding their progress with every step. Aurora's boots clung to the strands, releasing a soft, squelching sound as she attempted to disentangle herself.
"Brynn, help me out of this" said aurora stuck in the webs, flailing around to get free. "I think I'll just stand here and enjoy the show," said Brynn, chuckling at her. "Brynn!" shouted Aurora, irritated at her.
"Oh all right" said Brynn, walking over and pulling Aurora out of the spiderweb. The atmosphere grew increasingly oppressive, as if the forest itself recoiled under the arachnid invasion.

With every passing moment, the extent of the spiders' dominion became more evident. The intricate webs stretched across the canopy like a labyrinthine network, obscuring the sunlight and casting an otherworldly pallor upon the land. Each thread was coated in a substance so adhesive that even the gentlest touch threatened to ensnare the unwary.

Aurora's gaze fixed on a shadowy figure in the distance—a spider, its form silhouetted against the dappled light filtering through the tangled mass of webs. Its legs, thin as twigs yet undeniably menacing, carried the creature with an unsettling grace. Its movements were deliberate, weaving through its domain with a predatory awareness. Aurora's heart quickened with a mixture of trepidation and determination as she realized that her trusty bow and arrows would be ineffective against such a formidable adversary.

Aware of the limitations of her ranged weapon, Aurora turned to Brynn, her eyes filled with resolve.
"We need a different approach," she said, her voice tinged with a mixture of caution and determination. Brynn nodded, her grip on her mighty ax tightening. "Agreed. We must find a way to navigate this treacherous webbing and face these spiders head-on."

As they pondered their next move, a glimmer of insight illuminated Aurora's mind. "We'll need something to neutralize the stickiness of the webs," she mused, her eyes scanning their surroundings for a solution. And there, nestled between the gnarled roots of a nearby tree, she spotted a cluster of luminescent mushrooms—a rare breed known for their unique properties. "We can use these mushrooms to make torches, the oil on them will burn perfectly," said Aurora walking over to the group of mushrooms. "How do you know that?" asked Brynn with a confused look on his face scratching his head. "I have no idea, it just came to me," said Aurora, just as confused as Brynn.

Eagerly, the pair collected a handful of these bioluminescent fungi, their delicate caps emitting a soft, ethereal glow. Using a piece of cloth torn from their tattered garments, they fashioned impromptu torches. The mushrooms' natural oils, when ignited, released a subtle aroma that proved to be an effective deterrent against the sticky strands.

With their makeshift torches in hand, Aurora and Brynn gingerly stepped forward, cautiously testing the ground ahead with their flame-lit guides. As the radiant light cast flickering shadows upon the webs, a marvelous transformation unfolded. The sticky fibers, once formidable obstacles, dissolved and recoiled from the warmth, offering a pathway forward.

They progressed, their torches warding off the encroaching webs as they navigated the labyrinthine network. Occasionally, they encountered pockets of resistance, stubborn strands that clung tenaciously, but with each encounter, they persevered. The web's adhesive grasp weakened under the mesmerizing dance of fire and shadow.

As Aurora and Brynn advanced, they noticed the presence of the spiders intensifying. Faint skittering sounds emanated from the surrounding foliage, accompanied by an occasional hiss or click. It was an eerie chorus, a reminder that their adversaries lurked in the shadows, awaiting their moment to strike.

Steeling themselves, the duo pressed on, their senses heightened, ready to face the looming threat that awaited them. They knew that beyond the ethereal veil of webs, the true challenge awaited—a confrontation with the spiders that had claimed dominion over this once-majestic forest.

With their torches held high, their spirits aflame with courage, and their hearts beating in synchrony, Aurora and Brynn ventured deeper into the infected heart of the enchanted forest, determined to restore harmony and vanquish the eight-legged usurpers that had woven their dark web across the land.

Just as the anticipation reached its peak, three massive spiders descended from the canopy above, their eerie legs propelling them with alarming speed. The forest seemed to hold its breath, as if recognizing the gravity of the impending clash between the defenders of light and the grotesque arachnids that had claimed this realm as their own.

Aurora's muscles tensed, her grip firm on her trusty sword. With a battle cry that pierced through the dense silence, she swung her weapon in a sweeping arc, aiming for the closest spider. The blade connected with a resounding clash, striking against the arachnid's exoskeleton with a shower of sparks. The spider recoiled momentarily, its eight eyes glinting with a mixture of surprise and aggression.

Brynn, wielding her mighty ax with primal strength, lunged forward to engage the second spider. Her battle cry mingled with the clash of steel as her weapon cleaved through the air, seeking to sever the arachnid's vicious fangs. The spider, sensing the impending danger, unleashed a frenzied assault, its venomous mandibles snapping menacingly. But Brynn's resilience and skill proved unmatched, as she deftly parried and countered each strike, her ax biting into the spider's chitinous armor.

Meanwhile, the third spider, more cunning and agile than its companions, seized the opportunity to strike from the shadows. With astonishing speed, it skittered toward Aurora, its venomous stinger poised for a deadly injection. Sensing the danger, Aurora pivoted swiftly, narrowly evading the lethal attack. Her swift reflexes allowed her to counter with a swift kick, propelling the spider back momentarily, giving her a momentary respite.

The battle raged on, the clash of steel and chittering of arachnid mandibles echoing through the forest. Aurora, her movements fluid and precise, danced with the agility of a seasoned warrior, dodging the spider's relentless assault. With each swing of her sword, she aimed for vulnerable joints and weak points, gradually wearing down the creature's defenses. With each spider they killed, they gained 25xp.

Brynn, unyielding in her determination, engaged in a fierce contest of strength with her opponent. Her ax whirled through the air with controlled fury, striking with bone-crushing force. Each blow resonated with a thunderous impact, causing the spider to stagger and retreat under the relentless assault. Brynn's resilience and sheer might turned the tide of the battle, as the arachnid's resistance faltered, its once formidable carapace now weakened and vulnerable.

Despite the valiant efforts of the two warriors, the spiders fought with unmatched ferocity. They displayed a cunning that belied their monstrous nature, exploiting every opportunity to strike and retreat, aiming to exhaust their adversaries both physically and mentally. Yet Aurora and Brynn, fueled by a shared purpose and unwavering determination, stood resolute in the face of adversity.

The battle reached its crescendo as the forest bore witness to an epic clash of wills. Aurora, sensing an opening, unleashed a flurry of strikes, her sword arcing through the air with precision. With a final, powerful blow, she severed the first spider's connection to life, its monstrous form collapsing to the forest floor.

Not far from her, Brynn summoned every ounce of her strength, channeling her primal fury into a devastating blow. Her mighty ax cleaved through the air, connecting with the second spider's exoskeleton with an earth-shaking impact. The arachnid let out a piercing screech, its formidable legs crumpling beneath it as it met its demise.

As the echoes of battle subsided, only the third spider remained, its relentless tenacity undiminished. Aurora and Brynn locked eyes, a silent understanding passing between them. With a synchronized charge, they closed in on the remaining arachnid, striking in perfect harmony. The spider, now outnumbered and outmatched, fought desperately, its venomous fangs snapping futilely against the impenetrable wall of their combined defense.

In a final act of unity, Aurora and Brynn launched a simultaneous assault, their weapons finding their mark with surgical precision. The spider, its monstrous form wracked with pain, emitted a guttural shriek before succumbing to the inevitable. Its life force drained away, leaving only stillness and the echoes of their hard-fought victory reverberating through the enchanted forest.

Breathing heavily, covered in sweat and the grime of battle, Aurora and Brynn exchanged triumphant glances. Aurora took more than half her health in damage and was close to death. Their valor and skill had emerged victorious against the menacing arachnids that had plagued the forest. It was a testament to their unwavering resolve and the indomitable spirit that burned within them. They had managed to kill 12 spiders up to this point.

Just as Aurora and Brynn braced themselves for another grueling round, a sudden movement caught their attention. Emerging from the foliage, a massive figure strode forward with an air of stoic determination. It was none other than a tree-ent.

Tree-ent's towering form cast an imposing shadow over the battlefield, his immense presence commanding respect. With each step, the ground trembled slightly, as if nature itself acknowledged his authority. The spiders, sensing the imminent threat, skittered nervously, their eight eyes darting between the formidable warriors and the approaching tree-ent.

In a display of unmatched power and agility, tree-ent swiftly brought his massive foot down upon one of the spiders, its fragile form instantly reduced to a mere splatter of arachnid remnants. The ground quivered beneath the weight of his stomp, a testament to the force with which he had eradicated the creature.

Without missing a beat, tree-ent's unleashed another devastating blow, his mighty foot connecting with the abdomen of another spider. The arachnid was catapulted through the air, its trajectory interrupted only by a resounding crash against the trunk of a towering oak tree. The force of the impact sent a shockwave rippling through the forest, causing leaves to rain down like confetti.

The remaining spider, perhaps sensing the impending doom, scurried away in a panicked frenzy, desperate to escape the wrath of the tree-ent. It vanished into the undergrowth, leaving behind a trail of spider silk shimmering in the dappled sunlight.

Aurora and Brynn, their bodies fatigued and minds reeling from the intensity of the battle, collapsed to the forest floor in exhaustion. They were grateful for the timely intervention of the tree-ent, whose power and grace had turned the tide in their favor.

"Thank you, Tree-ent," Brynn managed to utter between labored breaths, her voice filled with gratitude and awe.
"We fought valiantly, but the spiders kept coming. Your help made all the difference."

Tree-ent's response came slowly, his words as measured as the centuries that had passed through his arboreal existence.
"We tree-ents are beings of peace and harmony," he explained, his voice carrying a tinge of sorrow.
"We do not engage in battle unless absolutely necessary. Our purpose is to guard and nurture the forests, to maintain the delicate balance of nature."

Aurora, her curiosity piqued, looked up at the tree-ent with genuine interest. "But why did you choose to aid us? We are mere travelers in this virtual realm."

Tree-ent's ancient eyes met Aurora's his gaze filled with a wisdom that transcended time.
"Verant has watched your journey, witnessed your bravery, and observed the depth of your spirit. Your quest aligns with the preservation of the enchanted forest. He sent me to help you out and It was an honor to offer my assistance in safeguarding this realm."

As the weight of tree-ent's words settled upon them, Aurora and Brynn felt a renewed sense of purpose. Their encounter with the tree-ent served as a poignant reminder that they were not alone in their quest. The forces of nature itself rallied alongside them, united in the common goal of protecting the delicate balance of the virtual world.

Together, Aurora, Brynn, and Tree-ent stood amidst the remnants of their recent battle, the echoes of their triumph mingling with the whispers of the enchanted forest. A bond, forged through shared struggles and mutual respect, linked their fates in this mystical realm.
"Here, let me heal you guys" said the tree-ent as he held out its hand. A magical ora surged out of his hand and swirled around Aurora and Brynn, healing them.

With renewed determination, they pressed on, their steps guided by the knowledge that they were not merely players in a game, but champions entrusted with a sacred duty to preserve the beauty and magic of the virtual world they had come to love.

The ancient tree-ent towered over Aurora and Brynn, his majestic branches swaying gently in the breeze. With deliberate slowness, he extended one of his long, gnarled limbs toward them in a gesture of friendship and camaraderie.

"If you ever find yourselves in need within the depths of the enchanted forest," tree-ent rumbled in his deep, resonant voice, "simply call out to the tree-ents, and we shall answer your plea. You have proven yourselves to be true friends of the forest, and in return, we offer our unwavering support."

Aurora, her eyes gleaming with gratitude, stepped closer to the tree-ent, her hand reaching out to touch the rough bark of his massive trunk. "We are humbled by your offer," she said, her voice filled with sincerity. "To be considered friends of the tree-ents and guardians of this sacred realm is an honor beyond words. We shall cherish this bond and call upon you when the need arises."

Brynn, too, approached tree-ent, her gaze alight with admiration. "Your presence and guidance have brought us strength and solace in our journey," she expressed, her voice carrying a hint of wonder. "The enchanted forest is a place of awe-inspiring beauty, and we promise to protect its secrets, its creatures, and the delicate balance that sustains its magic."

Tree-ent's ancient eyes twinkled with warmth as he regarded the two adventurers. "Your hearts are filled with reverence and respect for the wonders that reside within these woods," he acknowledged. "We, the tree-ents, have watched civilizations rise and fall, and we recognize the significance of kindred spirits such as yourselves. May your future adventures be blessed with courage and enlightenment."

Aurora and Brynn exchanged glances, their spirits lifted by the affirmation of their newfound alliance with the tree-ents. They knew that their journey in the enchanted forest would be fraught with challenges and trials, but they also understood that they had gained powerful allies who would stand beside them in times of need.

With a final expression of gratitude, Aurora and Brynn bid farewell to the tree-ent, their hearts brimming with excitement for the adventures that lay ahead. As they ventured deeper into the enchanted forest, they felt a sense of belonging, knowing that they were part of a grand tapestry woven by the interconnectedness of the natural world.

In the embrace of the forest's ethereal embrace, Aurora and Brynn pledged to honor their friendship with the tree-ents and safeguard the delicate harmony that pervaded the enchanted realm. They would forever cherish the memory of their encounter with Verdant, a symbol of wisdom and benevolence, and draw strength from the unyielding bond they had forged amidst the tree-ent wonders of the virtual wilderness.

Together, they set forth, their footsteps guided by the whispers of the trees, their spirits attuned to the pulse of the forest. With the blessings of the tree-ents and the enchantment of the world around them, Aurora and Brynn embarked on a new chapter of their adventure, eager to unravel the mysteries that awaited them and embrace the extraordinary journey that had become their own.

As the golden hues of the setting sun painted the sky, Aurora and Brynn bid their final farewell to tree-ent companions. Grateful for his wisdom and protection, they turned their steps toward the exit of the enchanted forest, their hearts filled with the lingering magic of their recent encounters.

The journey back through the dense foliage was as enchanting as their initial entry, with shimmering rays of sunlight filtering through the canopy, casting a soft, ethereal glow upon their path. They marveled at the interplay of light and shadow, the gentle whispers of the forest bidding them farewell.

Emerging from the enchanted forest, their surroundings transitioned to a vast open field, stretching out before them like an endless tapestry of green. The cool breeze danced through their hair, invigorating their spirits and carrying with it the scents of wildflowers and earth.

As they ventured across the field, the distant sound of birdsong accompanied their footsteps, creating a symphony of nature's melody. The open expanse brought a sense of freedom and serenity, contrasting with the intricate wonders they had left behind in the enchanted forest.

Finally, just as the sun began its descent below the horizon, casting a warm glow across the landscape, Aurora and Brynn arrived at the outskirts of their familiar town. The familiar sights and sounds welcomed them, evoking a comforting sense of homecoming.

Their exhaustion mingled with hunger, their weary bodies reminding them of the physical toll their adventures had taken. "I'm starving," Brynn exclaimed, her voice carrying a hint of playfulness, but also genuine longing. Her belly let out a low rumble, as if in agreement.

Aurora chuckled in response, her own stomach echoing the sentiment. "Indeed, my friend. The trials and triumphs of the day have left us famished," she replied, her voice filled with affectionate camaraderie. Together, they embarked on the familiar path leading to the inn, their footsteps resonating with a sense of contentment and anticipation.

The aroma of hearty meals wafted through the air as they entered the inn, captivating their senses and igniting a renewed vigor within them. The lively chatter of fellow adventurers and townsfolk filled the air, mingling with the clinking of glasses and the comforting crackle of the hearth.

Seated at a table in the corner, Aurora and Brynn eagerly perused the menu, their mouths watering at the descriptions of mouthwatering dishes. They placed their orders, their choice reflecting both their cravings and their desire to indulge in a well-deserved feast.

As they savored each delectable bite, their weariness slowly subsided, replaced by a warm sense of fulfillment. The nourishment not only satisfied their physical hunger but also rejuvenated their spirits, fortifying them for the adventures yet to come.

Conversation flowed effortlessly between the two friends, their voices interweaving with laughter and shared memories. They reminisce about their encounters with Verdant, the awe-inspiring beauty of the enchanted forest, and the countless wonders they had witnessed on their journey.

With every bite and every word spoken, a bond deepened between Aurora and Brynn, a bond forged in the crucible of shared experiences and unwavering trust. They revealed in the knowledge that they had each other to lean on, to confide in, and to celebrate their victories.

As the night grew darker outside the inn, the last remnants of their meal disappeared from their plates. Satiated and content, they bid the bustling inn farewell and made their way to their rooms, guided by the soft glow of candlelight.

Slipping beneath the covers of their beds, Aurora and Brynn reflected on the day's triumphs and challenges. The enchantment of the virtual world breathed life into their spirits, filling them with a sense of purpose and adventure. They drifted off to sleep, their dreams weaving new tales and whispering promises of the extraordinary tomorrow would bring.

In the embrace of the night, their bodies rejuvenated and their minds at peace, Aurora and Brynn surrendered to the sweet embrace of slumber. The inn fell silent, its halls filled with the hushed whispers of dreams and the anticipation of a new dawn, ready to greet them with boundless possibilities.

In the realm of the physical world, Hannah's father anxiously followed her virtual adventures with a mixture of anticipation and pride. The first two days of the tournament had taken a toll on him, as he wrestled with his illness. Despite his weakened state, he had mustered the strength to be present at the arena, cheering Hannah on from the sidelines, fueled by a deep-rooted determination to support his daughter in every possible way.

However, on the third day, mindful of his health and the need for rest, Hannah's father found solace and respite in the confines of the hotel room. With bated breath, he tuned into the live stream, his eyes fixated on the screen that connected him to the captivating virtual realm where Hannah's destiny unfolded.

As the moments unfolded before him, Hannah's father experienced a rollercoaster of emotions. His heart swelled with joy and pride as he witnessed her accomplishments, one by one. With every level gained, every monster defeated, and every new friend made, he couldn't help but feel a deep sense of admiration for his daughter's resilience and tenacity.

Through the pixelated lens of the live stream, he saw Hannah immerse herself in a world teeming with endless possibilities. The virtual realm had become a canvas for her dreams and aspirations, and she painted it with courage and determination. Her actions reverberated through the digital landscape, echoing a spirit of adventure that seemed to transcend the boundaries of the virtual and real worlds.

With each passing moment, Hannah's father became increasingly engrossed in the tapestry of her virtual journey. He found himself cheering and gasping alongside the virtual crowd, his emotions intertwined with the highs and lows of her experiences. Every victory she achieved resonated deeply within him, a testament to the indomitable spirit that had been passed down from generation to generation.

As Hannah ventured forth into the virtual world, her father marveled at the growth he witnessed. The virtual realm had become a crucible of personal development, where she honed her skills, conquered fears, and unearthed hidden strengths. The transformative power of the virtual environment had become evident, shaping Hannah into a person he could not have envisioned before.

Her father's heart swelled with love and pride as he watched Hannah flourish amidst the challenges and triumphs of her virtual existence. He saw her evolve not only as a skilled player but also as a compassionate friend and a pillar of support for those around her. The virtual world had become a testament to her character, revealing the depths of her empathy and the breadth of her capacity for growth.

And so, as the days passed and Hannah continued to make her mark on the virtual landscape, her father's admiration and pride grew exponentially. He cherished every moment, every shared victory, and every milestone achieved. Through the live stream, he felt a connection that transcended the boundaries of physical distance, and he found solace in knowing that his daughter was thriving and finding fulfillment in the virtual realm.

In the real world, Hannah's father and the rest of her family rallied around her, offering unwavering support and encouragement. They celebrated her victories as if they were their own, cherishing the profound impact her virtual journey had on their lives. Their pride in her accomplishments knew no bounds, for they recognized the incredible resilience and determination that propelled her forward.

As the tournament progressed and Hannah's story unfolded, her father couldn't help but marvel at the transformative power of the virtual world. It had become a catalyst for self-discovery, personal growth, and the forging of deep connections. And in that realization, he embraced the virtual realm not as a mere game but as a realm of boundless opportunities and profound impact.

With each passing day, Hannah's journey continued to captivate and inspire, serving as a testament to the potential of the human spirit. Her father eagerly awaited each new chapter, knowing that within the digital tapestry of her adventures lay the essence of her dreams and the embodiment of her indomitable will.

Chapter 14

Day 4 dawned in the virtual world, casting its ethereal glow upon Aurora as she lay in bed, her thoughts weaving a delicate tapestry of reflection and determination. Her gaze fixed upon the ceiling, her mind ventured into the realms of nostalgia and contemplation. It was hard to believe that she had made it this far in the game, defying the odds and surpassing her own expectations.

The player count had dwindled to 8432, a testament to the unforgiving nature of the virtual realm. Day by day, more players succumbed to the challenges and trials, leaving behind only the most skilled and resilient. Aurora, driven by a burning desire for triumph, set her sights on the ultimate goal: to face the last remaining player of pure skill and ability in an epic battle that would etch her name in the annals of virtual glory.

With unwavering determination, Aurora vocalized her aspirations, her voice echoing softly in the solitude of her room. She yearned for that climactic encounter, where her every skill and ability would be put to the test against a formidable opponent. The anticipation of that fateful day fueled her spirit, igniting a fire within her that burned brighter with each passing moment.

Aurora's fingers danced across the screen as she swiped up, summoning the game's menu before her. Her eyes fixated on the "Stats" tab, revealing her current standing in the virtual realm. It was a mere 275xp that separated her from reaching level 4, a tangible marker of her progress. However, before she could fully immerse herself in the pursuit of her own growth, she needed to turn in the quest they had yet to complete.

Verdant, the wise and ancient tree-ent, awaited their return in the enchanted forest.

Rising from her reverie, Aurora readied herself for the day ahead. As she made her way through the inn, she spotted Brynn already seated at a table in the tavern, a playful smirk on her face. "Look who finally woke up," Brynn teased, her eyes sparkling with mischief.

Aurora slid into the seat opposite Brynn, a faint smile tugging at the corners of her lips.
"I've been awake for some time, lost in my thoughts," she admitted, her voice laced with a touch of introspection.

Concern creased Brynn's brow as she leaned forward, her gaze gentle and empathetic.
"What's on your mind, Aurora?" she inquired, extending the warmth of her friendship.

Aurora paused for a moment, contemplating the depths of her emotions.
"I can't help but marvel at how far I've come," she mused. "Thoughts of my family linger in my mind, and I can't help but wonder what lies at the end of this journey."

The waiter approached their table, breaking the somber moment with a polite smile. Aurora's hunger surfaced, and she ordered a light breakfast, a carefully curated ensemble of eggs, sausage, potatoes, and cherry tomatoes. As their plates arrived, the aroma of the freshly prepared meal enveloped the table, casting a sense of comfort and nourishment upon them.

Brynn's eyes sparkled with admiration as she spoke words of encouragement.
"You love your family dearly, and they must be so proud of your achievements in the tournament. Keep this momentum, and you'll find yourself standing tall at the end, triumphant."

They savored their breakfast, allowing the flavors to mingle with their conversations, nourishing both body and soul. With the quest looming before them and the day draped in a cloudy embrace, they resolved to make the most of every precious moment, determined to forge their destinies before the potential arrival of rain that threatened to cast a shadow over their endeavors.

With renewed determination, Aurora and Brynn embarked on their journey once again, their steps purposeful as they made their way through the bustling village and across the vast field that led back to the entrance of the enchanted forest. Aurora's fingers brushed across the worn edges of her map, unfolding its creases to reveal the precise location where Verdant awaited their return.

As they delved deeper into the forest, their senses became attuned to the subtle whispers of the ancient trees. Shafts of sunlight filtered through the dense foliage above, casting an enchanting dance of light and shadow upon their path. Aurora's eyes flitted between the map and the surrounding flora, guiding them unerringly toward their destination.

After an hour of steady progress, the majestic figure of Verdant came into view. Towering above them, his branches extended in a welcoming gesture.

"Welcome back, Aurora," rumbled Verdant, his voice resonating with wisdom and age. "I trust your encounter with the spiders in the depths of the forest was a fruitful one. Your presence here attests to your success."

Aurora's eyes sparkled with satisfaction as she looked up at Verdant. "Indeed, we have emerged victorious against the spiders that plagued the heart of the forest. We have returned to turn in the quest," she declared with a touch of pride in her voice.

Verdant's gaze settled upon them, his voice slow and deliberate. "Very well, my little friend. As promised, here is your well-earned reward." With a gentle wave of his branch, a small box materialized before Aurora. The box shimmered with a faint, ethereal glow, signaling the completion of their quest. A notification popped up on Aurora's screen, displaying the words "Quest Completed - Spiders in the Enchanted Forest." The reward was not just the fulfillment of their mission, but also a substantial gain of 900xp, boosting their progress in the game.

Moments later, another notification sprang to life, accompanied by a cheerful charm. "Level Up - Level 4." Aurora's heart swelled with a sense of accomplishment as she celebrated the realization of her goal for the day. The new level brought with it a surge of power and unlocked potential, solidifying her status as a formidable player within the virtual realm.

As they prepared to leave the enchanted forest, dark clouds gathered above, releasing a gentle drizzle that soon evolved into a relentless downpour. The rhythmic pattern of raindrops on leaves echoed through the forest, creating a somber ambiance. Undeterred by the inclement weather, Aurora and Brynn pressed on, determined to reach the safety of the village.

"What's with the smoke," said Aurora as they neared the village, her heart racing. You could see the smoke for miles. "Whatever it is, we need to hurry," said Brynn as they picked up their pace.
Their arrival in the village was met with a scene of chaos and the destruction air was thick with smoke, and flames danced hungrily, consuming homes and structures.
The village had fallen under attack, overrun by a horde of malevolent goblins. Panic filled the air, mingling with the crackling of fire and the war cries of the invaders.

Aurora's heart pounded in her chest as she surveyed the chaos before her. This would be her first true test, a baptism by fire into the realm of intense combat. She knew she needed to approach this encounter with caution and strategy. Taking a deep breath, she steeled herself for the battle ahead.

With hesitation, Aurora and Brynn sprang into action. Their movements were swift and calculated as they engaged the goblins, their weapons flashing in the rain-soaked air. Aurora's sword cleaved through the ranks of the enemy, while Brynn's agile maneuvers allowed her to strike with precision and grace. During the battle, Aurora noticed 2 other players fighting. She'll have to watch her back even closer now.

The rain intensified, its torrential downpour adding a layer of complexity to the fight. The slick ground made footing treacherous, testing their agility and balance. Lightning streaked across the sky, briefly illuminating the chaotic scene and lending an ethereal quality to the clash of steel and the cries of combatants.

Amidst the chaos, Aurora's focus remained unyielding. She analyzed the battlefield, searching for strategic advantages. With each strike, she honed her skills, adapting to the relentless assault of the goblins. Brynn fought by her side, their synergy evident as they seamlessly covered each other's blind spots.

But the battle took an unexpected turn when the goblin chieftain, a hulking figure adorned with menacing armor and a wickedly sharp ax, emerged from the throng. He bellowed a war cry, his eyes locked on Aurora as if recognizing her as the greatest threat. The ground trembled beneath his colossal weight as he charged toward her with unbridled fury.

Aurora's heart pounded with a mix of fear and adrenaline. She knew she had to stand her ground against this formidable opponent. With a swift motion, she twirled her sword, channeling her inner strength and invoking a powerful enchantment. The blade crackled with energy, emitting a radiant glow that cut through the darkness of the storm.

As the goblin chieftain swung his massive ax down upon her, Aurora met the strike head-on. The clash sent sparks flying, illuminating the battle with a burst of light. The sheer force of the impact sent shockwaves rippling through the muddy ground, causing the goblins around them to stumble and lose their footing.

In that brief moment of distraction, Brynn seized the opportunity. With lightning speed, she leaped onto the back of the goblin chieftain, using him as a springboard. With a nimble flip, she somersaulted through the air, her daggers poised to strike. Like a whirlwind, she descended upon the goblins, slashing and dispatching them with unparalleled finesse.

Aurora, fueled by determination and driven by the adrenaline coursing through her veins, unleashed a barrage of strikes upon the goblin chieftain. Each swing of her empowered blade carried a surge of energy, battering against his defenses. +200xp popped up. With every blow, she drew closer to toppling this mighty foe.

With every defeated goblin, the villagers' hope began to rekindle. They watched in awe as Aurora and Brynn stood strong against the horde, their determination shining through the rain-soaked battlefield. The sound of applause and cheers carried on the wind, a testament to their bravery and skill. The villagers found solace in the realization that their defenders were not mere adventurers but true heroes, capable of turning the tide of battle with their unwavering spirit.

Their resilience and resourcefulness did not go unnoticed by the villagers, who watched in awe and admiration. They drew inspiration from the awe-inspiring display of skill and bravery, finding renewed hope in the face of seemingly insurmountable odds.

As the battle raged on, Aurora and Brynn's synergy grew stronger. Their movements became synchronized as if they were two halves of a whole, their individual skills complementing each other flawlessly. When Aurora engaged a group of goblins head-on, Brynn swiftly flanked from the side, catching the enemy off guard and diverting their attention. The duo fought with an almost preternatural cohesion, a testament to the trust and camaraderie they had forged on their countless adventures.

The goblin horde, initially caught off guard by the ferocity and skill of the two adventurers, slowly began to realize the tenacity of their opponents. They redoubled their efforts, launching a coordinated assault in a last-ditch attempt to overwhelm Aurora and Brynn. Yet, the duo stood firm, their resolve unshakable.

Time seemed to blur as the battle raged on, minutes stretching into hours. Fatigue tugged at their weary bodies, but their determination never wavered. The tides of the fight shifted, sometimes in their favor and other times against them, but they fought on with unwavering resolve. With each goblin killed, they gained 15xp.

As the last echoes of battle subsided, a sense of accomplishment washed over Aurora and Brynn. They stood amidst the aftermath, their bodies drenched and their breaths ragged. The village, though scarred and ravaged, was now free from the clutches of the goblin horde.

Aurora's gaze turned to Brynn, her eyes gleaming with a mixture of exhaustion and triumph.
"We did it," she whispered, her voice tinged with awe. "Against all odds, we prevailed."

Brynn nodded, a weary smile gracing her lips.
"Indeed, my friend. Together, we weathered the storm and emerged victorious. We have proven ourselves in the crucible of battle."

As they caught their breath and surveyed the village, Aurora's thoughts drifted to her family, hoping that they were safe and unaware of the turmoil that had befallen their digital world. The magnitude of their journey became more evident, and the weight of responsibility settled upon her shoulders.

But amidst the turmoil, a glimmer of hope shone through. Aurora knew that with each challenge conquered, she was one step closer to the ultimate goal, to face the remaining players of pure skill and ability in an epic battle of champions. The thought fueled her determination, reminding her of the adventure that still lay ahead.

The aftermath of the goblin battle left Aurora with a sense of accomplishment, but her triumph was short-lived as she realized that there were still two other players standing amidst the chaos. Her eyes scanned the wreckage, searching for any signs of movement. Only one figure remained upright, the other either vanquished or had fled the scene.

Aurora's grip tightened around her bow, her knuckles turning white as determination etched across her face. She knew that this encounter with the remaining player would be a pivotal moment, a test of skill and resilience. The rain continued to pour, the droplets blending with the sweat on her brow, as she prepared to face her opponent.

The female player approached Aurora, her lithe frame and elven features radiating an aura of grace and finesse. She moved with a fluidity that belied her agility, her eyes gleaming with a mixture of confidence and competitiveness. Aurora studied her, taking note of the other player's precise movements, seeking any advantage she could exploit.

"Let's end this," Aurora shouted, her voice carrying a mix of determination and resolve. With a deft motion, she notched an arrow and drew her bowstring, her aim focused on her opponent. The tension in the air was palpable as she released the arrow, intending to strike true. However, the female elf player evaded the projectile with a nimble sidestep, displaying a remarkable dexterity that left Aurora momentarily awestruck.

Refusing to be deterred, Aurora swiftly reached for another arrow, her muscles coiled like a tightly wound spring. She released the arrow once more, her eyes following its trajectory with anticipation. Yet, the elf player effortlessly sidestepped once again, narrowly evading the attack. It was evident that this opponent possessed an uncanny sense of timing and agility, making her a formidable adversary.

In the blink of an eye, the elf player closed the distance between them, moving with such rapidity that Aurora had little time to react. The clash of steel against steel reverberated through the rain-soaked air as their weapons collided. Aurora's armor absorbed the impact of a glancing blow, her body instinctively shifting to lessen the force. The intensity of the encounter surged, and both players locked in a fierce exchange of strikes and parries.

Aurora's mind raced as she analyzed her opponent's movements, searching for patterns and vulnerabilities. However, the elf player's speed and agility made it challenging for Aurora to land a solid hit. She could feel the strain on her muscles, the adrenaline coursing through her veins, as she fought to keep pace.

In a moment of vulnerability, Aurora's sword swing fell short, and the elf player seized the opportunity. With lightning-fast reflexes, she capitalized on the opening, delivering a swift strike to Aurora's left arm. Pain seared through her as the blow connected, registering as 5 damage on her health bar. Gritting her teeth, Aurora refused to succumb to the pain, channeling her resilience and determination into her next moves.

Their battle raged on, the clash of steel accompanied by the rhythmic drumming of raindrops. Aurora's mind raced, calculating her every move, seeking an opening to turn the tide in her favor. She adapted her strategy, focusing on agility and anticipation, aiming to match her opponent's speed and outmaneuver her with precision strikes.

Time seemed to stand still as they continued their intense duel, their stamina, and health dwindling with each passing moment. The rain-soaked ground beneath them became slick and treacherous, testing their balance and agility. The spectators, NPC villagers who had sought shelter from the chaos, watched in awe at the display of skill and determination unfolding before them.

As Aurora and her opponent danced through the rain, their weapons clashing in a symphony of battle, both players knew that victory hinged on a combination of skill, strategy, and sheer willpower. The outcome of this clash would determine not only their immediate fates but also their standing in the virtual world, as they navigated the treacherous path to become the last remaining players of pure skill and ability.

Aurora stood panting, her heart pounding with a mixture of exhilaration and exhaustion. The raindrops danced on her armor, blending with the echoes of the battle that had just transpired. At her feet lay the defeated elf player, their form still and lifeless. It was a hard-fought victory, one that would forever mark a turning point in Aurora's virtual journey.

As the onlookers erupted into applause, their cheers harmonizing with the rhythmic pattern of rain, Aurora couldn't help but feel a tinge of bittersweet emotion. She had emerged triumphant, showcasing her unparalleled skill and unwavering determination to all who witnessed the spectacle. Her victory reverberated through the virtual realm, captivating the attention and admiration of countless players who marveled at her prowess.

But amidst the jubilation and acclaim, Aurora's gaze fell upon the fallen elf player. Her hand instinctively reached out, a gesture of respect and acknowledgment in the aftermath of the fierce duel. The defeated player's eyes, now devoid of life, reflected a complex blend of admiration and acceptance—a silent testament to the price they had paid in their pursuit of victory.

Aurora stood there, her hand suspended in mid-air, caught between the conflicting emotions swirling within her. In this vast digital world, where battles could end in virtual death, she couldn't help but feel the weight of the consequences that came with her triumph. The line between the real and the virtual had blurred, reminding her of the significance of her actions even within the confines of a game.

She withdrew her outstretched hand, a solemn realization settling upon her. The fallen elf player would never rise again, forever entwined in the narrative of their shared virtual existence. Aurora's victory had come at a cost—one that she would carry as a lasting reminder of the complexities of this digital realm. 1000xp popped up as she watched the fallen elven player lay on the wet muddy ground.

The applause of the onlookers continued the cacophony of their appreciation, a backdrop to Aurora's contemplation. She took a step back, her eyes lingering on the fallen player, a silent vow to honor their memory. In this virtual realm of quests and battles, camaraderie and rivalry, she recognized the fragile threads that connected them all—a delicate balance of competition, compassion, and the shared pursuit of greatness.

"Brynn, help me move her body to bury her and give her the proper send-off a valent player deserves" said Aurora picking up her arms with a grunt, using her last bit of strength. Brynn walked over picking up the legs of the elven body. They carried her out into the open field, through the pouring rain. They picked a tree and propped the body up against it. They took the next half hour to dig a hole just deep enough to lay the body in. Once the body was in the hole, they covered her in the dirt. After they gave her a moment of silence to pay respect to the player. As they walked back to the village, a box popped up, "Moment Captured - Showing on highlights Livestream".

Aurora was taken aback by the notification.
"That must have been a powerful moment to be highlighted," said Aurora as she stopped in her tracks, taken back by it.
"That Was a noble thing you did, Aurora. Most people wouldn't have taken the time to do such a thing," said Brynn turning to Aurora, looking at her.
"You are a player most people could look up to. You are a model player," she said with pride.

As they headed back into the burnt-down village, the rain continued its gentle descent, Aurora joined the throng of players. The battle may have ended, but the journey persisted. In the distance, new challenges awaited, urging her forward with unwavering courage. And though the fallen player remained forever vanquished, their legacy would endure within Aurora's heart—a constant reminder that every victory bore a cost and that within this virtual tapestry, compassion and empathy held a vital place.

Her quest for greatness continued, fueled by the bonds she had formed and the battles she had overcome. Side by side with her comrades, she ventured forth, ready to embrace the next chapter of her virtual odyssey—a testament to her resilience, a testament to the fallen, and a testament to the complex tapestry of emotions that defined her virtual existence.

Leaving the devastation behind, Aurora and Brynn sought shelter from the rain, finding solace in the resilience of their friendship and the knowledge that they had grown stronger together. The relentless downpour may have soaked their clothes and chilled their bones, but it couldn't extinguish the fire within their hearts.

As they sought refuge, they vowed to make the best of the day, regardless of the weather. They knew that with each passing challenge, they were inching closer to the pinnacle of their journey. And so, with renewed determination, they set their sights on the horizon, ready to face whatever obstacles awaited them in the captivating virtual world.

As the rain poured relentlessly outside, Aurora and her companions sought shelter in one of the half-burnt homes that still stood amidst the chaos. The flickering light of a dying fire cast eerie shadows on the dilapidated walls, adding to the sense of desolation that hung in the air. It was in this grim setting that they huddled together, their weary bodies seeking respite from the drenching rain.

Exhausted and battered from the battle with the goblins, Aurora and her companions knew they needed a plan. With the village they once knew engulfed in flames, they were left with little choice but to seek refuge elsewhere. The question of their next destination loomed heavily upon them, the weight of uncertainty pressing down on their weary shoulders.

In an attempt to gather information, Aurora turned to the villagers scattered around the makeshift shelter. Their eyes were filled with fear and confusion, mirroring the turmoil that had befallen their once-peaceful village. The villagers stood silently, their presence a stark reminder of the fragility of their virtual existence.

Aurora's voice cut through the silence, her words directed at the villagers who surrounded them.
"Do any of you know where the nearest village is?" she asked, hoping for a glimmer of guidance amidst the chaos.

The villagers remained quiet, their faces etched with weariness and despair. However, amidst the somber crowd, a solitary figure emerged—an old man with a long white beard and a hunched posture. He leaned heavily on a gnarled cane, his eyes filled with wisdom earned through the passage of time.

"You must head north," the old man spoke, his voice frail but resolute.
"Travel for approximately two days, and you shall find yourselves at the bottom of Mount Sanctus," he continued, pointing towards the distant silhouette of a towering peak in the distance. "There, you shall discover a village larger than ours, a sanctuary amidst the storm."

Aurora's gratitude welled up within her as she thanked the old man for his guidance. The prospect of a larger village offered hope—a glimmer of possibility in their current predicament. They collectively decided to spend the night in the rundown home, finding solace in the warmth of a dwindling fire and the companionship of their fellow adventurers.

As the night wore on, thoughts of the upcoming journey swirled in Aurora's mind. She contemplated the challenges that awaited them on the road ahead—treacherous terrain, potential encounters with hostile creatures, and the constant threat of the unknown. But amidst the uncertainties, a flicker of determination burned within her heart.

With the first light of dawn, Aurora and her companions rose from their makeshift beds, their resolve strengthened by the knowledge that a new village beckoned them from the base of Mount Sanctus. They gathered their belongings, ensuring they were adequately prepared for the journey that lay ahead—a path fraught with perils yet ripe with the promise of new allies, quests, and discoveries.

With the rain finally subsiding, Aurora and her companions stepped out into the fresh morning air, the scent of wet earth mingling with the faint aroma of distant adventures. They set their sights on the north, their steps guided by the old man's words and their collective determination to find refuge and forge a new path in the face of adversity.

Hannah's family gathered around the large screen, their eyes fixed on the live stream that displayed the epic battle against the goblins unfolding before them. With bated breath, they observed every swing of the virtual avatars' weapons, each precise strike that felled a goblin. The intensity of the fight and the stakes involved held their attention captive.

As the rain poured down in the virtual realm, Hannah's family witnessed the magnitude of the challenge their beloved virtual heroine faced. The battle was grueling, each moment fraught with danger and uncertainty. Yet, Hannah, guided by her unwavering determination, fought valiantly to protect the village from the goblin menace.

With each swing of her sword, Hannah carved a path through the ranks of the enemy. Her movements were fluid and calculated, a testament to the countless hours she had dedicated to honing her virtual combat skills. Her strikes were executed with precision and strength, each one a testament to her courage and unwavering resolve.

Beside her, the virtual avatar of Brynn danced through the chaos with graceful agility. Her swift movements allowed her to strike at the vulnerabilities of the goblins, her blades cutting through their ranks like a whirlwind. The synchronicity between Hannah and Brynn was awe-inspiring, as if their avatars were extensions of their own spirits, united in purpose and unwavering determination.

Hannah's family watched in awe as the battle raged on. The screen was a window into a world where virtual avatars fought for the safety and well-being of the village's inhabitants. Every swing of their weapons, every expertly timed dodge, spoke of their dedication to their mission. It was a testament to the power of virtual reality, where emotions ran high and actions held consequences that transcended the boundaries of the screen.

As the battle wore on, a glimmer of hope emerged amidst the chaos. Hannah and Brynn's strategic maneuvers began to turn the tide in favor of the village. Together, they devised a plan to protect the most vulnerable areas, coordinating their efforts with precision and skill. Their unity inspired the villagers, instilling in them a renewed sense of determination and a belief that victory was within reach.

Hannah's family felt a surge of pride swell within their hearts. They understood that their daughter's decision to fight for the virtual village was not merely a game but a reflection of her character and values. Even though the inhabitants of the virtual realm were not real in the physical sense, the impact of Hannah's actions resonated deeply within their hearts.

Grace, Hannah's younger sister, looked up to her with admiration and awe. She was captivated by the way Hannah fearlessly took charge, making split-second decisions that shaped the course of the battle. Hannah's strategic thinking and unwavering resolve left an indelible impression on Grace, igniting within her a desire to follow in her sister's footsteps and embrace her own journey of virtual adventures.

As the battle reached its climactic finale, Hannah's family erupted into cheers and applause. The screen displayed the victorious avatars standing amidst the defeated goblin horde, triumphant and weary. Half the village had been saved, and most of the villagers had been rescued from the clutches of the enemy. It was a hard-earned victory, a testament to Hannah's courage and the collective efforts of all those involved.

Hannah's family exchanged proud glances, their hearts brimming with a sense of accomplishment. They understood that the virtual world held the power to inspire, bring people together, and showcase the strength of the human spirit. They marveled at how their daughter had embraced this digital realm, using it as a canvas to display her bravery and leadership.

Grace beamed with admiration as she gazed at her big sister, recognizing the incredible strides she had made in the virtual tournament. Hannah's decisions and actions had proven that she was not just a player in a game, but a true hero capable of shaping destinies and making a difference, even in a virtual world.

With newfound determination, Hannah's family vowed to continue supporting her on her virtual journey. They eagerly anticipated the next chapter of her adventure, knowing that with each challenge she faced, she would grow stronger, wiser, and more resilient. In their eyes, Hannah was not just a player, but a beacon of inspiration and an embodiment of the boundless potential that lay within each of them.

As they sat together, basking in the afterglow of the battle, they understood that the virtual realm had become a portal to new dimensions of courage, teamwork, and self-discovery. And they were grateful to have a front-row seat to witness the remarkable journey of their daughter, Hannah, as she ventured further into the realms of possibility and embraced the power of virtual adventures.

Chapter 15

Day 5 of the immersive virtual reality tournament had dawned, and Aurora found herself still immersed in the thrilling competition. The events of the previous day's battle with the goblins lingered in her mind as she prepared to embark on a new adventure in a different village. The aftermath of the goblin attack was evident as she surveyed the scene before her.

The village, once vibrant and bustling, now lay in a state of disarray. The fires that had ravaged through the structures had been extinguished, leaving behind a haunting reminder of the battle's devastation. Half of the houses had succumbed to the flames, their charred remains serving as silent witnesses to the fierce struggle that had taken place. Aurora couldn't help but feel a pang of sadness for the villagers who had lost their homes and belongings in the chaos.

However, amidst the destruction, there was a glimmer of hope. Aurora had stumbled upon a quest, a chance to bring a message of solace and reassurance to a family member in another village. The note would inform them of the events that had transpired, offering a small measure of comfort in knowing that their loved ones were safe, albeit in the face of great adversity.

As the morning sun peeked through the clouds, casting a soft golden glow over the village, Aurora and her companions gathered for a modest breakfast. The meal consisted of hard bread and cold, dry meats, their sustenance carefully rationed to ensure they had enough energy for the arduous journey that lay ahead.

As they ate, their eyes were drawn to the villagers, who had begun the difficult task of rebuilding their lives from the ruins. The resilient spirit of the community was evident as they joined hands to lift debris, salvage what they could, and pay respects to those who had lost their lives in the fire. The atmosphere was one of determination and unity, a collective effort to restore a sense of normalcy amidst the chaos.

After about an hour, Aurora and her companions felt a sense of readiness, both physically and mentally, to embark on their two-day journey to the next village. They carried with them only what they had managed to salvage from the inferno, their possessions reduced to the bare essentials. The inn, a place that once offered warmth and respite, now lay in ruins, claiming the lives of three unfortunate souls and swallowing their belongings in the relentless blaze.

As they set foot on the path leading away from the decimated village, their steps were filled with a mixture of weariness and determination. The road ahead promised new challenges and encounters, but also the potential for growth and discovery. They knew that the next village they were headed towards would be larger, offering a different set of experiences and opportunities.

With every stride, Aurora couldn't help but reflect on the resilience of the human spirit, both within the virtual world and in reality. The villagers they had encountered, though mere NPCs, had displayed a remarkable ability to rise above adversity, to band together in the face of catastrophe. Their unwavering resolve mirrored the strength she witnessed in the real world, a reminder that even in the darkest times, there is a glimmer of hope and a capacity for rebuilding what has been lost.

The two-day journey that lay ahead would test their mettle and fortitude. It would be a time of reflection, strategizing, and forging deeper bonds with her companions. Aurora knew that as they traversed the rugged landscapes and encountered new challenges, they would be pushed to their limits, but also granted the opportunity to discover hidden strengths within themselves.

As they ventured forth, the memory of the decimated village remained etched in their minds, serving as a constant reminder of the fragility of life and the importance of resilience. With every step, Aurora carried the weight of the village's struggle, the determination to deliver the note to a waiting family member, and the unwavering resolve to overcome whatever obstacles awaited them in the next village.

The path stretched out before them, winding through lush forests and rugged mountains, promising both trials and triumphs. They walked with a newfound sense of purpose and a shared commitment to rise above the challenges that awaited them. For Aurora and her companions, this journey was not just about winning a tournament but embracing the essence of their virtual odyssey—a quest for self-discovery, camaraderie, and the unwavering pursuit of greatness.

As Aurora and her companions continued their journey, the vastness of the virtual world surrounding them became increasingly apparent. The scenery stretched out in all directions, an intricately designed landscape teeming with immersive detail. Aurora couldn't help but marvel at the lifelike nature of their surroundings, even the non-player characters (NPCs) who, while somewhat rudimentary in their programming, possessed a spark of individuality that breathed life into the virtual realm.

"This place," Aurora whispered to herself, her voice filled with awe,
"It's so lifelike. Every aspect, from the towering mountains to the whispering trees, feels infused with its essence. It's as if this virtual world has taken on a life of its own."

As she gazed upon the expansive terrain, a sense of wonder washed over her. The scale of this virtual creation was staggering. Aurora imagined the countless hours, the meticulous attention to detail, and the sheer dedication it must have taken to bring this world to life. It was a testament to the boundless imagination and technical prowess of the creators.

Aurora's senses heightened as she immersed herself in the virtual environment. The grass beneath her feet felt real, each blade tickling her skin with a gentle caress. The wind, whispering through the trees, tousled her hair and carried with it the scents of the surrounding wilderness. She marveled at the intricacy of the weather system, as raindrops fell from the sky, splashing against her armor and creating a symphony of sound as they mingled with the earth.

At that moment, Aurora's mind began to wander, contemplating the profound implications of this immersive virtual reality experience. The level of realism and the depth of engagement offered the potential for more than just entertainment. It was a glimpse into a world that could redefine human existence—a place where people could forge new lives, escape the constraints of their physical reality, and explore uncharted territories of self-discovery.

As she trudged through the virtual wilderness, Aurora envisioned a future where these virtual realms could serve as a refuge, a sanctuary for those seeking solace, adventure, or a chance to start anew. It was a powerful notion, one that stirred a flicker of hope within her. Perhaps this virtual world could offer a lifeline to those burdened by the challenges of the real world, granting them a renewed sense of purpose and possibility.

"This could be more than just a game," Aurora murmured, her voice filled with conviction. "It has the potential to be a lifeline, a means to save lives and transform our existence. In this realm, we can transcend the limitations of our physical bodies and explore the depths of our potential."

She envisioned a future where virtual worlds became more than mere entertainment, but rather a platform for personal growth, healing, and connection. In these immersive experiences, people could find solace, discover untapped talents, and forge meaningful relationships. It was a vision that ignited a fire within Aurora, compelling her to push forward, to unravel the mysteries of this virtual world, and share its transformative power with others.

As she continued her journey, the weight of this realization settled upon her shoulders. She understood that the significance of this virtual reality extended far beyond the confines of a tournament. It was a gateway to a realm of infinite possibilities—a chance for humanity to redefine its collective destiny.

With each step, Aurora's determination grew, and her heart filled with a newfound purpose. She would not only conquer the challenges presented in this virtual world but would also strive to unlock its potential, to harness its power for the betterment of humanity. For Aurora, this adventure was no longer just a game; it was a catalyst for change, a catalyst that held the promise of reshaping lives and granting a new lease on existence.

Emerging from the dense forest, Aurora and Brynn found themselves standing on the banks of a mighty river, its rushing waters forming an imposing barrier in their path. The river, wide and swift, stretched as far as their eyes could see, its current churning with formidable strength. They knew they had to find a bridge to continue their journey, so they turned their gaze towards the east, hoping to discover a crossing point.

With determined strides, they followed the river's edge, venturing deeper into the unknown. The landscape unfolded before them, revealing towering trees, their branches swaying in harmony with the whispering wind. The rhythmic sounds of nature accompanied their footsteps, instilling a sense of serenity amidst the anticipation of what lay ahead.

After an arduous trek that seemed to stretch for an eternity, they finally caught sight of a bridge in the distance. Its wooden structure arched gracefully over the river, connecting the two banks and providing passage to those who dared to cross. Relief washed over Aurora and Brynn as they quickened their pace, eager to reach the bridge and continue their quest.

But their progress was abruptly halted as a commanding voice echoed through the air, piercing the tranquility of the surrounding landscape.
"Stop right there," came the stern warning. Startled, Aurora and Brynn turned their attention towards the bridge, where six figures stood, their presence exuding an air of danger and mischief.

The bandits, their ragged attire and unkempt appearances revealing a life of lawlessness eyed Aurora and Brynn with a mix of cunning and greed. Each bandit had a distinct look, emphasizing their distinct personalities. One had a scar across his face, his eyes glinting with a sinister glimmer. Another wore a patchwork leather jacket, adorned with various trinkets that hinted at a life of thievery. Each bandit exuded a sense of menace, their stance and expressions making it clear that they were not to be trifled with.

"Let us pass," Brynn shouted defiantly, her voice tinged with determination.

The bandits chuckled, their laughter filled with malicious intent.
"You must pay the toll or we kill you," declared one of the bandits, brandishing a wickedly curved sword in a menacing display of power.

From the other side of the bridge, another bandit chimed in, his voice dripping with a mix of sarcasm and hunger.
"If we don't get no toll, we don't get no rolls, and I'm hungry."

Aurora's brows furrowed in disbelief.

"We aren't giving you anything. It's free to cross here," she stated firmly, her voice resounding with unwavering conviction.

The bandits exchanged glances, their eyes narrowing with a combination of annoyance and greed. One of them, a particularly cunning individual, spoke up with a sly smile.
"It's not a lot, only two gold pieces per person," he stated, his tone filled with deceit.

"Two gold pieces? Two gold pieces?" Aurora responded, her voice dripping with sarcasm.
"That's not a lot at all. By any means."

The bandits grew restless, their patience wearing thin. Another bandit, fueled by aggression, stepped forward, his words laced with a chilling threat.
"One last chance. Give us the money, or we will gut you like a fish," he warned, his eyes gleaming with malice.

Brynn, her frustration boiling over, spoke up with fiery determination.
"First of, even if I had that much, I'd never give it to the likes of you," she retorted, her voice laced with defiance.

The tension in the air crackled, the standoff intensifying with each passing moment. Aurora and Brynn stood their ground, ready to face the bandits head-on. In their hearts, they knew that surrendering their hard-earned gold would only embolden the bandits and perpetuate their reign of terror. The bridge became a battleground, a line drawn between those who sought to exploit and those who would defend their principles at any cost. With their resolve steeled, Aurora and Brynn prepared themselves for a showdown, ready to prove that courage and righteousness could triumph over greed and intimidation.

Aurora's frustration grew, her mind racing to find a solution that would bypass the bandits' demands.
"How about we just find another place to cross?" she suggested, her voice tinged with exasperation. She scanned the surrounding area, hoping to spot an alternative route that would circumvent the confrontational bandits.

"Fine, go," one bandit sneered, his voice dripping with arrogance.
"But you'll be back. You can't escape us."

Aurora's eyes narrowed, her determination solidifying. She refused to be intimidated by their threats.
"Shut up," she retorted, her tone firm and unwavering.
"We don't need to cross your bridge. There are other paths available to us."

The bandits exchanged glances, their expressions morphing into a mixture of anger and disbelief. One of them, fueled by a volatile temper, stepped forward, his voice laced with venom.
"You think you can just walk away? You think you're above our authority? Think again," he spat, his eyes narrowing with malice.
"Either you cross here and pay the toll, or we will make sure you never cross anywhere again."

Aurora's grip tightened around her sword, the weight of the imminent battle settling upon her shoulders. Her eyes flickered with a resolute fire as she locked gazes with the bandits.

"Fine, then it'll be you that dies today," she declared, her voice filled with a steely determination.

The bandits erupted into mocking laughter, their crude amusement echoing through the air.
"That's a lot of talk coming from some girls," one bandit taunted, his voice dripping with disdain. The others joined in, their laughter echoing in a symphony of mockery.

Aurora's jaw clenched, her resolve strengthening amidst the bandits' derision. She understood the prejudice and underestimation that often came with being a woman in a world dominated by men. But she also knew that her skill, bravery, and unwavering spirit were more than a match for any adversary.

Brynn, standing beside Aurora, exchanged a knowing glance with her companion. Her eyes burned with determination, mirroring Aurora's unwavering resolve. Together, they formed a formidable duo, prepared to shatter the bandits' preconceptions and prove that gender had no bearing on one's ability to wield strength and courage.

The tension in the air became palpable as Aurora and Brynn readied themselves for the impending clash. The bandits, their laughter dying down, now wore smirks of arrogance and superiority. But little did they know that their condescending words and dismissive attitudes had only fueled the fire within Aurora and Brynn, igniting a determination that would carry them through the imminent battle.

Just as the tension reached its peak, the bandits surged forward, charging at Aurora and Brynn with a feral determination. The clash of steel against steel filled the air as the battle unfolded, each side pushing their limits. Despite being outnumbered, Aurora and Brynn stood their ground, their eyes locked onto their adversaries.

The bandits, driven by their false sense of superiority, underestimated the strength and skill of their opponents. Their reckless charge, fueled by arrogance, quickly turned into a desperate struggle for survival. The resolute determination in Aurora's eyes matched the unwavering resolve of Brynn as they expertly parried and countered the bandits' attacks.

The fight raged on, the sound of clashes and grunts filling the air. Aurora and Brynn moved in perfect synchrony, their movements seamless and calculated. They fought with a fierce determination, their skills honed through countless battles. Each swing of their weapons was delivered with precision, leaving the bandits scrambling to defend themselves.

However, amidst the chaos, a moment of vulnerability emerged. A bandit, driven by a surge of adrenaline, managed to land a swift strike on Aurora's side, causing her to stagger back, gasping in pain. The blow took her by surprise, but she refused to let it break her spirit. Gritting her teeth, she steadied herself and pressed on, determined to overcome the setback.

Aurora's health points rapidly dwindled as the battle progressed, the bandits relentlessly exploiting her momentary weakness. The pain surged through her body, threatening to slow her down. But she fought through the agony, her willpower igniting a stubborn fire within her.

As the battle raged on, Aurora's injuries only seemed to fuel her determination. Channeling her pain into a burst of adrenaline, she launched a series of fierce counterattacks, unleashing her pent-up strength. Her strikes were precise and deadly, cutting through the bandits' defenses with a relentless force.

One by one, the bandits fell under Aurora's skillful blade, their arrogant smirks replaced by expressions of shock and fear. The tides of battle had turned, and those who remained quickly realized that their lives were at stake. Fear gripped their hearts as they witnessed their companions fall.

In a desperate bid to save themselves, the remaining bandits turned and fled, their hasty retreat leaving behind an air of defeat. Aurora's victory was hard-fought but well-deserved. The bandits had learned a valuable lesson — underestimating their opponents had dire consequences.

Exhausted and battered, Aurora leaned on her sword for support, her breathing ragged. She surveyed the aftermath of the battle, her gaze shifting to Brynn, who stood tall and unyielding. The two warriors locked eyes, their mutual respect evident in the silent exchange.

Despite the injuries and the toll they had taken on Aurora, a sense of triumph surged through her veins. She had faced the odds and emerged victorious. The wounds she had sustained were badges of honor, testaments to her resilience, and unwavering spirit.

With a weary yet satisfied smile, Aurora turned her attention to Brynn. Together, they acknowledged the hard-fought victory and the battles they had overcome. They knew that this was just one step in their journey, and greater challenges awaited them. But at that moment, as the adrenaline subsided and the reality of their injuries settled in, they relished the victory and the camaraderie forged in the heat of battle.

Aurora's body ached from the battle, her health points were severely depleted. The wounds she had sustained served as a reminder of the risks she faced in this virtual realm. However, amidst the pain and fatigue, there was a silver lining. The defeated bandits had yielded valuable experience points, granting Aurora the opportunity to strengthen her character.

With each enemy vanquished, Aurora had gained 20 experience points, a testament to her prowess as a warrior. This bolstered her confidence, knowing that despite the toll it took on her, the battle had brought her closer to becoming a formidable force within the game.

However, the realization of her vulnerability in the middle of nowhere weighed heavily on Aurora's mind. The surrounding forest seemed to whisper threats, reminding her of the potential dangers lurking in the shadows. She understood that she had to remain on high alert, ready to respond to any potential threat that might come their way.

Brynn, perceptive to Aurora's heightened state of anxiety, attempted to ease her companion's worries.
"Why don't we talk to set your mind at ease?" she suggested, hoping to divert Aurora's attention from the looming dangers of their journey.

"Alright," Aurora replied, willing to engage in conversation as a means of finding solace amidst the uncertainties.
"What brought you here, playing this game and working for the company?" she inquired, genuinely curious about Brynn's motivations and backstory.

Brynn paused for a moment, her eyes scanning the surroundings before focusing back on Aurora.
"Well, the pay is what initially caught my attention," she admitted, a touch of bitterness seeping into her voice.
"It's far more than anything I could have earned back in the slums of the new USA."

Aurora listened intently, sensing that there was more to Brynn's story than a simple pursuit of monetary gain. Intrigued, she pressed further, "What did you do before this, and how did you get selected to join the game?"

A flicker of vulnerability crossed Brynn's eyes before she composed herself and began to recount her past.
"Before this, I was a skilled thief, surviving through quick fingers and stealth. Life in the slums taught me how to adapt and survive. As for joining the game, it was a stroke of luck, or perhaps fate. I caught the attention of one of the game's recruiters while demonstrating my abilities in a street skirmish. They offered me a chance to leave the grim reality behind and step into this virtual world. I do not wish my old life back for anything."

Aurora nodded, recognizing the shared experience of seeking refuge in the game from a harsh reality. She found a connection with Brynn, knowing that they both came from backgrounds shaped by adversity and the desire for something better.

Aurora's voice quivered with emotion as she shared the challenges she and her family faced back in the old Chicago area. The gravity of her father's illness weighed heavily on her, uncertain of how much time they had left together. Tears welled up in her eyes, reflecting the deep love and concern she felt for her family.

Brynn's expression softened, realizing the immense burden Aurora carried. "That's a noble thing to fight for, Aurora," she said, her voice filled with admiration and empathy.
"I hope you win, and I will do my best to support you and get you to your goal."

Aurora nodded, appreciating Brynn's words of encouragement and support. The bond between them grew stronger as they opened up to each other, sharing their deepest fears and aspirations. It was a powerful reminder that even within the virtual world, genuine connections could be formed.

However, a sense of surprise washed over Aurora's face as Brynn revealed her inability to harm other players.
"Wait, you can't kill any of the players?" Aurora asked, her astonishment evident.

Brynn nodded solemnly.
"That's right," she confirmed.
"If I were to swing my sword at you, nothing would happen. No damage, not even a scratch would be left behind. My purpose in this game is to assist and protect players like you."

Aurora took a moment to process this information, realizing the unique role Brynn played. While she couldn't directly engage in combat with other players, her dedication to safeguarding Aurora and aiding her in their shared adventures was invaluable.

A mixture of gratitude and relief filled Aurora's heart as she comprehended the depth of Brynn's commitment.
"I appreciate you helping me out," she said, her voice filled with sincerity and warmth. "I wouldn't have been able to fight off the goblins without you, and I know I can rely on you moving forward."

In an expression of gratitude and affection, Aurora pulled Brynn into a tight hug. It was a gesture that conveyed their growing friendship and the deep trust they had begun to develop in one another. In this vast virtual realm, they were not alone—they had each other to lean on and support through the challenges that lay ahead.

As they continued their journey, Aurora's mind eased slightly, finding comfort in the camaraderie they were building. The forest, though still harboring potential threats, no longer felt as ominous. They ventured forth over the great river, the sound of rushing water providing a soothing backdrop to their steps.

With each passing moment, Aurora's health points slowly regenerated, aided by her healing ability. She focused her energy, directing it inward to mend her wounds. Gradually, her health points climbed back to half their original value, currently resting at 24.

The journey through the forest continued, the dense foliage creating a sense of both enchantment and unease. Aurora remained on constant alert, her senses heightened, responding to every rustle of leaves or distant sound.

However, as the conversation between Aurora and Brynn deepened, their shared stories and shared determination brought a sense of comfort. They forged a bond, a mutual understanding that in this vast virtual world, they were not alone.

As the day wore on, the weariness in Aurora and Brynn's footsteps became more pronounced. Their legs ached from the constant walking, and the weight of their equipment felt heavier with each passing hour. But just as their energy dwindled, a stroke of luck came their way.

Through the dense forest, a glimmer of sunlight caught their attention, leading them to a serene clearing by a crystal-clear creek. The soothing sound of trickling water reached their ears, offering a momentary respite from the arduous journey. It was a sight that lifted their spirits and rekindled their determination to push forward.

Relieved to have found such a perfect spot to rest, Aurora and Brynn wasted no time in setting up camp. They carefully laid out their bedrolls on the soft grass, taking a moment to appreciate the natural beauty that surrounded them. The scent of wildflowers lingered in the air, creating an atmosphere of tranquility and renewal. They filled their waterskins from the fresh running creek.

As the sun dipped below the horizon, casting a warm golden glow across the landscape, Aurora skillfully gathered dry twigs and leaves to start a fire. With a spark from her flint and the crackling of kindling, flames danced to life, casting flickering shadows upon the trees. The warmth of the fire chased away the evening chill, enveloping them in a comforting embrace.

Their stomachs grumbled in protest, reminding them of the importance of nourishment. With practiced efficiency, they retrieved their rations from their backpacks. Aurora unwrapped pieces of dried meat, while Brynn carefully portioned out some hard bread. It was a simple meal, but their hunger lent it a certain satisfaction. They toasted the bread over the open flames, relishing the warmth and the aroma of the crackling fire.

Sitting side by side, they shared stories and laughter as they ate. The flickering firelight painted playful shadows on their faces, enhancing the camaraderie that was blossoming between them. The burdens of their respective pasts momentarily lifted, replaced by the shared purpose and the bond they had formed.

As the night sky unfolded above them, revealing a tapestry of stars, they marveled at the vastness of the virtual world they found themselves. It was a realm where dreams and possibilities intertwined, offering a chance for rebirth and a new sense of purpose. They contemplated the wonders they had witnessed so far, the battles fought, and the challenges yet to come.

With their bellies filled and their bodies reinvigorated, Aurora and Brynn settled into their bedrolls, staring up at the twinkling stars overhead. The soothing lullaby of the creek and the crackling fire lulled them into a peaceful slumber, their dreams interwoven with the magic of the virtual realm.

Tomorrow would bring new adventures, new quests, and new tests of their mettle. But for now, beneath the starlit sky, they found solace in the present moment grateful for the respite and the companionship they had found along their virtual odyssey.

The night settled upon the tranquil clearing, casting a blanket of darkness over the land. The hushed whispers of the wind rustled through the trees, creating a symphony of gentle whispers that seemed to echo through the night. The air carried a certain stillness as if nature itself held its breath in reverence for the weary travelers seeking respite.

Aurora took the first watch, positioned at the edge of their makeshift camp. She sat with her back against a sturdy tree, her senses heightened and alert. The crackling embers of the dying fire provided a soft glow, casting elongated shadows that danced upon the ground. With every flicker, her eyes scanned the surrounding darkness, searching for any signs of danger.

Her mind wandered as she sat there, thoughts swirling like the tendrils of smoke rising into the night sky. She pondered the events that had led her to this virtual realm, the choices that had shaped her path, and the challenges that awaited her. The weight of responsibility settled upon her shoulders, but she found solace in the presence of Brynn, her newfound ally.

As the hours passed, the night remained undisturbed, enveloped in a shroud of tranquility. Aurora's thoughts wandered to her family back in the real world, the worries and concerns that plagued her heart. She hoped they were safe, that they would find a way to overcome the obstacles that life had thrown their way. In this virtual realm, she sought not only adventure but also a respite from the hardships of reality.

After what felt like an eternity, Aurora's watch came to an end, and she gently nudged Brynn awake. As Brynn settled into her position, Aurora lay down on her bedroll, gazing up at the star-studded sky. The twinkling constellations seemed to hold secrets and ancient wisdom, inviting her to lose herself in their ethereal beauty.

Though her body yearned for rest, her mind remained restless. She contemplated the nature of the virtual world they inhabited, marveling at its intricacies and the limitless possibilities it offered. The line between reality and the game began to blur as if the virtual realm held a mirror to the depths of her soul.

The night remained a canvas of stillness, broken only by the occasional rustle of nocturnal creatures scurrying through the underbrush. Brynn maintained her vigilance, her senses attuned to the subtlest of sounds. With each passing hour, the weight of responsibility pressed upon her, and she found strength in knowing that Aurora relied on her.

In the depths of the night, the moon cast a soft glow upon the clearing, painting the landscape with a silver sheen. Shadows danced and swayed, seemingly alive as if the forest itself held its secrets. Brynn's thoughts turned to her reasons for embarking on this virtual journey. She reflected on the hardships she had faced, and the trials that had molded her into the resilient warrior she had become.

The night seemed to stretch on indefinitely, yet as dawn approached, the sky began to lighten in the east. The first hints of sunlight peeked through the canopy, painting the treetops with golden hues. Brynn's watch came to an end, and she gently nudged Aurora awake, their roles once again reversed.

As Aurora rose to her feet, stretching the stiffness from her muscles, she exchanged a tired yet reassuring smile with Brynn. They were in this together, united by a shared purpose and the bonds forged through adversity. With renewed determination, they prepared to face the challenges that awaited them, ready to continue their virtual odyssey with hearts full of hope and resilience.

As the sun began its ascent on the sixth day of their virtual reality journey, Aurora and Brynn counted their blessings for having endured the night unscathed. With a renewed sense of purpose, they briskly packed their belongings, ensuring to leave no trace of their presence in the quiet clearing. The embers of their campfire were doused and buried, erasing any evidence of their temporary respite.

Embarking on the next leg of their journey, the pair set forth toward the larger village that lay ahead. Their anticipation mingled with a hint of caution, for a larger settlement meant a greater potential for encounters with both non-player characters and other players. The awareness of lurking dangers heightened their senses, keeping them on constant guard.

As they continued their trek, the cold morning wind pierced through their clothing, causing them to shiver involuntarily. They nibbled on their meager breakfast, a reminder of the hardships they faced in this virtual realm. The taste of the cold food did little to warm their bellies, but the sustenance it provided was necessary for their endurance.

With each step, the dense forest gradually gave way to a sprawling expanse of rocky open plains. Towering cliffs and massive boulders punctuated the landscape, creating an obstacle course of nature's formations. The barrenness of the plains offered little cover, exposing them to the scrutiny of anyone who may be watching. It was a test of their stealth and survival instincts, forcing them to tread lightly and remain vigilant.

Carefully navigating through the rocky terrain, Aurora and Brynn sought refuge among the nooks and crannies of the imposing cliffs. They moved with calculated precision, using the natural formations as shields against prying eyes. Shadows became their allies, camouflaging their presence amidst the rugged surroundings.

Hours slipped by, marked only by the passing of a majestic herd of buffalo in the distance. Their synchronized movements and thundering hooves echoed across the plains, reminding Aurora and Brynn of the delicate balance of nature in this virtual realm. The sight offered a moment of tranquility amidst their journey, allowing them to momentarily forget the perils that lay ahead.

As the sun climbed higher in the sky, its rays casting long shadows upon the plains, the tension in the air grew palpable. The approaching village lay within their sights, its bustling presence a stark contrast to the desolate surroundings. It beckoned them forward, promising respite and new challenges alike.

With renewed determination, Aurora and Brynn set their sights on reaching the bottom of the mountain, their final hurdle before arriving at the village. The exposure to the open plains heightened their vulnerability, requiring them to exercise utmost caution. Each step was deliberate, ensuring they remained concealed from watchful eyes.

Time seemed to stretch, elongated by the anticipation and the weight of their quest. Yet, with unwavering perseverance, they pressed on. The rugged landscape seemed to test their resilience, pushing them to their limits. But they drew strength from each other, finding solace in the unspoken bond forged through shared hardships.

Finally, as the sun began its descent towards the horizon, painting the sky in hues of orange and purple, the bottom of the mountain lay within reach. The sight filled them with a mix of relief and trepidation, for the challenges that awaited in the bustling village would demand their utmost resourcefulness and resilience.

With deep breaths and hearts brimming with determination, Aurora and Brynn steeled themselves for the next chapter of their virtual odyssey. The journey thus far had tested their mettle, but it had also revealed their unwavering spirit and capacity for growth. With every step, they moved closer to uncovering the secrets that lay within the virtual realm, eager to forge their destinies and leave an indelible mark upon this vast and ever-evolving world.

As the weary adventurers trudged through the day, their eyes fixed on the distant glow of the village on the horizon. Every step brought them closer to their destination, filling their hearts with a renewed sense of hope. However, dusk settled upon them like a heavy cloak, casting long shadows that seemed to dance with malice in the fading light.

Nightfall in this virtual realm was no ordinary occurrence. As darkness blanketed the land, the boundary between the living and the dead blurred. Whispers of eerie legends and unsettling tales had circulated among players, warning of the dangers that lurked after sundown. It was a time when the restless souls of the departed roamed the world, seeking to inflict fear and chaos upon the unsuspecting.

Aurora and Brynn's anticipation turned to trepidation as they felt a chill permeate the air. The peaceful tranquility of the evening was shattered when, to their dismay, five skeletal figures materialized out of the ground with a bone-chilling screech. The eerie glow of moonlight revealed their bony frames, animated by some dark force that defied logic.

Aurora's heart raced as she unsheathed her sword, the cold steel gleaming ominously in the moon's pale light. The skeletons circled them, their hollow eye sockets fixed upon their intended prey. Panic threatened to take hold, but the two companions stood resolute, their instincts honed by countless battles prior.

"Where did they come from?" Aurora's voice broke through the tense silence, her voice filled with a mix of frustration and determination. Brynn, equally caught off guard by the sudden appearance of their skeletal adversaries, could only offer a bewildered shrug in response. They locked eyes, their unspoken agreement reaffirming their resolve to fight their way out of this unforeseen predicament.

With synchronized movements, Aurora and Brynn positioned themselves back-to-back, their gazes darting between the encroaching skeletons. The rustling of dried bones and the faint sound of their unearthly moans filled the night air, creating an unsettling symphony that only intensified their sense of urgency.

The battle commenced, and the clash of steel against bone reverberated through the stillness of the night. Aurora's sword sliced through the air with precision, striking at the unholy creature's relentless determination. Her movements were fueled by both fear and resolve, each swing of her weapon infused with a desperate plea for survival.

Beside her, Brynn showcased her agility and cunning, nimbly dodging the bony assaults aimed in her direction. With swift and calculated maneuvers, she exploited the skeletal creatures' weaknesses, striking with calculated precision. Her daggers danced in the moonlight, each strike aimed at dismantling her adversaries with ruthless efficiency.

But the skeletons, despite their decrepit appearance, possessed an eerie tenacity. They closed in, their skeletal hands reaching out with a haunting desperation. Aurora's heart pounded in her chest as she felt a bony finger graze her arm, sending an icy shiver down her spine. She could almost taste the cold breath of death itself, a reminder of the perilous nature of their current reality.

Their battle seemed to blur the line between the living and the dead, their surroundings illuminated by the flickering dance of combat. Aurora's health points steadily dwindled as each skeletal blow took its toll. The pain was real, despite the virtual nature of their existence, and she could feel her strength waning with each passing moment.

Yet, even in the face of adversity, their determination remained unyielding. Aurora's vision blurred with sweat and fatigue, but she summoned the last vestiges of her energy, fighting through the pain. She swung her sword with a ferocity born of survival, each strike punctuated by a burst of adrenaline coursing through her veins.

Their efforts began to bear fruit as the skeletons crumbled one by one under the onslaught. Bones shattered, crumbling into dust as their grip on this realm faded away. The final remnants of the skeletal horde realized the futility of their endeavor and, with an unearthly wail, retreated into the shadows from whence they came. With each skeleton killed, she gained 30xp. Getting her much closer to leveling up.

The night was silent once more, save for the labored breathing of the exhausted adventurers. Aurora's body ached, her health points almost depleted, but a glimmer of victory danced in her eyes. The battle had been won but at a great cost. She had survived, scarred but stronger, her will be tested and her determination renewed.

With caution, Aurora and Brynn pressed onward, making haste toward the village, their steps weighed down by weariness and the weight of their recent encounter. They were a little worse for wear, but their spirits remained unbroken. Each step forward brought them closer to the realization of their goals, propelling them toward the next chapter of their virtual odyssey.

As the worn-out adventurers stepped into the quiet town, their bodies hunched with fatigue, it was evident to any onlooker that they had endured a great ordeal. Aurora's once vibrant hair now clung to her forehead, damp with perspiration, and her clothes bore the telltale signs of battle—a few tattered patches and splatters of dried blood. Brynn, too, wore the remnants of their recent struggle, with a few scratches marrying her arms and a weary look etched upon her face.

Their arrival did not go unnoticed, and the innkeeper, a stout figure with a jovial demeanor, greeted them with a warm smile as they entered the cozy establishment. "Greetings, weary travelers. You look like you've seen a ghost," the innkeeper remarked, his eyes scanning their disheveled appearance with a mix of curiosity and concern.

Aurora, grateful for the respite and eager to find solace from the lingering chill that clung to her bones, mustered a weak smile and replied, "Indeed, it has been quite the journey. We would be grateful for two rooms, please."

The innkeeper nodded understandingly, his eyes filled with empathy. "Two rooms it is, my friends. And how about a hearty warm meal to accompany your stay? A hot meal can do wonders for the body and soul."

Brynn, her stomach grumbling in agreement, chimed in with enthusiasm. "Thank you, that would be most welcome after a night spent shivering as if we were standing in a snowstorm."

Led by the innkeeper, they made their way to a cozy table situated by a crackling fireplace at the heart of the bustling inn. The warm glow cast by the dancing flames enveloped them, offering a sanctuary from the harsh realities of their virtual journey.

After what felt like an eternity, the innkeeper returned, balancing two steaming bowls of hearty stew on a wooden tray. The tantalizing aroma of the simmering broth filled the air, teasing their senses and evoking a renewed sense of comfort and warmth.

"Here you go, girls," the innkeeper exclaimed with a warm smile, placing the bowls on the table before them. "Two warm, hearty stews with freshly baked bread to warm you right up. I hope it brings some solace to your weary souls."

"Thank you so much," Aurora murmured gratefully, her voice laced with a hint of lingering chilliness. She clasped the warm bowl between her hands, the heat seeping through her fingers and offering a momentary respite from the inner cold that still persisted.

They eagerly dug into the nourishing stew, relishing each spoonful filled with tender chunks of meat, savory onions, vibrant carrots, and the earthy sweetness of cabbage. The flavors melded together in perfect harmony, soothing their senses and rekindling their energy.

As they savored the comforting meal, conversation flowed between Aurora and Brynn, their voices carrying a mixture of exhaustion and camaraderie. Aurora, still feeling a lingering unease within her, finally spoke up, her gaze fixed on the flickering flames of the fireplace.

"The touch from the skeleton... it did something to me, and I don't know what," she confessed, her voice tinged with a mixture of confusion and concern.

Brynn's eyebrows furrowed with worry as she glanced at her friend. "You're just telling me this now? I thought we were both simply cold from the biting wind outside."

Aurora shrugged, trying to downplay her unease. "It's probably nothing, just a lingering effect. I'm sure it will pass."

Brynn's eyes narrowed a mixture of determination and concern reflecting in their depths. "Well, if you still feel that way in the morning, we must get you checked out. We can't take any risks with your well-being."

Nodding in agreement, Aurora gave a small smile. "Thank you, Brynn. Your concern means a lot to me."

With their conversation winding down, exhaustion finally claimed them. They bid each other goodnight, retreating to their respective rooms, longing for the rejuvenation that sleep would bring. The soft embrace of the inn's cozy beds beckoned them, promising a respite from the weariness that had settled deep within their bones.

As they closed their eyes, the echoes of their adventures danced in their dreams, mingling with hopes of a brighter tomorrow.

Chapter 16

Day 7 had dawned, marking a significant milestone in Aurora's journey. A full week had passed since she had entered the tournament, and the fact that she had managed to persevere thus far was both amazing and shocking to her. The sheer magnitude of her accomplishments surpassed her initial expectations, fueling a renewed sense of determination within her. As she glanced at the countdown, which now displayed a dwindling number of 6431 players remaining, the realization that victory was within reach ignited a flicker of excitement tinged with apprehension.

The morning sun cast a warm glow over the village, illuminating the cobblestone streets and painting the buildings in a golden hue. However, Aurora's mind was preoccupied with the challenges that lay ahead. She knew that she needed to find someone who could shed light on the mysterious cold sensation that gripped her from within. Additionally, there was the matter of delivering a crucial letter, a task that couldn't be delayed any longer.

As she prepared for the day, Aurora couldn't help but notice the absence of hunger gnawing at her stomach. It was a peculiar sensation, for she had always been known to have a healthy appetite. Nonetheless, she pushed aside any thoughts of breakfast, knowing that there were more pressing matters at hand.

With determination etched upon her face, Aurora approached the table where Brynn sat, devouring a plate of food. She interrupted him mid-bite, a sense of urgency in her voice.

"Brynn, we have bigger problems than food right now. I feel bone-chillingly cold deep within my core," she stated, her tone firm and resolute.

Brynn, taken aback by Aurora's sudden interruption, removed his hand from his plate and placed it on her arm. A jolt of surprise ran through her as she felt the warmth of his touch contrasted against her icy skin.
"Wow, that is mighty cold," Brynn remarked, his concern evident in his eyes.

Aurora nodded, her gaze fixed on the horizon.
"It's not just that. We still have the letter to deliver as well. Our day is shaping up to be quite eventful," she said, her voice laced with a mixture of determination and a hint of trepidation.

Leaving their unfinished meals behind, the duo stepped outside into the embrace of a bright and sunny day. The warmth of the sun's rays brought a temporary reprieve from the chill that enveloped Aurora's being. However, she knew that the coldness resided within her soul, defying the external elements.

"We'll have to find answers and fulfill our responsibilities," Aurora declared, her eyes scanning the bustling streets ahead. "We cannot afford to delay any longer. Our journey continues, and there is much to be done."

With that, Aurora led the way, her steps purposeful and unwavering. The weight of the letter pressed against her chest, a constant reminder of the task that awaited them. Little did they know that the path they were about to tread would lead them deeper into a world of intrigue, danger, and perhaps even answers to the mysteries that plagued Aurora's existence.

Aurora and Brynn embarked on a quest to find Elara Windrider, carrying a mysterious letter entrusted to them. They began their search by approaching the innkeeper, a friendly elderly man with a kind smile. Aurora politely inquired, "Excuse me, sir. Do you happen to know an Elara Windrider? We have a letter for her." The innkeeper paused, scratching his head thoughtfully.
"I'm afraid I don't, my dear. However, you might want to try speaking to the other innkeepers in town. They might have some information. If not, the taverns could be worth a shot," he suggested with a helpful tone.

Thanking the innkeeper for his guidance, Aurora and Brynn left the inn, their minds buzzing with possibilities. Brynn's sharp eyes caught sight of a bustling tavern just across the street. Curiosity sparked within them, and they entered the tavern, the sound of merry conversations filling the air. Approaching the bartender, Brynn leaned against the polished wooden bar counter and asked, "Excuse me, good sir. We're searching for someone named Elara Windrider. Have you heard of her?" The bartender, a stout man with a friendly demeanor, glanced at the letter in Brynn's hand. "Hmm, Elara Windrider, you say? I don't recall that name, but perhaps someone here might know." He paused, scanning the room before raising his voice, "Anyone here familiar with an Elara Windrider?"

Silence settled upon the tavern, broken only by the faint chirping of crickets outside. Disappointed glances were exchanged among the patrons, and the bartender shrugged apologetically.
"Sorry, folks. It seems you'll have to search elsewhere," he

said, regretting his words. Grateful for the bartender s efforts, Aurora and Brynn expressed their thanks before stepping back out into the cool evening air. Undeterred, they continued their quest, visiting two more taverns and an inn, yet luck remained elusive.

Finally, they reached the last inn in town, their spirits hanging in the balance. Nervously, they approached the innkeeper and presented the name once again. To their amazement, the innkeeper's face brightened with recognition.
"Ah, Elara Windrider! She's my second cousin," he exclaimed, taking the note from Aurora's outstretched hand.
"I'll make sure she receives this." Relief washed over Aurora and Brynn as they finally completed their quest. A notification box appeared before them, displaying the words "Quest Completed - Parchment Delivery." Aurora's heart skipped a beat as she saw the reward: she gained 1000 experience points (XP) for her successful accomplishment.

But the surprises didn't end there. Another notification box popped up, exclaiming, "Level Up - Level 5!" Aurora's eyes widened with excitement as she realized the significance of this achievement. It was time to choose a new skill or enhance an existing one. Reflecting upon her previous progress, she swiped up to open the abilities menu, where her current skills were displayed. She saw that she was already at level 3 in archery, level 4 in swordsmanship, level 2 in minor healing, and level 2 in bartering. Contemplating her options, Aurora's mind raced with possibilities.

After careful consideration, Aurora decided to invest her skill point in a new ability called "Shadow Stealth." This choice would enable her to become more adept at blending into the shadows, making it harder for enemies to detect her when she sought refuge in the darkness. Pleased with her decision, Aurora confirmed her selection and felt a surge of excitement, knowing that her newfound skill would aid her in future endeavors.

"Now we need to find someone to talk about this chilling feeling I have," Aurora expressed to Brynn, her voice laced with concern. They stood in front of the inn, contemplating their next move. Brynn, ever resourceful, suggested, "Let's start by seeking out a healer. They might possess the knowledge to shed some light on your condition." Determined, they reentered the inn, seeking the guidance of the innkeeper they had conversed with moments ago.

Upon seeing Aurora and Brynn returning, the innkeeper greeted them warmly. "Ah, back so soon? What can I assist you with this time?" he inquired, his eyes filled with curiosity. Aurora stepped forward, her voice steady.
"We are in search of a healer or perhaps a cleric," she stated, hoping the innkeeper could provide valuable information.

A thoughtful expression crossed the innkeeper's face as he pondered their request. "Well, I know of a healer residing on the other side of town in a small hut," he offered, reaching for a piece of parchment. Carefully, he wrote down the directions and handed them to them.
"He's more of a shaman than a traditional healer, but I believe he possesses unique abilities that might aid in your healing," the innkeeper explained, his voice carrying a hint of mystery. Grateful for his assistance, Aurora and Brynn expressed their gratitude before setting off to find the enigmatic shaman healer.

The journey to the other side of town took them roughly half an hour, guiding them through bustling dirt streets teeming with activity. Aurora couldn't help but marvel at the absence of other players along their route, or perhaps she simply hadn't noticed them in the midst of her thoughts. As they reached the outskirts of the town, the environment transformed, and the atmosphere grew more rustic and mystical.

Upon arriving at the shaman's humble abode, Aurora couldn't help but feel a sense of intrigue. The hut stood nestled amidst a grove of ancient trees, its exterior adorned with various bones and intriguing cave drawings. It exuded an aura reminiscent of a gypsy fortune-teller's den, filled with a sense of mysticism and ancient wisdom.

With a mix of anticipation and trepidation, Aurora and Brynn approached the shaman's hut. The door creaked open, revealing a dimly lit interior. The scent of incense wafted through the air, weaving an enchanting spell. Inside, they saw shelves adorned with curious artifacts, herbs, and potions. The walls were adorned with vibrant tapestries depicting mythical creatures and ancient rituals.

A wizened figure emerged from the shadows, his weathered face adorned with markings symbolizing a lifetime of spiritual connection. The shaman's piercing eyes seemed to hold secrets untold, and his presence commanded reverence. His voice carried a soothing yet authoritative tone as he beckoned them closer, his words seemingly whispered by the spirits themselves.

"Welcome, seekers of healing," the shaman greeted them, his voice carrying an otherworldly resonance.

"I sense the chill that lingers within you, young one," he addressed Aurora, his gaze penetrating to the core of her being. "Sit, and let us delve into the depths of your ailment, unraveling the threads of the unseen."

Aurora and Brynn settled into the cozy space, their hearts pounding with anticipation. They were about to embark on a journey of discovery, seeking answers to the mysterious coldness that plagued Aurora's very being. The shaman's words reverberated in the hut, intertwining with the ancient wisdom whispered in the bones and echoes of the past.

"Now, tell me the tale of how you come to possess this chilling feeling deep within you," the shaman requested, his voice carrying both wisdom and empathy. Seated in a circle around a crackling fire, Aurora and Brynn shared the details of their recent encounter with the skeletons. Aurora's voice trembled slightly as she recounted the moment she was touched, her body instantly succumbing to an icy coldness.

The shaman listened intently, his eyes gazing into the dancing flames, contemplating the words spoken.
"It seems," he began, his voice filled with a mix of solemnity and concern, "that you have been touched by death itself, a chilling reminder of its looming presence. You stand at the precipice, where the boundary between the realms of the living and the dead blurs."

Aurora's heart sank at the shaman's words. The gravity of her condition began to weigh heavily upon her, the realization that she was being slowly drawn towards the dark abyss of the underworld. She clung to a glimmer of hope and turned to the shaman, her eyes filled with anxiety. "Is there anything that can be done to cure me?" she implored, her voice trembling.

The shaman's face bore a mix of empathy and uncertainty. "I regret to inform you that there is no direct cure for your affliction," he responded, his words heavy with regret. "However, I possess the knowledge to slow down the insidious process, extending the time it takes for the corruption to fully consume your mind and body."

Aurora's heart sank further upon hearing the shaman's somber news. Her mind raced, contemplating the implications of her condition and the limited options available to her. "If you cannot cure me, then where must I go? Who can aid me in stopping this descent into darkness?' she asked, her voice quivering with genuine concern.

A brief moment of silence enveloped the hut as the shaman contemplated his response. Finally, his gaze met Aurora's, and he spoke with a tone laced with both caution and hope. "To find a cure, you must embark on a treacherous journey to the majestic High City of the Pixies," he revealed, his voice carrying a sense of reverence. "There, amidst the ethereal beauty and enchantment of their realm, you shall find extraordinary healers with the power to free you from this affliction."

Aurora's heart skipped a beat at the mention of the High City of the Pixies. She understood the gravity of the shaman's words, aware that reaching such a sacred place would not be an easy feat.

"How far must we travel? How long will this journey take?" she inquired, her voice tinged with a mixture of hope and trepidation.

The shaman's gaze softened as he offered a response. "The High City of the Pixies lies a great distance from here. The journey to their realm is a perilous one, and it will take approximately three months to reach their hallowed grounds," he disclosed, his words painting a vivid picture of the arduous path ahead.

Aurora's heart sank at the realization of the daunting journey that lay before them. Three months of unknown trials and tribulations, all in the hopes of finding a cure for her chilling affliction. She glanced at Brynn, silently acknowledging the challenges they would face together. Determination welled up within her, fueling her spirit with the resolve to overcome whatever obstacles may lie in their path. The quest for healing had just begun, and with each passing day, Aurora's inner fire burned brighter, igniting a spark of hope amidst the encroaching darkness.

The shaman, his face painted with intricate patterns symbolizing ancient wisdom, began the ritual to slow down the encroaching darkness that had taken hold of Aurora's being. With deliberate movements, he tossed a handful of fragrant herbs into the fire, which erupted in a burst of vibrant smoke. The flames, once a mere orange and yellow, transformed into a mesmerizing dance of orange and pink hues.

"Now, my child, gaze deep into the heart of the fire," the shaman instructed, his voice carrying a soothing cadence.

"Let the fire peer into the depths of your soul, illuminating every flicker of light within you. Recall all the moments of joy, the memories of kindness and compassion, and the essence of your being that gravitates towards the radiant path."

As the shaman rose from his seated position, he moved gracefully around the flickering flames, his feet tracing a pattern in synchrony with the rhythmic beat of his chant. The sound, reminiscent of ancient tribal melodies, resonated through the air, mingling with the crackling of the fire. Aurora's gaze, fixed upon the enchanting blaze, grew increasingly intense as if she had entered a trance-like state, guided by the shaman's enchanting presence.

In that sacred space between reality and the realm of spirits, memories washed over Aurora like gentle waves upon a shore. She delved into the treasury of her mind, summoning images of her loved ones—her family, Jane, her faithful companion Brynn, and Verdant, the wise old oak tree who had offered solace in times of need. Each recollection brought forth a surge of warmth and love, infusing her very being with a renewed sense of purpose and resilience.

Time seemed to suspend as the ritual continued, stretching into the depths of an hour. Brynn, seated steadfastly beside Aurora, observed the transformative process unfolding before her eyes. She marveled at the intensity of her friend's gaze, the ethereal glow that emanated from within her. The shaman, guided by ancient knowledge and intuition, intermittently added sacred dust to the flames, intensifying the energy swirling within the mystical fire.

The crackling of the fire seemed to sing a chorus of hope, intertwining with the shaman's melodic chants. Aurora's heartbeat was in harmony with the rhythm, her very essence attuned to the ancient power surrounding her. It was as though the collective force of her memories and the shaman's incantations wove a protective cloak of light around her, pushing back against the encroaching darkness that threatened to consume her soul.

As the final moments of the ritual unfolded, the fire erupted in a dazzling display of vivid colors, shimmering with an otherworldly radiance. The shaman, his eyes filled with both exhaustion and satisfaction, gradually ceased his chanting and joined Brynn beside Aurora. Their collective gaze remained locked upon the spectacle before them, their breaths held in anticipation of the ritual's culmination.

With one final surge of brilliance, the flames subsided, returning to their original gentle orange glow. The shaman, a sense of serenity etched upon his features, turned to Aurora and Brynn, a knowing smile gracing his lips.
"The fire has witnessed your light, my dear," he whispered, his voice filled with ancient wisdom.
"The journey ahead may be fraught with challenges, but you carry within you a resilience that can defy the encroaching shadows. Embrace the memories, the love, and the strength that reside within you, for they shall guide you towards the healing you seek."

Aurora, her eyes shimmering with newfound determination, rose from her seated position, her spirit rekindled by the transformative ritual. She felt the embrace of her companionship with Brynn, their unspoken bond strengthening with each passing moment. The journey to the High City of the Pixies stretched out before them, a treacherous path rife with uncertainties. However, they embarked upon it with renewed hope, knowing that within Aurora's heart burned a radiant light that could never be extinguished.

As the next crucial phase of the tournament loomed ahead, Aurora and Brynn knew that their journey to the esteemed High City of the Pixies would be arduous. The prospect of embarking on a three-month trek through untamed lands was daunting, and they yearned for a swifter means of transportation. They realized that acquiring horses would be the key to expediting their journey, reducing the travel time to a single month of relentless riding. Determined to find a solution, they returned to the innkeeper they had entrusted with the letter.

"Good day to you," Aurora greeted the innkeeper, her voice infused with a sense of determination.
"The shaman was able to extend the effects of the darkness, but he revealed that we must make our way to the High City of the Pixies."

The innkeeper furrowed his brow, his gaze fixed upon the adventurers.
"High City of the Pixies, you say? I cannot claim familiarity with such a place, which suggests it must be quite distant," he replied, his tone filled with genuine curiosity.

"Indeed," Brynn interjected, his voice tinged with anticipation. "According to the shaman, it lies roughly three months away from here if we were to travel on foot. However, we seek a faster method of transportation. Is there a way for us to acquire horses?"

The innkeeper scratched his chin, contemplating their request. "Horses, you say? Well, it just so happens that I have a few steeds available for purchase. They are sturdy creatures capable of enduring long journeys. However, they come at a price," he replied a glimmer of opportunity in his eyes.

Aurora and Brynn exchanged a glance, silently agreeing that securing horses would be a worthy investment for their expedition.
"We are willing to pay, as we understand the value of swift travel. What is your price?" Aurora inquired, her voice steady and resolute.

The innkeeper leaned in, lowering his voice as if divulging a secret.
"For each horse, I ask for ten gold pieces. Rest assured, these are no ordinary horses; they possess the endurance of the wind and the strength of the earth. With them, your journey to the High City of the Pixies will be expedited, ensuring you arrive within a month."

Aurora and Brynn exchanged a brief moment of contemplation, mentally calculating their available funds. They had managed to accumulate a modest sum during their tournament endeavors, but the innkeeper's price was higher than expected.

"Ten gold pieces per horse is indeed a considerable sum," Aurora mused.

"We may need to engage in additional ventures to gather the necessary funds. Do you have any quests or tasks that could assist us in acquiring the required amount?"

The innkeeper nodded knowingly, understanding their predicament.
"I do have a quest available, albeit one that offers meager compensation," he admitted with a hint of regret.
"Our supplies of boar meat are dwindling, and I require assistance in replenishing our stock. If you can hunt down ten boars and bring me their meat, I will reward you with one silver piece for every two boars slain."

Aurora's eyes sparkled with a mixture of determination and shrewdness.
"We will undertake this quest, but do you have any other opportunities that might offer a more substantial reward?" she asked, hoping to uncover an alternative means of income.

The innkeeper's gaze shifted to the northernmost inn in town, his voice carrying a note of anticipation.
"If you seek higher-paying endeavors, I suggest you visit the job board at the northern inn. There, you will find a plethora of requests from various individuals seeking assistance. It may present an opportunity more aligned with your desired compensation," he suggested, offering a potential path to greater financial gain.

With gratitude, Aurora and Brynn thanked the innkeeper for his guidance and promptly set out on their quest to replenish the inn's boar meat supply. Simultaneously, their minds whirred with thoughts of exploring the job board at the northern inn, where potentially lucrative opportunities awaited them. It was clear that to acquire the necessary funds for their horses, they would need to engage in a series of endeavors, both humble and grand. Determined to achieve their goal, they ventured forth, ready to seize every opportunity that would pave the way to the High City of the Pixies.

As the afternoon sun began its descent towards the horizon, Aurora and Brynn ventured into the surrounding wilderness in search of boars. Time was of the essence, for they were keenly aware of the perils that lurked in the darkness of night. They knew they had to accomplish their task swiftly to ensure their safety.

After some time, their perseverance paid off as they stumbled upon a group of boars. With practiced precision and coordinated teamwork, they swiftly dispatched each boar, their weapons finding their marks with lethal accuracy. The satisfying thud of each successful strike echoed through the forest, earning them not only the completion of their quest but also valuable experience points. Five experience points were awarded for every boar slain, reinforcing their growth as skilled participants in the tournament.

Carrying the spoils of their hunt, Aurora and Brynn returned to the inn, greeted by the innkeeper's expectant gaze.
"Ah, you're back so soon! Have you managed to gather all the boar meat for me?" the innkeeper inquired eagerly as they entered.

Aurora presented the innkeeper with the bounty they had collected, a proud smile gracing her lips.

"Here you go," she replied, handing over the requested boar meat. The innkeeper's eyes widened with appreciation, acknowledging their swift completion of the task.

Grateful for their hard work, the innkeeper rewarded them with the promised silver pieces. They each received a sum that reflected the number of boars they had slain. With the day drawing to a close and the sun casting its warm hues across the sky, Aurora and Brynn decided to secure a room for the night.

Taking a moment to savor the fruits of their labor, they settled down in the inn's cozy dining area, relishing in a meal prepared from the very boar meat they had so skillfully acquired. The tender and succulent meat, grilled to perfection, filled their senses with a delightful blend of flavors.

Having satisfied their hunger and indulged in well-deserved rest, they retired to their room, ready to conclude the eventful eighth day of their journey. As they drifted off into a peaceful slumber, dreams of the High City of the Pixies danced through their minds, anticipation and determination fueling their hearts for the days yet to come.

Chapter 17

Day 8 arrived, and the dwindling player count stood at 6239 participants. As the number continued to decrease, the intensity of the battles grew, for each encounter became a crucial step closer to victory. Aurora and Brynn commenced their day by fortifying themselves with a hearty breakfast, indulging in freshly baked bread and a variety of succulent fruits. They knew they needed sustenance for the arduous challenges that lay ahead.

Their first task led them to the northernmost inn in search of the renowned job board, which held promising opportunities for high-reward quests. With a pressing need to accumulate wealth rapidly, they hoped to secure a lucrative undertaking that would bring them closer to their ultimate goal. Brimming with determination, they navigated through bustling streets and winding alleyways, eager to reach their destination.

However, fate had a different plan for them. As they rounded a corner, they found themselves face-to-face with a formidable duo, two players united in their intent to cause harm. A chilling voice pierced through the air as one of the adversaries bellowed, "Halt! You shall meet your demise today, girls." The sneering grin on the other player's face revealed their malicious intent.

The pair that confronted Aurora and Brynn presented a striking contrast. One was a hulking orc, towering over them with bulging muscles and a menacing aura. The other, a nimble and cunning human, possessed a look of shrewd intelligence in their eyes. It was evident that these two adversaries would not be easily overcome.

Reacting swiftly, Aurora and Brynn instinctively decided to flee, darting between buildings and attempting to outpace their pursuers. Yet, luck was not on their side as Brynn, burdened by his shorter dwarf legs, struggled to match Aurora's speed. Realizing that escape was futile, they reluctantly resolved to stand their ground, preparing for an impending clash.

Aurora's agile fingers swiftly knocked her last arrow, her aim honed and her determination unyielding. With a single, fluid motion, she released the arrow, finding its mark and causing one of their pursuers to stagger, clutching their wounded arm. Seizing the opportunity, Aurora unleashed a defiant proclamation, attempting to intimidate her foes.
"This ends here! Know that I am Aurora, the legendary warrior of Earth, and you shall be vanquished!"

Confusion marred the face of the other player as they scoffed, oblivious to Aurora's reputation. Undeterred, the adversaries launched their assault, charging forward with relentless determination. The battleground was set, and an intense and protracted battle ensued, with each participant exhibiting unwavering resolve.

Aurora and Brynn fought valiantly, employing their unique skills and tactics in a dance of blades and arrows. The air crackled with the clash of weapons, the thudding of footsteps, and the echoes of grunts and battle cries. Blow after blow, strike after strike, the battle raged on, both sides fiercely resisting the encroaching darkness that threatened their existence.

Yet, despite their resilience, Aurora found herself pushed to her limits. Fatigue and wounds took their toll, her health points dwindling perilously low. The weight of the battle bore heavily upon her, threatening to snuff out her remaining strength. In her darkest moment, a surge of determination surged through her, a flicker of hope igniting within her soul.

Summoning every ounce of courage and resilience, Aurora rallied, pushing herself beyond her known capabilities. With a final burst of energy, she executed a daring maneuver, deftly evading an opponent's strike and retaliating with a devastating counterattack. The clash ended with a resounding victory as the adversaries lay defeated before Aurora and Brynn.

Breathing heavily, Aurora and Brynn surveyed the aftermath of the grueling encounter. A mix of relief, triumph, and exhaustion washed over them, the realization of their near brush with defeat sinking in. They had triumphed against all odds, emerging as victors in a battle that tested their mettle to the core.

As the dust settled, they took a moment to tend to their wounds, their hearts filled with gratitude for their hard-earned victory. With renewed determination, they pressed onward, their spirits bolstered by the knowledge that they had faced adversity head-on and emerged triumphant. The path to glory and the high city of the Pixies awaited them, and with each passing challenge, their bond grew stronger, their resolve unshakeable.

With their health points dangerously low, Aurora and Brynn tread lightly, their steps cautious and their senses heightened. Aurora, utilizing her minor healing ability, channeled her remaining energy to mend their wounds. The magical energy enveloped them, gradually revitalizing their battered bodies. As the healing energy subsided, they felt a surge of vitality coursing through their veins, bringing them back from the brink. Aurora's health points climbed to 26, while Brynn's reached 28, nearly half of their maximum capacity.

Determined to make the most of their day, the duo pressed forward, their eyes fixed on the job board. Countless quest postings adorned the board, each offering tempting rewards. Their objective was clear: they needed to amass a significant amount of gold quickly. Scanning through the listings, they came across several intriguing options, including "The Beast Slayer," "The Cursed Village," and "The Tournament of Champions." However, one particular quest caught their attention, standing out among the rest like a shining beacon.

"The Tower of Trials," the parchment read, its words etched in elegant calligraphy. The quest description described a towering structure, erected by a powerful wizard. Within its walls awaited a treacherous journey filled with intricate puzzles, devious traps, and formidable guardians. The wizard sought individuals who could prove their mettle by conquering the tower's myriad challenges, promising immense magical knowledge and coveted artifacts as rewards for each successful level completed.

Although the quest carried significant risks, the allure of the tower's promised rewards proved irresistible. It offered not only the chance to acquire substantial wealth but also the opportunity to gain invaluable experience points, propelling them closer to their ultimate goal. Aurora and Brynn exchanged glances, their determination mirrored in their eyes. They knew that embarking on this perilous undertaking would test their skills, courage, and teamwork to the utmost degree.

With their decision made, they set their sights on the towering structure, its silhouette visible on the distant horizon. The path ahead would be arduous, rife with unknown dangers, but they were prepared to face the trials that awaited them. Each step brought them closer to the tower, their anticipation building with every passing moment. They knew that within its ancient walls lay the key to unlocking their full potential and overcoming the darkness threatening Aurora's very existence.

Gathering their strength and mustering their resolve, they ventured forth, ready to face the Tower of Trials and all the challenges it held. The sun cast long shadows as they embarked on their journey, their hearts filled with a mixture of trepidation and excitement. The fate of their virtual world, as well as Aurora's salvation, hung in the balance. Little did they know that their encounter with the tower would test their limits, pushing them to the brink of their abilities and forging them into true champions. The epic battle they were about to face would be a testament to their resilience and unwavering spirit.

Their journey led them to the legendary Wizard's Tower of Trials, perched atop a towering mountain. The path ahead was a grueling six-hour hike, meandering through the rugged terrain. From the village below, the massive edifice could be seen, its spire reaching towards the heavens, a beacon of mystery and adventure. Eager to embark on their next challenge, Aurora and Brynn wasted no time in commencing their ascent.

The mountainous landscape presented a daunting obstacle, with the barren mountainside stretching out before them. Each step was a battle against the rocky and treacherous terrain. Loose rocks and falling boulders served as reminders of the inherent danger that accompanied their pursuit. But undeterred by the difficulties, they pressed onward, driven by their determination to reach the pinnacle of the tower.

Finally, after hours of arduous toil, they stood at the foot of the colossal tower. Its grandeur was beyond comprehension, defying the boundaries of scale and leaving them awestruck. The massive iron-clad doors guarded the entrance, exuding an aura of impenetrable strength. Towering several stories high, the doors stood as a testament to the secrets and challenges that awaited within.

As Aurora and Brynn approached, the doors groaned open, revealing a dimly lit room beyond. The soft glow emanating from within cast ethereal shadows, creating an atmosphere of mystique and anticipation. A handful of other players stood within the chamber, their presence a testament to the allure of the tower's trials.

As they stepped into the room, a notification box materialized before them, bearing the words "Non-PvP Area." The message reassured Aurora, dispelling any concerns about engaging in combat with fellow adventurers. The realization that they could focus solely on the tower's challenges and puzzles filled her with a renewed sense of purpose and relief.

Taking a moment to absorb their surroundings, Aurora and Brynn marveled at the intricate design of the tower's interior. The first floor, a testament to the wizard's craftsmanship, showcased a breathtaking blend of ancient architecture and magical elements. Massive stone pillars reached towards the heavens, their surfaces etched with arcane symbols and patterns. The air carried a faint scent of antiquity and untold secrets, invigorating their senses.

As they ventured deeper into the tower, they discovered a labyrinthine network of corridors and chambers. Each turn revealed a new vista, captivating their imagination and fueling their anticipation. Ornate tapestries adorned the walls, depicting long-forgotten legends and mythical creatures. Mysterious doorways beckoned, whispering tales of untold treasures hidden in the depths of the tower.

With every step, Aurora and Brynn could feel the energy of the tower pulsating around them, an enigmatic force that electrified their spirits. The first floor served as a mere glimpse into the Tower of Trials' grandeur, promising even greater wonders and challenges on the floors above. They were but the latest in a long line of brave adventurers who had embarked on this perilous journey, seeking glory, knowledge, and the chance to prove their mettle.

As they pressed onward, their hearts filled with a mixture of excitement and trepidation. The tower's trials awaited, each one more formidable than the last. But Aurora and Brynn were resolute, their camaraderie unyielding. They would face whatever lay ahead, drawing strength from their bond and the knowledge that their triumphs would bring them closer to their goals.

With anticipation building in their hearts, Aurora and Brynn stood before the small table in the middle of the room, where the bell awaited their touch. As their fingers gently pressed against the cool metal, a melodious chime resonated through the chamber, signaling the opening of a hidden door at the back. The door swung open, revealing a dimly lit staircase that spiraled upwards into the unknown.

Ascending the steps with cautious steps, their senses heightened, the air grew increasingly tinged with a sense of foreboding. Finally, they reached the top of the staircase and found themselves facing a pivotal choice. Before them lay two distinct paths, each marked by a sturdy door. A faded sign, etched with cryptic symbols, warned them of the impending decision: "Choose wisely, for one door conceals a challenge far greater than the other."

Pausing for a moment to evaluate their options, Aurora and Brynn weighed the potential risks and rewards. Their gazes met a silent understanding passing between them. With a shared determination, they opted for the left path, guided by a combination of intuition and the belief that fortune favored the bold.

Stepping through the door, they entered a vast, open room, bathed in an ethereal glow emanating from unseen sources. The air grew heavy with anticipation as their footsteps echoed through the chamber, seemingly swallowed by the vastness surrounding them. Across the expanse, two towering doors beckoned from the far side, their grandeur matched only by the mystique that shrouded them.
"This isn't so bad," said Aurora, looking around the room.
"Nothing even happened yet" mentioned Brynn with a smirk on his face.

As they began to formulate their next move, the silence was abruptly shattered by a resounding creak. One of the doors swung open, revealing a band of five goblins emerging with malevolent intent. Grinning maliciously, the goblins brandished their jagged weapons, eyes gleaming with cruel satisfaction.

Time seemed to slow as Aurora and Brynn prepared for the imminent clash. Their hands tightened around the hilt of their swords, muscles primed for action. Battle instincts kicked in, sharpening their focus and heightening their senses. The dance of combat was about to commence.

With a feral roar, the goblins charged forward, their movements swift and agile. Aurora and Brynn met their adversaries head-on, their swords singing through the air with precision and purpose. The clash of steel reverberated within the chamber, a symphony of warfare. Sparks erupted from the meeting of blades, casting fleeting bursts of light in the dimly lit room.

Aurora, swift and nimble, danced gracefully around the frenzied onslaught of goblin attacks. Her movements were like a whirlwind, evading strikes and retaliating with calculated precision. Brynn, stout and resolute, stood his ground, deflecting blows with the unwavering strength of his shield and counterattacking with calculated strikes that left the goblins reeling.
"Die goblin scum" shouted Aurora as she swung at the goblins.

As the battle intensified, the room became a chaotic battleground. Shouts and grunts mixed with the clashing of weapons, created a cacophony of combat. Bloodied wounds marred the bodies of both heroes and goblins alike, marking the toll exacted by the struggle.

Yet, the goblins fought with a tenacity that belied their small stature. They relentlessly pressed the attack, coordinating their strikes and exploiting any opening they could find. Aurora and Brynn found themselves locked in a desperate dance, defending against the onslaught, their bodies pushed to their limits.

As the minutes turned into an eternity, exhaustion began to seep into their bones. Aurora's movements grew sluggish, her strikes losing some of their usual finesse. Brynn's shield arm trembled under the weight of constant assault. The goblins sensed their faltering, seizing the opportunity to push forward with renewed vigor.

In a moment of peril, Aurora found herself surrounded by three goblins, their swords closing in from all directions. With lightning reflexes, she parried and dodged their attacks, but one managed to land a deep cut along her arm. Pain lanced through her body, and she staggered, her health points plummeting perilously low.

Fear surged within her, but the prospect of failure only steeled her resolve. With a burst of inner strength, Aurora unleashed a flurry of strikes, each blow fueled by sheer determination. One by one, the goblins fell before her, their bodies crumpling to the ground.

In the midst of the chaos, Brynn fought with unwavering resolve. The sweat-soaked hair clung to his forehead, obscuring his vision, but he pressed on undeterred. His shield became an impenetrable barrier, deflecting blows and shielding his companion when needed. With a mighty swing, he delivered a crushing blow to the skull of a goblin, the sound of bone shattering echoing through the room.

As the final goblin collapsed, defeated, the room fell into an eerie silence, broken only by the ragged breaths of the victorious duo. 15xp was gained from each goblin killed. Aurora stood, bloodied and battered, her health points hanging precariously by a thread. The battle had taken its toll, but she refused to yield. With a glance toward Brynn, a shared understanding passed between them—a silent acknowledgment of their resilience and unyielding determination.

The first trial had tested them to their limits, pushing them to the brink of exhaustion. Yet, as they caught their breath and surveyed the aftermath, a glimmer of triumph sparkled in their eyes. The Tower of Trials still loomed above them, holding more secrets and challenges within its hallowed walls. With newfound strength and an unwavering spirit, Aurora and Brynn prepared themselves for the arduous journey ahead, ready to conquer the next level and unveil the treasures that awaited them.

As the door swung open, revealing another set of stairs, Aurora and Brynn stepped forward, their determination unwavering. This time, they decided to take the right side, intrigued by the mystery that lay ahead. At the end of the stairwell, a single door stood, beckoning them toward their next trial.

Stepping through the door, they found themselves in a vastly different chamber from the previous one. The room stretched out before them, long and narrow, with towering walls adorned with ancient tapestries depicting long-forgotten legends. The atmosphere was tinged with an enigmatic aura, further heightened by the presence of large, meticulously placed tiles that spanned the floor. Each tile measured approximately four feet by four feet, forming a mesmerizing mosaic beneath their feet.

As Aurora and Brynn took in their surroundings, their eyes were drawn to a sign prominently displayed on the wall: "Answer this riddle to advance." The challenge before them was not one of brute strength but of intellectual prowess. Excitement mingled with a touch of trepidation as they prepared themselves for the mental test that awaited.

The riddle scrawled on the sign teased their minds, its enigmatic nature enticing them to unravel its secrets. It read:

"In the battle's fray, five goblins fell.
Their blades clashed, and their foes quelled.
Now gaze upon these tiles, each laid with care,
To find the answer that will lead you there.

Count the tiles, let numbers guide your way,
For they hold the truth you seek today.
With goblin's fate and room's design,
Reveal the sum and claim what's thine."

As Aurora and Brynn pondered the riddle's intricacies, their minds began to weave connections between the goblin adversaries they had vanquished and the tiles beneath their feet. They surveyed the room, counting the tiles with meticulous attention, their fingers tracing invisible lines as they sought patterns and meanings.

With each step taken, a number whispered in their minds, hinting at its significance. They considered the battles fought, the fallen foes, and the symmetrical arrangement of the tiles. Suddenly, a realization struck them like a bolt of lightning: the number they sought lay within the sum of the goblins they had defeated.

Carefully, they began to calculate the answer, their fingers tracing the edges of tiles, marking each one as they went. The room seemed to hold its breath as Aurora and Brynn's calculations neared completion, their excitement rising in tandem with their certainty.

Finally, as they reached the far end of the room, their calculations complete, they stood before the singular door, its presence now imbued with newfound significance. With a mixture of anticipation and confidence, Aurora and Brynn spoke their answer aloud, their voices ringing through the chamber.

They exchanged glances, silently contemplating the clues hidden within the words. With a spark of inspiration, Brynn whispered, "The answer is fifteen!" Their eyes met, a mixture of hope and uncertainty reflecting in their gazes.

Seconds passed, but the room remained eerily still. The tiles beneath their feet seemed to hold their breath, awaiting the affirmation of their answer. Yet, no magical response occurred, and the door at the far end of the chamber remained sealed shut. A ripple of doubt tinged their confidence, as they realized their answer may have been incorrect.

Just as they began to consider another attempt, an unsettling creak filled the air. Aurora and Brynn's hearts skipped a beat as they noticed the walls of the chamber slowly shifting inward, closing in on them with ominous intent. Panic surged through their veins, adrenaline spurring their next actions.

Frantically, they exchanged hurried glances, scanning the room for any signs of escape. But with each passing moment, the walls closed in further, leaving them with limited time to make a life-saving decision. In a desperate bid to find a way out, they scanned the surrounding tiles, seeking any hidden clues or mechanisms that could halt the encroaching peril.

Aurora's eyes widened as she noticed a faint inscription etched into one of the tiles nearby. Struggling against the mounting pressure of the closing walls, she read aloud, "When the answer eludes your grasp, seek the truth through reflection." The message fueled a renewed sense of determination, as they realized that the solution might not lie solely within the numbers.

With swift thinking, Brynn suggested, "Let's examine the tapestries on the walls. They may hold additional clues or symbols that could help us find the correct answer." Racing against time, they hurriedly analyzed the intricate weavings, tracing their fingers along the embroidered patterns.

Their eyes locked onto a tapestry depicting a battle scene, where goblins clashed against a group of adventurers. Intriguingly, numbers were subtly integrated into the artwork, cleverly concealed within the folds of armor and the swirling motion of weapons. Aurora and Brynn quickly deduced that these hidden numbers must hold the key to their salvation.

As the walls continued their relentless advance, they swiftly deciphered the hidden numerical clues within the tapestry. The realization struck them like lightning—the true answer had been right before their eyes. Taking a deep breath, Aurora steadied her voice and shouted, "The answer is twelve!"

Miraculously, the grinding sound of the walls' movement came to an abrupt halt. The chamber seemed to exhale, releasing them from the clutches of impending doom. The room regained its stillness as if acknowledging their triumph over the challenge.

The sealed door at the end of the chamber groaned open, revealing a pathway leading to the next stage of the Tower of Trials. Aurora and Brynn exchanged a mixture of relief and gratitude, their bond strengthened by the peril they had just overcome. They stepped forward, leaving the chamber behind, their determination unwavering as they embraced the unknown that awaited them in the ever-shifting labyrinth of the wizard's creation.

As they stepped into the next room, their eyes widened at the sight before them. The spacious chamber revealed two grand doors at the far end, promising new trials and dangers. However, their attention was quickly drawn to the sudden movement from one of the doors. Without warning, it swung open, and emerging from it were six Skrizzlethorn creatures.
"What are these creatures?" said Aurora with a confused, shocked look on her face.
"Never seen them," said Brynn, reading her ax.

The Skrizzlethorn was a perplexing sight. These hybrid beings embodied the fusion of goblin and rat, a result of twisted experimentation or perhaps a bizarre twist of nature. Their appearance was both fascinating and unsettling. Standing at around four feet tall, their lean and wiry frames were covered in a patchwork of mottled gray and brown fur, blending seamlessly with the shadows of the room. Their faces displayed an uncanny fusion of goblinoid and rodent features.

Their sharp, beady eyes gleamed with a mischievous intelligence, their long-pointed ears twitched with heightened senses, and their rat-like noses sniffed the air for any signs of prey. Slender, yet deceptively strong limbs adorned with wickedly curved claws hinted at their dexterity and deadly precision. A long, sinewy tail coiled and flicked, aiding in their agile movements as they skittered across the chamber.

Equipped with rusty short curved swords, the Skrizzlethorn exuded a sense of primal ferocity. Their weapon of choice mirrored their nature—a blend of goblin cunning and rat-like adaptability. Aurora and Brynn exchanged glances, both filled with a mix of curiosity and caution. They had never encountered creatures like these before, and their unfamiliarity added a new layer of challenge to their already arduous journey.

The Skrizzlethorn, aware of their intruders, emitted low growls that sent shivers down Aurora's spine. These agile creatures wasted no time, launching themselves into a relentless assault. With lightning-fast movements, they lunged and slashed at their adversaries, their rusty curved swords gleaming in the dim light.

Aurora and Brynn reacted swiftly, their reflexes honed by countless battles. They seamlessly coordinated their attacks, parrying and dodging the Skrizzlethorn's strikes with calculated precision. However, the Skrizzlethorn's nimbleness proved to be a formidable challenge, as they evaded many of their retaliatory strikes with uncanny agility.

The skirmish escalated into a chaotic dance of blades and bodies. The room echoed with the clash of steel, grunts of exertion, and the occasional yelp of pain. Aurora's bow became an extension of her arm, her arrows finding their marks with deadly accuracy. Brynn, with his dwarf strength, delivered powerful blows with his trusty ax, aiming to incapacitate their adversaries.

But the Skrizzlethorn were not easily deterred. Their rat-like agility allowed them to maneuver around their opponents, exploiting any opening or momentary lapse in defense. Their razor-sharp claws raked against armor and flesh, leaving trails of blood in their wake.

With each passing minute, the battle grew increasingly intense. Aurora's movements became more fluid and focused, her eyes locked on her opponents as she unleashed a barrage of arrows. Brynn, fueled by his dwarf resilience, pushed through the pain, his strikes gaining strength and precision.

But as the battle raged on, exhaustion began to weigh heavily on Aurora and Brynn. Their muscles burned, and fatigue threatened to slow their reflexes. The Skrizzlethorn, sensing their vulnerability, launched a ferocious onslaught, their coordinated attacks pushing the duo to their limits.

Aurora felt a searing pain as Skrizzlethorn's sword grazed her arm, leaving a deep gash. Blood trickled down her skin, but she refused to let the wound deter her. With gritted teeth, she drew upon her inner reserves, tapping into her warrior spirit to summon one last surge of energy.

Brynn, too, bore his fair share of injuries. The Skrizzlethorn's relentless strikes had taken their toll, leaving him with cuts and bruises across his stout frame. Yet, his determination burned bright, fueling his every swing and parry.

The room became a battleground of wills, a test of endurance and resilience. Aurora and Brynn fought on, their bodies and minds pushed to their limits. They refused to yield, their unwavering determination eclipsing the pain and weariness that threatened to consume them.

Time seemed to blur as the battle waged on, each passing moment a testament to their unwavering resolve. And then, in a moment of triumph, Aurora's arrow found its mark, piercing through the heart of a Skrizzlethorn. The creature let out a final, guttural cry before collapsing to the ground.

With the loss of their comrade, the remaining Skrizzlethorn faltered for a brief moment, their ferocity waning. Seizing the opportunity, Brynn unleashed a powerful strike that connected with one of the creatures, sending it sprawling backward. The room fell silent, save for the heavy breathing of Aurora and Brynn, their bodies covered in a sheen of sweat and dirt. Aurora gained 35xp for each Skrizzlethorn killed.

The battle was won, but the toll it had taken on them was evident. Aurora clutched her bleeding arm, her breath ragged, while Brynn leaned heavily on his ax for support. They exchanged a glance, their eyes reflecting both exhaustion and triumph. Their health was now extremely low. With a nod of understanding, they knew it was time to tend to their wounds and gather their strength for the challenges that awaited them on the higher floors of the tower. Aurora used her minor healing to bring back some of their health points. They rested for sometime to regain their health points.

With caution in their steps, Aurora and Brynn ventured forward, their eyes scanning the room for any signs of danger. The stench of battle lingered in the air, mingling with the acrid smell of charred stone. As they passed the fallen bodies strewn across the chamber, they couldn't help but feel a somber weight upon their hearts, a reminder of the perilous journey they had undertaken.

The door at the far end of the room beckoned them forward, its aged wooden panels worn from countless encounters. Beyond that door lay another choice of stairs, and this time they were resolute in their decision to ascend the left side. With each step, the anticipation grew, and their minds braced for whatever trials awaited them.

As they reached the top of the stairs and crossed the threshold of the next room, their senses were immediately engulfed by the grandeur of the chamber. It was vast, stretching out before them with a sense of both awe and trepidation. The floor dropped off sharply on either side, revealing a perilous abyss that sent shivers down their spines. In the midst of this chasm, tall pillars rose from the depths below, reaching towards the heavens like the skeletal fingers of ancient giants.

At the far end of the room, a solitary door stood, seemingly the gateway to their next challenge. But it was not the door that captured their attention—it was the imposing statue that commanded the center of the chamber. A massive knight, standing at a towering eight feet, carved from stone with meticulous detail. Its presence exuded an aura of strength and unwavering resolve.

Bathed in the dim light filtering through the room, the statue held a colossal sword, its length spanning six feet. The blade gleamed with an ethereal glow, hinting at the power it possessed. It stood as a silent sentinel, observing their every move with an intensity that sent a chill down their spines.

A small sign rested before the statue, bearing a riddle that challenged their wits and forced them to ponder their next move. The words etched upon it seemed to dance before their eyes, urging them to decipher its cryptic meaning. This riddle held the key to their progress, yet failure to unravel its secrets would awaken the dormant knight and set it upon them in a furious onslaught.

They exchanged glances, their determination mirrored in their eyes. The weight of their choices bore down upon them as they contemplated the riddle's enigma, their minds racing with possibilities and potential consequences. Each step they took could either lead them closer to triumph or plunge them into a perilous fight for survival.

With bated breath, Aurora and Brynn embarked on a cautious exploration of the chamber, their eyes darting from pillar to pillar, seeking clues that would unravel the riddle's mystery. They tested the ground beneath their feet, wary of triggering any unforeseen traps that might unleash the wrath of the stone knight.

Carefully, they deliberated on their options, analyzing the significance of each pillar and its relationship to the statue. Every decision they made carried the weight of their lives, urging them to choose wisely and with calculated precision. A single misstep could awaken the knight from its slumber, transforming it from a mere statue into a formidable adversary.

Their hearts pounded in their chests as they carefully considered the riddle's intricacies. The pillars and the statue held the key, their interplay concealed within the riddle's verses. The tension in the air was palpable, each passing moment amplifying the weight of their choice.

Aurora's eyes widened as a realization struck her. The riddler's clues aligned with the position of the pillars, each one representing a crucial element that would unlock the path to their salvation. With newfound clarity, she motioned for Brynn to follow her lead, guiding their footsteps toward the pillar that held the answer to the riddler's conundrum.

Step by step, they traversed the chamber, their eyes fixed on the designated pillar. With each footfall, their anxiety heightened, the fear of awakening the stone knight gripping their souls. Time seemed to stretch into eternity as they advanced, the room enveloped in tense silence.

And then, as their final footfalls reached the predetermined pillar, the room erupted with a resounding rumble. The ground beneath them quivered, and the colossal knight shook with a newfound vitality. The statue's eyes blazed with an otherworldly light, and the massive sword lifted from its stone pedestal with an air of impending menace.

Aurora and Brynn braced themselves for the onslaught, their swords at the ready. They had gambled their lives on their intelligence and resolve, and now they must face the consequences of their choice. The battle that unfolded would test their mettle like never before, as they engaged in a dance of survival against the awakened stone knight, its strikes fueled by an ancient power.

Their swords clashed with the colossal blade, the clash of steel reverberating throughout the chamber. Each movement was a testament to their skill and determination, as they fought tooth and nail against the formidable adversary. The air crackled with tension, the outcome of the battle hanging precariously in the balance.

As they fought, their bodies dripping with sweat and their muscles strained, they knew that this was not just a physical test but a battle of wills. The stone knight's relentless assault pushed them to their limits, demanding every ounce of their strength and resilience. Their bodies bore the scars of their struggle, but their spirits burned bright with unwavering resolve.

Time seemed to blur as the clash between warrior and statue raged on, each moment blending into the next. Sparks flew as their blades clashed, the sound of steel ringing through the chamber like a symphony of war. Aurora and Brynn fought side by side, their movements harmonized through unspoken understanding.

In the face of seemingly insurmountable odds, they persevered. They channeled their fear and exhaustion into a fierce determination, their eyes locked onto the stone knight, unyielding in their pursuit of victory. Blow after blow, strike after strike, they weathered the storm unleashed upon them, their resilience a testament to their unbreakable spirit.

And finally, after what felt like an eternity, their combined efforts paid off. With one final strike, their swords found their mark, shattering the stone knight's defense. The colossal figure crumbled, its existence returning to a motionless state of stone. They gained 200xp for killing the knight.

Exhausted and bruised, Aurora and Brynn stood amidst the remnants of their battle, the room engulfed in a heavy silence. The victory was hard-fought, the scars on their bodies a testament to the trials they had overcome. They exchanged a weary smile, a shared acknowledgment of their triumph amidst the perils of the Tower of Trials.

With aching muscles and determination etched upon their faces, they pressed forward, eager to uncover the secrets that awaited them on the higher floors of the tower. The journey was far from over, but they had proven their worth and resilience, inching closer to the ultimate goal that lay at the summit of the tower.

As they retreated from the battle-scarred chamber, the echoes of their victory reverberated within the walls. They were warriors tested by fire, their spirits unyielding. With each passing obstacle, they grew closer to their ultimate goal, determined to emerge victorious from the Tower of Trials.

As the creaking door swung open, revealing the hidden passage beyond, Aurora and Brynn were greeted once more by the familiar sight of two ascending staircases. This time, they made their choice and opted for the right side, their footsteps echoing against the stone walls as they ascended.

The room that awaited them was unlike any they had encountered thus far. It stretched out before them, seemingly endless in its length, with no visible end in sight. The ceiling loomed high above, casting elongated shadows that danced along the worn stone floor. A solitary sign, weathered by time and adorned with faded ink, caught their attention.

Its inscription offered a chilling warning, for it spoke of impalement and consequences that awaited those who failed to decipher the riddle presented to them. The weight of their previous encounters and the mental strain of relentless challenges bore heavily upon Aurora's mind, and she couldn't help but express her frustration.

"I grow weary of these riddles," Aurora muttered, a tinge of exhaustion seeping into her voice. She rubbed her temples, attempting to alleviate the strain that had accumulated from countless hours of mental exertion.
"My brain aches from the constant thinking and deciphering."

Brynn, ever the optimist, placed a comforting hand on Aurora's shoulder. His voice, laced with determination, cut through the weariness that hung in the air.
"Fear not, my dear friend. We have braved these trials together, and we shall emerge victorious. Trust in our abilities and the knowledge we have acquired thus far."

Aurora managed a faint smile, reassured by Brynn's unwavering faith in their partnership. With renewed resolve, she straightened her posture and focused her gaze on the sign before them. The riddle's cryptic message demanded their attention, compelling them to embark on a mental journey of deduction and observation.

Examining the intricacies of their surroundings, Aurora's eyes traced the patterns etched into the walls. The interplay of light and shadow revealed a subtle rhythm, an unseen cadence that held the key to unraveling the riddle's enigma. Each stroke of the brush that had painted these walls carried a purpose, a message waiting to be deciphered.

Together, they analyzed the patterns, searching for clues that would guide them toward the correct path. With painstaking precision, they pieced together the intricate dance of shadows and the arrangement of shapes. They hypothesized and tested, stepping with caution and meticulous attention to detail.

As they progressed, Aurora's fatigue began to dissipate, replaced by a surge of exhilaration. The riddle became more than just a mental challenge; it became a quest for enlightenment, a journey to unlock the secrets of this mysterious room. Brynn's unwavering support and their shared determination propelled them forward, their bond growing stronger with each passing moment.

And then, as if a divine revelation had struck them, Aurora's eyes widened with a newfound understanding. The pattern on the wall revealed itself in all its intricate glory. It was not a mere sequence of shapes but a map, a guide to navigating the treacherous path that lay before them.

Eagerly, they followed the pattern, stepping in sync with the invisible melody that the room had orchestrated. Their feet found solace on the specific tiles that matched the cryptic design, avoiding the dangers that lurked beneath the false steps. With each correct footfall, they moved closer to their objective, their confidence bolstered by their astute observation.

Their progress was marked by a resounding silence, broken only by the steady rhythm of their breathing and the faint echoes of their footsteps. They advanced through the chamber, never straying from the path dictated by the enigmatic pattern. It led them further into the heart of the room, closer to the door that beckoned them with promises of both trepidation and reward.

Aurora couldn't help but feel a mixture of relief and anticipation. The mental strain had transformed into a sense of accomplishment, a testament to their resilience and ingenuity. With each passing trial, their bond grew stronger, their trust in one another unyielding.

The final step fell into place, and the door before them swung open, revealing what awaited on the other side. Their journey was far from over, but they had proven once again that they possessed the wit and determination to face any challenge that the Tower of Trials dared throw their way. With renewed determination, they stepped through the threshold, ready to conquer whatever lay ahead.

As they stepped through the doorway, their eyes were met with another set of ascending stairs, stretching upward into the unknown depths of the tower. The sight of yet another daunting climb weighed heavily on their shoulders, a reminder that their journey through this formidable structure was far from its conclusion.

The stairs seemed to extend endlessly, disappearing into the shadows that veiled the upper reaches of the tower. Each step they took echoed through the dimly lit chamber, amplifying the sense of isolation that surrounded them. The air grew colder, carrying a subtle hint of ancient whispers and forgotten secrets.

Aurora and Brynn exchanged a weary glance, their resolve tested by the seemingly unending ascent before them. However, their shared determination refused to waver. With gritted teeth and unwavering determination, they pressed onward, their footfalls echoing resolutely against the stone steps.

As they ascended, the architecture of the tower revealed itself in all its grandeur. Intricate carvings adorned the walls, depicting scenes of mythical battles, arcane rituals, and lost civilizations. The flickering torches that lined the stairwell cast dancing shadows, breathing life into the ancient artwork as if whispering tales of triumph and tragedy to those who dared listen.

With each passing step, the weight of the tower's history and mystique settled upon their shoulders. The realization that they were but small, insignificant figures in a grand tapestry of stories filled them with a humbling sense of awe. The tower had witnessed the rise and fall of countless heroes, the echoes of their triumphs and defeats forever etched into its very essence.

Time seemed to lose its grip within the tower's confines. Minutes melded into hours, blurring the boundaries between day and night. The passage of time became an abstract concept, overshadowed by the relentless pursuit of progress. The weariness in their muscles and the strain in their minds were a testament to the arduousness of their endeavor.

As they continued their ascent, the architectural design of the tower began to shift subtly, reflecting the changing nature of the challenges that lay ahead. The stairs twisted and turned, sometimes spiraling upward, other times leading them through narrow corridors that seemed to defy the laws of space and geometry.

The air grew increasingly dense with an otherworldly aura, suffused with ancient enchantments and the lingering presence of powerful beings. Wisps of ethereal energy danced around them, carrying whispers of forgotten spells and untold secrets. Every step felt like a journey through time and realms, their very beings resonating with the hidden magic that permeated the tower's core.

Through perseverance and sheer will, they pressed on, fueled by the tantalizing prospect of what awaited them at the pinnacle of the tower. The challenges they faced and the sacrifices they made were not in vain. They had come too far to turn back now.

With each step, their determination grew stronger, forged by the trials they had overcome and the unyielding spirit that burned within them. The tower's infinite expanse no longer intimidated them but fueled their desire to unravel its mysteries, to stand as triumphant champions within its hallowed halls.

And so, they climbed, their hearts and minds attuned to the rhythm of the tower's pulse. Each step brought them closer to the summit, closer to the ultimate test of their mettle. With every weary ascent, they carved their names into the annals of the tower's storied history, leaving an indelible mark upon its ancient stones.

The tower loomed above them, an imposing testament to their resilience and unwavering determination. Though the journey was far from over, they were ready to face whatever awaited them on its highest floor. Their spirits unyielding, they continued their ascent, eager to prove themselves worthy of the challenges that lay beyond.

Chapter 18

As they pushed open the heavy, metal doors, a rush of anticipation filled the air, revealing a round chamber bathed in an eerie glow. At the far end of the room stood a towering figure, an imposing Minotaur whose sheer presence commanded attention. Standing at an impressive height of 8 feet, the Minotaur's muscular frame rippled with raw power, every sinew and vein pronounced beneath its matted fur.

The Minotaur's head, adorned with a pair of massive bull-like horns, loomed above its broad shoulders, exuding an air of primal ferocity. Its eyes glowed with an otherworldly intensity, betraying an ancient wisdom hidden within the depths of its gaze. The snarl that etched across its face revealed jagged rows of razor-sharp teeth, evidence of its insatiable appetite for battle.

Clad in battle-worn armor, the Minotaur's form was a testament to its prowess in combat. Its massive hands gripped a colossal battle ax, its blade etched with runes that pulsed with a foreboding energy. Each swing of the weapon threatened to cleave through the very fabric of reality, leaving destruction in its wake.

The chamber itself was a testament to the Minotaur's might. The walls, adorned with intricately carved reliefs depicting epic battles and mythical creatures, exuded an aura of ancient power. Beams of ethereal light pierced through small, stained-glass windows, casting vibrant hues upon the scene as if the very essence of magic and legend converged within this sacred space.

Aurora's heart raced as she and Brynn exchanged a resolute glance. They knew that this encounter would test every ounce of their skill and strength. The Minotaur's presence alone exuded an overwhelming aura of danger and challenge, reminding them of the countless battles they had faced throughout their journey within the tower.

As they stepped forward, their footsteps echoed through the chamber, resounding like a battle cry. The Minotaur's eyes locked onto them, its stance unwavering, a silent invitation to engage in an epic clash of blades and wills. Aurora and Brynn tightened their grip on their weapons, their resolve unshaken, ready to face this formidable foe.

With a surge of adrenaline, Aurora lunged forward, her sword slashing through the air with precision and grace. Brynn followed suit, his ax swinging in powerful arcs, its momentum carrying the weight of their shared determination. The clash of steel reverberated through the chamber, a symphony of battle that echoed the struggle between mortal limits and the indomitable spirit.

The Minotaur responded with primal fury, its movements fluid yet calculated, each swing of its mighty ax a testament to its fearsome strength. Its hooves pounded against the stone floor, sending shockwaves through the chamber as it closed the distance, horns lowered in a display of sheer aggression.

Aurora and Brynn danced with the Minotaur, their every move a testament to their years of training and unyielding camaraderie. They weaved through the chamber, dodging the Minotaur's bone-shattering strikes, retaliating with their deft maneuvers and calculated strikes.

The battle raged on, an intricate dance of skill and survival. Each clash of weapons filled the chamber with a symphony of metallic echoes, the rhythm of their battle resonating with the very heartbeat of the tower itself. Their collective strength, honed through countless trials, pushed them beyond their perceived limits, fueling their determination to emerge victorious.

Time seemed to slow as Aurora, her senses heightened by the urgency of the situation, saw the impending danger. With a surge of adrenaline and unwavering determination, she threw herself between Brynn and the Minotaur's deadly blow. The clash of steel against steel resounded through the chamber as Aurora's blade intercepted the devastating strike, sparing Brynn from certain doom.

Aurora's muscles strained under the force of the impact, her entire being dedicated to protecting her companion. The weight of the Minotaur's blow threatened to overpower her, but fueled by a combination of love, loyalty, and sheer willpower, she held her ground. Every fiber of her being screamed with the intensity of the moment, a testament to her unwavering resolve.

Brynn, startled by Aurora's selfless act, regained his senses just in time to witness her act of sacrifice. A profound sense of gratitude and admiration swelled within him, igniting a newfound determination to fight alongside her, to ensure her sacrifice would not be in vain.

With renewed vigor, Brynn launched herself back into the fray, his battle cries harmonizing with Aurora's as they fought in perfect synchrony. Their movements became a seamless dance of trust and instinct, each anticipating the other's needs, and supporting and protecting one another in the midst of the chaos.

The Minotaur, enraged by its failed strike, redoubled its efforts, launching a relentless assault against the duo. Its monstrous strength and ferocity tested their resilience, pushing them to the brink of exhaustion. But fueled by a shared purpose and an unbreakable bond, Aurora and Brynn refused to yield.

As sweat trickled down their brows and exhaustion threatened to claim their bodies, Aurora and Brynn drew upon the reserves of their willpower. They fought with unwavering focus, their every movement an embodiment of the indomitable spirit that burned within them. With every strike, they chipped away at the Minotaur's defenses, their relentless assault slowly wearing down the formidable adversary.

Time seemed to blur as the battle raged on, the minutes stretching into eternity. The chamber bore witness to their unyielding resolve, each clash and parry etching a testament to their unwavering determination. Despite the weight of fatigue settling upon their shoulders, Aurora and Brynn pressed forward, their belief in their shared purpose unshaken.

And then, with a final, thunderous strike, the Minotaur's resistance crumbled, its formidable form crashing to the ground. The chamber fell silent, the echoes of battle dissipating into the air. Aurora and Brynn stood victorious, their breaths ragged but triumphant, their blades stained with the blood of their fallen foe. They gained 400xp, but it wasn't without a loss. Aurora was very low on health and Brynn almost died. This tower might be what sends them home in the tournament.

As they caught their breath, a sense of accomplishment and relief washed over them. They had overcome yet another arduous trial within the tower, pushing themselves to the very limits of their abilities. But they knew that this victory was merely another step in their journey, as the tower still held untold challenges awaiting their arrival.

With their heads held high and their spirits bolstered by their recent triumph, Aurora and Brynn steeled themselves for what lay ahead. The tower, unforgiving and relentless, awaited their continued ascent, promising even greater tests of strength, wit, and endurance. And together, they were ready to face whatever

trials awaited them, determined to conquer the Tower of Trials and claim its legendary rewards.
As the adrenaline from their battle with the Minotaur began to subside, Aurora's focus shifted to the well-being of both herself and Brynn. The exertion had taken a toll on their health, and their dwindling energy reserves signaled the need for respite. With a calm and determined demeanor, Aurora channeled her healing abilities, her hands emitting a gentle glow as she tended to their wounds. The minor healing spells worked their magic, gradually replenishing their health points and soothing their aching bodies.

However, Aurora knew that merely relying on her healing prowess would not be enough to sustain them in the arduous trials that lay ahead. They required nourishment and sustenance to restore their energy levels fully. Searching through their provisions, they found dried meats and hard bread, the last remnants of their meager supplies. Though meager, these rations would serve as their lifeline, providing the necessary sustenance to revitalize their weary bodies.

As they consumed the dried meat and hard bread, the taste may have been far from gourmet, but each bite was savored, knowing that it would replenish their strength. The morsels they consumed were not only physical sustenance but also a symbol of their resilience and determination to push forward.

Yet, a nagging thought crept into their minds. The slain Minotaur's massive form lay before them, an untapped source of potential sustenance. If only they had the means to start a fire, they could utilize its meat for a more substantial and satisfying meal. However, they lacked the necessary wood to ignite a flame within the tower's confines, leaving their desire for a hot meal unfulfilled.

Acknowledging their need for rest and recognizing the importance of conserving their energy, Aurora and Brynn settled into a quiet corner of the room. Finding a comfortable spot, they eased their bodies onto the cold stone floor, using their equipment as makeshift pillows. Their eyes, heavy with exhaustion, closed as they sought solace in the realm of sleep.

Hours passed as they slumbered, their bodies recharging and recuperating from the strenuous trials they had endured thus far. The tranquil silence enveloped them, broken only by the soft sounds of their steady breathing. Within the depths of their dreams, their minds wandered through fragmented memories and visions of the tower's challenges yet to come.

As the last vestiges of fatigue gradually dissipated, Aurora and Brynn stirred awake, their bodies refreshed and their minds reinvigorated. The brief respite had granted them a renewed sense of determination, a clear focus on the path that lay ahead. They rose from their resting place, ready to face whatever obstacles awaited them within the Tower of Trials.

With their health points replenished, their bodies nourished, and their spirits rekindled, Aurora and Brynn stood side by side, their bond stronger than ever. The tower's challenges had tested them, but they had emerged resilient, ready to conquer each trial that awaited them. They ventured forth, their steps echoing through the chamber, as they continued their ascent through the enigmatic and treacherous labyrinth of the Tower of Trials.

With a renewed sense of purpose, Aurora and Brynn pushed open the heavy door that led them to the next stage of their journey. The room beyond was dimly lit, casting eerie shadows along the stone walls. Their footsteps echoed through the chamber as they ascended the left set of stairs, each step bringing them closer to the unknown challenges that lay ahead.

As they climbed, the air grew colder, sending a shiver down their spines. The winding staircase seemed to stretch on indefinitely, making it difficult to gauge just how far they had ascended. Yet, their determination remained unwavering, fueling their resolve to overcome whatever obstacles awaited them.

The stone steps beneath their boots were worn and weathered, evidence of countless adventurers who had ventured through this tower before them. The ancient stones seemed to whisper tales of triumph and defeat, their echoes intertwining with the whispers of unseen specters that lingered in the shadows.

Reaching the top of the staircase, they emerged into another chamber, bathed in an ethereal glow. The room was vast, its ceiling soaring high above them, adorned with intricate carvings depicting long-forgotten legends and mythical creatures. The air crackled with arcane energy, and the faint scent of magic permeated the space.

At the far end of the chamber, two imposing doors stood as gateways to the next phase of their trial. One door was adorned with intricate engravings of celestial beings, while the other bore symbols of fiery dragons. Each door emanated an aura of mystery and danger, presenting Aurora and Brynn with a pivotal decision.

They exchanged a knowing glance, their unspoken communication conveying a mutual understanding. They had come too far to turn back now. Resolute in their choice, they approached the door marked with celestial engravings. Its surface was cool to the touch, adorned with a faint glow that danced along the intricate patterns.

With a creak, the door swung open, revealing a passage that seemed to stretch into infinity. The path ahead was shrouded in darkness, concealing both treacherous pitfalls and untold treasures. Undeterred, Aurora and Brynn stepped forward, their footsteps echoing with each stride.

As they ventured deeper into the unknown, the air grew thick with anticipation. Each passing moment brought a heightened sense of awareness, their senses attuned to the slightest shift in the environment. They traversed through winding corridors, their path illuminated by sporadic torches flickering in the gloom.

The silence was broken only by the distant sound of dripping water and the occasional flutter of wings from unseen creatures skittering across the ceiling. Shadows danced along the walls, their movements seeming to mock their progress. But Aurora and Brynn pressed on, their determination unyielding.

With each step, the trials grew more challenging, pushing their physical and mental limits to the brink. They encountered rooms filled with ancient puzzles and mechanisms, their intricate designs requiring wit and intuition to unravel. They faced fearsome guardians, wielding weapons honed by centuries of battle.

In one harrowing moment, Brynn found herself on the brink of collapse, a formidable opponent poised to deliver a fatal blow. But in a display of unwavering loyalty, Aurora, her eyes ablaze with determination, rushed to his aid. With a swift and precise strike, she incapacitated their adversary, her timely intervention saving Brynn from certain doom.

Their bond forged through countless battles, Aurora and Brynn fought side by side, their strengths complementing each other flawlessly. They had become a force to be reckoned with, their synergy evident in the fluidity of their movements and the precision of their attacks.

As they pressed onward, the Tower of Trials revealed its secrets gradually, rewarding their resilience with glimpses of ancient knowledge and coveted artifacts. Yet, each victory only served as a prelude to the next challenge, as the tower's depths seemed to stretch into eternity.

Undeterred by the trials that tested their resolve, Aurora and Brynn forged ahead, driven by a shared purpose and an unyielding spirit. They were determined to overcome every obstacle, to reach the pinnacle of the tower and claim the glory that awaited them. With each step, the legends of their journey grew, etching their names into the annals of the Tower of Trials.

Just as they were about to exit the room, their hopes of progress were dashed when the heavy door slammed shut with a resounding thud. The suddenness of the noise reverberated through the chamber, signaling the commencement of a new trial that would test their mettle like never before.

A deafening roar erupted, echoing within the confined space as a monstrous silhouette descended from above. The ground quaked beneath the weight of the colossal presence that now stood before them. It was a lesser dragon, its immense form casting an ominous shadow over Aurora and Brynn.
"Now this will be a challenge," said Aurora, looking at Brynn with a surprised look on his face, reading her sword.

The lesser dragon loomed above them, its massive frame reaching a towering height of fifteen feet. Its wings, spanning an impressive twenty feet, were poised for flight, their membranous expanse lined with formidable spines. The dragon's body was encased in shimmering, crimson scales that glistened with an otherworldly radiance as if they were forged from the molten fire itself.

The dragon's eyes glowed with an intense, predatory gaze, fixated on its prey with unwavering focus. Its snout was adorned with rows of razor-sharp teeth, each gleaming ominously in the dim light. Every breath it took seemed to send a wave of heat rippling through the chamber, hinting at the infernal power contained within its mighty lungs.

As the battle ensued, Aurora and Brynn found themselves locked in a perilous dance with the fearsome beast. Their swords clashed against the dragon's impenetrable scales, their strikes aimed at vulnerable spots between armored plates. Each swing of their blades was met with a retaliatory swipe of the dragon's massive claws, threatening to rend flesh and bone.

The air was thick with tension, filled with the sounds of steel clashing against scales and the thunderous beat of the dragon's wings. Aurora's agility and precision allowed her to evade the dragon's ferocious attacks, while Brynn's strength and endurance provided a sturdy defense against the relentless onslaught.

Yet, despite their valiant efforts, the dragon's sheer power and relentless assault began to take its toll. Brynn, battered and weary, found herself momentarily vulnerable. In a swift and calculated motion, the dragon seized the opportunity, jaws gaping wide as it engulfed Brynn whole, his form disappearing into the darkness of its cavernous maw.

Aurora's heart sank as she witnessed her companion's plight, a surge of determination and fury coursing through her veins. With renewed fervor, she channeled her inner strength, refusing to succumb to despair. She focused her energy, directing it towards a desperate strategy to save Brynn from the belly of the beast.

Summoning every ounce of her magical prowess, Aurora unleashed a torrent of fire and lightning, striking the dragon's vulnerable underbelly. The dragon writhed in agony, its fiery breath faltering as it released Brynn from its clutches. With a violent burst, Brynn emerged from the dragon's stomach, battered but alive, his determination shining in his eyes.

Together, Aurora and Brynn rallied, their shared resolve stronger than ever. They fought as one, exploiting the dragon's momentary weakness, striking with precision and unwavering resolve. Blow after blow, they relentlessly assaulted the beast, their determination fueling every swing of their blades.

As the battle raged on, the once-mighty dragon's strength waned, its movements growing sluggish and labored. Sensing the end was near, Aurora and Brynn unleashed a final, coordinated assault. With a resounding roar, the dragon succumbed to its wounds, massive from crashing to the ground in a storm of dust and debris.

Breathing heavily, their bodies bruised and bloodied, Aurora and Brynn stood victorious. They gained 1000xp from slaying the dragon. A box popped up "Ability Gained - Dragon Slayer - 10% extra damage against dragons." Another box popped with a cheerful charm "Level up - Level 6."

The room was filled with a tense silence, broken only by the fading echoes of their battle. They shared a moment of relief, knowing they had triumphed over an adversary that seemed insurmountable.

With their victory secured, Aurora and Brynn collected their thoughts and readied themselves for the next stage of their arduous journey. Brynn sat against the dragon, all sticky and covered in stomach acid.
"I don't know about you, but that was the worst thing I ever experienced in my life. Never again" said Brynn to Aurora as she sat next to her.
"I thought I lost you there. Almost gave up too" said Aurora, having a heartfelt moment with Brynn sitting next to her.
"These trials are going to get us killed. I just almost died. I know it wasn't for real, but it felt so real that everything flashed before my eyes" said Brynn, scared to continue the tower of trials.

"We've already come this far and we managed to kill a lesser dragon. How could it get any worse" said Aurora, trying to reassure Brynn.
"Ya, we've come this far, we have to be at the end," said Brynn standing up.
"We have to continue"
"That's the spirit," said Aurora with excitement, standing up next to Brynn.

The trials of the Tower of Trials were far from over, but with each triumph, their bond grew stronger, and their determination burned brighter. They were ready to face whatever lay ahead, prepared to conquer the challenges that awaited them.

As the door creaked open, revealing another set of stairs, Aurora and Brynn ascended, their anticipation mounting with each step. They were determined to conquer the Tower of Trials, their hearts brimming with the resilience of seasoned warriors. They had faced numerous challenges and triumphed against formidable foes, but the tower seemed determined to push them further, testing the limits of their strength and courage.

This time, they chose the left path, venturing through the door into a vast chamber that stretched out before them. The room was bathed in a dim, flickering light, casting elongated shadows that danced across the stone walls. In the distance, they spotted three doors, an air of mystery hanging heavily in the space between them.

Moments ticked by, each second laden with anticipation, until the doors swung open, revealing their adversaries. Three towering figures emerged from the darkness, their immense frames casting an imposing presence. It was clear that among them was a hulking cave troll, its gnarled skin and brutish features a testament to its raw power.

Aurora's gaze fixed upon the troll, a glimmer of concern flickering in her eyes. She knew firsthand the devastating strength possessed by these creatures, their ability to rend stone and crush bone with ease. Her instincts told her that this battle would be their most formidable yet.

"Ah, they have a troll," she voiced her observation, her voice betraying a hint of apprehension. Brynn tightened her grip on her weapon, the weight of his determination palpable.

The chamber seemed to shrink in the face of the trolls' looming presence, their heavy footsteps resonating through the room. The clash of metal against stone reverberated, echoing their intent to vanquish their foes. The battle had begun.

Aurora and Brynn fought side by side, their synergy and trust forged through countless trials. Their blades sliced through the air with precision, each strike aiming for vulnerable points on the trolls' thick hides. The scent of battle filled their nostrils as adrenaline coursed through their veins.

The skirmish raged on, the clash of steel against flesh and the grunts of exertion creating a symphony of combat. The trolls fought with primal fury, their massive fists delivering bone-crushing blows that threatened to shatter their resolve.

As the battle reached its climax, only one troll remained standing, its crimson eyes glinting with an unhinged ferocity. Sensing victory within reach, Aurora mustered her remaining strength, her determination igniting like a blazing fire within her.

However, in a cruel twist of fate, the troll lunged forward, its massive hands seizing Aurora in a vice-like grip. She struggled against its relentless grasp, her muscles straining against the overwhelming force. The troll swung her through the air with brutal force, like a ragdoll at the mercy of a monstrous puppeteer.

The room seemed to spin as Aurora's body collided against the unyielding stone wall, the impact sending shockwaves of pain coursing through her. Agony enveloped her senses as she felt her health points dwindling, a stark reminder of her vulnerability in the face of such overpowering might.

Brynn's heart pounded in his chest as he witnessed the brutality inflicted upon his companion. Rage mingled with concern, fueling his every move as he unleashed a torrent of strikes upon the remaining troll. Each blow was fueled by a burning desire to avenge Aurora's suffering.

With a final, thunderous strike, Brynn incapacitated the troll, causing it to collapse to the ground, defeated. His breaths came in ragged gasps as he rushed to Aurora's side, his hands trembling with a mixture of fear and determination.

Brynn's heart pounded in his chest as he rushed to Aurora's side, a surge of panic and desperation gripping his every fiber. His eyes widened in disbelief and anguish as he beheld the sight before him—the lifeblood of his dearest friend seeping through her wounds, each drops a cruel reminder of the fragility of their existence in this treacherous tower.

Time seemed to slow as Brynn knelt beside Aurora, his hands trembling with a mix of fear and determination. He had faced countless adversaries, and battled formidable creatures, but none had prepared him for this heart-wrenching moment, where the life of someone he cherished hung in the balance.

With a sense of urgency and a single-minded focus, Brynn set to work. He tore a piece of fabric from his tattered cloak, pressing it against Aurora's wound, desperate to stem the flow of crimson. The air was thick with tension as he applied pressure, his hands slick with both his perspiration and the blood of his companion.

Aurora though weakened and in pain, remained resilient, her eyes reflecting a determination that matched Brynn's own. She fought against the encroaching darkness, summoning the last vestiges of her magical prowess to aid in her healing. Waves of ethereal energy emanated from her trembling hands, swirling around her wounded body in a delicate dance.

Brynn watched with bated breath, his heart aching with a mixture of hope and despair. His mind raced, conjuring memories of their shared adventures, the laughter, and the camaraderie they had forged. How could it all be jeopardized by a single, fateful encounter?

As Aurora's healing magic intermingled with Brynn's desperate efforts, a flicker of vitality returned to her pale features. A glimmer of hope pierced the gloom that threatened to envelop them both. Yet, the battle was far from over. The room seemed to close in around them, the air heavy with an oppressive sadness that mirrored their precarious situation.

Minutes stretched into eternity as Brynn continued to tend to Aurora's wounds, his touch gentle yet urgent. Every movement was laced with profound sorrow as if he were trying to convey through his touch the depth of his love and friendship for her. The weight of the world rested upon his shoulders as he prayed for her survival.

In the stillness of the room, the silence was shattered by the rhythmic thump of their racing hearts. Each passing moment felt like an eternity as if time itself had conspired to prolong their suffering. Brynn dared not imagine a world without

Aurora, their destinies entwined like threads in the tapestry of their shared adventures.

The room seemed to hold its breath, its walls witnessing the raw intensity of Brynn's desperate struggle to save his beloved friend. Every passing second felt like a lifetime, and the room became a vessel for their collective anguish.

Finally, as the last vestiges of hope threatened to slip away, Aurora's eyelids fluttered open, her gaze locking with Brynn's. In that fleeting moment, a multitude of emotions passed between them—an unspoken gratitude for Brynn's unwavering devotion, and a silent promise to face whatever lay ahead, hand in hand.

Though the battle was not yet won, a sliver of relief washed over Brynn's weary soul. He knew that their journey was far from over and that more trials awaited them within the tower's depths. But at that moment, as the weight of their emotions hung heavy in the air, they found solace in the strength of their bond—a bond forged in blood, tears, and unwavering loyalty.
"Thanks, Brynn for caring so much. Helping me out" said Aurora slowly catching her breath.
"You almost died this time. We need to stop before you're out of the tournament" said Brynn, concerned for her, kneeling by Aurora.
"We have come this far, I'm not giving up now," said Aurora slowly, determined to finish the tower of trials.

"Well, let's keep on going then," said Brynn, unsure of how things will turn out.

Together, Aurora and Brynn would face the challenges that lay ahead, their spirits intertwined in a dance of resilience and determination. For as long as they drew breath, they would fight side by side, their friendship defying the cruel whims of fate, their hearts beating as one.

They headed through the door to another set of stairs. They headed up the right side, headed to a door to the unknown. Through the door lay a large open chamber just like the last. One single door on the far side of the room. A shadowy man in a black clock, holding a staff, stood there.

Brynn and Aurora stood at the precipice of their exhaustion, their bodies weary and their spirits tested. The daunting presence of the necromancer loomed before them, his dark intentions and malevolent power palpable in the air. The weight of their journey bore down upon them, threatening to crush their hopes and dreams of triumph.

Brynn's voice trembled with a mix of exhaustion and determination as she contemplated the daunting task that lay ahead. Doubt gnawed at the edges of her resolve, whispering in her ear the tempting allure of surrender. But Brynn's unwavering faith in their shared purpose served as a beacon of strength, urging her to press on.

"We have come too far to turn back now," Aurora's voice resounded with unwavering conviction. "This tower has tested us at every step, but we have overcome every challenge together. Our journey doesn't end here; it culminates in this final confrontation."

Aurora allowed Brynn's words to seep into her weary bones, reigniting a spark of determination within her. She closed her eyes, drawing upon the reserves of her strength, both physical and mental. The weight of the world seemed to settle upon her shoulders, but she refused to buckle under its crushing force.

Hours passed as Aurora reclined against the cold stone wall, her eyes closed, her body replenishing its energy reserves. The wounds that marred her once-vibrant form slowly began to heal, the magic within her knitting her torn flesh back together. The rejuvenating embrace of rest granted her a precious reprieve, but time was of the essence, and the necromancer's sinister presence beckoned them forward.

Finally, with newfound vitality coursing through her veins, Aurora rose to her feet, her once-fatigued limbs now steady and resolved. The glint of determination gleamed in her eyes as she surveyed the room, her gaze fixated on the door that beckoned them forward.

Chapter 19

As her fingers brushed against the cold metal surface of the door, a shiver ran down Aurora's spine. The foreboding atmosphere within the dimly lit room enveloped her senses, the dense fog clinging to her skin like an ethereal veil. Shadows danced and writhed as if concealing the secrets of the chamber.

Suddenly, a voice, dripping with malevolence, pierced the silence, sending a chill down Aurora's spine. The necromancer emerged from the shadows, his presence cloaked in darkness and menace. His eyes glowed with an unholy light as he revealed his intentions—to end their journey, to snuff out their flame of hope.

Brynn's voice rang out, undeterred by the necromancer's ominous pronouncement. "Who are you to stand in our way? We have faced every trial this tower has thrown at us, and we will not falter now."

A smirk played upon the necromancer's lips as he raised his hand, commanding the very essence of death to do his bidding. From the bowels of the room, the ground beneath them erupted, and skeletal figures emerged, their hollow eye sockets fixed upon Brynn and Aurora.

Fifteen skeletal warriors, stripped of their humanity, stood ready to obey the necromancer's every command. The chill of despair settled upon the heroes' hearts as they realized the magnitude of the battle before them. Each bone rattled with malevolent energy, threatening to crush their spirits.

But Brynn and Aurora, bonded by friendship and purpose, refused to be overwhelmed by the horde of undead. They locked eyes, their unspoken vow echoing between them. With weapons at the ready, they steeled themselves for the fight ahead, their minds focused, and their determination unyielding.

The clash of steel against bone reverberated through the room as the battle erupted in a cacophony of desperate cries and resolute determination. Brynn's blade danced with calculated precision, deflecting the skeletal onslaught, while Aurora, with her restored vitality, weaved intricate spells, unleashing bursts of radiant energy that obliterated their undead adversaries.

The battle raged on, and each swing of their weapons met with an unholy resistance. The skeletal warriors, driven by their master's dark will, fought with unrelenting ferocity. But Brynn and Aurora, fueled by their shared bond and indomitable spirit, refused to yield. They fought as if their very existence depended on it, their every strike and parry a testament to their unwavering resolve.

As time stretched on, weariness crept back into their weary bodies, threatening to undermine their efforts. Aurora's movements grew sluggish, her magical prowess waning, while Brynn's muscles screamed in protest with each swing of her blade. Yet, even in the face of exhaustion, their determination burned bright, refusing to be extinguished.

With each fallen skeletal warrior, the room seemed to shrink, their numbers dwindling, until only one remained—a towering skeletal figure, imbued with the necromancer's darkest magic. Its bony fingers clenched into a fist, and with a surge of unholy power, it lunged toward Aurora, it's intent clear: to snuff out the light that still flickered within her.

In a moment of brutal force, the skeletal creature seized Aurora, its cold grip constricting her fragile form. The air escaped her lungs in a gasp of pain as she was flung against the unforgiving stone wall. Blood trickled from her wounds, staining the ground beneath her, and her health points dwindled perilously.

Brynn's heart twisted with anguish at the sight of her friend's vulnerability. Every fiber of her being screamed to rush to Aurora's aid, to strike down the skeletal abomination that threatened to consume her. Her muscles tensed, her grip on her weapon tightened, but a flicker of hesitation held her back.

Aurora's eyes, though clouded with pain, met Brynn's, conveying a silent plea for her to continue the fight. Through the agony and despair, a glimmer of determination still burned within her, a testament to her unyielding spirit. She mouthed the words, "Don't give up."

The weight of the moment bore down upon Brynn, a torrent of conflicting emotions raging within her. Her fists clenched, her jaw set in determination, she made a vow—a vow to protect her friend, to triumph against all odds.

With a battle cry that echoed through the chamber, Brynn unleashed her fury upon the skeletal monstrosity. Her strikes were fueled by a ferocity born of love and desperation. Blow after blow rained down upon the skeletal creature, until finally, with a resounding crash, it crumbled to the ground, reduced to a lifeless pile of bones. With each skeleton they killed, they gained 40xp.

Silence settled over the room, broken only by the labored breaths of the victorious heroes. Aurora, bloodied and bruised, struggled to rise from the cold stone floor. Brynn rushed to her side, offering a steady hand, their fingers intertwining in a gesture of unspoken solidarity.

"You did it," Brynn whispered, her voice filled with a mixture of relief and admiration. "You faced death itself and emerged victorious."

Aurora's lips curved into a weary but triumphant smile. "We did it," she replied, her voice laced with a quiet strength. "Together, we conquered the necromancer and his vile minions."

Their eyes met a silent exchange of gratitude and unspoken words passing between them. They knew that this battle was but one chapter in their arduous journey, but with their bond unbroken and their spirits unyielding, they were ready to face whatever lay ahead.

As the heavy door swung open, it revealed a grand sight that took their breath away. The room stretched out before them, adorned with intricate details and opulent furnishings. Bathed in the ethereal glow of the stained glass windows lining the walls, the chamber seemed to come alive with vibrant hues that danced across the polished marble floor.

At the center of the room, upon a raised dais, sat a magnificent golden throne, its craftsmanship exuding an aura of timeless elegance. The throne was embellished with delicate engravings, depicting mythical creatures and arcane symbols that shimmered in the soft light. Embedded within its structure were precious gems of various colors, their facets catching the light and scattering dazzling reflections across the room.

Seated upon this regal seat was an elderly sorcerer, his visage weathered by time and wisdom. His long, flowing robes, adorned with intricate patterns and symbols of power, cascaded around him, accentuating his aura of authority. His eyes, though aged, sparkled with keen intelligence and a deep well of knowledge that seemed to transcend mortal understanding.

Before the sorcerer, resting on a gleaming pedestal, was a treasure chest of exquisite craftsmanship. Its wood, polished to a lustrous sheen, revealed intricate carvings of mythical creatures and epic battles. The chest itself was bound with bands of pure silver, adorned with precious gemstones that glimmered with a hypnotic allure. It stood as a testament to the trials and tribulations endured by those who had come before, an embodiment of their quest's ultimate reward.

The room itself was a marvel to behold. The towering stained glass windows depicted scenes of ancient legends and heroic feats, their vibrant colors casting ethereal shadows upon the chamber's vast expanse. Elaborate tapestries adorned the walls, woven with threads of gold and silver, depicting the history and mythos of the wizard's Tower of Trials.

As Aurora and Brynn approached the sorcerer, a hushed reverence fell upon them. They felt the weight of their journey, the culmination of their efforts, as they stood before this venerable figure. The sorcerer's gaze met theirs, his eyes shimmering with a mixture of wisdom, pride, and perhaps a touch of sorrow.

"Welcome, brave adventurers," the sorcerer spoke, his voice resonating with a timbre that commanded attention.
"You have overcome the trials and tribulations that few have faced. You have proven yourselves worthy of the treasures that await."

Aurora's heart raced with anticipation as she exchanged glances with Brynn. This was the moment they had been striving for, the culmination of their arduous journey. They approached the treasure chest, their hands trembling with a mix of excitement and trepidation.

As they lifted the lid, a soft glow spilled forth, illuminating their faces with a warm radiance. The treasure within glittered and shimmered, a dazzling array of ancient artifacts, enchanted weapons, and untold riches. It was a sight that would have made the most seasoned adventurers weak at the knees.

But amidst the allure of the treasures, Aurora's gaze returned to the sorcerer, his expression both somber and proud. She could sense that there was more to this encounter than mere riches and rewards. There was a depth of knowledge and understanding that he possessed, and she yearned to learn from him.

The sorcerer nodded as if acknowledging their unspoken questions. "You have shown great bravery and resilience," he said, his voice carrying a note of solemnity. "But remember, true power lies not in the treasures you acquire, but in the wisdom and compassion you cultivate on your journey."

Aurora and Brynn exchanged a knowing look, their hearts filled with a newfound sense of purpose. They had braved the trials, fought countless foes, and now stood on the threshold of their destiny. The journey had changed them and molded them into something greater than they were before.

With a renewed determination, they bowed before the sorcerer, their voices filled with gratitude and reverence.
"Thank you, wise one, for guiding us on this path. We shall carry your teachings with us as we venture forth, forever grateful for the lessons learned within these hallowed walls."

And as they turned to depart, their hearts brimming with newfound knowledge and an unwavering spirit, they knew that the end of the Tower of Trials was only the beginning of their greater purpose. The echoes of their footsteps reverberated through the chamber, carrying with them the legacy of their triumphs and the promise of a future filled with adventure and wonder.

As Aurora and Brynn approached the treasure chest, their anticipation grew, and their eyes fixated on the array of enchantments that lay within. Carefully lifting the lid, they beheld a treasure trove of extraordinary weapons, each radiating its unique aura.

Aurora's heart skipped a beat as her gaze fell upon a sleek and elegant longbow. Crafted from the finest materials and imbued with ancient magic, this bow possessed an extraordinary ability. Its arrows grew more deadly the further they traveled, ensuring that her enemies would be struck down from afar with pinpoint accuracy. The weapon resonated with her affinity for precision and strategy, making it a perfect match for her archery skills.

Beside her, Brynn's eyes widened in awe as she beheld a massive battle-ax unlike any she had ever seen. The ax's weight defied logic, for despite its formidable size, it felt surprisingly light and nimble in her grasp. Its razor-sharp blade gleamed with an otherworldly luster, promising devastating strikes that would cleave through the toughest of armor. Brynn could feel the raw power surging through her veins as she envisioned the ax's potential to unleash swift and devastating blows upon her adversaries.

In addition to their newfound weapons, a sense of fortune smiled upon them as they discovered a pouch filled with 200 gold coins and a scroll inscribed with ancient text promising a wealth of knowledge and experience. Their hearts leaped with excitement at the prospect of further growth and mastery.

With the spoils of their triumph in hand, Aurora and Brynn exchanged glances, their eyes shining with a shared understanding. This was not merely about personal gain or self-indulgence; it was about embracing their roles as champions of justice and defenders of the innocent. The sorcerer's words echoed in their minds, a gentle reminder of the weighty responsibility that now rested upon their shoulders.

"Now, take all that you have learned within these hallowed walls and wield it for the greater good," the sorcerer's voice resonated, infused with a blend of wisdom and urgency. "The world cries out for heroes like you, those who can vanquish darkness and restore hope. Go forth and save the innocent, for they depend on your bravery."

Their resolve hardened, Aurora and Brynn nodded in unison, accepting their charge with unwavering determination. Their spirits ignited with purpose, fueled by the realization that their journey had only just begun. As if responding to their intentions, the sorcerer summoned forth his mystical powers, weaving a tapestry of arcane energies that enveloped the adventurers.

In an instant, they found themselves transported back to the village, their surroundings shifting from the grandeur of the tower to the familiarity of their humble origins. Though physically back where their journey had begun, they were forever changed, carrying with them the gifts of knowledge, power, and purpose.

As they emerged from the teleportation, the village's denizens looked upon them with awe and gratitude. The sorcerer's presence still lingered in their hearts, his teachings etched in their minds. Aurora and Brynn exchanged a knowing smile, ready to face the challenges ahead and embark on a new chapter of their quest. With the enchanted weapons at their side, gold in their pouches, and the wisdom of the sorcerer guiding their steps, they were now prepared to venture forth to the Grand City of the Pixies, where new adventures and untold wonders awaited.

Under the cover of night, Aurora and Brynn made their way to the familiar inn, seeking respite and a chance to purchase the horses that would carry them to the grand city of the Pixies. The warm glow of the inn's windows beckoned them, promising comfort and a momentary escape from the trials they had faced.

As they stepped through the doorway, the innkeeper, a friendly and slightly grizzled man, greeted them with a mix of surprise and relief.
"Well, well, if it isn't the daring adventurers! I must admit, I thought the wild might have claimed you both. Glad to see you're still among the living," he remarked, his voice filled with a hint of jest.

Aurora chuckled, her fatigue momentarily lifted by the innkeeper's banter.
"We've had our fair share of close calls, but we managed to persevere. It's not so easy to get rid of us," she replied, her tone brimming with a sense of pride and accomplishment.

With their goal in mind, Brynn approached the counter, laying down the agreed-upon sum for the horses. However, the innkeeper surprised them by mentioning a price increase.

"Actually, it's 15 gold each now," he stated matter-of-factly, his shoulders shrugging in a gesture of feigned helplessness.

Brynn glanced at Aurora, a silent exchange passing between them, before reluctantly adding the additional gold to the counter.
"Alright, we'll pay the extra. We understand you need to stay competitive," she conceded, albeit with a hint of mild annoyance.

Curiosity gleamed in the innkeeper's eyes as he counted the gold.
"If you don't mind me asking, where did you manage to amass such a fortune in such a short time?" he inquired, genuine interest lacing his words.

Aurora's smile widened, a spark of excitement evident in her eyes.
"We stumbled upon an advertisement for the wizard tower challenge. Intrigued, we decided to venture forth and test our mettle. Turns out, we were up against dragons, trolls, necromancers, and a whole lot of riddles. It was an incredible challenge, to say the least," she shared, her voice tinged with a mixture of pride and nostalgia.

The innkeeper's eyebrows shot up in astonishment, a mix of admiration and curiosity playing across his features.
"Few dare to enter that tower, and even fewer emerge. You two must make quite a formidable team. What was it like inside?"

he inquired, leaning in slightly, eager to hear tales of their adventures.

Brynn, ever the nonchalant one, shrugged casually.
"Oh, you know, just your typical assortment of mythical creatures and mind-bending puzzles. It kept us on our toes, that's for sure," she replied, downplaying the enormity of their feat.

The innkeeper's eyes widened, captivated by the snippets of their journey they had shared.
"You both are a rare breed indeed. I do not doubt that the grand city of the Pixies will be astounded by your presence. Safe travels, and may your adventures continue to be filled with glory," he said, his voice laced with a mixture of admiration and well-wishes.

With a nod of gratitude, Aurora and Brynn bid the innkeeper farewell, their minds already filled with visions of the grand city and the myriad of adventures that awaited them. They were determined to make the most of their hard-earned horses, embarking on a new chapter of their quest with the spirit of resilience and camaraderie that had carried them through the challenges of the wizard's tower.

Despite the late hour, Aurora and Brynn found themselves in need of a hearty meal, something more substantial than the rations they had subsisted on during their perilous journey.

They made their way to the cozy inn, seeking solace in the warm crackling fire that danced in the hearth.

Seated at a sturdy wooden table, they eagerly awaited their meal, their stomachs growling in anticipation. The innkeeper, ever attentive to the needs of his weary guests, brought forth a platter adorned with steaming dishes, filling the air with an enticing aroma. The main course consisted of succulent roasted venison, expertly seasoned with fragrant herbs and accompanied by a medley of roasted vegetables, still glistening with natural juices. The venison's tender flesh practically melted in their mouths, a testament to the skillful culinary artistry of the inn's kitchen.

As they savored each mouthful, the flavors danced upon their tongues, providing nourishment and a sense of comfort that had been sorely missed. The meal was a welcome respite, providing not only sustenance but also a moment of respite from the trials and tribulations they had faced.

Engrossed in their meal, Aurora and Brynn engaged in conversation, their voices hushed but filled with determination. They discussed their next steps, formulating a plan that involved replenishing their supplies, acquiring the horses they needed, and setting forth on their journey come morning. Despite the urgency of their quest, they couldn't help but acknowledge the allure of the village they had only just arrived in. There was a sense of curiosity, a longing to explore and unravel the mysteries that lay hidden within its streets and alleys.

With their plan in place, they savored the last bites of their meal, the warmth of the fire casting a soft glow upon their faces. Their eyelids grew heavy with fatigue, a testament to the arduous journey they had endured. It was clear that a restful night's sleep was essential for the long road that lay ahead.

Thanking the innkeeper for the satisfying meal and the comforting ambiance of the inn, they bid him farewell, their steps slow and deliberate as they made their way to their designated chambers. The rooms were cozy, adorned with simple but comfortable furnishings, providing a tranquil sanctuary for their weary bodies.

As they settled beneath the covers, their minds teemed with the experiences they had gained, the victories and close calls that had shaped them. The village's whispers and secrets would have to wait, for now, the lure of a well-deserved rest beckoned. With the knowledge that the morning would bring new adventures, they surrendered to the embrace of sleep, knowing that they would awaken refreshed and ready to face the challenges that awaited them on the long and winding road ahead.

As the sun's golden rays began to peek over the horizon on day 10 of their quest, Aurora and Brynn rose from their beds, eager to embark on the next leg of their journey. Having spent two arduous days within the treacherous depths of the wizard tower, they now sought to replenish their supplies and fortify themselves with new armor for the challenges that lay ahead.

With determined strides, they made their way to the bustling market, the air alive with the chatter of vendors and the tantalizing aroma of freshly baked goods. Aurora, valuing agility and flexibility in combat, sought out a set of finely crafted leather armor that would grant her both protection and freedom of movement. The armor bore resemblance to the noble riders of Rohan in the tales of Middle-earth, featuring supple leather adorned with intricate etchings and a sturdy leather helmet that shielded her head without sacrificing visibility or comfort.

Meanwhile, Brynn's attention was drawn to a display of formidable scale mail. The armor's dark hue, reminiscent of the shadows that cloaked them during their encounters, caught her eye. Its design showcased wide, diamond-shaped scales that overlapped, providing both resilience and flexibility in battle. With each movement, the armor seemed to ripple like waves upon a moonlit sea, exuding an air of mystery and strength.

Their armor selections made the duo turned their focus to restocking their provisions. They gathered an ample supply of dried meats, fruits, and hearty bread, enough to sustain them for a fortnight. The thought of replenishing their stores in a distant village spurred their determination, for they knew that with each passing day they drew closer to the climax of the tournament and the fabled Great City of the Pixies.

Before bidding farewell to the market, they sought out a skilled fletcher, where Aurora acquired a quiver of twenty arrows, each meticulously crafted to ensure true flight and deadly accuracy. The arrows, their slender shafts adorned with feather fletching promised to be valuable companions in the battles yet to come.

Finally, their attention turned to the stables, where the sturdy horses they had purchased from the innkeeper awaited. The horses stood strong and proud, their glossy coats reflecting the morning sunlight. Aurora's steed possessed a sleek ebony mane that cascaded down its powerful neck, while Brynn's mount displayed a rich chestnut coat, its muscular frame exuding strength and endurance. The horses were well-trained, their eyes intelligent and their gaits smooth, ready to carry their riders through untamed lands and uncharted territories.

With their supplies secured and their new armor adorning their bodies, Aurora and Brynn mounted their noble steeds. The weight of responsibility and anticipation settled upon their shoulders as they bid farewell to the familiar comforts of the village. The wind whispered promises of new adventures and the lure of the Great City of the Pixies beckoned them forward.

With resolute determination, they set forth on their trusty mounts, their path veiled in mystery yet filled with purpose.

The virtual reality tournament had become their reality, their lives intertwined with the quests and challenges that lay ahead. With hearts aflame and minds sharpened, they rode onward, their spirits unyielding as they ventured toward the grand finale that awaited them on the horizon.

As Aurora and Brynn embarked on their journey, their horses' hooves rhythmically pounding against the earth, they navigated the winding path that encircled the towering mountain before them. The majestic landscape unfolded before their eyes, revealing a tapestry of awe-inspiring sights. Verdant valleys stretched out in undulating waves, adorned with vibrant wildflowers that danced in harmony with the gentle breeze. Majestic waterfalls cascaded down sheer cliffs, their crystalline droplets sparkling in the sunlight, while ancient trees whispered secrets with their rustling leaves.

As they traversed this picturesque terrain, their senses remained heightened, ever watchful for the presence of other players who roamed the vast expanse of the virtual world. The dwindling count, now at 5327, indicated the decreasing number of adventurers who had managed to survive the perils of the game thus far. While the count continued to decline, the magnitude of the game's world posed a challenge in itself, making chance encounters with fellow players increasingly rare and precious.

Aurora, her mind a kaleidoscope of thoughts and emotions, couldn't help but wonder about the fate of James, a fellow player she had hoped to meet within this virtual realm. The mere possibility of joining forces and venturing through the trials together had filled her heart with excitement and anticipation. Yet, as the miles stretched on, their paths had not yet crossed, leaving a tinge of disappointment mingled with lingering hope.

Lost in her reverie, Aurora contemplated the intricate design of the game. Surely the creators had devised a mechanism to adapt and compensate for the diminishing player count. She imagined hidden quests and challenges that would become more elusive and complex, designed to test the mettle of those who dared to continue their journey. The virtual creatures that inhabited this realm were likely attuned to this transformation, their behaviors, and strengths evolving as the player count dwindled. The game world was a living entity, responding to the ebb and flow of the adventurers' progress, shaping itself into a formidable adversary.

But amidst these musings, Aurora's thoughts always circle back to James. She wondered if he had encountered the same trials and tribulations as she had if he too had faced dragons and trolls, riddles, and necromancers. Would their paths intertwine at a critical juncture, uniting their skills and forging an unbreakable bond? The unknowns hung in the air, intertwining with the scent of wildflowers and the gentle melody of birdsong.

With each passing day, as they ventured further into the virtual realm, the camaraderie between Aurora and Brynn deepened. They shared tales of past victories and near-fatal encounters, forging an unspoken trust and synchronicity in battle. Their partnership grew like the ancient trees that stood sentinel in this realm, their roots intertwining, granting strength to weather the storms that lay ahead.

As the sun began its gradual descent, casting golden hues across the horizon, Aurora's gaze shifted from the stunning vistas to the path that lay before her. The game had become her reality, and every twist and turn in this fantastical world held the promise of discovery, triumph, and the potential for a reunion with a fellow adventurer. With hearts filled with determination and a spirit that refused to yield, Aurora and Brynn continued their arduous journey, their eyes firmly fixed on the Grand City of the Pixies, a beacon of hope and the ultimate destination of their virtual odyssey.

As the moon rose high in the inky sky, casting an ethereal glow upon the land, Aurora and Brynn pressed on with unwavering determination. The horses' hooves thundered against the earth, their rhythmic gallop propelling the adventurers forward with an urgency born from their desire to reach the grand city of the Pixies as swiftly as possible. Rest and sustenance became fleeting moments, brief pauses in their relentless pursuit of their goal.

Yet, as the night cloaked the world in its mysterious embrace, a presence began to stir in the shadows. Unseen eyes watched their every move, lurking just beyond the limits of perception. The air grew heavy with an otherworldly aura, and a sense of foreboding crept into the adventurers' hearts.

It was then, in the veil of darkness, that the first signs of their pursuers emerged. A whisper of movement, like a wisp of smoke dancing on the wind, caught their attention. Turning their gaze to the periphery, they beheld the haunting sight of wraiths—ghostly apparitions draped in ebon shrouds. These creatures, neither of the living realm nor the realm of the dead, materialized with eerie grace, their forms shifting and undulating in the moonlight.

Aurora and Brynn recognized the danger that accompanied the presence of these wraiths. Legends whispered tales of their deadly nature, their ability to drain life force and shatter the spirits of those who dared to cross their path. The duo knew that combating these ethereal adversaries head-on was a futile endeavor, for the wraiths' corporeal forms proved impervious to mortal weaponry.

With urgency in their hearts, Aurora and Brynn spurred their steeds onward, urging them to their limits in an attempt to shake off the relentless pursuit. The shadows of the night seemed to writhe and coil as if conspiring against their escape. The wraiths, undeterred by fatigue or fear, matched their every stride, an ever-present reminder of the peril that loomed just behind.

The adventurers relied on the power of light, the flickering flames of their campfire serving as a fragile shield against the encroaching darkness. The wraiths, repelled by the radiance, kept their distance, their malevolent gazes fixated upon their prey, patiently biding their time for a moment of weakness.

With each passing mile, the tension in the air grew palpable, and weariness threatened to seep into Aurora and Brynn's bones. But the fire within their hearts burned brighter, fueled by the determination to overcome this spectral torment. They drew strength from one another, their bond a beacon of resilience amidst the encroaching gloom.

As the night wore on, the adventurers clung to the hope that the first light of dawn would scatter the wraiths, banishing them back to the shadowed realms from whence they came. With every stride, they pushed harder, and their willpower steeled against the encircling darkness.

And then, as if in response to their unwavering resolve, the first gentle tendrils of dawn's embrace began to illuminate the horizon. The pale hues of pink and orange painted the sky, casting a gentle warmth upon the land. The wraiths, sensing their inevitable retreat, receded into the shadows, their ethereal forms dissolving like mist.

Relief washed over Aurora and Brynn, mingling with the exhaustion that clung to their weary bodies. They had survived the harrowing night, their spirits tempered by the encounter with the otherworldly. With renewed determination, they continued their journey, the memory of the wraiths etched into their minds as a testament to the perils that awaited them on this arduous path.

Together, they rode forth, resolved to reach the grand city of the Pixies and face the trials that lay ahead. For even amidst the darkness and the specters that haunted their every step, they knew that their indomitable spirit and unwavering bond would light the way, guiding them toward the culmination of their virtual odyssey.

Chapter 20

As the sun began to rise the next morning, casting its warm golden hues across the land, Aurora and Brynn resumed their journey. Their weary bodies yearned for rest, but the call of adventure pushed them forward. The road stretched endlessly ahead, promising another challenging day of travel. Day 11 of their epic quest had arrived, and Aurora could feel the weight of destiny pressing upon her.

Their path now led them toward a sprawling city, its reputation preceding it. Tales of its grandeur had reached their ears, depicting a metropolis teeming with life and bustling with activity. Aurora couldn't help but feel a mixture of excitement and trepidation. The thought of navigating through crowds of countless players, each with their own goals and ambitions, sent a shiver down her spine. She knew that in such a vast and populous city, she had to remain inconspicuous, avoiding unnecessary attention that could potentially expose her true identity. This realization instilled a sense of caution within her, reminding her to keep her guard up and blend into the background.

But before they reached the towering city's gates, they had the luxury of time. Along the way, they made strategic stops at various villages and settlements, taking advantage of the opportunities to replenish their supplies and engage in a few side quests. The quests not only provided them with valuable experience points to further develop their skills and abilities but also offered glimpses into the intricate tapestry of this fantastical world they found themselves. Each quest brought them closer to uncovering hidden truths and unraveling the mysteries that permeated this realm.

As they traversed through rugged landscapes and picturesque vistas, Aurora couldn't help but marvel at the diverse landscapes that unfolded before her eyes. Rolling hills embraced by blankets of wildflowers, dense forests whispering ancient secrets, and babbling brooks that danced merrily along their path—all served as a reminder of the breathtaking beauty that coexisted alongside the perils of their journey.
"This must be what our world looked like back before the ice age, " said Aurora, thinking of what life would have been like.
"It must have been something magical like this," said Brynn wishing she was born much more earlier than it was.

The days blended into nights, each campfire serving as a flickering beacon of respite amidst the darkness. Aurora and Brynn took solace in these quiet moments, reflecting on the trials they had overcome and the battles they had fought. Their bond grew stronger with each shared hardship, forging a connection that transcended mere companionship.

With every step they took, the grand city loomed closer on the horizon. It's colossal spires and ornate architecture seemed to beckon them forth, promising a convergence of fate and possibilities. Aurora's heart quickened with anticipation, aware that the challenges awaiting her within those bustling streets would test her resolve like never before.

But for now, they pressed on, embracing the adventure that lay ahead. With renewed determination and a glimmer of excitement in their eyes, they continued their journey, knowing that every step brought them closer to the realization of their destiny.

They rode relentlessly throughout the day, their steeds galloping tirelessly beneath them. The passing hours seemed to blur into a seamless tapestry of landscapes and distant horizons. Despite the monotony of the journey, they pressed on, fueled by a shared determination that refused to waver.

As the sun began its descent, casting a warm orange glow upon the world, they made a brief stop to rest and replenish their energy. The quietude of the moment provided a temporary respite from the weariness that clung to their bones. They savored their meager meal, allowing the flavors to revive their spirits, before mounting their horses once again.

Night fell like a dark shroud, enveloping the land in an ethereal stillness. The moon cast an eerie glow upon the winding road, illuminating their path as they rode steadfastly through the darkness. However, their peace was short-lived as a familiar sense of foreboding gripped Aurora's heart.

Out of the depths of the night, the wraiths emerged, their ethereal forms swirling and undulating with otherworldly grace. They seemed drawn to Aurora like moths to a flame, their presence almost palpable. The realization struck her like a thunderbolt, causing her to ride with a mix of fear and anger.

Aurora's voice echoed through the night, piercing the silence as she shared her revelation with Brynn. The words spilled out, laden with frustration and a tinge of despair. It was as if she had stumbled upon the key to a puzzle she never wanted to solve. The darkness that had been steadily growing within her seemed to have become a magnet for these vengeful apparitions.

Brynn listened intently, his eyes narrowing in concern. The gravity of the situation was not lost on him, and a surge of protectiveness welled up within him. He understood that they couldn't afford to ignore this newfound realization. The threat the wraiths posed to Aurora's very existence was too great to be taken lightly.

"Are they trying to harm you?" Brynn asked, his voice laced with worry and determination.

Aurora shook her head, her gaze fixed ahead, focused on the road.
"I don't know, but we shouldn't wait around to find out," she responded, her tone resolute and tinged with a hint of unease. The urgency in her voice underscored the need for immediate

action, for they knew all too well the danger that lurked in the shadows.

Together, they urged their horses forward, their pace quickening as they sought to outdistance the encroaching wraiths. The rhythmic pounding of hooves against the earth resonated in the night, mirroring the cadence of their racing hearts. They rode as if their very lives depended on it, pushing their mounts to their limits in a desperate bid to escape the clutches of the spectral pursuers.

In the face of this new threat, the bond between Aurora and Brynn grew stronger. They relied on one another, their unspoken trust weaving an unbreakable thread that fortified their spirits. Their determination to overcome this ominous darkness that plagued them fueled their relentless pursuit of safety and answers.

As they rode into the unknown, the looming shadows of doubt and uncertainty threatened to consume them. Yet, they remained resolute, their spirits unyielding in the face of adversity. The path ahead was fraught with peril, but they rode on, their hearts aflame with a courage born of necessity.

Little did they know that this encounter with the wraiths would only be the beginning—a prelude to the trials and tribulations that awaited them on their grand quest.

The first rays of dawn painted the sky in delicate hues of pink and gold as Aurora and Brynn sought respite within the shelter of a vast forest. Exhaustion clung to their weary frames, prompting them to seek solace in the embrace of peaceful slumber. Nestled amidst the comforting canopy of trees, they allowed themselves to succumb to the call of sleep, their minds and bodies yearning for restoration.

It was within this fleeting moment of respite that Aurora's dreams were interrupted by an ethereal presence. Like a specter emerging from the depths of the unknown, a wraith materialized before her, its form an unsettling blend of translucence and shadows. The air grew heavy with an otherworldly aura, causing Aurora's eyes to flutter open, her heart racing in her chest.

The wraith, emanating an eerie glow, whispered in a language foreign to her ears. Its words carried a haunting melody, a sibilant cadence that seemed to echo within the depths of her consciousness. Aurora's senses were heightened, every fiber of her being attuned to the enigmatic whispers that filled the air.

With trembling hands, she attempted to rouse Brynn from his slumber, desperation etched upon her features. But no matter how urgently she shook her, she remained undisturbed, lost in the realm of dreams. Fear and confusion gripped Aurora, intensifying the terror that coursed through her veins. She was left to face the enigmatic wraith alone, her heart pounding in her chest like a captive bird desperate for escape.

In an instant, the wraith, with a sudden burst of ethereal energy, surged towards Aurora, its form merging with hers in a horrifying fusion. A bloodcurdling scream pierced the air, shattering the tranquility of the forest and rousing Brynn from her slumber. Startled and disoriented, he jolted upright, his eyes wide with alarm as he beheld the scene unfolding before him.

"Aurora! What's happening? Are you alright?" Brynn's voice quivered with concern as he rushed to her side, his presence a much-needed anchor amidst the tumult of emotions that threatened to engulf her.

Tears streamed down Aurora's face as she struggled to find her voice amidst the residual echoes of her nightmares.
"I...I don't know," she stammered, her gaze fixed upon the rising sun as if seeking solace within its warm embrace.
"It felt so real, Brynn. The wraith spoke to me, but in a language I could not comprehend. It was foreign, unlike anything I have ever encountered before."

Brynn's brows furrowed with a mix of worry and curiosity. She grasped Aurora's trembling hands, her touch a source of comfort and solidarity.
"Perhaps it is a language of the realm beyond, a tongue of the ethereal or the depths of the underworld," he mused softly, his voice laced with empathy.

"It seems we have yet to face the full extent of the challenges that lie ahead."

Gazing into each other's eyes, Aurora and Brynn found strength in their shared connection, their hands interlocked like a lifeline in the face of the unknown. They knew that this encounter with the wraith was but a harbinger of the trials they would face on their journey. Together, they vowed to navigate the shadows that lurked in their path, drawing upon their unwavering determination to overcome the obstacles that lay ahead.

With the forest around them stirring to life, a symphony of birdsong filling the air, Aurora and Brynn took solace in the beauty of the waking world. Their hearts beat in tandem, an unspoken pledge echoing within their souls. Whatever lay beyond the boundaries of their understanding, they would face it together, unwavering in their commitment to protecting each other and the fragile balance of light and darkness that hung in the balance.

On the twelfth day of their arduous journey, Aurora and Brynn awoke with renewed determination, their spirits undeterred by the trials they had faced thus far. As the first rays of dawn bathed the horizon in a gentle golden glow, they set their sights on another demanding day ahead. With a light breakfast to sustain them, they mounted their trusty steeds and embarked on the path that stretched before them, beckoning with the promise of both peril and triumph.

The hours melded into one another as they rode steadily, the rhythm of their horses' hooves echoing the steady beat of their resolute hearts. The landscape unfolded around them, a tapestry of untamed wilderness and fleeting glimpses of distant peaks. Yet, despite their tireless efforts, the day remained devoid of noteworthy events, with only the occasional rustle of leaves or distant cry of a bird to punctuate the quietude.

As the sun began its descent towards the western horizon, casting long shadows across the land, the duo pressed on, determined to make the most of their fleeting daylight. They rode through the twilight hours, their path illuminated solely by the pale glow of the moon and the faint twinkle of distant stars. Day thirteen emerged on the horizon, painting the sky in hues of soft rose and amber, signaling the start of a new chapter in their odyssey.

The weariness that had settled into their bones prompted them to seek refuge in a quaint village nestled amidst rolling hills and emerald fields. Dismounting their horses, they led them to the safety of a nearby stable, ensuring their noble companions were well taken care of before turning their attention to their own needs.

The tantalizing aroma of home-cooked meals wafted through the air as they entered the local inn, greeted warmly by the innkeeper whose jovial countenance seemed to radiate a genuine sense of hospitality.

"Welcome, weary travelers," the innkeeper chimed, a glint of curiosity sparkling in their eyes.
"How may I be of service to you on this fine eve?"

Aurora offered a weary smile, her voice laced with a hint of exhaustion.
"We need two rooms for the night, a good innkeeper, as well as any information regarding quests or tasks that may be available to us."

The innkeeper's face brightened, eager to assist.
"Of course, dear adventurers! I shall arrange the rooms for you immediately. As for quests, you need to look no further than the bustling market square just beyond those buildings," they gestured towards the bustling activity beyond the inn's windows. "There, you shall find a vibrant job board brimming with opportunities for grand endeavors and thrilling escapades. May your stay in our humble village be one of grandeur and fulfillment."

With grateful nods, Aurora and Brynn settled into their comfortable accommodations, feeling the weight of their fatigue slowly lifting from their shoulders. As they embraced the embrace of a well-deserved slumber, their dreams danced with visions of untold treasures and noble quests that awaited them on the morrow.

In the heart of the village, beneath a starlit sky, the inn hummed with the stories of weary travelers and vibrant souls seeking purpose and adventure. The tapestry of fate continued to weave its intricate threads, entwining the destinies of Aurora and Brynn with the hopes and dreams of those they would encounter in their quest. Little did they know that the path they had chosen would soon lead them to unforeseen challenges and encounters that would test their resolve and reshape the very course of their lives.

As the night unfolded its star-studded veil, enveloping the weary adventurers in a realm of restful tranquility, Aurora and Brynn found solace in the embrace of peaceful slumber. The moon, a luminescent guardian, cast its gentle glow upon their faces, infusing their dreams with whispered promises of a new day dawning.

As the sun ascended the horizon with a vibrant burst of radiance, its golden rays heralding the arrival of a fresh chapter in their journey, Aurora and Brynn arose, their spirits rejuvenated by the rejuvenating embrace of a restful night's sleep. With newfound vigor coursing through their veins, they eagerly set forth, their destination the lively market square that beckoned with its bustling activity and vibrant energy.

Navigating through the vibrant tapestry of stalls and eager merchants, Aurora's gaze shifted towards the questing board, a veritable treasure trove of opportunities awaiting the intrepid souls who sought the thrill of daring exploits and heroic endeavors. The board, adorned with a myriad of parchment notices, showcased an array of quests, each bearing promises of rewards and challenges that stirred the adventurers' hearts.

Aurora's eyes darted from one parchment to another, her fingertips tracing the edges of each proclamation, her mind analyzing the risks and rewards embedded within the words. Suddenly, in a moment that seemed to stretch in suspended animation, a searing pain pierced through her back like an arrow finding its mark. A cry of anguish escaped her lips as she felt her health points diminish with alarming speed.

Instinctively, Aurora sought refuge behind the questing board, seeking cover from the unseen assailant. Her heart pounded with a potent mixture of adrenaline and fear, her eyes scanning the surroundings for any signs of danger. The commotion in the market square swirled around her, oblivious to the peril that had befallen her. It was clear: they were under attack, and the source of their torment was likely another player, concealed amidst the chaotic hubbub of the market.

Brynn's eyes widened in alarm as she swiftly moved to Aurora's side, her protective instincts flaring to life. "Aurora, stay behind me!" she urged, her voice resolute despite the tremor of concern that coursed through her. Her grip tightened around her weapon, her gaze intently scanning the crowd for any signs of the assailant's presence.

In the midst of the bustling market, chaos and confusion became Aurora's shadow, as the weight of pain lingered in her wounds. She gritted her teeth, determination etched upon her face, vowing not to let this assault define her. Her mind raced, seeking a strategy amidst the turmoil, a means to thwart their attacker and safeguard their lives.

Whispers of suspicion filled the air, as speculative glances darted between merchants and passersby, each wondering who among them concealed the cloak of malevolence. The vibrant atmosphere of the market square had turned into a treacherous labyrinth of uncertainty, every shadow a potential threat, every face a mask of suspicion.

With a resolute glint in her eyes, Aurora steeled herself, ready to face the unknown adversary that had chosen to target her. She knew that survival demanded both cunning and valor, a willingness to adapt and overcome in the face of relentless adversity. She silently vowed to protect not only herself but also the bond she shared with Brynn, for their destinies were irrevocably intertwined, and together they would weather any storm that dared to cross their path.

As the echoes of chaos reverberated through the market, a battle of wits and resilience commenced, two souls bound by fate confronting the shadow that sought to undermine their very existence. Little did they know that this encounter would serve as a crucible, forging them into formidable warriors, their spirits aflame with a determination that could not be extinguished.

With hearts united and weapons brandished, Aurora and Brynn prepared to face this unexpected threat head-on. Their journey, fraught with danger and adversity, had prepared them for such moments, and they would not falter in the face of darkness. For within their veins caused the spirit of true heroes, driven by an unyielding desire to triumph over adversity and bring light to a world shrouded in shadows.

Aurora's heart pounded within her chest, the rhythmic thumping echoing in her ears as she peered cautiously from behind their makeshift cover. Her eyes darted back and forth, scanning the shadows, desperately searching for any sign of the elusive assailant closing in on them. Each passing second felt like an eternity, the weight of impending danger bearing down upon them with an oppressive force.

"This is not how I wanted to die," Aurora whispered, her voice laced with a mixture of fear and determination. She clutched her weapon tightly, her knuckles turning white as she prepared herself for the imminent confrontation. The thrill of the battle mingled with the cold tendrils of dread that coiled around her heart.

Brynn stood resolute by Aurora's side, her presence a steadfast shield against the encroaching darkness.
"I won't let that happen," she declared, her voice filled with unwavering loyalty and unwavering resolve. The bond between the two friends was unbreakable, their commitment to each other a testament to their unyielding spirit.

With bated breath, Aurora and Brynn strained their senses, honing in on every subtle shift in the environment, every whisper of movement that threatened to betray the position of their unseen adversary. And then, like a phantom materializing from the depths of the abyss, they caught a glimpse of the other player, their form fleeting yet unmistakable.

Aurora's heart quickened as adrenaline surged through her veins. She had the advantage of surprise, the first strike at her fingertips, and a keen sense of the assailant's whereabouts. Without hesitation, she carefully calculated her aim, drawing upon her newfound proficiency with her enchanted longbow.

A taut silence enveloped the battlefield as Aurora steadied her trembling hands. The tension in the air was palpable, an electric current charging the atmosphere. And then, with precision and timing honed by countless battles, she released the bowstring, the arrow slicing through the air with deadly accuracy. It found its mark, striking the assailant's arm with a resounding impact, inflicting additional damage upon them.

The enemy retreated, disappearing into the murky shadows, leaving Aurora and Brynn momentarily breathless, their gazes locked on the spot where their assailant had vanished. Minutes turned into eternities as they maintained their vigilance, wary of any signs of a possible return. The forest whispered its secrets, but no trace of the enemy emerged from the depths of the tree-line.

However, in a cruel twist of fate, their momentary respite was shattered as the assailant stealthily circled them, seizing the advantage. Aurora's heart skipped a beat as a searing pain tore through her chest, her vision blurred by the onslaught. Blood seeped from the wound, staining the ground and the board upon which they sought refuge.

Time seemed to slow to a crawl as Aurora grappled with her mortality. Thoughts raced through her mind in a chaotic whirlwind, questioning the very fabric of her existence and the destiny she had carved for herself.
"Is this the end?" she wondered, her voice lost amidst the chaos of battle.
"Am I destined to die here with my dreams left unfulfilled?"

But Brynn, ever the beacon of unwavering support, stood strong, deflecting the enemy's subsequent strikes with unwavering resolve. The clash of weapons rang through the air, each clash an embodiment of their indomitable spirit. Aurora's senses sharpened, her adrenaline-fueled survival instincts surging forth, as she snapped out of her momentary haze.

Gripping her sword tightly, Aurora joined the frenzied dance of combat, her movements a symphony of calculated strikes and cautious evasions. She teetered on the edge of vulnerability, her diminished health points a constant reminder of her perilous state. Yet, driven by a tenacity that defied her dwindling strength, she refused to retreat. Every swing of her blade was infused with desperation and an unyielding determination to fight until her last breath.

Together, Aurora and Brynn battled on, the clash of steel and the thunder of their resolve reverberating through the surrounding landscape. The outcome remained uncertain, hanging in the balance like a delicate thread. Yet, at that moment, they knew that victory was not solely measured by their physical prowess or the number of health points remaining. It was their unwavering bond, their unyielding spirit, and their refusal to succumb to the darkness that defined their true triumph.

As the defeated player fell lifelessly to the ground, a sense of triumph and relief washed over Aurora and Brynn. Their victory had come at a heavy cost, though, as Aurora's wounds throbbed with agonizing intensity. Weakened and on the brink of exhaustion, she sank to her knees, her body trembling with both exertion and pain. The battle had taken its toll, and immediate attention was needed to mend her battered form.

With a steely determination, Aurora mustered what little strength remained within her. Focusing her energy, she called upon her minor healing abilities, harnessing the latent magic coursing through her veins. The soft glow of healing energy enveloped her, knitting together the torn flesh and revitalizing her weary body. Although not a complete restoration, the spell provided a respite, bringing her health points to a level that allowed her to continue, albeit cautiously.

Aware that their current location offered little safety, Aurora and Brynn swiftly retraced their steps, their senses heightened by the lingering adrenaline. The innkeeper, his cheerful demeanor now clouded with concern, met them with a knowing gaze. Sensing the urgency in their eyes, he directed them to a nearby healer, a beacon of hope amidst the tumultuous aftermath of their encounter.

Following the innkeeper's directions, they hurried through the labyrinthine streets, their footsteps muffled by the hushed atmosphere that hung over the village. Finally, they arrived at the healer's humble abode, a small stone building nestled amidst a cluster of bustling shops. The healer, a wise and compassionate soul, greeted them with a kind smile, her eyes filled with empathy.

"What can I do for you?" the healer inquired, her voice filled with warmth and understanding. Aurora, her voice tinged with a mixture of apprehension and gratitude, explained her desperate need for healing. The healer's experienced gaze swept over Aurora's wounded form, assessing the severity of her injuries. With a calm demeanor, she directed Aurora to lie upon a sturdy cot, preparing to work her restorative magic.

Aurora handed over the requested fee, the jingling of silver coins serving as a reminder of the sacrifices made along their perilous journey. Minutes turned into eternity as the healer channeled her ancient knowledge, her hands moving with purpose and grace. The air hummed with a soothing energy, an ethereal symphony of healing power enveloping Aurora's body.

Finally, as the healing session drew to a close, Aurora felt a surge of vitality coursing through her veins. The wounds that had once married her flesh were now nothing more than fading memories. Gratitude filled her heart as she expressed her heartfelt appreciation to the skilled healer, who smiled knowingly, recognizing the indomitable spirit that burned within Aurora.

With renewed vigor and a sense of resilience, Aurora and Brynn ventured once again towards the quest board, their eyes scanning the myriad of postings for a new adventure to undertake. The challenges they had faced thus far had only steeled their resolve, instilling within them a determination to triumph over the trials that lay ahead. They were ready to once again heed the call of destiny and embark on their next chapter.

With their wounds tended to and a renewed sense of purpose, Aurora and Brynn turned their attention to the quest board. Among the numerous parchment notices, one request caught their eye—a seemingly straightforward task that entailed retrieving a lost artifact, a golden ring, hidden deep within a treacherous cave. The promise of a worthy reward sparked their curiosity, but as twilight approached, the prospect of delving into the darkness of the cave during the night gave them pause.

In a calculated decision, they opted to postpone their expedition until the following day, unwilling to risk the perils that darkness could bring. Seeking respite and sustenance, they returned to the welcoming embrace of the inn, their footsteps light with anticipation. The aromatic symphony of culinary delights filled the air as they entered the bustling dining hall, adorned with flickering candlelight and the comforting crackle of a roaring hearth.

Seated at a table, their weary bodies sinking into plush cushions, Aurora and Brynn eagerly perused the menu. A feast fit for heroes awaited them, the tantalizing array of dishes invoking a symphony of flavors that set their taste buds ablaze with anticipation. The succulent aroma of roasted meats, infused with herbs and spices, mingled with the hearty aroma of sizzling potatoes, freshly plucked from the fertile earth.

As their meal arrived, plated with exquisite precision, the sight before them was a feast for the eyes. Thick cuts of tender steak, seared to perfection, glistened under the soft glow of candlelight. Juicy poultry, succulent and dripping with savory juices, beckoned temptingly from its golden-brown exterior. The robust symphony of seasoned vegetables, meticulously arranged in a kaleidoscope of colors, added a touch of vibrancy to the culinary masterpiece.

Each bite was a revelation—a symphony of flavors dancing upon their palates. The steak, cooked to a mouthwatering medium-rare, melted upon contact, releasing a burst of rich, savory goodness. The poultry, moist and succulent, boasted a tantalizing blend of herbs and spices that enlivened the senses with every tender morsel. The roasted potatoes, crispy on the outside and fluffy on the inside, offered a comforting contrast of textures, their earthy flavors complementing the hearty meats.

Time seemed to stand still as Aurora and Brynn savored each bite, their spirits lifted by the culinary indulgence. Amidst the clinking of cutlery and hushed conversations that swirled around them, they found solace in the simple pleasure of nourishment, refueling their bodies and souls.

Satiated and content, they bid the dining hall farewell and retreated to their quarters, their weary bodies craving the solace of a restful slumber. The inn's cozy rooms enveloped them in a cocoon of tranquility, offering respite from the trials of their quest. Lying beneath soft blankets, their minds filled with dreams of valor and adventure, they surrendered to the embrace of sleep, knowing that the challenges of the following day awaited them with both trepidation and excitement.

Chapter 21

Day 12 dawned upon Aurora and Brynn, their spirits fueled by determination and the promise of adventure that lay ahead. Rising later in the morning, they fortified themselves with a hearty breakfast, savoring each bite with a mix of anticipation and trepidation. Their destination awaited—the fabled cave nestled deep within the dense forest on the outskirts of the town.

Armed with a sense of purpose and a well-worn map, they navigated the winding paths of the forest, their footsteps guided by the flickering sunlight filtering through the ancient trees. The hushed whispers of leaves rustling in the wind accompanied their journey, lending an air of mystique to their quest.

As they arrived at the mouth of the foreboding cave, Brynn took the lead, fashioning a makeshift torch to pierce the shadows that shrouded the entrance. The dim light cast eerie silhouettes upon the rocky walls, revealing glimpses of the unknown that lay ahead. Aurora's heart fluttered with a mix of excitement and apprehension—this was the moment they had prepared for.

Venturing deeper into the cavernous abyss, their steps echoed against the cold, stone floor. Aurora's eyes scanned the surroundings, searching for any sign of the elusive golden ring. The cave's labyrinthine passages twisted and turned, making their quest seem like searching for a needle in a haystack.

Their hopes began to wane, clouded by the overwhelming darkness that threatened to engulf them. But then, like a beacon in the night, they caught sight of a flickering glow and the distant murmur of voices. Intrigued and cautiously optimistic, they pressed on, following the light that grew brighter with each step.

Finally, the cavern opened up to a vast chamber, bathed in an ethereal radiance. It was an awe-inspiring sight—a spectacle that could rival the grandest arenas of the world. And within this grandeur stood eight goblins, their eyes gleaming with malicious intent. To Aurora's astonishment, amidst the chaos, she spotted the golden ring, glimmering like a star in the darkness.

Aurora's heart skipped a beat, a mixture of disbelief and amusement washing over her. How could the goblins, so close in proximity to the ring, remain oblivious to its presence? She exchanged a hushed comment with Brynn, marveling at the stroke of fortune that might befall them. But fate had other plans.

As if sensing their presence, one of the goblins locked eyes with Aurora, a blood-curdling screech escaping its lips. Panic spread through the ranks of the goblins as they charged forward, their weapons drawn, a frenzied symphony of chaos and conflict echoing through the chamber.

Reacting swiftly, Aurora notched an arrow in her bow, her skilled fingers finding their mark with uncanny precision. The projectile whizzed through the air, finding its home in the vulnerable nape of a goblin's neck, silencing its menacing presence with a swift demise. But there was no time for celebration—the battle had just begun.

With weapons in hand, Aurora and Brynn engaged in a fierce dance of steel and fury. The goblins, fueled by their primal instincts, fought with ferocity, their blows raining down upon our heroes like a tempest. The clash of metal and the cries of combat reverberated throughout the chamber, a testament to the sheer intensity of the struggle.

In the midst of this chaotic fray, a figure emerged from the shadows—an imposing silhouette that towered above the rest. It was the Chieftain, a hulking orc with a bellowing roar that sent shivers down their spines. The ground trembled beneath his weight as he charged toward them, his eyes burning with a primal fury that matched his formidable presence.

Now, the battle had transformed into an epic struggle—a test of skill, strength, and sheer willpower. Aurora and Brynn stood resolute, their eyes locked onto the Chieftain, their determination unyielding. This was the moment that would define their mettle—a true challenge that would push them to their limits.

The clash of weapons intensified, the crescendo of battle reaching its zenith. Aurora's heart pounded within her chest, her every movement fueled by a combination of adrenaline and a fierce desire to emerge victorious. Brynn fought valiantly by her side, their swords intertwining in a symphony of precision and agility.

As the battle raged on, time seemed to distort, the seconds stretching into eternity. Each swing, each parry, was executed with calculated precision. Blood was spilled, wounds were inflicted, but Aurora and Brynn stood tall, refusing to falter in the face of adversity.

Though fatigue threatened to consume them, their resolve remained unbroken. Their swords sang through the air, striking blows with unwavering determination. Every strike against the Chieftain was met with unyielding resistance, his sheer strength and resilience pushing them to their limits.

But in the heat of battle, a sudden surge of energy coursed through Aurora's veins—a burst of determination that transcended her mortal limits. With a renewed focus, she mustered her remaining strength, drawing upon every ounce of skill she possessed. The world around her blurred as she channeled her inner power, striking with unparalleled precision.

With a final, thunderous blow, the Chieftain staggered, his imposing figure swaying like a titan on the brink of collapse. The battle had taken its toll, but Aurora and Brynn refused to yield. In a final, coordinated assault, their weapons found their mark, delivering a resounding defeat to the mighty Chieftain. 200xp was gained once the Chieftain had fallen. 15xp for each goblin rang out.

The chamber fell silent, save for the echoes of their labored breaths and the soft crackle of flickering torchlight. The battle was won, the goblins scattered, and the golden ring lay before them, a testament to their triumph. Though wounded and weary, a surge of elation flooded their beings—they had emerged victorious from a battle that would be etched into their memories for eternity.

Filled with a mix of relief and elation, Aurora and Brynn stood before the coveted golden ring, gleaming in the dim light of the cavern. Aurora delicately picked it up, her fingers trembling with anticipation and a sense of accomplishment. "We finally found it," she whispered, a hint of awe in her voice. She carefully slipped the ring onto her finger, ensuring it was secure and wouldn't be lost in the chaos of their journey.

To Brynn's astonishment, as soon as Aurora adorned the ring, a mesmerizing transformation occurred. Her figure blurred and wavered as if she was becoming one with the shadows. Within moments, she had vanished from sight, leaving behind nothing but a faint shimmer in the air. Brynn's eyes widened in disbelief. "Wow, how'd you do that?" he exclaimed, his voice filled with a mix of astonishment and curiosity.

Aurora, still invisible, chuckled softly. "I'm not entirely sure myself," she replied, her voice carrying an air of intrigue. "It seems this ring possesses enchantments of its own, granting me the power of invisibility." With a swift motion, she slipped the ring off her finger, and just as mysteriously as she disappeared, she reappeared before Brynn's eyes. The ring sparkled with an otherworldly glow in her palm. "Truly, it must be an enchanted ring," she mused, her eyes glimmering with excitement.

Brynn's gaze locked onto the magical artifact, his mind filled with possibilities. "Perhaps we are destined to keep it," he suggested, a sense of hopeful anticipation creeping into his voice. Aurora nodded in agreement, a mischievous smile playing on her lips. "Indeed, luck seems to be on our side. Let's hope this enchanted ring becomes our ally on this grand adventure."

With the golden ring carefully stowed away, they embarked on their journey back to the entrance of the cave, retracing their steps through the labyrinthine forest. Hours passed, the sunlight filtering through the dense canopy above as they navigated the familiar path, their minds filled with the memory of their epic battle and the newfound treasure they had acquired.

Emerging from the forest's embrace, they rejoined the bustling streets of the village, their steps guided by the directions provided in the quest posting.

Following the winding path, they soon arrived at a modest house—a quaint dwelling that seemed to exude an air of mystery. Aurora raised her hand and knocked gently on the door, the sound echoing through the quiet neighborhood.

After a brief moment, the door creaked open, revealing an older woman peering through the narrow gap. Her eyes widened with surprise at the sight of the two adventurers standing before her. "Can I help you?" she inquired, her voice tinged with curiosity.

Brynn stepped forward, holding the golden ring aloft. "We found your ring, ma'am," he said with a warm smile. The woman's expression transformed into a mix of delight and relief, her hand reaching out to accept the returned treasure. Opening the door fully, she invited them inside, grateful for their assistance.

As Aurora and Brynn handed over the ring, a sense of fulfillment washed over them. A small notification appeared in their vision, declaring the completion of their quest. "Quest Completed - Lost Ring," it announced, accompanied by a satisfying chime. They felt a surge of accomplishment as their efforts were rewarded with 250 experience points, inching them closer to the next milestone in their journey.

The woman paused for a moment, gratitude evident in her eyes. "I don't have much to offer in return, but you have my deepest gratitude," she said earnestly. After a brief contemplation, she reached for a nearby jewelry box and gently removed a delicate, silver band adorned with intricate engravings. "Take this as a token of my appreciation. May it aid you on your future endeavors," she offered, extending the ring to Brynn.

With a mix of surprise and gratitude, Brynn accepted the gift, his fingers carefully tracing the intricate patterns. "Thank you, ma'am. We are honored," he replied, his voice filled with genuine appreciation. They had acquired not only the fabled ring of invisibility but now a new artifact of power—an enchanted ring that carried the blessings of the woman they had helped.

As they left the house, the weight of their newfound possessions filled their hearts with a renewed sense of purpose and excitement. The streets of the village seemed to hold endless possibilities, and with their enchanted rings in tow, Aurora and Brynn knew that their adventure had taken a thrilling turn. Little did they know what other wondrous discoveries and treacherous challenges awaited them on the path ahead.

With the enchanted ring securely adorning Brynn's finger, the power of stealth surged through their veins, granting them a newfound advantage in their perilous journey. The ring's enchantment heightened their senses, honed their reflexes, and bestowed upon them an ethereal grace. As they basked in the glory of their acquisition, they couldn't help but envision the countless possibilities that lay before them.

The world seemed to transform around them as if the very air whispered secrets of hidden paths and concealed treasures. Their steps became lighter, their movements more fluid, as the ring's magic intertwined with their beings. With this newfound ability, they knew they could navigate through the shadows undetected, silently dispatching foes with lethal precision. It was a power they would wield with caution, using it to tip the scales in their favor when the odds seemed insurmountable.

As the sun began its descent towards the horizon, casting an amber glow over the land, they returned to the quest board, their eyes scanning the myriad of postings in search of a task that could be swiftly completed. They sought a quest that would allow them to utilize their newly acquired ring, putting its stealth-enhancing abilities to the test.

After some careful deliberation, their gazes settled upon a request to retrieve a sacred relic from a nearby forgotten temple. The relic, known as the Tear of Seraphia, was said to possess healing properties beyond imagination—a priceless artifact that could potentially turn the tide of battles in their favor. It was a quest that piqued their interest, both for the potential rewards and the opportunity to showcase their enhanced stealth.

As they set out towards the temple, anticipation coursed through their veins. The setting sun bathed the landscape in hues of orange and gold, casting long shadows across their path. The forest whispered with secrets, and the leaves rustled with the promise of adventure. Every step brought them closer to their destination, the air growing thick with anticipation.

Arriving at the temple's entrance, they found themselves standing before a massive stone structure, ancient and weathered. Vines clung to its crumbling walls, and moss blanketed the ground, bearing witness to the passage of time. The temple exuded an aura of mystery, as if it held ancient guardians and untold secrets within its hallowed halls.

Taking a deep breath, Aurora and Brynn stepped into the temple, their footsteps barely making a sound. The air inside was heavy with the scent of incense and the faint echo of forgotten prayers. Torchlight flickered, casting eerie shadows along the stone corridors. It was a labyrinth of mystery and danger, but they navigated through it with a newfound sense of confidence.

Their stealth was their shield, allowing them to evade lurking traps and elude the attention of long-dormant guardians. They moved as one, their footsteps synchronized, their senses attuned to every sound and movement. The ring of invisibility became their ally, enabling them to slip past patrolling spirits and ancient sentinels with ease.

With every step deeper into the temple, the tension mounted. They could feel the presence of the Tear of Seraphia drawing closer, its mystic energy calling out to them like a siren's song. Yet, they remained ever vigilant, for they knew that the temple's ancient defenses were not to be taken lightly.

Finally, after what felt like an eternity, they reached the inner sanctum—a chamber bathed in a soft, ethereal glow. There, upon an intricately carved pedestal, rested the Tear of Seraphia. Its radiance illuminated the room, casting a warm and soothing light.

Aurora and Brynn approached the relic with reverence, their hands trembling with a mixture of excitement and awe. As they carefully lifted the Tear of Seraphia from its resting place, a wave of healing energy washed over them, enveloping their weary bodies and revitalizing their spirits. It was a tangible reminder of the power they now possessed, both in their enchanted ring and the artifacts they acquired along their journey.

With the sacred relic safely in their possession, they retraced their steps, their hearts lighter and their confidence soaring. The Tear of Seraphia would prove to be a valuable asset in the battles that lay ahead, providing them with healing energies that could mend wounds and restore vitality in even the direst of circumstances.

As they exited the temple, the moon rose high in the night sky, casting its gentle glow upon the world below. Aurora and Brynn, united by their shared victories and the artifacts they had acquired, made their way back to the town, ready to embark on their next chapter of adventure and triumph. The ring of invisibility and the Tear of Seraphia served as constant reminders of the wonders they had encountered and the trials they had overcome. Their journey was far from over, and they eagerly embraced the challenges that awaited them on the path ahead.

Chapter 22

Day 13 had arrived, signaling yet another arduous leg of their journey. Determined to make progress, Aurora and Brynn rose before the break of dawn. Their weary bodies yearned for rest, but the looming task ahead demanded their resilience. With a somber farewell to the village that briefly offered solace, they braced themselves for the challenges that awaited them.

As they set out, the sky still draped in shades of purple and orange, they left behind the familiar sights of lush green fields and dense forests. The landscape transitioned gradually, unfolding into an expansive desert of golden sand that stretched as far as the eye could see. A sense of trepidation clung to the air, for they knew the desert would test their endurance like never before.

Aurora's gaze swept across the vast desert expanse, her voice tinged with concern, "I hope our water supply will suffice for this daunting journey." Brynn's brow furrowed as he surveyed the barren terrain, unsure of the challenges that lay ahead. "Regrettably, there is no alternative route. We must traverse this desert," he replied, his voice betraying a hint of uncertainty.

The moment their steeds ventured onto the sun-scorched sand, they realized the enormity of the task at hand. The shifting dunes, like waves frozen in time, presented an unpredictable and unstable path. Progress was hindered as the horses struggled to maintain their footing, their hooves sinking into the soft, shifting grains.

With each stride, they encountered an unyielding solitude—a desolate landscape bereft of life. The absence of any discernible landmarks amplified the feeling of isolation as if they were mere specks in a sea of sand. The searing rays of the sun relentlessly beat down upon them, amplifying the desert's scorching embrace. The temperature soared to a sweltering 90 degrees Fahrenheit, further draining their strength and resolve.

Aware of the strain on their faithful steeds, Aurora and Brynn paced themselves, allowing the horse's frequent rests and replenishing their water supply at every opportunity. The sound of their hooves merged with the hushed whispers of the wind, creating a haunting melody that reverberated through the vast expanse.

Days melted into one another as they pressed on, their bodies growing accustomed to the rhythm of desert travel. They marveled at the ever-changing hues of the sand, from burnished gold to amber, as the sunlight danced upon its granulated surface. The silence became their companion, broken only by the occasional gust of wind that carried with it grains of sand, stinging their faces like whispers of the desert's secrets.

During the long stretches between oasis, they rationed their water and sustenance meticulously, aware that their survival depended on these precious supplies. The parched landscapes forced them to rely on their resourcefulness, seeking out hidden pockets of shade to find respite from the relentless sun and using their cloaks to shield their faces from its scorching intensity.

As they forged ahead, a sense of awe washed over them, for the desert revealed its unique beauty. The shifting sands formed mesmerizing patterns, undulating like a vast ocean frozen in time. Occasionally, they caught sight of delicate desert flowers, resilient plants that defiantly bloomed in the face of adversity, their vibrant colors providing fleeting moments of resplendence amidst the desolation.

Finally, after what seemed like an eternity, the horizon revealed the subtle contours of an oasis—an oasis whispered of in tales of old, the Lost Oasis. Its mere presence breathed hope into their weary souls. The promise of shade, refreshment, and the chance to rejuvenate their bodies and spirits beckoned them forward.

With grit and determination, they pressed on, eagerly anticipating the oasis's arrival, for within its verdant embrace lay the secrets they sought—mystical waters, hidden knowledge, and the next chapter of their extraordinary adventure.

As Aurora and Brynn embarked on their journey, little did they know that they were about to uncover the secrets of an ancient and mythical city known as the Lost Oasis. The mere mention of its name had always intrigued adventurers and historians alike, for it held the key to the origins of the enigmatic sand people.

Guided by the whispers of folklore, they ventured deep into the vast desert until they stood at the gates of this fabled city. Its weathered stone walls rose from the shifting sands, telling tales of a bygone era. This was the last known refuge of the sand people, a civilization whose existence had long been shrouded in mystery.

As they stepped foot into the Lost Oasis, the travelers were immediately struck by the ethereal beauty that surrounded them. The city seemed frozen in time, with remnants of a once-thriving civilization now scattered across the landscape. The homes of the sand people were unlike any architectural marvel they had ever witnessed.

Constructed with remarkable ingenuity, the sand people's dwellings blended seamlessly with the vast dunes that embraced the city. These unique structures were a testament to the ancient techniques employed by the sand people. The desert's golden sands were meticulously shaped and compacted into walls and roofs, forming sturdy adobe-like structures. The sand itself, mixed with straw and clay, was utilized to create a natural insulation against the extreme temperatures of the desert.

Clothed in garments that echoed an era long past, the sand people exuded an aura of resilience and adaptation. Their attire, meticulously woven and embellished, bore witness to the interplay of practicality and the rich tapestry of cultural traditions meticulously passed down through generations. Each thread, each intricate pattern held a story, a testament to their connection with the land and their ancestors.

Despite their primitive lifestyle, the sand people possessed an innate wisdom that had allowed them to survive in the harsh desert environment for centuries. Their lives revolved around simple yet profound practices, drawing from their intimate knowledge of the land and the skills acquired from their ancestors. Each member of the sand people community played a vital role, whether it be tending to livestock, cultivating small oases, or crafting tools and weaponry with ancient techniques passed down through generations.

Aurora and Brynn, overwhelmed by the awe-inspiring sight before them, couldn't help but feel a profound sense of reverence for the sand people and their way of life. The city of the Lost Oasis had opened a window into a world long forgotten, a place where ancient traditions and survival instincts intertwined with breathtaking beauty. It was an encounter that would forever leave an indelible mark on their souls, as they stood humbled by the magnificence of the sand people's existence.

In that moment, Aurora and Brynn realized that their journey had only just begun, for within the depths of the Lost Oasis lay countless untold stories and untapped knowledge, waiting to be unraveled. With eager hearts and minds filled with curiosity, they set forth to explore this mysterious land, ready to discover the wonders that lay hidden within its sands.

Within the realm of the sand people, a veil of linguistic mystery shrouded their ancient civilization. Utterances flowed from their lips in an enigmatic tongue, an ethereal language that remained indecipherable to Aurora and Brynn. However, amidst the confounding linguistic barrier, fortune smiled upon them, for they fortuitously encountered an individual well-versed in the sand people's speech, who offered a glimmer of hope in navigating their intriguing realm.

Guided by their newfound interpreter, the travelers traversed the sprawling city, their footsteps resonating against the sun-bleached stone streets. As they ventured deeper, an awe-inspiring sight materialized before them—the magnificent temple, resplendent amidst the desert's unforgiving landscape. This sacred sanctuary stood as the heart of the city, its presence emanating an aura of profound significance.

The guide, with a reverent gleam in their eyes, regaled Aurora and Brynn with tales that awakened their imaginations. They spoke of an exceedingly rare and ancient artifact, a treasure of unparalleled allure—the legendary golden glove. Enshrined within the temple's hallowed halls, this fabled relic was whispered to grant unimaginable strength to its wearer.

Legends swirled like desert winds, carried through generations of storytellers, leaving tantalizing fragments of truth that danced on the edge of myth and reality. The golden glove had become an emblem of aspiration, inspiring awe and wonder in the hearts of the sand people. Its origins, like the shifting sands, became obscured by the passage of time, lending an air of mystique and uncertainty to its existence.

Yet, the guide cautioned against complete surrender to the allure of myth. They revealed that very few had been bestowed the privilege of witnessing the golden glove in person, its radiant splendor kept veiled within the temple's hallowed chambers. The hushed whispers of those fortunate few echoed tales of its iridescent glow and the profound aura that enveloped it. Its reputed ability to bestow superhuman strength upon its wearer remained a matter of speculation, for the truth lay confined within the annals of the sand people's history.

As the guide gestured toward the temple, a gesture that bridged the gap between the physical and the mystical, a sense of reverence hung in the air. The temple stood as a testament to the sand people's profound spiritual connection, a beacon of their ancient wisdom and the embodiment of their devotion to the mysteries of their existence. It beckoned the intrepid souls to venture forth and uncover the secrets locked within its hallowed confines.

That moment, Aurora and Brynn found themselves at the precipice of a remarkable odyssey—one that transcended the realm of ordinary exploration. Their quest was not merely to lay eyes upon the legendary golden glove, but to peel back the layers of history, to grasp the untold stories woven into the fabric of the sand people's civilization. With a newfound sense of purpose and anticipation that tingled in their very beings, they prepared to embark upon a journey that would unveil the truths concealed within the sacred temple and, perhaps, unravel the mysteries of the golden glove.

As the vast expanse of the desert stretched before them, a sudden shift in the atmosphere heralded the arrival of an impending sandstorm. The swirling vortex of sand loomed on the horizon, a tempestuous juggernaut threatening to engulf everything in its path. The urgency of the moment compelled the guide to act swiftly, his voice resonating with a sense of urgency.

"Quick, to my humble abode!" he exclaimed, his voice infused with a blend of concern and determination. With nimble steps, he led Aurora and Brynn through the treacherous winds, navigating their way to his sanctuary amidst the chaos of the encroaching storm. It was a race against time, each stride serving as a testament to the guide's unwavering knowledge of the land and his commitment to the safety of his unexpected guests.

Within the confines of his dwelling, a humble one-room hut, the travelers found solace from the unforgiving elements. The interior exuded an air of simplicity, constructed primarily from locally sourced materials of sand and clay. The walls, molded with painstaking care, held the mark of the guide's resourcefulness and adaptability in the face of the desert's formidable challenges. The flickering light of a solitary oil lamp cast dancing shadows on the uneven surfaces, imbuing the space with an otherworldly ambiance.

Taking their seats around a rudimentary table, the guide offered a welcoming smile, his eyes shining with curiosity and genuine interest. It was a rare occurrence for him to receive visitors in this isolated realm, where the harsh conditions and scarcity of resources created a natural deterrent for most wanderers.

"What brings you to our humble abode in the midst of this forsaken land?" he inquired, his voice laced with a genuine sense of curiosity. His humble demeanor conveyed the resilience and adaptability that characterized the sand people, a community forged by the uncompromising desert landscape.

With a shared glance of determination, Brynn leaned forward and began to unravel their purpose. "We are on a pilgrimage to the Great City of the Pixies," he revealed. "But the vastness of the desert lies between us and our destination. It would take an impractical amount of time to circumvent it, so we must brave its challenges."

The guide's expression shifted, an amalgamation of admiration and caution. "You are indeed fortunate to have found our humble settlement," he mused, pouring water from a small earthenware vessel into cups for his guests. "There is little else in these harsh conditions—a relentless environment that demands tenacity in the face of scarcity."

Aurora, thirst quenched by the life-sustaining liquid, couldn't help but express empathy for the guide's predicament. "Have you ever considered leaving this place behind and seeking refuge in a less inhospitable land?" she gently inquired, her voice brimming with genuine concern.

A flicker of contemplation danced in the guide's eyes, a testament to the internal struggle he had grappled with in his solitary existence. "I have pondered such thoughts," he admitted, his voice tinged with a blend of longing and loyalty. "But my bond with my people, our ancestral ties to this unforgiving landscape, tether me to this place. Moreover, the prospect of venturing into the unknown and leaving behind all that is familiar haunts me."

Aurora's eyes sparkled with a sense of adventure as she leaned forward, her voice brimming with enthusiasm. "But imagine the wonders you could behold, the experiences you could gather if you were to journey with us," she suggested her words carrying a hopeful melody. "You could explore the world, savor its diversity, and then return to this cherished home, enriched by the stories and memories gathered.

A moment of contemplative silence hung in the air as the guide weighed the words that resonated with both curiosity and trepidation. His eyes danced with flickering uncertainty, the weight of a decision unexplored pressing upon his shoulders. His voice, laced with a touch of vulnerability, finally broke the silence.

"I confess, the thought of venturing beyond these familiar sands both captivates and daunts me," he confessed, his gaze shifting between Aurora and Brynn. "For as long as I can remember, I have found solace and belonging in this land. It has shaped my identity, imbued me with a profound connection to my people and their resilient spirit."

Aurora and Brynn nodded empathetically, their expressions suffused with understanding. They recognized the weight that tradition, loyalty, and the embrace of home held within the guide's heart. They knew that stepping into the unknown could be an unsettling prospect, one laden with uncertainties and the relinquishment of the familiar.

"We understand," Brynn interjected, his voice brimming with sincerity. "Our journey is one of personal choice and discovery. We would never wish to impose our desires upon another. It is a path that each individual must undertake willingly, embracing the challenges and rewards that come with it."

The guide's eyes flickered with gratitude at Brynn's reassuring words, a sense of relief settling upon his features. It was as if the burden of expectation had been gently lifted from his weary shoulders. The knowledge that his newfound acquaintances would respect his decision, whatever it may be, brought solace and renewed clarity.

"I am grateful for your understanding," the guide responded, his voice infused with a newfound sense of serenity. "Although my feet may never tread upon distant shores, my heart shall travel with you as you embark upon your odyssey."

Aurora and Brynn exchanged appreciative glances, their admiration for the guide's resolve growing with each passing moment. They recognized the courage it took to remain steadfast in the face of unexplored possibilities, choosing instead to nurture the roots that had been anchored in this harsh yet cherished terrain.

With a renewed sense of camaraderie, the trio settled into a comfortable rhythm of conversation, their shared experiences and tales intertwining within the walls of the humble hut. The guide shared anecdotes of encounters with rare desert creatures, the whispers of forgotten legends passed down through generations, and the ancient rituals that formed the bedrock of their society.

As the winds howled outside, the sandstorm's fury unabated, the humble abode provided a sanctuary not only from the physical onslaught of nature but also from the uncertainties that lay beyond its protective walls. Within those moments of respite, bonds of friendship deepened, nurtured by mutual respect, and the understanding that journeys take many forms, intertwining lives in unexpected ways.

Ultimately, the guide's decision remained firm, rooted in the wisdom and strength forged by a lifetime spent embracing the challenges of the desert. As Aurora and Brynn prepared to resume their voyage, their hearts were filled with gratitude for the brief yet profound connection they had forged. In the face of their departure, the guide's farewell carried the weight of unspoken camaraderie, a silent understanding that their paths had converged for a reason, leaving an indelible mark upon their respective journeys.

Just as the tempestuous sandstorm raged outside, a knock echoed through the humble abode, interrupting the tranquility that had settled within its walls. The guide, ever hospitable, hurried to answer the door, his movements synchronized with the storm's relentless fury. With a welcoming smile, he gestured for the visitor to seek refuge within.

"Come on in, seek respite from the storm," the guide invited, his voice laced with warmth and genuine concern. As the newcomer stepped inside, he unraveled a cloth from his face, revealing features that exuded an otherworldly charm—a visage that belonged to an elf. The familiarity of their shared language bridged the divide between them.

"Hey, guys," the elf greeted with a glimmer of recognition in his eyes. "I was told that you speak my language, and I see that you do." The guide's face lit up with recognition as he replied, "Why yes, I am (give the guide a name)." The elf nodded, introducing himself in return, "I'm (give this guy a name)." A moment of curiosity swirled in the air, binding the unexpected gathering together.

Then, a spark of surprise ignited within Aurora as she recognized the elf before her. "Wait, James, is that you?" she exclaimed, her voice tinged with astonishment.

Made in the USA
Monee, IL
10 November 2023

46174905R00216